Kill Me
If You Can

Also by Nicole Young

Patricia Amble Mystery series
Love Me If You Must

Kill Me If You Can

A PATRICIA AMBLE MYSTERY
BOOK 2

Nicole Young

Revell
a division of Baker Publishing Group
Grand Rapids, Michigan

Published by Revell
a division of Baker Publishing Group
P.O. Box 6287, Grand Rapids, MI 49516-6287
www.revellbooks.com

Printed in the United States of America

Library of Congress Cataloging-in-Publication Data
Young, Nicole, 1967–
    Kill me if you can / Nicole Young.
        p.   cm. — (A Patricia Amble mystery ; bk. 2)
    ISBN 978-0-8007-3158-8 (pbk.)
    1. Dwellings—Remodeling—Fiction. 2. Family secrets—Fiction.
3. Upper Peninsula (Mich.)—Fiction. I. Title
PS3625.0968K56 2008
813′.6—dc22   2007046654

Published in association with the literary agency of Janet Kobobel Grant, Books & Such, 4788 Carissa Ave., Santa Rosa, CA 95405.

For my children . . .
and theirs.

1

Who said you can never go home again?

What a bunch of hooey.

I was home. Again.

And while perhaps not a single soul that passed me tonight on the frozen highway would recognize me, I still knew where to find home: Number Three Valentine's Lane, a dilapidated log cabin in the middle of a cedar woodland squashed between the creek and the bay.

Yeah. I knew where I was going.

Now I just had to figure out where I came from.

I squinted through swirling snowflakes and squeaking wipers to see the turn ahead. I barely missed the bank of white made by the plow as I maneuvered my Explorer onto the narrow two-track that led a half mile down to the house.

Around the final curve, the porch light blazed a welcome through the storm. The realtor must have left it on for me. She had hated to hear I was driving up in the worst blizzard of the year but obviously had faith enough that I'd arrive safely.

I pulled into the driveway, which already had several

inches of new snow since the plow had last been here, and turned off the engine.

Silence. A balm to my nerves.

My boots crunched in the drifts as I walked around to unload my suitcase and sleeping bag. How many times had I done this in the past? Pull up to the new home, take out the suitcase, bring in the sleeping bag and cot . . .

I did a quick calculation. This would be my fifth renovation project. The last one had just about ended my career. The spooky old Victorian had been home to a body buried in the basement. Finding the corpse had almost been too much for me. But God knew not to give me more than I could handle, and I finished the project unscathed—physically and mentally, at least.

But as for my heart . . .

I slammed the hatch closed. It didn't merit a trip down memory lane.

Better to keep my mind here in the present, down Valentine's Lane, and the project ahead of me.

And if the porch were any indication, I'd have plenty of work come spring. The boards bounced as I walked to the door. The thin layer of ice crackled into spidery veins.

The realtor had warned me not to buy anything sight unseen. But I had seen it—twenty-some years ago. How much could it have changed? It still felt like yesterday that I'd run around in these woods and swum at the sandy beach out front. I knew when I called Northern Realty a few months back and found out this cottage was for sale, the one I'd spent my summers in as a kid, that God had made it all possible. I knew He meant for me to come here. To come home.

I put my hand on the doorknob and paused, hoping the agent hadn't let me down. When I'd asked her how I'd get in the house tonight, she'd laughed.

"Nobody up here locks their doors. I'll leave the keys on the table for you, if you think you'll need them."

"Up here" was the Silvan Peninsula, a stretch of land that stuck down into Lake Michigan in the state's dislocated top half. On one side of the narrow strip were the unpredictable waters of the big lake, on the other, the calm, sheltered shores of Nocquette Bay. I'd survived the cities and towns of lower Michigan, now I'd discover if I could hack the wintry weather and isolation of Michigan's Upper Peninsula, or the U.P. as the natives called it.

The door swung open into the kitchen and I flicked on the overhead light. The room looked so . . . small. I hadn't realized how a place could shrink in a little over two decades. But, I guess I wasn't a scrawny seven-year-old anymore. Tonight, the red-and-gold-speckled '50s countertops reached my hips instead of my chin. And if I put my hand up, I could almost touch the white asbestos ceiling tiles. Back then, I'd had to climb on a stool piled with books to retrieve my stuck gum.

Still, everything was as I remembered: tacky beyond compare.

I dropped my gear by the door and walked through to the great room. I hit the switch, but nothing happened, the fault of either ancient wiring or burned-out bulbs.

The light from the kitchen spilled onto the fireplace

against the far wall. The massive limestone chimney would probably still be standing long after the rest of the house collapsed around it.

A few pieces of furniture were scattered around the room, left by the previous owners. I sat on a tatty green sofa, and gave a test bounce. The spring beneath me gave a *twang*. My eyes misted. It was the very couch I'd jumped on as a kid.

Boing, boing, boing . . .

"Patricia Louise Amble," my mother had yelled from the kitchen, "get off that sofa!"

I smiled at the memory and leaned back.

Mom died young and beautiful. While I only remember the smiles and fun, there were apparently dark times that she kept from me. I was later told that when my father left her, Mom changed. Gone were the carefree days of youth. She was single and had a child to support. She was alone and afraid. And without a church upbringing, she had no Jesus. No one on whom to lay her burdens.

Before the summer of my eighth year, she was dead, entangled with the metal of her Ford pickup at the bottom of Mead Quarry. A cry for help that was never heard until it was too late.

I wiped at a tear that trickled down one cheek. I used to be angry when I thought how Mom abandoned me. I considered suicide to be an act of pure selfishness. Then time passed, and suddenly the tables were turned, and I found myself recovering from another self-inflicted death, but this one under completely different circumstances.

Either way, whether from being a martyr to oneself or to others, suicide made a cruel tonic for those left behind.

Now that I was thirty-three, six years older than my mother had been when she'd killed herself, I had a little more understanding of the trials of life. How they can beat you down and poison you. How they can make you weary and fill you with despair. The little twists and turns I encountered on my narrow road often threatened to plunge me into my own abyss of hopelessness. It gave me compassion for my mother. It made me yearn to travel back in time and tell her of my one salvation, my one hope.

I stood up and headed back to the kitchen. The past had drifted up and captured me again. But wasn't that what I was here for? To discover my past? To discover my mother? Her loves, her hates, her favorite color, her shoe size?

Only after the death of my grandmother, who'd raised me from the age of eight, could I even entertain the thought of looking into the past. As long as Grandmother had been alive, she'd discouraged probing questions. It must have been like a knife in her heart the night she'd gotten the call that my mother was dead. Even years later, she couldn't talk about Mom except with vague descriptions and scattered details that left an incomplete picture of the woman who'd birthed me.

I might be off to a late start, but I wanted to know my mother. I wanted to know everything about her. Her life held the key to crates of unanswered questions that cluttered my mind and kept me locked in limbo. How could I love someone else, commit to someone else, if I didn't know diddly about myself or my heritage?

I grabbed my gear and climbed the staircase to the second-story balcony. From here I could look down into the great room. Tomorrow, I'd be able to gaze out the high picture windows and see across the bay to the silo-like tower, a factory incinerator from a bygone era, on the other side. But tonight, the blackness was broken only by an occasional swirl of snow against the glass.

I set down my things and leaned against the rail. I almost gave a contented sigh, but I knew better than to celebrate my inner happiness. At any minute, all chaos could break loose in my life.

Though I held my pensive pose, I was still thanking God in my mind. I couldn't believe I was actually here. As a kid, I'd promised myself that when I grew up, I'd buy this cottage and live in it, and bake pies for the Fourth of July celebration down in Port Silvan, and make lemonade for all the children who would come to swim on Saturdays.

I'd never baked a pie, but I could probably figure out the lemonade. Would I be breaking my promise if I drank it alone?

A yawn, punctuated by a squeak in my throat, sent my thoughts in the direction of bed. Ghosts of the snowflakes I'd battled on the road the past eight hours danced before my eyes. Time for some sleep.

I dragged my stuff into my old bedroom and set it by the door. I flicked on the light and stood in numb surprise. It looked like I wouldn't need my cot after all. The room was furnished with a twin bed, a table, and a chair. A puffy patchwork quilt was turned back to reveal crisp white sheets and a plush pillow.

Who would have taken time to make up a bed for me? As nice as the realtor was, I couldn't imagine that she'd done it.

A piece of paper was angled on the pillow. Perhaps it was a note from my fairy godmother. I stepped across a braided rug and reached for the page.

My hand jerked back as if slapped. It wasn't a note, it was a photograph. Of my mother. Her high school graduation picture lay torn in two pieces on the pillowcase.

Written in thick black script across her smiling face were the words "DON'T ASK WHY."

2

My hands shook as I picked up the halves of glossy paper. I stuck the jagged edges together, trying to make what was broken whole again. The corners of my eyes stung. Who would do such a thing? Back in the last town I'd left, I'd had enough veiled threats and attempts on my life to keep me on constant red alert. I hadn't expected to run into the same thing up here. No one even knew I was coming. I'd specifically told the real estate agent to keep my purchase of the log home confidential. All I wanted was peace and quiet and anonymity while I got in touch with the past. Yet it seemed my first night home would be no different than anywhere else.

But tonight I was too tired to care. I snuck to the end of the hall and used the crusty porcelain. A flick of the handle failed to render a flush. I groaned and turned on the faucet. Nothing. I'd been a fool not to heed the agent's warning. But any self-reproach would have to wait until tomorrow. Fairly certain I'd locked the back door after coming in, I fumbled into a warm pair of sweats and climbed under the quilt. For a while, I listened to the logs creak and groan, hoping it was only the wind blowing against the rafters. Then I fell asleep.

The next morning, gray light poured through the naked bedroom window. I squinted, trying to pinpoint my surroundings. Blue wallpaper flecked with shiny silver leaves told me I was in my old room at the cottage. The bed pulled me into its saggy warmth, and I indulged the urge to lie there a little longer.

I stared at a crack in the wallboard and thought about the kiss he'd given me just before I drove away. Was that only yesterday morning? His mouth had been so soft, so comfortable touching mine. And gentle. He'd barely pressed against my lips. Then, he'd pulled back just as heat rushed to my face.

I scrunched my nose into the coolness of the pillow, trying to drive away the burning sensation that coursed over my cheeks at the memory. The linen smelled of an overdose of fabric softener, the kind my grandmother used to use. The scent brought me back to the memory of last night's discovery.

Leaning off the edge of the bed, I picked up the halves of my mother's picture from the rug where they must have fallen while I slept. I matched the ragged inner edges and looked past the fat black script that marred the surface.

Mom had had beautiful eyes. The bottom lid curved up when she smiled, giving her an exotic look. I forced a smile to my own face and ran a finger along my bottom lid. My eyes did the same thing.

Memories of him snuck back into my mind.

Our final weeks together had been wonderful. I'd been

recovering from the sting of a short but disastrous relationship, so I'd known better than to let things get romantic. We were friends. Just friends. But I suspect he'd felt differently about the romance department. He'd called my eyes bewitching. He loved how the color changed with the lighting: turquoise in dim light, bright green when the sun hit them. One day, he touched my hand. And instead of camaraderie, I'd felt a jolt of lightning deep in my stomach. And I knew I had to leave. Fast.

I threw back the quilt and landed on the floor. If I was going to get anything done today, I had better get started.

The bedside table had a slim drawer, and I set Mom's picture on the bottom. I shut it, cutting off thoughts of her, and anybody else, until later.

I wiggled out of my sweats and put yesterday's clothes back on. The first thing I'd have to do was crank up the heat in the drafty old cottage. The propane wall furnace down in the kitchen did nothing for the rest of the house, which still used an ancient boiler system. I remember huddling near the wall heater on a cold U.P. summer morning as a kid. Now, I pulled on fat wool socks and raced down the steps, anxious to snuggle up to its warmth in the dead of a U.P. winter, twenty-odd years later.

Holding my hands to the heat of the steel grate, I felt my circulation pick up. All I needed was a cup of hot coffee and I'd be ready to tackle my first day at the new place.

I pulled on my boots and stepped onto the porch. The air crackled with cold. Clumps of snow dropped from the trees onto the ground, breaking the silence with muffled thuds. Low white clouds raced through the sky. Above them, a solid sheet of gray promised more snow to come.

I scurried out to the car for my coffeemaker, one of my few possessions. My quick move to the U.P. was made easier by the fact that I owned only enough to fit in the back of my SUV. I'd always rented furniture to fit the houses I'd renovated, and only to aid in schmooze-appeal. I wasn't into personal comforts. My cot and sleeping bag had served me well enough over the years. Of course, last night had seemed like heaven in a real bed.

I opened the back hatch of the Explorer and dug through suitcases, duffels, and tools for the coffeepot and accessories. Arms full, I picked my way through the drifts, rushed inside, and slammed the door against the cold.

I stomped my boots, leaving Abominable Snowman tracks on the tattered welcome mat. I walked in stocking feet over to the sink and stuck the carafe under the faucet. I turned the handle.

Again nothing.

Of course. The cottage would have been winterized to keep the pipes from freezing. That meant no flushing the toilet, taking a shower, or washing the dishes until the water situation was cured. And as for the coffee, I'd have to use bottled water until the tap was available.

I wrinkled my nose. I used to be a big bottled-water proponent. But back in Rawlings, I found out I was being slowly poisoned by arsenic in my personal supply of bottled water. After that, I decided to accept whatever the ground had to offer.

17

I walked down the hall to the first-floor bedroom. The summerhouse must have been a hunting lodge back in the '30s or '40s, with its six bedrooms and three bathrooms. But by the time Mom got a hold of it, the place was in such a state of disrepair that we'd always used the most functional bathroom in the downstairs bedroom. And for the ridiculously low price I'd paid, I couldn't imagine that subsequent owners had made any upgrades. I'd make time later to give the home a complete inspection.

The bedroom door squeaked open. I poked my head in. The bare, blue-striped mattress of a full-size bed caught my eye. The scent of musty wood caught my nose. I sneezed.

The walls and ceiling of the room were paneled with cedar that had darkened to a rich golden hue over time. A good washing would take care of the dust. The floor, on the other hand, had been done over in the '50s with some gray-and-black-speckled linoleum-type stuff.

I smiled. Things were the same as when my mom had slept here, although she'd had a soft white comforter on the bed, a colorful braided rug on the floor, and a vase of wildflowers on the dresser. When I was scared, I'd slept in here with her.

I traced a finger in the dust on the dark oak dresser. It was odd that whoever had made up my bed had known which room I'd slept in as a kid. Anyone else would have made the bed in this room for me. It was the logical choice.

I looked at the trail I'd made in the dust. DON'T ASK WHY, I'd written.

But I would ask why. And I wouldn't stop asking until I had some answers.

I walked into the bathroom. The toilet bowl was filled with pinkish liquid, probably anti-freeze, but I used it anyway, reserving the flush for later when the water was turned on.

I checked my hair in the mirror. I'd been growing it out from its former chin length to its now shoulder length. I had chosen the shorter style to avoid looking too much like another resident of my old town. But with five hundred miles between me and Rawlings, Michigan, I was free to look any way I wanted.

I ran my fingers through reddish-brown tangles, deciding I looked good enough for a run to the store the day after a snowstorm.

The driveway had drifted over during the night, but the Explorer cut through scattered three-foot-high snow mounds without any trouble. I would never have made it in my inherited classic Buick, the one I'd finally unloaded for this dream machine.

The end of my driveway sloped upward where it joined the two-lane highway to Port Silvan. I slowed to look for traffic. All clear. I pressed the gas. My wheels started to slip. The car skidded sideways on the incline. I punched the vehicle into four-wheel drive and burst onto the lonely highway like a colt trying out its new legs.

"Woo-hooo!" I grinned at the swell of exhilaration rushing through my veins.

The county plow had already been through. Salt left clear patches on the otherwise slippery blacktop. I put the Explorer back in two-wheel drive and took it easy for the eight-mile trip to Port Silvan. Just down the road, a red wooden sign with white letters identified Cupid's Creek. This time of year the creek was nothing more than a trickle of water at the bottom of an icy trough. The sign had been there when I was a kid. I wondered what else had stayed the same even after all these years.

Farther ahead, the roofs of farmhouses and barns were white with caked-on snow. Horses huddled over bins of hay. The fields around them looked like wrinkled sheets of bleached cotton.

A little ways up, the road straightened. In the distance rose the blue water tower of the Village of Port Silvan. The houses grew closer together as I neared town. Some I remembered from my time here as a kid, some looked new.

I reached the village limits. I nearly choked on the dry air in the SUV. Or was it nerves? I turned the fan to low and cleared my throat. There was no reason to be nervous. No one would recognize me. I wasn't seven anymore. I was all grown up.

I pulled into Sinclair's Grocery and shifted into park. I left the car running while I scoped out the neighborhood. The ancient building in front of me had been recently updated with a bright white coat of stain on its clapboard siding. The store's name was traced in blue on a sign swinging over the entry. Painted-on letters in the big picture window said OPEN. Across the full length of the front ran a snow-covered boardwalk. I could picture its row of benches filled with kids eating ice-cream cones in the summer. I'd been one of them, of course. Blue Moon had been my favorite. Next door, a house had gotten new vinyl siding. So had the old gas station. Behind me across the street, a couple buildings, at least a hundred years old, had gotten fresh paint jobs as well. Port Silvan Museum, one of the signs said. Blinds covered the windows and the place had a vacant look.

I was beginning to think the whole town was vacant. Then I heard a rumble off to my right. A red four-wheeler pulled up next to me. Its driver wore a ski mask, though whether to protect from the bitter cold or to burglarize the place, I couldn't be sure. I activated my power locks, thinking as I did that I couldn't have done that in Grandma's old Buick. The man glanced over at the sound and shook his head. He went in the store. I waited. He came out a few minutes later carrying a case of soda. His mask was folded back to his forehead. I scrunched in concentration as I studied his face. He was a notch older than me and good-looking in a rugged sort of way. But there was nothing familiar about him. He bore no resemblance to any nine- or ten-year-olds from the past. With a narrow-eyed look in my direction, he got on his four-wheeler and rode away.

I stepped out of my vehicle and walked into the store. A bell jangled overhead as I entered. The scent of fresh, sweet donuts met me at the door. To one side, candy bars and treats were laid out at kid-level beneath the front window. Directly in front of me, racks of DVDs promised night after night of entertainment. The covers were sprinkled with yellow Post-it notes that said "Sorry, Out." The blizzard must have boosted rentals.

To the other side, a fifty-something woman with a poof of blonde hair stood behind the checkout. I gave

21

a nod and smiled as I pulled a cart from the stack and headed in search of the bottled water aisle. I couldn't shake the feeling that she was watching me, even after I turned the corner out of sight. I glanced up at one of the large, round security mirrors and met her eyes. I looked away, focusing on the choice of bottles and jugs in front of me. I ignored the suspicion that nagged at me. I was new in town. She was curious. That was all.

I loaded the water and went down the remaining aisles of the miniature supermarket. I grabbed the basics on my way through, then ordered up six assorted donuts at checkout.

"Expecting company already?" the woman asked.

"Me? No, just figured I'd have some treats handy the next few days." I stared at her, wondering if I should know her, and why she seemed to know something about me.

Her cheeks were rosy with makeup and her maroon lipstick looked freshly applied. She kept a pleasant smile as she checked price tags and punched buttons on the cash register. Stick-on fingernails flashed a metallic pink in the fluorescent lighting.

"That'll be twenty-nine dollars and sixteen cents," she said in a raspy smoker's voice.

I grimaced at the high cost of groceries in this out-of-the-way burg as I groped through the pocket of my ski coat for the money. I laid two twenties on the counter.

The cash drawer popped open with a *bing* and she passed me my change.

"Oh," she said, "this is for you." She fished around

next to an old-fashioned rotary phone and found a slip of paper. "Candice wanted you to have her number. Said to call her as soon as you got in."

I reached for the note in slow motion. "Who's Candice?"

The woman smiled. "Candice LeJeune. She figured you wouldn't remember her. You used to visit her all the time when you were a kid."

I stared at the folded paper with "Tish" written across the top. Whoever this Candice was, she had a lot of nerve calling me by the pet name my mother had given me. I only liked people to call me Tish after I'd given my permission.

"Was Candice a friend of my mother's?" I asked.

"And your grandmother's, God rest her soul," the woman said.

My glance shot up at the reference to my grandmother. I couldn't be sure, but there might have been a hint of accusation in her eyes.

"My grandmother was a wonderful lady. Did you know her?" I asked.

"Everybody knew Eva Nagy. There's a ton of Nagys around here. Eva was related to half the peninsula."

My forehead rose in surprise. I guess I never knew my grandmother's maiden name. She'd been Eva Amble for as long as I could remember. I had a feeling there would be a lot more surprises coming my way. Questions I'd asked Gram about my mother, my father, my early years had all carried the same response: "Let it lie, Tish. No sense living in the past. Just let it lie."

A tiny nuclear bomb had exploded in my chest every

time I'd heard the words, until fallout had built up to the point I could no longer ignore it.

I looked at the note in my hand. It pulsed in my fingers like some mystical Pandora's box. Dare I open it and step into the past? Or should I heed my grandmother's words of warning and leave well enough alone?

3

I slid the note open.

Call me! Aunt Candice.

A local telephone number accompanied the scribbled letters.

No friendly face popped to mind at the inscription. I had no memory of an "Aunt Candice," nor any other relations. Maybe I'd recognize her once I saw her face.

I gathered up my purchases, gave the cashier a parting smile, and headed out.

"Welcome home, Tish," she called behind me. I let the words get lost in the wind as I pushed open the door.

A patch of blue sky broke through the cloud cover, sending sunlight glinting off the fresh snow. The sudden glare made my eyes water. I loaded the groceries in the Explorer. Before I left town, I stopped at the bank to open a new account. The teller seemed to recognize my name, but allowed me the dignity of my privacy. At least one institution in town practiced confidentiality.

I ducked my face against the wind, jumped in my car, and headed north. I'd already come to the realization that there was no such thing as anonymity in this day and age. One word from the real estate agent, one look at the national headlines ten years back, and anyone would know who I was. Patricia Louise Amble, Grandma Slayer. I thought I'd shaken the feeling that people were judging me. But I guess it would take more time. And if Gram had been related to half the peninsula as the clerk said, then I could expect a few evil eyes for my past deed. I'd just have to hold my head up and not let it get to me. They weren't going to run me out of Port Silvan like some Frankenstein's monster. I planned on sticking around awhile.

I slowed and took the turn down my driveway. Snow flew from the tires in my rearview as I gunned the engine through the drifts. I pulled up to the cottage feeling like a cowboy who'd just rounded up a herd of cattle. *Yee-haw.* I loved the power beneath the hood.

I brought in the groceries and water jugs. While I put things away, I thought about where I might find the water shutoff valve so I could get the faucets working again. I couldn't remember seeing any doors on the first floor that might conceal waterworks. That meant there had to be a crawl space or a freestanding pump house somewhere nearby.

I tried picturing the yard without snow, as I'd seen it every summer back when. The only structure that came to mind was a garden shed that stood about a hundred feet from one end of the house, at the edge of the woods. That left the probability of a crawl space. Hopefully the access door was inside the house.

The sound of an approaching vehicle seeped through the thin glass of the kitchen windows. I headed toward the back door, wondering who would brave the driveway in this weather.

I stepped onto the porch. Snow dust blew down the neck of my jacket. I zipped against the ice-cold pinpricks. The roar of a diesel engine reverberated through the trees. A truck pulled into sight. Snow flew to one side in front of it like a white geyser. The driver slowed, angled into a snow bank, then backed up, revealing a rusty red plow attachment. The truck took another swipe at the opposite bank. After a few more maneuvers, the vehicle parked on the cleared driveway. The engine cut out. The rust-eaten driver's side door opened. A pair of brown Sorels, laces dangling, appeared.

"Morning, young lady." A burly man wearing tan canvas-type outerwear stepped into view. Curly white hair and a matching beard circled his face. He carried a to-go cup in one hand.

"Hi." I held on to the rail as I went down the porch steps.

"Thought you might need some help cleaning up this mess." He spit a stream of tobacco into the snow.

"Thank you." I put my hand out. "I'm Patricia Amble."

He took my fingers in a loose grip. "I know who you are. You're Beth's little one."

Beth. That was a name I hadn't heard in years.

"Did you know my mother?" I couldn't contain my excitement.

His eyes roved my face. "'Course I did. You look a lot like her." The old guy shook his head. "Too bad how things ended up for your mom."

"Yeah." Tears stung my eyes. Dead at the bottom of a quarry was a pathetic end for anybody. I sniffled. "So how did you know her?"

"I'm hoping for a fill-up on my coffee. Got any?" He lifted his travel mug.

"Oh, gee." I ran a hand through my hair. "I was working on that when you pulled up. Come on in."

He followed me inside. He leaned against the wall and started to pull off a boot.

"Please," I waved a hand. "Leave those on. It's too cold in here for stocking feet." I poured water from a jug into the coffeemaker. "Besides, nothing can hurt this old linoleum." I wrinkled my nose at the tan-and-black-flecked tiles.

I scooped some coffee into the filter and turned on the pot. The machine belched, then dripped fragrant, steaming liquid. "It just takes a few minutes."

"I hear you're going to fix this place up." The old gentleman surveyed the kitchen.

I shook off my annoyance. I'd moved from one small town to another. Of course everyone knew who I was and what my plans were.

"It'll probably take awhile, but with all that lakefront, it should do well on resale," I said.

"Resale? Papa B is going to let you sell the place?"

Somewhere along the way, the guy had lost me. "Pardon? I'm the new owner. That's why I bought this place. Fix it up and sell it for a profit."

He put his hands up and shook his head. "None of my business. Just surprises me is all."

I crossed my arms and leaned against the cupboards.

On the opposite counter, a sprinkling of coffee grounds betrayed my hasty prep job. I ripped a piece of paper toweling off the roll and held it under the faucet. I turned the handle. Nothing. Frustrated, I wiped the grounds up with the dry toweling and flung it in the trash.

I turned to my visitor. "You were going to tell me how you knew my mother. Maybe you can start with your name."

"Jim Hawley. I live down in the village. I'm related to the Russo family on Olivia's side. Second or third cousins. I can't remember."

"Sorry, Jim. Name-dropping is wasted on me. I haven't been around here since I was a kid."

"Oh." He stroked his beard. Droplets of melted snow came off in his fingers. "I just figured since you're a Russo yourself, you'd know who Olivia was."

I stepped back. "The last name is Amble. My grand-mother used to be a Nagy." I reached for the steaming coffee decanter. "How about that cup to go? Do you take it black?"

He nodded. "Sure your grandmother was a Nagy. I remember Eva. But your dad is a Russo. Olivia is his grandmother." He smirked through his whiskers. "She's the local matriarch around here. If something's going on in this town, you better believe Olivia knows about it."

I held the coffeepot suspended. My dad. I'd almost forgotten I had one of those. And now I had a busybody great-grandmother named Olivia.

"Olivia must be pretty old by now," I said. I hadn't been up here in close to thirty years. My father would have had to be young, and his parents young, in order for Olivia to still be kicking.

"The town just celebrated her ninety-third birthday last month," my visitor told me. "That gal's too ornery to die."

There must have been something in the water up here. The people drank from a regular fountain of youth. Even with cancer, my grandmother had lived years past what the doctors had predicted. Too bad the water hadn't extended my mother's life any.

I poured coffee into his mug. "So you knew my mother through my dad?"

The old guy took a sip and nodded. "Sweet girl. She was always bailing Jacob out of some sort of trouble or another. She wanted to marry him real bad. Next thing you know, Beth was pregnant and Jacob took off."

I swallowed hard at the story. To hear Mom's version, theirs had been a fairy-tale romance. Two people so in love. Two families determined to keep them apart. Then I came along, the apple of their eyes. Dad worked out of town, Mom said, and that's why we didn't see him. But she'd always loved him. I could tell.

Once Mom was gone, however, I'd been fed Grandma's version of things. My perfect mother fell in love with a perfect loser, who'd left town the moment he heard I existed. I remembered how Gram squirmed whenever I asked about my parents' wedding. I'd eventually figured out there probably had never been one, though Gram always insisted I was "legitimate," as if the term somehow made me a real person as opposed to a phony. But the fact that my name, Mom's name, and Gram's name were all Amble pretty much said it all.

I fixed myself a cup of sweetened coffee. I held the hot mug in my palms, soaking in the warmth as I sipped.

"Want some help getting that water back on? If I'd have known you were going to be staying here, I would have had everything hooked up for you. But Ethyl just told me to keep the road open."

I smiled. Ethyl Merton was the real estate agent. "I don't think she believed me when I told her I planned on moving right in. A little too rustic for her taste, she said."

"She was shocked, let me tell you, when you called her. Papa B had this place waiting for you all these years. Then out of the blue, here you are."

My neck crawled with heebie-jeebies. "You've mentioned Papa B before. Who is he?"

"B for Bernard." He looked at me like I knew what he was talking about. "Bernard Russo. Your grandfather."

4

At the mention of another long-lost relative, pressure built in my sinuses.

I remembered the phone call to Northern Realty a few months back. The agent had seemed utterly thrilled to hear from me, total stranger though I was.

"Did you say your name is Patricia Amble? How wonderful. I have just the thing."

I'd been equally thrilled to hear she had the old lodge up for sale. "That's where I spent summers as a kid," I'd told her.

"Isn't that a nice coincidence? Are you sure you don't want to see it before I get the papers ready?"

But I'd been too excited. "Fax everything to me. I'll sign this week." I hadn't paid any attention to the seller's name.

Not that the name Russo would have meant anything to me.

I glared at Jim Hawley as if he were somehow to blame for the faults of my paternal relatives. At any rate, I wasn't prepared to discuss family I barely remembered as if they had always been a part of my life. What was their excuse for disregarding me, anyway? And what kind of grandfather kept a log home around for a granddaughter he'd never even given the time of day? Did he think I was just going to move in and pretend there were no hard feelings?

Jim shifted his weight and cleared his throat. "I'll get that water hooked up. The shutoff's in the crawl."

I watched through the narrow window by the door as he pulled a shovel from the bed of his truck and walked to the side of the house. He pushed back the bare branches of a towering shrub. A moment later, chunks of snow landed in the yard as he cleared the hidden access.

Five minutes passed. The faucet gurgled, then spit water into the sink. I rushed over to turn it off. I headed toward the first floor bathroom to check that sink as well. I flipped the handles to the "off" position, then went upstairs to make the rounds.

My feet made hollow *thunks* as they landed on the slabs of cedar logs that made up the steps. The worn remains of bark still clung to the outer edge of each riser. The rails were constructed of peeled cedar trees, about six inches in diameter apiece, and supported by chunky cedar spindles. The banisters were cedar stumps, complete with roots.

At the top, I slowed and looked out at the lake. A mass of white blanketed the once-blue waters. Wind kicked up walls of snow in the center of the bay. I'd have to wait until another day to see all the way across.

I walked down the hall of the north wing. Two bedroom doors hung open on opposite sides of the hall. I peeked in each one. Both rooms were long and narrow. Neither had furniture. Daylight came in through double dormers, leaving rectangular patches of gray on wide plank flooring. I was relieved to see the original wood had escaped the vinyl updates the first story had endured. I shut both doors and continued down the hallway to the bathroom at the end, toward the sound of running water. Thankfully, the plumbing still worked in the claw-foot tub and matching pedestal sink, regardless of the deplorable condition of the room.

The south wing was a mirror image of the north. I turned off the faucets in the bathroom and shut the doors to the bedrooms. I poked my head in my own bedroom at the top of the stairs, just to see that nothing had moved from where I'd left it this morning.

Jim was just coming in the back door when I reached the kitchen. He grabbed his insulated mug from the counter. "Thank you for the refill. Call me if you need anything." He headed toward the door.

"Thanks, Jim. I really appreciate all you've done."

He lifted a hand in the air without turning around. The diesel fired up, backed out, and fled down the driveway.

Opening my box of fresh donuts, I chose a chocolate-filled powdered one. Jim's new slant on my dysfunctional upbringing gave me plenty to think about while I cleaned the white sugar from my fingers.

I spent the rest of the morning scrubbing down the kitchen. The sponge in my hands made a good replace-ment for the necks of the Russo clan. I couldn't imagine any excuse great enough to pardon their neglect of both me and this house over the years.

I dried off and took a look around. If I stuck to my unwritten Rules of Renovation, the kitchen required a complete face-lift. But I'd learned at the last house that some things are better left alone. This time I'd settle for removing the asbestos tiles in order to expose the original nine-foot-high walls and ceiling. That, along with a shiny new oak floor, would make the room feel dramatically bigger. Then I'd simply hop on the latest home-decorating bandwagon and play up the '50s flavor.

I grabbed some turkey and cheese from the fridge and made a wrap. I wandered into the great room and plopped with a rusty *boing* onto the sofa.

I'd taken my jacket off at the start of the kitchen project. Now as I relaxed with my feet up, work boots and all, I thought how nice a fuzzy throw would be. I'd have to find one to complement the lime upholstery. After all, this was an heirloom sofa that had a permanent home at the lodge, regardless of its color and condition.

A blast of wind whistled in the chimney. I shivered from cold. I'd only been here one day and already I felt like I'd relocated to an Arctic wasteland. Thank goodness winter wouldn't last forever.

I jumped up and huddled at the kitchen wall heater. With all the surfaces in my kitchen sparkling, I had no fear of drop-ins. Maybe now was a good time to invite dear Aunt Candice over for a visit. She was probably as curious about me as I was about her.

I dug in my jeans pocket and pulled out the scribbled note. I rubbed at the wrinkles with my thumb. Why would Candice have left a note for me at the local grocer's? Granted, I had to buy food sometime. But why not tape her phone number to the back door, or better yet, greet me in person? Leaving a message in the hands of that clerk was like putting a billboard in downtown Port Silvan, flashing TISH AMBLE IS BACK.

I found my phone in my ski coat. The signal was weak, but I dialed the number anyway.

"Hello, Patricia. I'd hoped to hear from you."

I was silent while I processed the sultry, mature voice. Something in the tones made me feel seven years old again.

I cleared my throat. "I got your note from the clerk down at Sinclair's. You asked me to call."

"I wanted to welcome you home. It's been a long time."

Yeah. My whole life, I could have reminded her. "I'm sorry, but I don't remember you. Maybe we could meet in person. I'm living in the lodge on Valentine's Lane. Would you like to come by for coffee?"

"That's not a good idea. Why don't you stop by my place instead?"

I hated the thought of going back out in the cold after my feet had finally thawed, but curiosity got the best of me.

"Okay. Where are you?"

She gave me directions to her home, and within a few minutes of disconnecting, I was ready to tackle the winter roads again.

I headed south toward Port Silvan and turned left at the cider mill sign before town. About a mile later I came to a fence of fieldstone and wrought iron, nearly buried beneath the drifts. Behind it sat the Victorian farmhouse

Candice had described. White gingerbread trim accented the wraparound front porch. A second-story dormer was decked with bric-a-brac siding in cream to match the rest of the house. Soft blue shutters trimmed the windows.

I didn't know anything about the woman, but I liked her taste in homes.

I swung into the drive and parked up by the house.

The slam of my car door echoed across the snowy fields. I stared at the residence, remembering the wise words of my grandmother. *Let it lie.*

It wasn't too late to get in my vehicle and gun it back to my own stretch of woods. I'd learned from my last renovation project that curiosity could definitely kill the cat. For the duration of my stay in Port Silvan, minding my own business should be my personal credo.

The front door opened. A woman dressed in equestrian-type clothing stepped into the cold.

"Tish. Welcome," she called from the porch in her Bette Davis voice.

A breeze brushed my cheeks. I could always get back in the car, I reminded myself.

"Come in. We've got so much to talk about," said the spider to the fly.

I wanted to buzz off in the worst way. But minding my own business could begin tomorrow, right after I figured out who this Candice was and where she fit into my mother's life.

I took a step forward. The hole in my jeans suddenly felt the size of a baseball instead of a marble. Why couldn't I have put on something a little more stylish? Candice looked like she'd stepped straight off the pages of *Vogue*. Next time I visited, I'd dress up and give her a better impression. I did have a few nice pieces in my wardrobe.

I put on a smile and walked up the front steps. She probably didn't realize how intimidating she came off. Her short hair was dyed pure silver. Her sixty-something face looked wrinkle-free under a meticulous makeup job. Her trim physique would put most twenty-year-olds to shame.

She reached out and pulled me toward her.

"Look at you. You're beautiful. And so much like your mother." Her eyes seemed misty. She blinked a few times and shook her head. "Well, let's not stand out here. Let's go in where it's warm."

The light changed from snowy white to warm yellow as I entered the cozy parlor. The room was done in cream with satin white trim lining both the top and bottom of the walls. Framed black-and-white photographs hung from various length ribbons attached to thin molding that circled the perimeter. Flames flickered in a corner fireplace. Atop the dark oak mantel sat a miniature grandfather clock, its *tick tick tick* muffled by silky curtains striped in deep mauve and butter yellow. The tapestry furniture had a Victorian flair, but looked more comfortable than formal. Keepsakes and antique books were displayed in orderly chaos around the room. It was exactly the way I would have decorated my last house if I had lived in it for twenty years instead of a few months.

"Your home is gorgeous." I couldn't hide the awe in my voice.

"Thank you. Have a seat by the fire. I'll get us some tea."

She took my coat and left the room. I sank into an overstuffed armchair. The back reclined and a footrest popped out in front of me. I imagined having a set of these, perhaps in leather, flanking the hearth at my log cabin. I sighed. No use getting my heart set on furniture. The same rules that had applied to the last four renovations also applied to Port Silvan. Rent, don't buy. The fewer possessions I owned, the easier it would be to pull up and move to the next project. Things just weighed you down. They made you get emotionally involved with four walls that should remain strictly a business transaction.

I put my hands behind my head and listened to the clinking of dishes coming from a kitchen somewhere. Things and people. Both were best avoided if a girl like me wanted to keep her head together. It was already hard enough that I'd bent my people rule back in Rawlings.

I stared at the ceiling and did a quick calculation. I'd gone almost forty-eight hours now without hearing his voice. I could get through the next forty-eight. And the next forty-eight after that. By then he should feel more like a distant memory, like my old friend Anne or my old cat Peanut Butter, and less like I'd had open heart surgery and the doctor forgot to put my heart back in and the only thing left was a huge, empty cavity where a lot of joy used to be.

I swallowed the lump in my throat.

Time. It was all a matter of time.

"Here we go." Candice entered the room and set a tray

of delicate china tea service on the low table between us. Orange-and-cinnamon-scented steam rose as she poured.

I reached for my cup. My fingers grabbed clumsily at the handle. The first swig singed my lips and burned a trail down my throat.

Across from me, Aunt Candice relaxed in her chair, cup and saucer in hand as she waited for the boiling liquid to cool.

"So how old is this place?" My s's lisped out. I set my cup back on the table and nursed my lips with a suffering tongue.

"It turns twenty-five this spring."

I scrunched my forehead. "Well, that explains why there're no cracks in the plaster. It looks so authentic. I thought for sure you had renovated an original."

She pursed her lips. "Unfortunately, the original burnt down. It was an exquisite craftsman-style home built in the 1940s, complete with secret doors and hidden passages. Entirely irreplaceable." She took a sip of tea. "I've always loved Victorian architecture, so at the opportunity, I designed this farmhouse."

"It's really nice." I wanted to get straight to the point and ask her to recite everything she knew about my mother. But the way she looked at me with that intent stare, seeming to check out every line on my face, made me nervous. It was better to keep the conversation impersonal until I knew what was running through her mind.

She set her tea on the table and leaned forward. "You're probably wondering about me. Who I am, how we're related, why I wanted to meet you."

I grinned. "All of the above."

"I'll give you the short, sweet version." She stared into the fire. "I got to know you and your mother quite well when you were young. You visited with me almost every weekend." Her eyes met mine. "Perhaps as you spend more time on the peninsula, you'll begin to remember."

I concentrated on her features, hoping to stir some vague memories. Nothing rose to the surface. "Maybe." I reached for the note that was still in my pocket and dropped it on the glass tabletop. "How did you know I'd be arriving in town?"

"Ethyl Merton kept me posted. She and I go way back. She said she'd promised not to tell anyone of your arrival, but she remembered how special you were to me and couldn't resist passing on the good news. I hope you're not angry with her."

I considered whether or not to forgive Ethyl's misconduct while Candice sipped her tea.

She looked over the edge of her cup. "I'm surprised you'd drive through a snowstorm to get here."

I shrugged. "My grace period was up at the last house and I had nothing better to do, I guess." Nothing better to do except meet Brad for lunch at Sam's Coney and plan our downhill ski trip with the gang after church on Sunday. But why put off the inevitable? I simply said goodbye and meant it instead of dragging out some long, agonizing relationship that was doomed to failure before it even began.

"You do have Russo blood in you, I see. Anyone else would have waited until spring," Candice said.

I'd decided that facing a blizzard was definitely less scary than looking Brad in the eye and telling him why I couldn't hang around Rawlings anymore.

I waved a hand. "Oh, I'm not so brave, really."

Her brow lifted. "I'm not talking bravery. I'm talking stupidity."

My jaw dropped and my eyes fluttered. Had she just insulted my entire family?

"Don't look so offended. The Russos are known for having their priorities out of kilter. I only hope you won't make the same mistakes."

Too late, I wanted to tell her. "Thanks for the warning," I said.

Aunt Candice leaned back and crossed one tall leather boot over the other. "You've been away a long time, Tish. I can only assume you're back because your grandparents kept you in the dark all these years." She folded her hands in her lap. "Art and Eva did a commendable job snatching you away from the peninsula. I'm sure I'm not the only one astounded that you've returned. That's why I had to see you before they got to you."

"Before who got to me?"

Her eyes narrowed. "The Russos, of course."

5

The clock on the mantel marked a new hour. Its musical chimes blared like gongs in the silence. I took a sip of tea. It had cooled to lukewarm. The bitter brew clung to my taste buds.

"Would you care for some honey?" Candice asked.

"Thank you." I stirred some into my cup. I had a feeling I'd need more than a spoonful of the sweet stuff to make whatever Candice had to say palatable.

"How much did your grandmother tell you about the Russo family?" Candice asked.

She sat forward and sipped her tea, watching me over the rim.

"Nothing. I never even heard the name until this morning."

"She probably thought she was protecting you. I'm sure she couldn't have guessed you'd eventually move back to the area."

"Protecting me from what?" Candice made it sound like my dad's side of the family was out to get me.

She sighed and pursed her lips. "This may be a beautiful area, but every garden has its snakes. I can't tell you what to do, Tish, I can only urge you not to get mixed up with the Russos. And believe me, as soon as they find out you're back, they'll try luring you into their viper's nest. They're not the only ones to watch out for, of course. They're just the most obvious."

I hadn't come five hundred miles to stick my head in the sand. If finding out about my mother meant going nose to nose with the Russo clan, then so be it. "I appreciate your concern, but I'm not passing up the opportunity to get to know the family that was denied me all these years."

Candice's eyes flared. "Art and Eva Amble did what was necessary to ensure your survival. If Bernard Russo had known your whereabouts, your life would have been a few chapters short of what it is today."

I shook my head in confusion. "What are you saying?"

"Just that I would hate to see history repeat itself. Your mother was a beautiful woman with a bright future until the Russos got a hold of her. Bernard virtually lured her to her death."

"I don't understand. Is he somehow responsible for my mother killing herself?"

"Is that what Eva told you—that it was suicide? Bernard couldn't be more guilty of her death if he drove her car into the quarry himself."

"What did he do that was so terrible? Why would she kill herself because of him?"

"You'll have to trust me and keep your distance. You have a bright future, Tish. Don't throw it away on people who aren't worth the dirt they walk on."

Candice's intentions were probably kindhearted, but being told that half my genes were lower than dirt didn't endear her to me. I set my teacup down with a clumsy *clink*. "Thank you for inviting me over today." I stood. "I appreciate the advice. I really do. I just can't promise I'll follow it."

Candice sucked in a deep breath. "Just be careful, Tish. That's all I can say."

She rose and brought my coat to me.

"Thanks for the tea." I bundled up and stepped into the cold, sorry to leave the cozy haven for the harsh winter winds.

I drove home. The scenery blurred over with thoughts of feuding relatives and the image of my mom's Ford merging with bedrock.

Afternoon was already fading to evening by the time I got back to the cabin. I trekked upstairs and flopped on my bed, breathing in the yummy baby-fresh scent that lingered on my pillowcase. Maybe tomorrow I'd give Ethyl Merton a call and find out who else she'd told of my arrival. Right after I found out their brand of fabric softener, I'd bawl them out for ripping up my mom's picture and writing those three maddening words across the front.

Don't ask why.

As if that were possible. Whoever had done the deed might as well have written, "Definitely ask why."

I rested my eyes for a few minutes, then got back to work downstairs making the bathroom presentable. The fixtures were old, but functional. Nothing a little caulk and white paint couldn't cure, at least temporarily.

Afterward, I washed up, then heated a mug of tomato

soup in my travel-size microwave. I took the steaming brew into my drafty great room. I sat in the dark and looked through the tall windows at the stars. Tomorrow promised to be clear and bright. If the wind died down, I'd get out and exercise.

I sipped my soup. Brad had been the one to get me walking three times a week on top of daily stretching. By the time I left Rawlings, he and I had become a regular sight along a three-mile route.

My lip scrunched. Somehow, hitting the trail wouldn't be the same without my walking buddy. But that was the choice I'd made, I reminded myself. And it was a good one. Because here I was, close to the people who had known my mother. I'd find out what I came to learn. Only then could I be in a relationship and be happy about it. I wouldn't have to feel dumb when I said, "I don't know," to every question about my parentage. I frowned as I remembered Candice's disparaging attitude toward my dad's side of the family. Still, at least I'd have answers, even if I didn't like them.

I rinsed out my mug and hit the sack early.

Another day, another donut.

I spent the morning washing down the staircase with wood oil soap. I paused at the top to gaze at the tower across the bay, rising black against the miles of ice and snow. I smiled and remembered the visit to the burn tower when I was a kid.

Mom had taken me for the day, the summer before she died. We parked the car at the boat dock behind the old hotel there and walked a narrow path through sun-washed grass. Monarch butterflies had been everywhere that day, feasting on milkweed and wildflowers. A little way up we crossed a rickety bridge that spanned a man-made channel. And just around the next clump of trees rose the tall, black tower.

We walked into its cool shadow. The rust-covered grate that once blocked the entrance lay over in some weeds. Mom and I poked our heads through the wide-open hole. Hundred-year-old ashes and coals were crusted over in a lumpy mound. We stared up at the dome. Daylight shot through sooty screens a long way up. I remember I was staring in awe at the sight, and the next thing I knew, a spider was crawling up my freckled arm. I screamed and danced to get it off me. My voice bounced off the walls of the chamber along with Mom's laughter. Later, we found a spot by the lake and ate our picnic lunch. Then we held hands and walked, still laughing, back to the car.

Up in the loft of my log cabin, I slouched against the rail. My chin rested on the back of my hands. Through my tears, the tower blurred until it disappeared into the glaring white around it. I straightened. If I could remember my visit to the burner with Mom as clearly as if it had happened yesterday, there had to be other memories waiting to rise to the surface. I just had to be patient.

I finished my task and bundled up with coat, hat, and scarf for a walk up the driveway before dark set in. I'd never been to the cottage in the winter as a kid, so today, every turn along the way held a snow-covered wonder. Pine branches hung low and mysterious beneath their fluffy white burdens. The creek where Mom and I waded

47

in the summer was iced over. Critter tracks crossed its winding path.

I came around a curve. Just ahead, a deer stood on the road. I jerked to a halt and watched its ears flick back and forth like furry radars. It spotted me and we locked eyes. Neither of us moved. Then the doe bolted into the forest. I raced ahead, slipping and sliding in the tire ruts. I paused where the deer had stood. Its cloven hooves left deep imprints in the snow. I followed the tracks with my eyes. Just through the trees, the doe watched me.

I made kissing sounds with my lips and held out a hand.

"Here, girl," I said in a falsetto voice.

The doe tensed.

"Come on, I'm not going to hurt you." I took a step toward her. She turned and fled into the woods.

"Goodbye! Come back soon!" I jumped up and down, feeling a little like Snow White's protégée.

I reached the end of the drive and turned right toward Cupid's Creek, keeping to the edge of the highway. I had to walk at least another mile before I could backtrack and call it three miles, although with the weight of my winter boots, it would feel like I'd walked six by the time I was done.

The wind picked up. I tied my scarf around my face. The sound of a car rumbled behind me and I hoped the driver would give me a wide berth. Across the road, a path led off to the east. Someone's tires had already packed the snow. I looked over my shoulder and crossed the highway before the car overtook me. I felt safer walking off the main road.

I headed along the two-track. The route curved up a hill back in the direction of my house. I followed the bluff to a clearing that looked out over Valentine's Bay. I paused to catch my breath after the rigorous climb. The trees below resembled ultra-shag carpet fit for a giant. And where the trees ended, the giant left his heel-print, a huge ice-covered semicircle called Valentine's Bay, a tiny part of the larger expanse of Nocquette Bay. Nestled along the shoreline was the roof of my cottage. Captivated by the view, I kept moving along the trail even though I'd already surpassed my mileage quota.

I looked ahead, farther on through the trees, and saw red. My face had begun to sting a little ways back, so at first I thought I was experiencing wind-burnt eyeballs. But as I blinked and squinted for a better view, I could make out a cherry red four-wheeler parked near a clump of brush. Curious, I drew closer. The outline of another four-wheeler, this one dark green, became visible through the bare limbs. Standing next to the vehicles were two men. One was dressed in a camouflage snowsuit, the other in black winter gear. Their voices came in muffled bites, blown by the wind, too low to distinguish words. The man in camouflage passed something to the man in black. And the man in black passed something back to him.

The action stopped my progress cold. Perhaps I'd seen too many cop movies, Brad's favorite Saturday night pastime. But instinct told me I was witnessing a drug deal. I crept backward, hoping to make a quick escape without drawing attention to myself. I backed into a bush and fell with a resounding *crunch*. The men jerked their heads in my direction.

6

The man in camo looked at me from behind his ski mask, jumped on his four-wheeler, gunned the motor, and sped toward me on the two-track.

I scrambled to my feet, pivoted, and ran back the way I came. The engine roared in my ears and I lurched sideways to get off the trail before the maniac ran me over. I fell and rolled. Before I could stop myself, I slipped over the edge of the bluff. I grabbed handfuls of snow, groping at anything to hinder a plunge down the hillside. Gravity mocked me and I gained momentum, sliding like a human toboggan through the trees. My ski parka and sweater crept up until my bare stomach scraped against the cold, harsh slope. Halfway down, my hip collided with a tree trunk. I bounced off and found myself hurtling headfirst down the hill. Brush raced past me at a dizzying speed. Straight ahead, a tree trunk loomed on a collision course. I screamed and reeled to one side. The move spun me around and I was feet-first again. I grabbed at a passing shrub and pulled back at the sting of needles biting into my flesh. Raspberries. I hated those.

The next moment, I was on my tush in the ditch. A semi-truck roared past on the highway, not ten feet from where I sat wet, bruised, and cold. I turned and looked up the hill behind me. The black-clad man stood at the top, looking down. Even at this distance, I recognized him as the man I'd seen going into Sinclair's Grocery yesterday morning.

I got up, just to prove I still could. Every muscle in my body ached. I gave the guy a look I hoped would kill and brushed the snow off my clothes.

I crossed the highway and limped homeward. I thought about calling the police, but I didn't want to start my stay in Port Silvan as the head Wolf Crier. Then someday when I really needed help, they'd drag their feet coming to my aid. After all, what had I really seen? Two guys riding four-wheelers in the woods. At least I'd had my scarf over my face so they wouldn't recognize me if we ever crossed paths again.

I looked down at my white ski parka. The fabric was sliced and shredded from top to bottom after that short-cut I took. I guessed it was time for a new one anyway. I'd bought the thing my first year in college, almost fifteen years ago. Letting go of the jacket meant letting go of the fact that I'd never completed my college degree. I'd been sidetracked in prison instead, after helping my grand-mother end the pain of her terminal lung cancer. But my life hadn't really been so bad. A few disappointments, a couple letdowns, one super-big setback . . . overall a pretty good existence, if I focused on the bright spots. And up ahead was the most beautiful bright spot of all, my log cabin in the woods. I rushed toward it, eager to walk the same floor my mother had all those years ago.

Before I knew it, Sunday morning rolled around. Instead of getting dressed in ski gear for an outing after church like Brad and his sister Samantha would be doing back in Rawlings, I put on a mid-calf-length denim skirt over tall boots. Long johns underneath and a turtleneck over top along with my jean jacket completed my winter fashion.

I started my Explorer and let it warm while I had a cup of coffee. I'd seen the community church at the top of the hill in Port Silvan. I had no idea what to expect, only that I'd really enjoyed the people and sermons at the church back in Rawlings. I hoped I'd get the same warm welcome at my "home" church that I'd gotten as a stranger downstate.

I climbed behind the wheel and pulled down the driveway. Ten minutes later, I parked behind the traditional white church building. Bells in the steeple rang as I walked through the door. I snuck into a vacant back pew and fumbled to find the opening hymn.

The music swelled against the white walls of the spacious sanctuary. Stained-glass windows in cheerful colors showed simple renderings of Noah's ark, a rainbow, a dove, and other religious symbols. A plain wooden cross filled the space above the altar.

There were about thirty people in attendance, many a trifle on the elderly side. I looked down at the notes in front of me, disappointed there weren't more people my age.

Off to my left, a baby cried. I craned for a peek at the parents. Along the opposite aisle, a young woman stood at a pew with an infant around six months old in her arms. Blonde hair fell in thick waves to the woman's shoulders. She looked frazzled as she tried first a pacifier then a bottle to soothe the baby. Next to them, a golden-haired girl not more than four years old doodled with a crayon.

The hymn ended and the congregation sat. A man wearing khakis and a flannel shirt stood at the podium and began the service.

The baby let out a wail.

"Was that an 'amen' I heard from the back corner?" the leader joked, getting a round of chuckles. He launched into announcements.

His jovial voice blurred into the background as I watched the woman try frantically to stop the crying. She looked on the verge of tears as she grabbed the four-year-old's hand and left the sanctuary.

Empathy pulled at me. I snuck out the door behind her into the large fellowship hall. A rear corner served as a makeshift nursery, its boundaries formed by a sofa and plush rug. The woman sat in a glider, soothing the baby. The young girl picked through a toy box.

"Hi." I stepped toward the little family. "Any way I can help?"

The mother looked like she was holding back tears herself. Her golden hair was tousled and one edge of her blouse had pulled out of her skirt. "He'll stop in a minute. He's just cranky this morning." The woman patted the baby's back. "I'm sorry if he disturbed you. I try not to let the kids get too carried away in there."

"Disturb me? It's so wonderful to see children at church." I gave a quirk of my lip. "Not too many at this one, huh?"

"No." She managed a smile. "Are you visiting relatives in town? We don't get many tourists this time of year."

I hesitated, not wanting to share too much information. Still, what did it matter after the clerk at Sinclair's probably already broadcast the news? "Actually, I just moved to the area. I bought an old log cabin that I used to spend summers in as a kid."

"Oh? Whereabouts is it?" she asked. The baby in her arms calmed to whimper level.

"Just past Cupid's Creek."

Her eyebrows lifted. "That must be the old Russo place. I'm surprised they let it out of the family."

"It turns out they didn't." I shifted, giving a sidelong glance at the floor. "Bernard Russo is my grandfather."

Her eyes opened wide. For some reason, I rushed to explain, or apologize, or something. "But I only found out I was related to him after I bought the house. I don't even remember my grandfather and now I own his old hunting lodge. Weird, huh?"

"Was your mom the one that . . ." Her voice petered off.

"Killed herself? Yep. That was my mom."

"I'm sorry. I didn't mean to—"

"Oh, you didn't. Don't worry about it. It's all water under the bridge. I'm okay with it. Really." The more I babbled, the less believable I sounded. Even to myself.

54

I gave a half grin. "Let's start over. My name is Patricia Amble. You can call me Tish."

"Hi, Tish. I'm Melissa Belmont. Everybody calls me Missy. I live up on River Street, in that rose-colored house toward the end." She reached over and smoothed the toddler's curls. "This is Hannah. And the baby is Andrew."

"They're beautiful kids. I hope they get some playmates here soon."

Missy's pretty features collapsed into a pained frown. "Oh, they will. I've already got another one on the way."

I blinked, surprised at her forlorn tone. "Congratulations."

"I wish I could say I was happy about it. But it comes as a big surprise. And at a bad time."

I didn't want to minimize her situation, but I also didn't want to play into some pity party. "I'm sure you'll make the best of it," was all I could think to say.

At my words, a veil dropped over her face. I flinched with guilt. Maybe she'd wanted to talk to me about her situation and I'd just slammed the door in her face.

I backtracked. "What I meant to say was, is there anything I can do to help?" She'd probably never take me up on it, but it felt good to make the offer.

Missy gave a look of hope. "I'll think about that. Thank you for asking."

I glanced at her left hand and saw the flash of a diamond ring. "Is your husband in there? Because if you want to join him, I can watch the kids."

She shook her head. "He doesn't come to church."

I reached for the baby. "Even more reason for you to get back in there. No sense in dressing everybody up and rushing over here if you don't even get to hear the sermon."

She hesitated a brief moment, then let me take the baby.

"I'll come rescue you if he cries." She stood and headed for the sanctuary. "Thank you, Tish. Hannah, you be a good girl."

The door closed behind Missy. I sat in the glider with baby Andrew on my lap. He twisted up his face. For a minute I thought he was going to cry. But soon he found the zipper pull on one side of my jean jacket. Chubby fingers strained to drag the mechanism up and down the track. His forehead furrowed in concentration. Pudgy baby lips jutted out with the effort.

I drank in his clean, fresh baby scent. His warmth and weight there on my lap sent love flooding through my veins like a caffeine fix. I pictured my own kid bouncing on my knee. His head would be topped with Brad's dark hair, he'd have Brad's straight, serious lips . . .

Baby Andrew held his breath and grunted. Suddenly, a mini mortar exploded on my thigh. With my self-preservation instinct operating in full gear, I lifted the baby like a hot-air balloon and set him on the floor. I dug through the diaper bag Missy had left behind and found a rattle. Andrew shoved the toy in his mouth and sucked on it. His face turned red, then back to white, like an errant Christmas bulb.

The next few minutes passed in relative peace. Hannah occupied herself with a chunky manger scene puzzle.

Andrew continued a project of his own. Then the odor hit.

Hannah spoke without looking up. "Andrew's got a stinky."

"I know. I think church is almost over. Your mom will be here soon."

Hannah paused and swung her blue eyes my way. "You should change him so he doesn't go ballistic."

Her matter-of-fact tone as she said the big word made me smile. "Think you can help me with that?"

"'Course." She went for the shoulder bag and pulled out a disposable diaper and a box of wipes. She spread out a cushy vinyl mat, then seized the baby under his arms, dragging him to the changing pad.

I intervened, laying the baby gently on the soft surface. "You're going to be a really great mom when you grow up."

"I know," the girl said, already unsnapping the baby's bottoms.

With Hannah in charge, we cleaned Andrew and had him back in action by the time the grown-ups started trickling out of the sanctuary.

The moment Missy reached us, she scooped up Andrew and hugged him. She knelt to Hannah's level.

"How'd it go, sweetie?"

"Good. I had to show the lady how to change a diaper."

Missy smiled. "Thank you, pumpkin." She rose. "And thank you, Tish. I really appreciate it. Sometimes those sermons are the only thing that gets me through the week."

I patted Hannah's head and smiled. "I have a hard time believing life could be less than perfect with these two cuties around."

Missy stepped closer and dropped her voice to a whisper. "Can we get together sometime soon? I'd like to talk to you about something."

I looked at the congregation around me, milling about with smiles on their faces, as if life was nothing short of heaven. No wonder Missy singled me out to talk to. Spiritual Journey in Progress was stamped all over my forehead. "Do you want to come out to the cottage? I'm pretty much available anytime," I said.

"No. Not the cottage." She crouched to pack the diaper bag one-handed. "Let's meet in Manistique instead. How about Tuesday around noon at the public library? There's a nice kids section there."

"Okay. Sure. I'll see you Tuesday."

Missy rattled off quick directions. Then in a few swift moves, she had herself and the kids bundled up and out the door.

I stood in the corner of the large hall and watched them leave. With the Belmonts went my sense of belonging. Now I was merely a strange face once again. I willed a friendly person my way, but got only polite smiles and quick glances from those who even bothered to look at me. I refused to read anything into the standoffish behavior other than general discomfort regarding strangers.

I zipped up my jacket and raced through the cold out to my car.

7

That afternoon, I treated myself to hot tea and the last pages of a romantic mystery along the lumpy length of my sofa. I had on three layers of clothes and a sleeping bag to guard against the chill. By evening, I knew I'd have to break down and invest in a new heating system and maybe some storm windows. While it didn't faze me to live like a refugee, I knew the next owners wouldn't be able to hack it.

Monday morning I opened the skinny Manistique area phone directory and dialed the number of a Silvan Township–based heating professional. I got an answering machine.

"Hi, my name is Patricia Amble and I'm at Number Three Valentine's Lane," I said after the beep. "I'd like a quote on a new heating system, please." I left my cell number and hung up. If he were like the contractors in the rest of the state, a call back was questionable.

I spent the remainder of the day washing down the great room. The stone surround of the fireplace presented my biggest challenge at the cabin so far. Dust had collected on the uneven ledges between every rock.

I stretched as tall as I could and began wiping the chimney and hearth. I was exhausted by the time dark rolled around, but at least the stones sparkled with new life in the glow of my work lamp. Another day I'd borrow a ladder and clean all the way to the ceiling that soared above. While I was up there, I'd change the bulbs in the light fixture. For now, I called it quits and went to bed early, looking forward to meeting with Missy and the Belmont kids the next day in Manistique.

The sun hadn't even considered rising yet when I heard my cell phone ringing somewhere down in the kitchen. I jumped up and careened groggily down the staircase. Maybe it was Brad. He hadn't forgotten about me.

"Hello?" My lips were thick from sleep.

"This is Ted from General Heating calling you back."

My heart shriveled. Brad had forgotten me after all. I cradled my forehead in my hand and leaned against the counter. "Thanks for calling, Ted." I couldn't keep the disappointment out of my voice. "I've got a big old cottage on Valentine's Lane that needs a whole new approach to heating. I'm hoping you'll have some good ideas." I swallowed the lump in my throat.

"Normally I would." His voice became curt and gruff. "But I don't do business with drug dealers."

I looked around the kitchen to see if there was someone else in the room that he could possibly be talking to. "Excuse me? My name is Patricia Amble and I just moved up here."

"I know who you are. Tell your granddad to get one of

his buddies to help you out. I don't get involved in that stuff." The line clicked and went silent.

Okay. I'll tell my granddad as soon as I meet him for the first time, I thought to myself as I flung my phone on the counter. Of all the family skeletons I'd imagined, drug dealers hadn't been among them. I yawned and rubbed at my eyes. As long as I was awake, I might as well make coffee and get the day started.

The last Sinclair donut became breakfast as the sun lit the icy landscape outside the kitchen window. Six donuts. Six days. The sugary bear claw wasn't the only thing getting stale. I couldn't wait to meet Missy at noon. I had to get out of this house. I'd grown accustomed to a social life my last months in Rawlings. Being trapped behind four walls just wasn't working for me anymore.

I showered, dressed, and put on my regimen of light makeup, then frittered around to pass the time. About 11:00 a.m., I'd had enough. I started up the SUV and came back inside while it warmed.

A corner closet held a broom. I swept the kitchen floor. I gathered dirt into a central pile, deciding to spend the rest of the day exploring Manistique. Maybe I'd come across some of the places Brad told me about. I remembered how pleasantly surprised I'd been to find out he'd visited the Upper Peninsula—and loved it. I simply couldn't wait to try the pizza at Buddy's Pub, drop in at the Olive Branch gift shop, and browse the books at Merchant's Pointe Deli. Some of the other things Brad mentioned, like tackling the rocky jetty in Manistique Harbor to get to the lighthouse and strolling the boardwalk in the moonlight, would have to wait until summer.

I found the dustpan under the cupboard and swept the pile in. Somehow not having Brad around to share my new experiences dampened my enthusiasm. But I'd thought that through before I moved. Back in Rawlings, Brad taught me a lot about taking time to enjoy God's creation. And now I went for walks, went to town, and even went to church. He'd helped me start a whole new batch of great habits. I could keep up the routine even without him. I'd gone for one walk already this week, hadn't I? I rubbed the bruise on my backside. That walk might have ended on a less brutal note if Brad had been with me.

I stowed my cleaning tools, locked the back door in opposition to Ethyl Merton's shaky advice, and started the drive to Manistique. The trees along US-2 looked like they'd sprouted crystals. Soon the forest gave way to Lake Michigan. Turbulent black waters beat against mounds of ice along the shoreline. Towers of spray shot up at random and settled atop the wall of white. A few minutes later, houses cropped up on the narrow strip of snow-covered dunes between the highway and the lake. I crossed the bridge over the Manistique River and took the first left. After three blocks of quaint shop fronts, I came to the high school. I navigated into the parking lot and took a space reserved for public library patrons. I snatched my purse and headed in, excited for a lunch date, minus the food, with my new friend.

Teens peered out at me as I walked past their class-rooms. I found the library entrance halfway down the hallway. I entered and passed between the stanchions of a security device, surprised to see the sophisticated system in a U.P. town. But, it was the twenty-first century, even in the Upper Peninsula. Although it seemed like a hundred years since I had last been up here, it was reassuring to know that time hadn't totally passed the place by.

I paused to get my bearings. A bank of computers filled the center of the large, square room. Tall shelves with numeric and alphabetic guides on the ends took up the right side. And straight ahead, past the librarian's desk, was the modestly proportioned children's section. Through the racks, I could make out the back of Missy's shoulder-length hair. I smiled at the sweet older gal manning the desk on my way by. I rounded a bookcase and stepped into the kids' section. Missy sat at a child-sized table, flipping through the pages of *Curious George* with Hannah. Andrew slept peacefully in his car seat next to them on the floor.

Hannah looked up at me as I approached. "Mommy, that lady's here."

I smiled. "How are you today, Hannah?"

She ducked her head into the book. Missy barely turned to greet me.

"Thanks for coming," she whispered.

I circled the table and slid into a seat made for a bottom half the size of mine. I met Missy's eyes across the Formica top. She looked wiped out. Her eyes were puffy and she'd used heavy makeup to hide the dark circles under them. Her blush had been over-applied, making one cheekbone look almost purple.

I squinted and leaned closer. "Is that a bruise on your face?" The words spewed out before I could add any tact.

63

Hannah looked up from her book. Missy's fingers rose to cover the dark spot.

She bent forward and whispered to the girl. "Hannah, honey, why don't you go find some more stories we can take home with us?"

The four-year-old placed *Curious George* on a stack on the table and wandered over to a kiddy pool filled with picture books. She gave a long look in our direction before scrounging for new reading material.

Missy slumped and closed her eyes. A tear slid down one cheek. She struggled with her breathing before finally looking up at me.

"I don't know what to do. I don't know how to make him stop."

"Did your husband do that to you?" I asked. My hand made a move to touch the bruise, but I pulled back, not wanting to make a scene with Hannah so near by.

Missy nodded. "It's been going on for years. I watched my mom put up with it. But I want it to stop." Her shoulders shook and her voice croaked. "I don't want Hannah to think it's something she has to live with."

I peeked over toward the pool. Hannah skimmed blissfully through some illustrations. My eyes watered as I turned back to Melissa. "Why don't you leave him?" I asked.

"I've threatened to. But he swore I'd never see the kids again, if he didn't kill me first."

"There has to be a women's shelter in the area. You've got the kids. You could go today. He'd never know. He'd never find you."

She sobbed silently into one hand. "I wish I could. But

he would find me." She exhaled sarcastically. "My own father would probably help him. Between the two of them, they wouldn't stop until I was back with Drake. He'd want to make sure I wouldn't tell about the marijuana he grows and the sick friends he sells it through."

I swallowed hard. I recalled what happened back in Rawlings when someone else had tried to turn over a new leaf at the expense of a career criminal. She'd ended up buried under the concrete in my basement. All the details of the villain's devious life would have died with her, if I hadn't somehow ended up unearthing the body, nearly costing me my own life.

"Don't you know anybody who could help you? Don't you have somewhere to go?" I asked. The last thing I wanted was to be in the bad graces of some Port Silvan drug ring.

Her eyebrows rippled. "That's why I'm talking to you. Your grandfather could help me. Ask him. He'd do it for you, I know he would."

I snorted. "According to popular belief, he's one of the dealers. Besides, I haven't even met him yet. I don't see how he'd do anything for either one of us."

"Please. Just ask him." She looked over at her daughter. The girl gave a surreptitious glance in our direction. Missy pleaded to me with her eyes. "Do it for Hannah and Andrew. Please. It's our only way out."

I nodded. "I'll ask my grandfather at the first opportunity. But I can't make any guarantees. I think you're better off leaving him on your own."

"Thank you." She reached forward and grabbed my arm across the table. "If you see me again, pretend you don't know me. If Drake ever suspects I talked to you, I don't know what he'd do."

"Pretend I don't know you? Are you nuts? I'm so excited to have you for my friend." I gripped her wrist with my other hand.

Missy cocked her head. "I mean it, Tish. I'll look past you like you don't even exist. It's safer that way. For both of us."

Missy was overreacting, of course, but I wasn't the one who had to face Attila the Hun at bedtime every night. I only hoped she and the kids could weather it through until Drake Belmont got put behind bars.

"I understand." So much for my first friendship in Port Silvan. My time here looked like it would be riddled with the isolation I'd finally managed to shake off back in Rawlings. It was probably just God trying to teach me how to be happy on my own again. It seemed every time I got close to mastering the lesson, I botched it by getting too attached to someone or another. Maybe this time I'd get the point down pat. Goodness knew it shouldn't be any problem with the heritage I'd been dealt. Drugs, suicide, and murder certainly didn't fall on the list of how to win friends and influence people.

I pulled out my golf pencil and scratch pad. "Here." I scribbled my cell number. "Call me anytime." As an afterthought, I wrote down Candice LeJeune's name and number as well. "I have a feeling this woman could do more for you than my grandfather." I tore the slip off and handed it to her.

She looked at it. "Thanks, but I hope I'm never so desperate I'll have to call her."

"I met her last week. She was a little uptight, but seemed like she had things together. I'm sure she'd help if you ever needed her to."

"That woman sits in judgment over everyone in this town. You, me, and especially your grandfather. He's one of the most decent people I've ever met and she's got nothing but venom for him." Missy stared at the slip of paper and shook her head. "It's hard to believe they were once in love."

"Candice and my grandfather in love? You're right. That is hard to believe."

"Just rumors you hear from gossipy old ladies. Supposedly, Candice had left her husband for your grandfather, but then her husband was killed in a fire and she blamed Papa B for starting it. Nothing was ever proven, but she's hated the Russos ever since."

I remembered my meeting with Candice and all her warnings about my family. I couldn't blame her for being angry with my grandfather if he'd taken matters into his own hands. But I couldn't condemn the man either. Hadn't I done the same thing where my grandmother was concerned? The only difference was, I got caught, while he'd apparently gotten off the hook. Perhaps he'd mended his ways after so many years. Missy's generous portrayal of him gave me hope.

I strummed my fingers on the table. "Like I said, I can't make any promises. I really don't know anything about the Russos anymore." I shrugged a shoulder. "I don't even know how to get a hold of them."

Missy nodded. "I'm sure they'll be getting in touch with you soon."

"They haven't bothered trying to reach me the past twenty-five years. What makes you think they'll start now?"

"Something I overheard." She reached up and touched her bruise. "It earned me this." She half-laughed. "I should know better than to throw in a load of wash when Drake's buddies are hanging in the garage."

I shook my head in disbelief. "Missy, none of this is your fault. You don't have to accept that treatment."

Missy bit her lip. "I know. But it's just the way it is right now." She wiped moisture from her eye. "You better get going, just in case Drake decides to check up on me."

I huffed. "I can't let you go back there. I'll make some phone calls. I'll find you a place to stay."

Missy gave a vehement shake of her head. "Just tell your grandfather. Please, nobody else." She looked over her shoulder at the library entrance. "Thank you for meeting me today. Now please go. And forget we ever met."

I stared at her as I stood up. It took all my willpower not to race up to the desk and dial 9-1-1 and put out a bulletin for Drake Belmont's arrest.

"Bye, lady." Hannah gazed at me from the pool of books. I tried not to cry.

"Bub-bye, honey." My voice came out like the bleat of a goat. I turned to go.

I averted my eyes as I walked past the librarian. Missy was a grown-up. She could make her own decisions. But she was pregnant now. And that meant keeping herself and all of her beautiful children out of harm's way. If she wasn't going to help herself, I'd have to do it for her.

8

I'd lost my appetite for sightseeing after taking on Missy's personal problems as my own. I drove home, the once riveting lake and woods now a dreary backdrop to my thoughts. Ignorance would have been bliss. I could have said hi to Missy and her cute babies once a week at church, confident that everything was hunky-dory back home. But after hearing her story, and her refusal to take the steps I felt were necessary, I couldn't exactly ignore the situation. If something ever happened, I'd have to live with myself. And my action or inaction under the circumstances would determine whether I'd hold my head up because I'd done the right thing, or hide in shame because I'd neglected to do what I could.

But what was the right thing? Missy insisted I contact my grandfather and tell him alone of her situation. Yet I really couldn't see that helping her at all. It would be like having her go from one drug dealer to another. In my opinion, getting the authorities involved and getting Missy and those kids to safety was the better plan.

But what if I called the police and everything back-fired and Drake didn't end up in jail? Drake would know

Missy had talked to someone and she'd be in an even bigger mess.

By the time I pulled up to the house, all the extrapolation had launched a headache the size of Kadavu, that faraway isle in Fiji where I should have gone instead of here. Was it just a few months ago that Brad had taken me to the Rawlings Public Library and introduced me to Google? I'd typed in "remote tropical island" and up popped the most beautiful stretch of sand and water I'd ever seen.

I slammed the car door and waded through the snow. I'd need at least a year to get this place shipshape, but I promised myself the beaches of Kadavu would be my next stop. I'd promised myself that before. But this time I meant it.

I hung my coat by the door and kicked my boots off on the rug. I'd turned the thermostat down before I left, hoping to be a wise steward of something called *propane*, a natural gas alternative that enabled this middle-of-nowhere cottage to have heat at all. I had a feeling I'd get to know a good deal about that sewer thing called a *septic system* as well. Rural life sure wasn't like living in town where all the necessities were magically provided as long as you paid the bills. Out here, I half expected to find my electric running off some nearby windmill.

After cranking up the wall heater, I headed for the phone book. If I called a heating contractor from Manistique, maybe my anonymity would garner some service. I flipped through the slim guide, hesitating at the "R" page. I ran a finger down the column. Raymond, Reno, Richard, Roberts . . . Russo. Three were listed: Bernard,

Gerard, and Joel, all of Port Silvan. I stared at the print. I tapped at the names with my finger.

No.

I wouldn't make the first peace offering. My family had wronged me, not me them. They'd have to make first contact. I wasn't here for them anyway. I was here for myself, to put the past behind me and move on.

I tore through the book until I came to the yellow pages. Manistique Plumbing and Heating. They'd do. I put in the call, got the machine, and left a message.

Missy would simply have to be patient 'til my grandfather got around to calling me. She'd lasted this long without his intervention. She could hold out a little longer—or just do things my way and call the cops.

My stomach growled. I'd been so preoccupied with solving Melissa's misfortunes that I'd forgotten to stop for groceries at the supermarket in Manistique. Now I'd have to stock up with the pathetically overpriced and limited selection of goods available in Port Silvan. I chugged a cup of reheated coffee, hoping to boost my attitude along with my heart rate before heading down to the village.

I walked into Sinclair's thinking that a fresh glazed donut while I shopped might keep me from impulse buying.

"Hello," I said to the bouffant blonde clerk as I scrutinized the selection under glass. I salivated over a powdered sugar one with red gel oozing out the side.

"Haven't seen you in a while," the clerk said. "How's things going down at Valentine's Bay?"

I ripped my eyes from the white confection and looked

at her. "Great. The place needs a new heating system, but other than that, there are no surprises." Except for the defaced photo of my mother I found on my bed. I pointed through the glass. "Hey, do you mind if I get that donut in front?"

"No problem." She took a square of waxed paper and pulled it for me.

I savored its sweetness as I pushed my small-town, reduced-capacity shopping cart down the narrow aisles. I rounded the end of the dried cereal row and headed for the meat counter. A woman stood with her back to me, peering at the rows of Styrofoam-and-plastic-wrapped cuts. I recognized her tall leather boots and fur-lined barn jacket as an Aunt Candice special.

She glanced up at the squeak of my cart. "Hello, Tish."

"Candice." I nodded.

Her warm smile caught me off guard.

"How did your first week home go?" she asked.

I stared at a family pack of New York strips. My first week. Let's see. Pictures torn in two, murderous drug dealers, abusive husbands, neglectful relatives, not to mention uncooperative heating contractors.

I met Candice's eyes. "Overall it went pretty good."

She lifted her eyebrows. "I'm glad to hear that. Surprised, but glad."

"Why are you surprised? Of course it went well." A defensive tone crept into my voice.

"I thought perhaps you'd be disappointed with Port Silvan. So many wonderful childhood memories, only to find that everything had changed."

"Heavens, no. Everyone is so helpful and friendly and full of information." Jim Hawley had been helpful, Missy Belmont had been friendly, and Candice herself was full of information. I popped the last bite of donut into my mouth.

"I'm glad to hear that." Candice picked up a package of chicken breasts. She weighed it in her hands. "And was your family everything you had expected?"

I dusted powdered sugar off my fingers. "Oh, absolutely. We're going to get along great."

She glanced at me with a "yeah, right" look on her face. "That's wonderful. I guess I'd worried for nothing." She placed the chicken in her blue plastic shopping basket. "You know, we really didn't get a chance to chat long the last time you were over. I hope you'll join me for tea again this week. Is Thursday good for you?"

My instincts said no way, but maybe Candice could help me with my Missy conundrum.

"Thursday's fine," I told her.

We agreed on a two o'clock teatime at the farmhouse.

I picked through the meats and settled on a tray of ground round and some lean steaks. I grabbed a few more staple items and ended up in line behind Candice at the checkout.

As the clerk rang up her selection, the bells on the door jangled. A tall, distinguished-looking man with gray hair and mustache entered and strode over to us. His dark blue peacoat set off the brilliant blue of his eyes. He stopped two feet from Candice.

He prodded a finger at her. "I thought I told you to stay off Russo land."

73

I swallowed hard. My grandfather. With all the bad press Candice had given him, I'd expected some deformed ogre with a forked tongue. But the handsome man didn't fit the stereotype of a viper-in-waiting.

Candice lifted her chin. "I would never dream of trespassing on your little kingdom."

I stared at Bernard Russo, seeking some feature that I could claim in common. High cheekbones. Roundish chin. Wrinkles slashing across his forehead in an angry scowl. Maybe I looked like that when I was ready to blow a gasket.

He inched closer to Candice. "Then how come Joel saw your car pulling out down by Valentine's Bay last week?"

She held her ground. "That was such a long time ago, I don't recall where I was. Why not accuse me on the day the crime supposedly took place instead of waiting until the trail is cold?"

"Don't get smart with me, Candice. If I so much as hear that you even looked at my granddaughter, I'll track you down."

"Why, Bernard, I wouldn't recognize your granddaughter if she were standing in line with me at the grocery store." Candice shot playful eyes my way.

Bernard followed her glance and saw me for the first time. His eyes opened wide. Maybe Jim Hawley was right. I really did look a lot like my mother.

He swayed back and forth a few times, perhaps debating whether to hug me or shake my hand. He rubbed the back of his neck. Then he broke into a huge grin.

He skirted past Candice and wrapped me in an embrace that knocked the wind out of me.

His jagged breath rushed past my ear. "My baby. My little baby. You're all grown up."

I buckled into his arms.

"Puppa," I gasped through tears. The word came to me as naturally as the grip of my elbows around his neck. Here was my family. My blood. My heritage.

When the moment ended, I stared at him, wiping the streaks from my face. "I've been here a week. Why didn't you come see me? Why didn't you call?"

His hands lingered on my shoulders. "I wanted to, but I didn't know how you'd feel. I figured we'd take it slow."

I swatted at his chest like a child. "Slow? I haven't seen you in twenty years. Isn't that slow enough?" But his blue eyes looked with love into my own, and I forgave any insult caused by his delay.

"Closer to twenty-six years. But now that we're together again, let's forget we were ever apart." He dropped his hands to his sides. "Come up to the house for supper tonight. Everyone wants to meet you." He turned. "Candice, you . . ." His voice petered out.

Candice and her groceries were gone.

9

I hummed and boogied and did my hair in the bathroom mirror while I waited for five o'clock to roll around. I couldn't believe I was finally going to meet the aunts and uncles and cousins that comprised the "everyone" my grandfather said wanted to meet me. For the first time in years, I had family.

"Fam–i–ly," I sang at the top of my lungs. I barely heard my cell phone ringing from its place on the kitchen counter. I raced down the hall.

I flipped it open, so rushed to make the connection I didn't even glance at the caller ID. "Hello?"

The other end was silent for a beat. Then he spoke. "Tish."

I almost choked at the sound of his voice. "Brad?" I slumped to the floor and leaned against a cupboard. "How are you? I'm so surprised to hear from you."

Silence again. "I guess I thought I'd be hearing from you. What happened? Why didn't you call me?"

I scanned the specks on the floor for some valid excuse. "It's been hectic. New house, new grocery store, new church. I guess I'm just getting settled in." How could I tell him the truth—that we were just too different, that things could never work out between us? Or was it simply that I was too afraid to enter uncharted territory?

He delayed his answer. "I've been worried about you. I know you don't want a relationship right now. You made that plain enough. But, Tish, I thought we were friends. Friends call each other to say they made it to their new house. They call each other to ask how the ski trip went. They call each other just because." His voice dropped off. "I guess I thought you'd call me."

My throat knotted up. "It goes both ways, you know. You should have called me last week if you were so worried."

Silence.

"I'm glad you're all right," he said at last. "Did you find what you're looking for?"

I rubbed my face. What was I looking for? Oh yeah, just trying to figure out who I was by figuring out my mother. But she was dead. It seemed her trail had been washed away by the years. And really, what difference would it make to know whether she liked dark chocolate or milk chocolate best? Would it change the fact that I would always prefer dark? I stared at the perforations in the ceiling squares. Maybe it was all just an excuse not to get involved in a relationship. Who could understand it? I'd have to be crazy not to return Brad's love.

I sighed into the receiver. "I'm just starting to figure things out."

"Gonna take awhile, huh?" Brad's voice was little more than a whisper.

"Yeah. Pretty sure it is. Hey, I'm going to my grandfather's tonight. I get to meet my dad's side of the family."

"That's great."

"Yeah. I bumped into Puppa by accident. Kind of funny how it happened." I looked at the stove clock. "In fact, I have to get going soon if I'm going to get to supper on time."

"Well, enjoy yourself. I hope it's everything you thought it would be."

"Thanks. Thank you a lot." I cleared my throat. "Well, I guess I'll talk to you later."

"Sure. Yeah. Call me sometime."

"Okay then. Bye."

"Bye."

The phone went silent.

I flipped it closed and stared at it for a while. I just wanted Brad here. I wanted him with me. I wanted things to be like they were in Rawlings. Phone calls, walks, supper together four nights a week, and church on Sundays. But I'd left him. I'd moved away from all that. And now it was a phone call once a week, walks on my own, and meals all alone.

I stood up and put on my jacket. I stuffed the cell into my pocket. Why'd Brad have to call me anyway? I'd been doing great without him. I'd hardly given him a thought. He'd nearly been relegated to that distant place called the Past. And I would have been fine without him.

The kitchen door slammed behind me, a little harder than I intended. I was fine without him. I didn't need his "Boo hoo hoo, why didn't you call me" pressure in my life. I had another mission to focus on. Maybe I'd get back to him when it was completed, or maybe not. Only time would tell.

I drove through Port Silvan, taking the curve past town and heading out along Lake Michigan. Silvan Bay, a once thriving harbor in the now defunct port town, was covered over with ice. Fishing shanties dotted the white expanse. A snowmobile, nothing more than a black speck, made its way to shore.

I passed the sign to the public boat launch, right where my grandfather said it would be. A line of white fences cropped up, barely visible against the mounds of snow. Puppa's house. I turned into the driveway and slowed, stunned by the view ahead. A quarter mile down, across the serene, snow-covered lawn, rose a massive lake house. A pillared porch wrapped the front and sides. Weathered gray shakes covered the exterior. Bright white trim and shutters provided relief from the dreary color. Above, third-story dormers broke up the vastness of the charcoal roof. A fieldstone chimney topped the structure. Just beyond the house lay the icy harbor.

I blew out a breath of anxiety and pressed on the gas.

I parked along the circle drive that flanked the sweeping front stair. A red four-wheeler was parked to one side. Those things must be a dime a dozen up here. I tucked my keys into my pocket, took a deep breath, and headed toward the door. I took a closer look at the dwelling as I walked up crimson steps. The canopy of the porch dwarfed me with its ten-foot height. The width was at least ten feet as well, providing plenty of space for outdoor furniture, which was now covered in cheerful striped tarps and clumps of snow. The front door itself was double-wide with a transom above. Stained glass in a colorful red and green tulip pattern trumped the overbearing gray shakes to extend a belated welcome.

I pressed the bell.

Deep inside the walls, I heard a *bing bong bing*. The notes sounded rich, an upper-class interpretation of the boring, traditional *ding dong*.

A shadow approached the door. The handle turned. The white wood swung open. I put on my happy face, expecting my grandfather.

I got the man from the bluff instead. The one on the red four-wheeler. Candice's accusations about my grandfather being a bad apple appeared to be dead-on.

I wiped off my smile and squinted at the doorman. He was handsome in an overactive testosterone gland sort of way. Dark whiskers gave the hint of a beard without him actually having one, as if his watch read five o'clock perpetually. Black hair, blue eyes, more bulk under his plaid flannel shirt than seemed natural. He reminded me how Brad had looked that day on the porch when he'd opened his door in just his sweats and tank.

I cleared my throat. "Please tell me I'm not related to you."

A grin broke out on his face. "You want me that bad, huh?"

I sputtered, indignant. "Pardon me? I do not want you." My arm muscles twitched as I contemplated whether to strangle him. "What I meant was, I hope I'm not related to the maniac who stood there on the bluff and watched me nearly plummet to my death."

"I saw you get up. You looked okay to me. You'll probably stay clear of the bluff from now on, huh?" He stepped to one side. "Come on in. I'll tell Papa B you're here."

I glared at him as I entered the foyer. Who was he, anyway? The right-hand man of the local godfather? Next to me, a grand stairway shot straight up to the second floor. Dark cherry floors and woodwork against a backdrop of bare, white walls gave the interior a clean, uncluttered feel. The Spartan approach to decorating made me wonder if the house was just some elaborate bachelor pad. How could a woman resist a throw rug at the front door or a plant in the corner?

"Well, are you coming?" he said over his shoulder.

I hurried to keep up. We stepped out of the hall and into a room that stretched the entire width of the house. One end served as a dining area, the other the living room. Wall-to-wall windows framed the view of the bay. On the opposite shore, a row of historic buildings made the snowy scene look like a Currier and Ives rendering.

"Patricia."

I turned at the sound of my grandfather's voice. The attractive seventy-ish man approached me with a smile and held me in a gentle embrace. He stepped back and looked toward the plaid-shirt guy.

"You've met Gerard, my brother Sid's oldest boy Owen's son."

His attempt at explaining the relationship left me dizzy. I looked toward Gerard. He gave me a mischievous double eyebrows-up as if letting me know I was eligible to be on his radar.

I rolled my eyes.

81

"Joel," my grandfather called over his shoulder. "Get in here and meet Patricia."

A man entered from the front of the house, wiping his hands on a dishtowel.

Gerard dropped into a lounge chair. "My derelict little brother."

I had no doubt which side of the family my height came from. Cousin Joel towered as tall as the other two Russo men. His light brown hair was disheveled. His moustache made him seem a younger copy of his great-uncle Bernard. A black sweatshirt and blue jeans showed traces of flour.

He nodded. "Patricia."

"Hi." My smile must have stretched from ear to ear. I was so excited to have cousins—boy cousins. Finally, the playmates I never had. I wanted to run outside and throw a football or something.

I looked at the strapping men. "You know, that Patricia stuff is a little too formal for family. I think you guys qualify to call me Tish."

"Sounds like a sneeze," Gerard said in his dry, cynical way.

My grandfather glowered in his direction. Puppa turned back to me. "Patricia is a lovely name. I wouldn't dream of shortening it."

"Uh . . ." I squirmed. "I kind of like the name Tish better. Do you mind?"

"Of course he minds," the brash Gerard piped up. "That's the name Eva and Beth called you. He wouldn't be caught dead using that name for his little princess."

My eyes dropped to the floor at the mention of my

mother and grandmother. Besides, me a princess? Maybe in some other life. I glanced up. The clouds had thickened as they moved across the bay. The room darkened with their approach.

Joel wadded up his towel. "Supper's almost ready." He left the room.

"Need any help?" I tossed my coat onto a nearby chair and ran after him. He seemed by far the least volatile of the Russo clan. I skirted the dining table and pushed through a swinging door into the kitchen.

The room had a long chopping board island down the center. Chunks of lettuce, shreds of carrots, and evidence of broccoli lay scattered on the surface. Worn cupboards in the same dark wood as the rest of the house circled the perimeter. A fry pan on the oversized gas stove sent up a cloud of meat-scented steam.

"That smells delicious." I poked my nose in the air and gave a whiff. "What is it?"

"Tenderloin."

He lifted the lid and stirred the contents.

"Mmm. Thanks for having me down tonight," I said, hoping to break the ice.

"Wasn't my idea." He put the lid back on, set down the spatula, and wiped his hands on the front of his sweatshirt.

"O-kay." I blew off the comment. "So, when is everyone else getting here?"

"Everyone else, like who?"

"Like all the people Puppa said couldn't wait to meet me. You know, all the aunts and uncles and cousins that live around here."

Joel shook his head. "I've got news for you. There are no other relatives. Me and Gerard are it, little cousin."

I crossed my arms. He might be taller than me by several inches, but I had to be older than him by at least two years. Who did he think he was calling "little cousin"?

"What about Olivia?" I asked. Jim Hawley had mentioned the matriarch of the Russo clan.

"She's in her room. Says she won't come out to meet you."

"Won't come out to meet me?" I stared at the gaps in the chopping block. Hurt oozed from some long-healed wound on my heart. "Can't be anything I did, right?"

Joel shook his head. "You want the sugarcoated version or the straight version?"

I gulped. "Sugarcoated, please."

He pulled a bowl of lettuce topped with shredded carrots from the fridge.

"She didn't like your mom."

"That's it? So now she doesn't want to meet me?"

"You said you wanted it sugarcoated. Put this on the table, please." He passed the salad to me. I staggered through the swinging door and placed the bowl on one end of the stretched-out dining set. Even though the table could seat about twelve people, there were only four of us tonight.

I looked at the far end of the room. Cousin Gerard and my grandfather sat in flavorless brown upholstery, watching me. Gerard leaned forward with his elbows on his knees. He rubbed his hands together as if he couldn't wait to get his fingers on a fork. Puppa's hands gripped the ends of his recliner as if reluctant to ever get out of it.

Well, he had to face me sometime. And so did Olivia. She wasn't getting off the hook so easily. I didn't care what she thought of my mother. It was probably some inane gripe, anyway.

I scooted back into the kitchen. "So," I said to Joel, "if that's the sugarcoated version, what's the straight version?"

He gave me a look that asked if I really wanted to know. I gave him a look that said lay it on me.

He walked to the sink and started banging around some dirty pans. "The straight version is that Olivia blames your mother for the death of her son, my grandpa Sid. And when you get to be ninety-three years old, I suppose if you want to hold a grudge against someone, who's going to stop you?"

I sputtered. "What do you mean, she blames my mother? Mom would never have killed anybody. She didn't have it in her."

He gave me a look that asked if I really wanted to go down that path. I blinked. I'd killed somebody, hadn't I? And I'd done it because I'd been sure my mother would have done the same thing. Maybe I didn't want to go down that road just yet.

"Truce," I said and raised my hands in the air in mock surrender. "Olivia can have her grudge for now."

Joel excused himself to deliver a tray of food to the stubborn woman. When he returned, we sat at the dinner table, the four of us, in near silence as we ate.

I looked at the strong faces that surrounded me and wondered what events had shaped their lives the past three decades. How had they all ended up living in the

85

same house? Where were the wives and the children? Where were all the aunts and uncles and cousins? The three of them seemed like star-crossed heroes from some skewed Greek tragedy. The sad thing was, I fit right in.

I couldn't take the silence anymore. "The tenderloin is delicious," I said.

Gerard answered. "Shot it opening day. Big eight-pointer."

These guys even spoke Greek. "What do you mean?" I asked. "This is beef, right?" My stomach clenched while I waited for affirmation.

"Venison. Joel makes it better than anybody I know." Gerard dug in for another bite.

I set my fork down and reached for the water glass in front of me, hoping to wash down the taste. Deer meat? I couldn't eat a deer. I pictured the beautiful doe I'd encountered on my walk the other day. How could anyone shoot such a lovely creature?

I stuck to the salad and rice and bread for the remainder of the meal. Afterward, the men worked together to clean up the kitchen while I spun in useless circles trying to figure out their system.

Joel threw a washcloth in my direction. "Go wipe off the table, Tish."

"Yes, Patricia," my grandfather reiterated, "please wipe off the table."

Joel rolled his eyes and I tried not to laugh as I headed to the dining room. I had a feeling my grandfather should give up trying to put polish on those two boys.

With the kitchen spic and span, we all got a cup of

coffee and sat in the living room. A million questions flitted through my mind. I decided to start with the most basic ones.

"So how'd you all end up living here together?"

Gerard spoke first. "I wouldn't be caught dead living with these meatheads. I live in the village. Orchard Street."

His reference to the village reminded me that I had to fulfill my obligation to Melissa Belmont. I'd do it later, when I could get my grandfather alone.

Joel leaned back in his chair. "If it weren't for me living here, this place would fall apart at the seams. And I'm not about to let my inheritance go to shreds." He gave my grandfather a long look. I could feel the tension rising.

"This is the Russo homestead," my grandfather said without breaking eye contact with Joel. "It belongs to Patricia as well as you two."

"Only after you're dead," Joel replied.

All eyes in the room narrowed. Except mine, which grew huge at the thought of a fistfight breaking out.

"Don't worry about me," I threw in. "I don't need any homestead. I've got too much gypsy in me."

My grandfather took a deep breath. "I'd say you got that from your father."

The three men relaxed now that they had a new target for their bottled-up rage.

I bristled at the shot. "So where is dear old Dad, anyway?"

"Hopefully as far from Port Silvan as he can get," Gerard piped up.

87

My eyes started to water. I blinked fast. There was no way these big buffoons were going to see me cry.

"Gerard." My grandfather jerked in his grand-nephew's direction. His tone was sharp. "Watch your manners."

Gerard looked to the floor. "Yes, sir."

The tears weren't going away. One escaped and landed on the back of my hand.

I stood up. "Well, this was so much fun"—I grabbed for my coat—"I hope we can do it again sometime."

I was at the end of the hallway before my grandfather made a halfhearted attempt to stop my hasty departure.

"Patricia! Patri—"

His voice disappeared when I slammed the front door behind me.

10

I couldn't tell which blinded me more, the snow or the tears. I kept my speed around twenty miles an hour while I picked my way home through the latest blizzard conditions.

How could I have had such totally wrong expectations of the Russos? All the information leading up to tonight had pointed to a dysfunctional unit, but still I'd clung to the fairy-tale hope of smiling, happy people who would love me, accept me, and invite me to be part of their family.

All my hopes dashed again. I had to quit going down the trail of optimism and stick with my tried-and-true pessimistic outlook on life. You couldn't be disappointed by dreams you never had.

By the time I pulled down my drive, it was clogged with more snow. I hoped Jim Hawley would make another swing through in the morning. I couldn't take the thought of getting stuck all alone in these miles of woods for the rest of the winter. I didn't want to end up like Jack in *The Shining*.

I cut the engine and trekked through the drifts into the

house. To top the whole night off, I'd let Melissa Belmont down. I'd had the opportunity to share her situation with my grandfather, and I'd passed it up because of some lame comment about my dad. Poor Missy. She should lean on someone with more backbone.

I locked up and climbed the stairs to my cozy bedroom. There was still the opportunity to tell Candice LeJeune of Missy's dilemma. She'd know what to do. I'd see her on Thursday for tea.

I opened the slim drawer of my bedside table and blew a kiss toward the two halves of my mother's picture.

"Night, Mom," I whispered.

I turned out the light.

I dragged through Wednesday with my pessimistic attitude firmly in place as I removed the layer of old yellow wax from the linoleum in my mother's bedroom. I ran through my list of dashed expectations while I rubbed. The heating guy was never going to return my call. Missy would never leave her husband. Brad and I were never going to be an item. I was never going to get a decent price for this piece-of-junk cottage. I was never even going to find a buyer for it. In fact, I was going to rot back in these woods.

Cheery ring tones broke through my downward spiral.

It was the heating guy.

"Yah, no problem. I can take a look at your place on Friday," he said with his U.P. twang.

I sighed in relief. At least that was taken care of.

Instead of giving the black voice in my head another

chance to berate my future, I put on my boots and went for a walk.

My head cleared the instant fresh air hit my lungs. Powdery white puffs flew with each step. Jim Hawley apparently hadn't thought the new round of snow merited plowing. Halfway up my road, I saw the doe. I stopped and put out my hand, making kissy sounds like I had done the first time I'd seen her. She stared at me. Her ears twitched with curiosity. I took a step closer. She stiffened. I took another step. She stayed rooted in place. I stepped closer . . . closer . . . She turned and ran.

"Goodbye, little deer," I called after her. Next time I'd put an apple in my pocket. One of these days, she'd come to me. I was sure of it.

I finished a three-mile loop, keeping clear of the bluff this time. I made it back to the house just as darkness fell. I threw together a quick supper, grabbed a book, and wilted onto the sofa. When the letters on the pages started to divide and multiply, I climbed off to bed.

Thursday was my tea date with Candice. I tinkered around in the morning so I wouldn't get grungy enough to have to take another shower. After a light lunch, I put on my finest blue sweater. A silky bow tied it shut at the side. I slipped on the slacks that completed the outfit. I stood in front of the bathroom mirror. I'd bought the pair for a date back in Rawlings. The guy had turned out to be a conman. Thankfully all he'd stolen from me was my heart. I realized now that I'd given it to him all too willingly. I wasn't about to let that happen again.

I smoothed the fuzzy fabric and put my jean jacket

over it. I'd have to get to Manistique again soon for a proper winter coat, before I froze from exposure in my lightweight denim.

I let the Explorer warm up, then headed toward Port Silvan, once again taking a left at the cider mill sign before town.

Jim Hawley was just pulling out of Candice's drive in his plow truck as I turned in. I waved and sent a telepathic message to please plow my road before the next storm rolled through.

I parked on the cleared area and went up the shoveled walk. Candice met me at the door.

"Glad you made it, Tish," she said, giving me a peck on the cheek as I entered. A crackling fire and a row of flickering candles on the mantel lent an extra measure of warmth to the room.

We sat down and she poured the tea. This time I relaxed about my wardrobe, knowing I looked impeccable.

"So how is it really going with your relatives?" Candice asked. "I saw your car down at Bernard's when I drove past last night."

I loved the way she small-talked to break the ice before bringing up a gut-wrenching topic.

"Not so good," I said. No use trying to pull the wool over Candice's eyes. She had my relatives figured out. "It was awful. At first things were going well and I was so happy to have cousins. Then I found out Grandma Olivia refused to meet me, and there was a fight about who got to inherit the house. Then they insulted my dad." I closed my eyes and shook my head. "That's when I left. I guess family isn't all it's cracked up to be."

Candice sat silent, sipping from the delicate china. She set her cup on the table. "I'm sure they must be a disappointment to you."

"I expected too much. Of course they're not happy to have me show up in their lives after so many years." I humphed. "I mean, Joel was pretty sure he got the old homestead all to himself after Puppa dies. Then I come out of nowhere, the long-lost cousin, supposedly entitled to some share in that place." I leaned forward and played with my cup and saucer. "I don't want anything from them. Especially not their stuff." I wiped at my nose. "I just wanted to feel like family again."

Candice looked at me with eyes that glimmered in the light from the fire. "They weren't always that way. There was a time when family was everything to them."

"Must have been a long time ago."

Candice nodded and stared into the flames. I wondered if she regretted throwing away the love she and Bernard once shared.

"I don't mean to pry," I said, gripping my teacup for courage, "but what happened to your husband? Missy Belmont said you blamed Papa B for his death."

Her eyes snapped up, filled with anger. "Missy Belmont? When did you talk to that piece of trash?"

I gasped at her crude words. "At church last Sunday."

"She should go to church, the little tramp. Maybe she can pray her way to heaven."

Candice seemed overly vicious toward my new friend. My voice took on an edge. "She's not a tramp. She needs help. I was supposed to talk to my grandfather for her."

"As if Bernard would do anything to help her. She and her lowlife husband are a plague to this town. Bernard should run them both out of Port Silvan."

"What did Missy Belmont ever do to you? She's just a frightened mom trying to get out of a tough situation."

Candice's face twisted with hate. "Don't believe her, Tish. She's a liar. If she wanted out, she'd go. She's right where she wants to be. She just wants to suck you—and your grandfather—into her drama. If you know what's good for you, you'll stay far away from that woman."

My leg started to jiggle. Whom should I believe? Missy had warned me that Candice didn't have anything good to say about anybody in Port Silvan. But was there a grain of truth in Candice's opinion of Melissa? If Missy wanted help, she had to be willing to do something for herself. Otherwise, Candice was right. She was just looking for more participants in her life's drama.

"I appreciate the advice," I said. "I'd be wise not to believe everything people told me around here." Including Candice, I thought to myself. Who knew what hidden agenda she had going? She'd completely avoided the topic of her husband, instead diverting the attention to poor Missy. With a reaction so fierce, Candice's secrets must be big, black, and ugly. Just like mine once were.

"Come here, Tish. I want to show you something." Candice stood and headed through an arched hallway that led to the rear of the house. We walked past the kitchen, with its tidy country clutter, to a spacious area that served as a hobby room. A row of windows stretched across the rear, giving view to open pastureland. The white expanse looked uninviting this time of year. But I could imagine the beauty spring would hold. Indoors, along the bright, salmon-colored walls, more black-and-white photos were arranged in artsy order.

Candice opened the top drawer of a map-type storage chest. She lifted out a stack of glossy 8x10 photos and passed them to me.

"Recognize this little girl?" she asked.

I stared at the top picture. The child in the black-and-white close-up looked about six or seven years old. A sweet, innocent smile lit her round face. Wisps of hair blew across her cheeks. The corners of her eyes turned up with an exotic flair.

My lids stung. I flipped to the next picture. The same girl, holding the hand of a young woman as they walked away from the photographer along a path in the woods. I squinted at the woman. Her profile barely peeked through the edges of her hair.

I flipped through the pile. The girl at the beach. The girl and the woman perched on a horse. The girl swinging at a park, the woman pushing her.

A tear trickled down and dropped to my wrist, barely missing the shiny print.

I glanced up at Candice. "It's me," I whispered. "And my mom."

11

Candice watched as I studied each picture.

"I saved those for you," she said.

"Where did you get these? Who took them?" I cycled through the photos again.

"They're mine."

"But how? Were you with us?"

She nodded. "Your grandfather and I were together then. Your mom was like the daughter I never had. And you . . . ," she looked away, ". . . you were like my own grandchild."

I searched my data banks once more. "Why can't I remember having an Aunt Candice?"

She crossed her arms and leaned back against a filing cabinet. "I wasn't Aunt Candice back then. You had a special name for me." She grinned and a tear trickled out. "I told you to call me Aunt Candi and you said you'd call me by the name of your favorite candy."

"Jellybeans." I looked around in wonder. "Puppa and Jellybean. I do remember." My childhood rose up out of the ashes of time, just snips and bits and impressions of people and smells and sounds. "You were at the lake house. Me and Mom would visit on dress-up day." I closed my eyes in concentration. "We'd all eat together, then we'd do something fun." Playgrounds and laughter, a walk along a pier, scooping up sand at the beach. The images were brief but real.

"Dress-up day. Is that what you called it?" Candice wiped at her cheek. "We always looked forward to weekends with you and Beth. You were such a bright spot in our lives."

Candice opened a cabinet filled with camera equipment, and pulled a bulky metal box from the lowest shelf. "Look at these." She opened the lid, revealing a heap of photos.

I knelt and began sifting through them. Some were color, others black and white. A drop of dew on a leaf, a wildflower bent in the wind, a rickety old barn, the burn tower with clouds rolling in across the bay, a pair of tiny sandals and beach towel left forgotten near the shore, a younger Candice perched on a rock and looking out at the waves.

"These are all so amazing. Who took this one?" I asked, passing Candice the photo of herself.

She stared at the picture, quiet for a moment. She cleared her throat. "These photos were all taken by your mother."

My chest heaved. "My mom took those?" I squeaked. "They're beautiful. I had no idea. Grandma never said anything."

"I'm sure it was difficult for her to talk about your mother. There wasn't a person on the planet that didn't love Beth Amble."

97

"Except my dad. What was his problem, anyway?" I didn't expect Candice to answer my pity-coated question.

She sighed. "He loved your mother very much. But the Russo family flaws were too much for him. It's good that he was never in your life. Perhaps you'll be free of the curse that seems to follow the Russos through time."

My throat balled up. "Why do you always think the worst of everyone? I don't care what his flaws are. He's my dad." I felt the fortress guarding my heart grow stronger as I defended my father. Gasping breaths choked out of me. It took me a minute to gain control. "Someday I'm going to find him. He's not cursed. You'll see."

Not caring if I seemed childish, I sank to the floor and tucked up my knees. My silky pants turned blacker with each teardrop.

Candice reached around behind me, rubbing her hand across my back in slow, soothing circles.

She spoke in a lulling whisper. "You must never look for him, Tish. Let him stay in a far-off place. Some things are better left alone."

I knew as she spoke the words that I would go after my father someday. Her speech was the verbal equivalent of the "Don't ask why" scribbled across my mother's picture.

I stuffed my anger back into some hidden corner of my heart. When I felt calm, I stood. "I think I'd better get going."

"I didn't mean to upset you. Our lives are what they are. No sense trying to force them into something they're not." Candice turned toward a worktable scattered with photos. "I have a few prints for you to take home."

She chose several shots of my mother and me from the assortment. "These are my favorites," she said, handing them my way.

I took them without looking, my eyes caught up instead with some photos sitting on the top right corner of the table. The nature shots had thick black lines running parallel to the sides, forming a square around each central scene. A chunky black pencil sat next to them. A gooseneck lamp lit them from above.

"Why did you draw on those photos?" I asked, pointing.

"Those are crop lines. I use a grease pencil to mark how much of the photo I want to include in the finished product." She demonstrated. "If I mess up, I can wipe off the pencil lines and do it over. I'm too old-fashioned to deal with all that digital stuff they're doing nowadays."

I looked around at all the paraphernalia in amazement. "You must really like to take pictures."

"It's what I do. It's my profession."

"Oh."

"Your mother was studying photography with me when she died," Candice said.

I took a deep breath. "She wanted to be a photographer? Wow. That's so cool."

"She had a good eye for it. She was an artist at heart." Candice played with the pictures on the desktop until they were arranged in neat columns. "I'm betting you're an artist at heart too, Tish."

99

I shrugged. "I guess so. My medium is the houses I renovate."

"Well, I hope you don't plan on selling the lodge. I'm glad you're fixing it up, but it really does belong in your family. And you belong in it." She gave me a stern look.

I lifted a firm eyebrow. "Like you, my art is my profession. If I don't fix up the cottage to sell it, then it becomes simply a hobby, and I'll have to go out and get a job." I wrinkled my nose. "And me and jobs just don't work out." I shrugged a shoulder. "I don't take orders very well."

Candice humphed and shook her head. "Just like the rest of the clan."

She packaged my photos in a black faux-leather box and sent me home with the promise that I'd come for tea again the following Thursday.

I lay in my droopy twin bed that night flipping through the pictures from Candice. I'd been so happy in all of them. My mother smiled with me in each photo she was in. I could tell by my age in a few of the shots that some were taken just before my mother killed herself. How could those eyes that seemed so filled with happiness lie to the camera? What terrible thing had happened to take away her smile and make the bottom of Mead Quarry seem a better place than the cottage on Valentine's Bay and the arms of her little daughter?

I was doing the very thing I was warned not to do. I jerked upright, the black scribbles across my mother's graduation photograph flashing through my mind. DON'T ASK WHY. I scrambled for the two halves in the bedside drawer. I pulled them out and stared at the writing. I scratched at the *D* with my thumb. The black lines rubbed off, leaving a greasy residue behind.

Candice.

She'd known which bedroom was mine when I was a kid. She must have been the one to make this room comfortable for my arrival. And she was the only one who could have written those words across my mother's photo and left it on my pillow. Hadn't my grandfather accused her of being on Russo land? Joel must have seen Candice's car down here right before I showed up.

I flopped back on my pillow, holding one side of the torn photo in each hand. But Candice had loved my mother. And she'd loved me. Why would she so cruelly rip my mother's face to shreds?

From somewhere downstairs came the ringing of my cell phone. Brad. I hadn't given him a thought since our brief exchange Tuesday night. I jumped up and raced downstairs. ONE MISSED CALL, the display read by the time I found the phone. I checked caller ID and sighed. It wasn't Brad. A message came through and I listened to it. The heating guy. Just wanted to remind me that he'd be here around ten the next day.

I dragged back up the steps, placing the phone by the bed in case Brad should call.

The heating guy arrived as scheduled and prescribed a new high-efficiency forced-air unit. Between the crawl space and the generously thick walls, the ductwork would go in with minimal hassle. He wrote up the estimate and handed it to me.

"Can't get to you until April, though," he said. "I'm putting in under-floor heat at a new build down the peninsula. Takes awhile to install, but, boy, is it nice."

I took the slip from him. "Thanks. I'll get back to you with my decision."

Now, I sat at the counter, sipping coffee and staring at the proposed bill. The figures in the bottom right corner soared far beyond my imagined total. I wondered what genie in a bottle would make that wish come true.

I crumpled the paper. A woodstove or corn burner would be better suited to my budget. But they wouldn't exactly contribute to the resale value. The wealthy Chicagoan who would pick this place up wanted effortless heat. No cutting, chopping, or hauling required.

I sighed. I could always put off the decision until next fall. Warm weather was only a few months away.

In the meantime, I'd keep doing what I could.

I sanded a section of cedar paneling in the downstairs bathroom. The wood had been damaged by water from the sink area and was nearly black. When my efforts yielded little gain, I rounded up some bleach, diluted it, and applied it to the wall. Gradually, the original color reappeared. I added polyurethane to my list of things to purchase during my next trip to Manistique. A thick coat on the bathroom walls should prevent future damage and look crisp next to cabinetry painted bright white.

At dusk, I cleaned up my project and puttered around in the kitchen trying my hand at homemade chicken noodle soup. I'd been entirely spoiled back in Rawlings by the neighbor's scrumptious blends. Her yummy varieties had sustained me through the whole Victorian ordeal.

I stirred celery and onions into the chicken and broth, remembering Brad's humorous attempt at homemade soup a few days after I'd discovered the body in that basement. Nothing had lifted my spirits more than seeing him in a checkered apron that barely covered his broad form. The soup had boiled over, sending up a cloud of steam that filled the room. We'd laughed and cried and hugged while he helped me work through the whole killer-in-the-neighborhood trauma.

I chopped the carrots and added them to the boiling pot. Brad had always been there for me. He'd cared so much, even when I pushed him away. He could have kept his distance and let me pout over the holidays, my least favorite time of year. As crabby as I'd been, I certainly deserved to be left alone. But instead he'd made the two days I dreaded most, Thanksgiving and Christmas, so special. We hadn't done anything spectacular, just turkey or ham and all the fixings with his sister Samantha and a few other friends. But the fact that he'd included me, that he'd wanted me with him, made my holiday season the best I could ever remember.

Then there was New Year's Eve, and the toast at midnight, and the way our foreheads leaned together and stayed that way long past when the others had given a celebratory kiss and been done with it. His hands had lingered on my shoulders and things unsaid were spoken between us. His kiss was gentle but momentary, nothing that required a response. But the touch of our lips held all kinds of promises and commitments and questions and dreams. Afterward, our eyes met and conversed unblinking . . . until Samantha had broken between us to lay a smooch on her brother.

And in one panicked moment, one slam of my car door ten days ago, I'd ended it.

I at least owed him a phone call.

I put the lid on the pot and went in search of my cell phone.

12

It had been three days since I had spoken to Brad. I found the phone upstairs next to my bed and dialed Brad's number. I returned to my soup project as the line rang.

"Hello."

At the sound of his voice, my heart raced.

"Hi, Brad. It's me, Tish."

"Hey. How's things?"

Why did I feel like I was talking to a stranger? Not so long ago we'd been inseparable. "Good. Things are real good."

"I'm glad to hear it."

We suffered through a prolonged silence.

I said anything to fill the air. "I'm making chicken noodle soup tonight. Hopefully it turns out as good as yours." I picked up the lid and stirred the contents.

He laughed. "I'm sure you can't miss."

The steam rose in a puff around my face. "I forgot to buy spices. All I have is salt."

"Hmm. Did you add celery?"

"Yeah." I replaced the lid.

"Then it should be fine. Celery's got plenty of flavor. Add a little salt and pepper and that should do it."

I smiled with one hand to my forehead, fighting back the pressure in my sinuses. "Have you been doing good? Everything's okay with you?"

"Oh, sure. There was a fire up on Oak Street last night. Family lost their home. I guess they're staying with some relatives up in Flint 'til they get things settled."

I took in a sharp breath. "Where on Oak Street?" Brad and I had tackled most of Oak Street during our three-mile walks.

"It was that big gray house on the corner of Oak and Elm. It had that picket fence you liked."

"Oh, no. That's too bad. There were always kids playing in the yard. Nobody was hurt?"

"They were lucky. Everyone got out safely."

I missed Rawlings with its houses and sidewalks and shop fronts. Port Silvan with its blink-and-you-miss-it business district seemed a little too small town. And the people up here just weren't the same. There was no Brad.

"Hey," I said. "I really miss you guys."

"Yeah. Everyone misses you too."

"So how was the ski trip?" I asked.

"Fun. But it just wasn't the same without you."

I laughed. "Thanks, but I don't believe you. You know I flunked the bunny hill."

"Maybe. But you would have graduated one of these times."

I swallowed hard and ventured into dangerous territory. "Do you think we'll ever get together again?"

"Of course we will."

I started to cry. I couldn't help it. I sounded like a chipmunk in its dying throes.

"Tish? Is everything all right?"

I walked to the bathroom and pulled a wad of toilet tissue off the holder. I set the phone on the sink and gave a good blow.

I picked up the cell and slouched on the floor next to the vanity. "I'm okay. Sorry about that."

"You're worrying me. What's really going on up there?"

The soft rumble of Brad's voice calmed me momentarily. Then I started to cry again. "They don't love me," I bawled.

"Who? Who doesn't love you?"

I hiccupped between blubbers. "My family."

"Tell me what happened. We can work through this."

I gave him a hiccup-ridden rundown of current events, including Missy's sob story, but leaving out the bad guys on four-wheelers.

"Hang in there, Tish. You'll do the right thing. Don't let that stuff get you down. You're not the type to give in and give up. You're a fighter. You're a conqueror."

At his words, a feeling of peace washed over me. I smiled through misty eyes. "Thanks, Brad. You're such an encouragement to me. I don't know how I made it this long without you. Believe me, it won't happen again."

"That's good to know. So it's my turn to call same time tomorrow night?" he asked.

"Yes, sir. I need my daily pep talk."

"I can't give you a definite time, because sometimes things come up on my shift. But I'll be as punctual as I can."

"I understand."

"Okay then."

"Okay then." I didn't want to let him go, but I couldn't think of another intelligent thing to say. "Bye."

"Bye, Tish."

The sound of breathing, then the click of the disconnect.

I sat there scrunched in a little ball, wishing and wishing and wishing.

As the cold weather wore on, I settled into a routine. Four days a week, I worked on projects around the house. I took one day to get supplies in Manistique. Then on Sundays, I worshiped in Port Silvan. Thankfully, most of the churchgoers had loosened up over time, or maybe I had. I now enjoyed visiting over coffee before going back home and plopping on the couch with a book. Missy Belmont, however, held to her promised cold shoulder, regardless of my efforts to reclaim our friendship. As usual, Thursdays were spent at Candice's house, gently picking her brain. I never let on that I knew what she'd done to my mother's photo. And fortunately, I didn't have to worry about avoiding my paternal relatives over the weeks. The first encounter must have soured them to any repeat reunions. We said a polite hello at any chance meeting but never went beyond the perfunctory "How are you?" Brad and I enjoyed our phone calls, but as time marched on, we'd cut them back to three times a week due to time and scheduling constraints. Or maybe it was the effect of distance on a cooling relationship.

April showers arrived with full fury. One morning the ground had been covered in snow. The next, mini lakes dotted the yard wherever the ground dipped. I sat in the kitchen listening to rain batter the roof. A thumping had begun sometime during the night, possibly a loose gutter. I took a final sip of coffee and put on my new rain slicker. I'd found a ritzy department store in Manistique and splurged on several necessities, the bright melon jacket included.

I opened an umbrella and walked around to the source of the clanging. A downspout had detached from the gutter above and now dangled from two loose fasteners. Rain gushed from the unprotected hole, cutting a ditch into the ground below. I'd have to wait until the storm was over before tackling the repair.

I dashed across the yard and jangled open the latch on the garden shed. I tipped my red umbrella and let the water run off, then I entered. One window lit the dank, musty interior. The stone and log building was a trim 10x10 or so in size, but held every tool imaginable for some serious landscaping. A ramshackle old ladder leaned in the corner. At least I had a way to reach the spout and reconnect it when the time came.

I futzed around on one wall, rearranging the gadgets and dusting off cobwebs with an old rag. The place would look great with a fresh coat of white on the wooden slats. I could even spray some of the rusty tools bright colors to make a tidy wall display that no man could resist. It would be a fun project as soon as the weather warmed up and dried out. For now I tabled it, grateful that I knew where to find a ladder.

I opened the door and my umbrella. I checked the latch to make sure the door fastened behind me. The forest around the shed dripped and crackled with rain. The temperature hovered around forty-five degrees these days, and I couldn't resist a walk. I headed up the driveway. My breath misted in the clammy air. I sloshed through potholes that seemed to merge into one endless puddle. I loved the way my feet stayed dry in my new yellow rubber boots. Swampers, the saleslady had called them.

The exercise felt invigorating after long weeks of winter when walks were short and sparse. I branched to the right when I reached the highway, then crossed the road and headed up the bluff as I'd done once before. I didn't worry about the men on four-wheelers this time. I figured my wayward cousin had been smart enough to find a new location for his drug buys.

Up on the bluff, the view was drab. The skies threw a gray wash over the bay. Masses of black ice covering the water's surface seemed to gasp as they drowned beneath the rain. From my vantage point, the trees showed no signs of spring. Bare branches added to the dismal panorama, broken only by my driveway that ran like a charcoal-colored ribbon across the forest floor.

On the highway below, a car slowed and turned down the two-track toward my house. I squinted. A tan four-door I didn't recognize. I hated to miss a visitor. I folded my umbrella and hooked the loop around my wrist. I took the shortcut down the face of the bluff, picking my way from tree trunk to sapling. The umbrella pulled at my arm like a red kite in a brisk wind. I made it to the bottom of the incline safely this time and crossed the highway to my drive. I splashed at top speed toward the cottage. After a ways, I slowed to catch my breath. The tan car pulled toward me on its way back to the highway.

I waved. The car stopped. The driver's window rolled down.

I smiled. "Hi, Joel. What's up?"

My cleaner-cut cousin gave a big sigh and set one arm on the car door.

"Get in. Olivia's asking for you."

I patted my hair, drenched with rain. "What's the rush? How about if I finish my walk, shower up, and then head down to your place?"

His fingers tapped. "It can't wait. She wants you now."

I stepped back and crossed my arms. "Why the sudden change of heart? Not so long ago I was chopped liver."

He looked at me with arched eyebrows. "Get in, Tish. She's dying."

13

"Olivia's dying?" I sloshed around to the passenger side and jumped in. I slammed the door and fastened my seat belt. Joel moved in slow motion to put the car in gear.

"Well, hurry up. She could pass at any moment," I urged. I didn't want to miss out on my last opportunity to meet my great-grandmother.

"So she says," Joel replied.

The car pulled forward at a snail's pace.

"You don't seem to be taking this very seriously." I pushed my foot against the floorboard, hoping the car would accelerate in response.

"Nope." Joel stopped at the top of the drive, sending a lengthy gaze in either direction before pulling onto the highway. "She's been dying for the past twenty years." He glanced at me with cynical eyes. "Leverage, you know."

My lips formed a silent "oh." I nodded and looked out the window. I knew firsthand how weighty the threat of death could be to the living. My grandma Amble had used her illness to guilt me into dropping out of college to take care of her in her last days, which had stretched out for more than two years. Recently, I'd given thought to what I should have done instead of playing into her death drama. I should have continued to live. I should have stayed at college and finished my degree. Hospice and visiting nurses would have been more than sufficient to provide for my grandmother's physical needs. I would have been home with her on weekends and breaks anyhow.

I sighed. That reasonable scenario had seemed so selfish at the time. But Gram and I would have enjoyed each other so much more without the martyrdom that brought anger, resentment, and eventually murder into my heart.

Joel kept below the speed limit as he drove toward Port Silvan.

"So remind me again why you live with Olivia?" I said.

He gave me a glare that told me my question didn't merit an answer.

"I'm not trying to be nosy," I said. "I just don't think it's healthy for a guy your age to be living with his great-uncle and great-grandmother." The sign for the cider mill passed by on my right. "I mean, don't you plan on dating or getting married and having a family? What kind of woman is going to want to move in with Papa B and Olivia?"

He looked at me tight-lipped, then glanced back at the road. "I suppose I should just lace their morning coffee with cyanide and be done with them?" He shook his head. "Oh, wait. I don't feel like going to prison for three years."

I swallowed and stared ahead. "Point made," I whispered.

He tipped his head at me. "Listen. I don't want to fight with you. I live at the lake house because I choose to. Uncle Bernard and Grandma Olivia are both good people and I like helping them out. I like hearing stories about the old days. And to me, it's better than living alone. But"—he made sure he caught my eye before continuing—"they're not perfect. Watch what you say in front of Olivia. She's not a big believer in confidentiality. If you cough in front of her, Port Silvan is going to hear that you've got pneumonia."

I waved a hand. "You're exaggerating."

"No, I'm not. You've been warned. And that's all I'm going to say about it."

Joel navigated the curve out of town. A few minutes later we pulled into the drive at the lake house. Joel parked in the detached garage, pushing a button to shut the garage door behind us. The noisy clanking meant I didn't have to say anything as we got out of the vehicle. I followed him outside and across the cobblestone walk.

We came in the house through a side door that led into an entry room. From the landing where we stood, steps forked up to the kitchen or down to the basement. Behind us hung at least twenty coats and jackets in denim, canvas, camouflage, nylon, and flannel. Boots and shoes were scattered across the floor near the back wall. Paint that had once been bright white was covered with black scuff marks.

Joel took my coat and slung it over an open hook. I

removed my swampers and lined them near the wall. My socks made contact with a pool of water. I cringed.

"You want a cup of coffee to take in there with you?" he asked.

I'd worked up a dose of perspiration on my walk and now that my slicker was off and my socks were wet, I couldn't stop shivering. "Coffee sounds good." I rubbed my arms to chase away the chill. I could already feel the pneumonia setting in.

"You want a fresh sweatshirt or something?" Joel asked.

I nodded. "Slippers, too, if you have some."

"Come on," he said. "You can change upstairs." He motioned for me to follow him.

The front steps made a steep run to the second floor. My socks slid on the smooth cherry treads. At the top, I paused to view Silvan Bay. Most of the snow had melted from the shore, with only an occasional patch still lingering in shaded areas. A lone ice-fishing shanty, patched together with a hodge-podge of boards and old siding, sat half submerged in the retreating ice, perhaps destined to bob as a menace to boaters until sinking at last to the bottom of the bay.

"Here," Joel said from a door at the end of a long hallway. "After you change, come back downstairs and I'll bring you to Olivia." He handed me the warm garments I'd requested and walked off.

I entered the bedroom. The air was cold, as if the room had been shut off from the rest of the house. A pink comforter with lace edging covered a white wrought-iron bedstead. Candles in colorful holders lined the window ledge. A wreath of dried wildflowers hung above the round mirror of the '50s-style dresser. I wondered how the room had been allowed to exist in the mostly male household.

A photo on the wall showed a smiling *Leave It to Beaver* family of three. I took a closer look. I recognized a young-twenties Puppa sans moustache and dressed in a coat and tie. The woman next to him would be my deceased grandmother. She was beautiful, with dark hair and happy, gleaming eyes. That made the toddler in the picture my father. He looked about three years old when the photo was taken. An abundance of curls topped his head. Baby teeth peeked out from his wide-mouthed smile.

I ran a finger across the glass. Surely the little family had held such promise. Who could have known the tragedy in store for their lives?

I turned my back on the past and put on the thick sweatshirt. I stepped into the slippers, closed the bedroom door behind me, and made my way downstairs.

"Joel?" I called when I got to the entry hall.

"This way."

His voice came from a door that hung open underneath the steps. I hadn't even seen it my first time through.

I entered what must have been at one time the nursery. Small and square, the room was painted a pale blue that had darkened unevenly over the years. From the light fixture in the center hung a child's mobile, with a circle of giraffes that remained forever just out of reach of the jaws of a smiling lion. A door in the far corner of the room probably connected to the master bedroom.

A hospital bed sat against one wall. Joel's shoulders blocked the view of the woman under the covers. Her feet moved beneath the white spread.

"Joel. Move so I can see Patricia." The voice was sharp and strong. An underlying waver revealed the speaker's advanced age.

My cousin stepped aside with a flourish of his arm, as if to say, "She's all yours."

I smiled and moved to the edge of the bed. The lovely Olivia wore carefully coifed and silvered hair. Her lined face was still pert and attractive for a woman her age. A touch of rouge brightened her cheeks.

"Hi. It's nice to meet you." I held out a hand in greeting. Though her bones looked as delicate as a bird's, she nearly crushed my fingers with her feisty grip.

"You look just like your mother." Olivia shook her head as if disappointed.

"Thank you," I said anyway. "I've seen pictures of my mother and she was very beautiful."

"Just be careful you don't end up like her," Grandma Olivia said.

I broadened my smile. "I have no plans to kill myself, if that's what you mean."

"Good. I'm glad she's dead after killing my boy."

I pulled my hand out of her grasp. "I don't know the whole story. I'm sure if she killed Uncle Sid, it was an accident."

"She had no business going to the cops. He was just doing what he had to do to get by. He wasn't hurting anybody."

Mexico - Audrain County Library
305 West Jackson
Mexico, Missouri 65265

I scrunched my forehead. "I don't understand. She killed him by calling the cops?"

"It was none of her business. People got scared that Sid might talk. And they started that fire." Olivia struggled to sit up. "Some things are better left alone."

Joel pushed me aside to get to our great-grandmother. He laid his hands on her shoulders and eased her back down on the bed. "Calm down, Olivia. No sense getting worked up over old news."

Olivia pulled in a few deep breaths and closed her eyes. "Sit with me awhile, Patricia."

I looked at Joel. He shrugged and left the room. I sat in a wooden upright chair and scooted it close to the edge of the bed. The old gal held my fingers. Within ten minutes she had fallen asleep.

I looked at her face, now lying in peaceful slumber. The lines in her forehead came together in the center like an arrow, evidence of a lifetime of worry. The skin around her mouth lay in a deep frown, betraying disappointment and bitterness. How sad that she'd held on to all her griefs. I realized how fortunate I was to have been able to let go of so many of my own.

The door squeaked open behind me. My grandfather came into the room.

"Hello, Patricia," he whispered.

"Hi, Puppa." I kept my voice low.

He lifted a matching chair and set it next to mine. "I see Olivia broke down and asked you over."

I looked at him funny. "Joel drove to my house and picked me up. She told him she was dying and had to see me right away."

118

My grandfather smiled and looked at his mother's quiet form. "Maybe. She probably just feels foolish for shunning you earlier. What better way to save face?"

"I guess so." I stared at Olivia's fingers intertwined with mine. Even in sleep she hadn't relaxed her grip.

I looked at my grandfather, realizing we were alone for the first time. I remembered my promise to Missy Belmont. "Uh, I have a favor to ask of you."

"Sure. What is it?"

I struggled for the right words. "A friend of mine is hoping you'll help her out."

He furrowed his forehead. "What do you mean?"

I bit my lip. "Back in March, Melissa Belmont asked me to tell you that her husband was dealing drugs and beating her. She said you'd know what to do to help her out."

He held a finger to his mouth to quiet me. He stood and pointed to the far door. I wriggled my hand from Olivia's hold and tiptoed after my grandfather.

We entered a large master bedroom that apparently served as a study as well. A huge desk sat against the windows overlooking the front yard. Papers littered the surface. Rows of filing cabinets filled a whole corner. A double bed was scrunched against a wall, as if an afterthought.

"Wow. You're a little behind with your filing." I smiled as I made the comment.

Puppa ignored me and sat down at the desk, with pen perched over a scratchpad. "So when exactly did Missy ask you to talk to me?"

14

I put a hand to my forehead, trying to remember the events surrounding Missy Belmont's plea for help. "I met her the Sunday after I moved up here. The next Tuesday we met at the library in Manistique, and she told me everything."

Puppa glanced up at a twelve-month wall calendar. He wrote on his paper.

"And what exactly did she say to you?" he asked.

I relayed the details the best I could. "Then I told her she should take the kids and go to a shelter."

My grandfather nodded. "That works for most people, but Missy knows she's in a little deeper than that."

"What do you mean?"

"There's a drug network involved. It's not just Drake she's got to break away from. As with a lot of the wives and girlfriends, Missy has seen and heard too much. If she runs, she could be dead."

I sucked in a breath. "So what can you do?"

Puppa shrugged. "Make a few phone calls. Call in a few favors. We'll see."

"But why would Missy think you could help her?"

"I used to be in law enforcement. Maybe she thinks I still have an inside track."

"Do you?"

"We'll see." He scribbled a few more notes on his pad. "Or, maybe there's something else going on altogether." He paused, pencil in midair as he concentrated. He looked over his shoulder at me. "Go back in there and check on Olivia."

I hesitated at the door. Puppa strode to a file cabinet and started flipping through folders.

"So, you're like a retired cop?" I asked him.

"No, I'm like a fired cop." He turned his back to me.

I gulped and nodded and walked back into Olivia's room.

She was awake.

"How are you feeling?" I went to the bed and touched her hand.

"I'm fine," she snapped. "Tell Joelly I'm hungry."

"Sure."

I found him in the kitchen, putting supper together.

"Mmm. Smells good," I said.

He glanced up from his place at the stove where he was mixing something in a fry pan. "Hey, little cousin."

"Hey, yourself." I snuck a peek in the skillet. "Stir-fry. Looks yummy."

"I take it Olivia's not dead?" he asked.

"Nope. She'll be kicking for a long time yet. In fact, she's hungry."

His spatula slowed. "Uh-oh. What'd you tell her? She only gets hungry when she's gearing up for the gossip circuit."

121

"You heard everything. She insulted my mother and I thanked her for it. She fell asleep right after you left." Fat scraps and veggie ends were scattered across the top of the island. I scooped up a handful and put it in the trash. "So. Papa B was a police officer?"

Joel looked up from the stove. "State cop. How'd you know?"

I shrugged. "He told me. Said he was fired. What happened with that?"

His spoon halted mid-stir. "I'm surprised he said something to you. He never talks about it."

I grabbed a dishcloth and wiped down the island. "So? What's the scoop?"

Joel shook his head and went back to stirring. "I was pretty young at the time. Four or five years old, I guess." He tapped the spoon on the edge of the pan. "In fact, it was right around the time Lizard died."

"Lizard?"

Joel's cheeks blushed red. "Elizabeth. Beth. Your mom. That's what me and Gerard called her. She was a lot of fun."

My forehead bunched. I could see two freckle-faced boys jumping out in ambush along some forest path.

"Nice try, boys," I heard my mother say. "But I saw Joelly's white socks from a mile away."

"No fair," the boys whined as they ran ahead to find a better hiding place.

I looked at my cousin, all grown up. "You called my mom Lizard and me Toilet Tissue."

Joel looked sheepish. "You see why Uncle Bernard will only let us call you Patricia these days?"

I crossed my arms. "Yes. Remind me to thank him."

Gerard showed up in time for supper and the four of us shared a pleasant meal. Grandma Olivia had her tray in the bedroom again. She had to make it look like she was still dying, Puppa said when she wouldn't come to the table.

Joel drove me home around seven.

"You want to come in and see what I've done?" I asked.

He looked straight ahead, as if debating. "Why not? I haven't been in there since I was a kid." He turned off the ignition and came after me.

"Nice kitchen," he said, kicking his shoes off on the rug.

"Think so? I thought about changing some things because it feels so small."

He looked around the room. "It has everything a good chef needs. Nice work triangle, a prep island, and stools for company. No need to change a thing."

"Thanks. I'll go easy on it."

We walked from room to room. I gave Joel the rundown on the improvements. He made all the right comments.

Upstairs, I leaned against the banister overlooking the great room.

"So what's the history behind this place, anyway?" I asked him.

His hands rested on the log railing. "I'm not sure. Some big family hunting lodge from back when there was still family to fill it, I guess. Unfortunately, the years haven't been kind to the Russos. They just petered out 'til there's just me and Gerard—and now you—left to carry on."

I looked out over an orange sky. "Seems sad, doesn't it? I mean, what is it about our family that causes us to self-destruct?"

Joel was quiet for a minute. "Is it just us? Or is it everybody? We're not the only ones living lonely and afraid. It's everywhere you look."

I thought about his words. Lonely and afraid. Yep. That about summed it up. Yet I really didn't have an excuse for feeling that way. I'd heard enough Sunday sermons about abundant life in Christ that I should feel happy and joyous by now. I guess I just needed to try harder.

I put on a smile. "Listen to us whining. We're some of the luckiest people I know. Young, healthy, and miles of future ahead."

Joel grinned. "You're right." He rubbed his hands together. "Nice job here, Tish. All the best with the rest of your improvements." He went down the steps two at a time. At the bottom, he stopped and looked back up at me. "By the way, I owe you an apology." He cast his eyes onto the stair treads. "I didn't know you were going to be such a decent person. I thought you might be . . . well, I figured you'd just want to barge in here like you had some right . . . Anyway, I'm sorry I was rude at Papa B's house last time. You didn't deserve it." He gave a final glance up at me, then disappeared under the arch. A moment later I heard the back door close.

I stood at the rail. Maybe Joel had been disrespectful the other night. But his apology made up for it in a big way. It took a big person to humble himself like that.

Twiddling my thumbs, I stared at specks of dust floating in the beams of a setting sun. Humility sure wasn't my strong point.

I sighed. Tonight was my night to call Brad. I dropped my head on my arms, dreading the call. It had been hard conversing with him lately. I just wanted to be with him. But he had his job, his family, his roots down in Rawlings. And I had my roots to plant here in Port Silvan. It seemed there could never be a way for us to be together.

I contemplated not calling him. The pain always spiked after I heard his voice. Maybe if I just let him go, just let him become a long-forgotten memory, then that place in my chest would quit hurting.

Eight o'clock passed and I didn't call him. I breathed a sigh of relief. It hardly hurt at all. I sat on the couch with my book. After ten minutes staring at the words, I hadn't understood a sentence. I reread the page. Then I gave up and checked the clock. Eight twenty.

I should call him. That would be the right thing to do. I could say, "Please don't contact me anymore. Every time I hear your voice, I'm jerked back into loving you. And what good is that doing? We can't be together right now and it hurts too bad to be apart. So just don't call me anymore. Just leave me alone."

Tears ran down my face just thinking the words. I couldn't bear to be without Brad. As much as it hurt to be away from him, it would surely kill me to never speak to him again.

I dialed the phone.

"Brad?" My voice quavered with emotion.

"Tish, are you alright?"

I laughed into the mouthpiece. "Yes. I'm just glad to hear your voice." I laughed again to hide my feelings. "Hey, remember the day we went shopping for garage door openers?"

He gave a quiet chuckle. "Oh, man. What were we thinking?"

I smiled and closed my eyes as I relived the afternoon we'd spent at the home improvement center in Flint, just north of Rawlings. We'd gone to buy his-n-hers openers for our own separate detached garages. But somehow we'd gotten distracted on the way to the hardware department and ended up in kitchen cabinets, choosing our favorite styles and colors. He picked a medium hickory with an arch top, I picked a light oak square top. We laughed at our differences, together choosing a lighter arched hickory as our joint favorite. We did the same thing in the bath department, then the lighting department, and finally the whole store, until we built an entire house for ourselves.

"Yeah," I sighed into the phone, "what were we thinking?"

In the end, we bought our separate garage door openers and drove home to our separate houses and went to sleep in our separate beds and woke up to our separate brews of coffee, which we drank alone each morning in our separate kitchens.

I swallowed hard so I could speak. "Hey," I said, "did you ever think it might have been fun—to build a house together?"

"Yeah," he said, "I thought about that. It would have been a lot of fun."

Then why don't we do it, I wanted to say. Why don't we figure out a way to get together and make it work?

Instead, I made a little grunt through my tears. "What do you think happened to that idea, anyway?"

He paused a moment. "We decided to just be friends."

I nodded, wiping my face. "Just friends" didn't get married and have babies and build houses together. No, "just friends" called each other on the phone every once in a while. Just like we were doing now. I tried not to sniffle into the receiver. "Thanks for being my friend, Brad. It really means a lot to me."

Comforted in the knowledge that he was at least still my good buddy, I relaxed a little. We talked for over an hour. I could almost hear the dinging of a cash register at my cell phone company as each minute passed, but decided not to let my usage minutes rule my relationships.

I mentioned my great-grandmother's death scare, my grandfather's former career, and my cousin's take on life.

"Your family sound like good people. I'm glad they're there for you."

He said it like such a true friend. I wanted to think that underneath the words he was really saying, "I love you." But that would have been reading too much into it.

"Good night, Tish."

Brad's gentle farewell dredged up that gush of agony.

"Night."

I sniffled and disconnected. Then I carted myself off to bed.

15

The weeks that followed brought an amazing transformation to the peninsula. Bare branches now glowed bright green as tiny leaves began their temporal journey. New grass poked through last year's tangle of dried yellow blades. Each new morning dawned crisp and bright as the sun drew closer to Port Silvan.

It was the first Thursday of May. I stood on the ramshackle front deck, careful to avoid the rotted sections. It was warm enough for a sweatshirt and my navy windbreaker. Just beyond my perch, small brown birds twittered in and out of the brush. Farther out, Valentine's Bay stretched smooth and blue in front of me. I savored the scent of newly warmed soil laced with cool lake breeze. I had a hard time imagining ever making a move back to civilization.

In fact, tea with Candice was the maximum human interaction I wanted today. Afterward, I planned on getting intimate with the local worms and grubs as I dug up a section of yard for a flowerbed. Besides, burying my hands in dirt up to my elbows would take my mind off the significance of the day's date. But then again,

burying anything was probably the exact thing I should be avoiding.

I made the drive to Candice's house, memorizing every new and brilliant spring creation along the way.

She waved from the porch as I pulled up. A gust of wind pushed at the sides of her wide-brimmed straw hat. She tightened the black polka-dot scarf that kept it from blowing away.

"Hello!" I called as I approached the house.

"Happy Thursday." She kissed my cheek. "I can't hug you until I've washed up. I've been getting the beds ready."

I looked at the rectangles of newly turned soil on either side of the steps. "What are you planting?"

"Nothing yet," she said. "Not until Memorial Day. That's the rule of thumb around here." She held the door open for me. I waited in the parlor while she washed. A few minutes later she served up the tea.

"It'll be iced tea soon enough, won't it?" Candice said.

"I know." I took a sip. A hint of lemon tickled my tongue. "This winter has flown by. Just when I got settled in Rawlings, it was time to make the move to Port Silvan. And now summer's almost here."

"What projects do you have planned for the warmer weather?" Candice nibbled a circle of rye topped with cream cheese and a cucumber.

I reached for a tiny tuna on wheat. "The porches need all new decking and the log siding needs restoration. I'll be going through a truckload of bleach to kill the mold and get the logs back to their original color. Then of course I have to stain everything."

Candice knit her brows. "Is that really something you can handle on your own? That place is huge. You'll be spending your summer up on a ladder."

I smiled to reassure her. "It's all part of the job. And it's a great excuse to get outdoors in sunny weather."

"I sure hope you know what you're doing. Jim Hawley could probably finish the project in a week. Maybe you should think about letting him help you."

I waved a hand to reject her offer. "No, no. I can handle it." After all, I didn't want to get the place fixed up too quickly. What excuse would I have for sticking around Port Silvan if everything was done by September? And figuring out my mother's life wasn't like baking a cake. It was more like refinishing a piece of fine furniture. The old varnish had to be removed layer by layer until the true wood was revealed. Only time and patience could bring an accurate depiction of my mother.

Candice and I talked more about my renovation schedule. Then the mantel clock *bonged*.

"Is it that time already?" I stood to go.

Candice gathered the cups and saucers and set them on the tray. "I forgot to mention that Drake Belmont was arrested yesterday. Had you heard?"

My hand flew to my throat. "Is Missy alright? He didn't hurt her, did he?" I could kick myself for not forcing my way into Melissa Belmont's life instead of letting her dictate a code of silence.

"From what I gather, he was picked up for possession of marijuana with the intent to distribute, or something like that."

I closed my eyes and breathed a sigh of relief. "As

130

long as Missy and the kids are okay, that's what matters. Hopefully she can leave safely now that he's in jail."

Candice arched a doubting eyebrow. "We'll see. Some women are tenacious about staying in an abusive situation even when the way out is staring them in the face."

I pursed my lips. I hated that Candice always thought the worst of Missy. "I know she'll do the right thing." I turned to go. "See you next Thursday," I called over my shoulder.

As I drove toward home, I tossed around the bright possibilities for Missy now that Drake was sitting in a jail cell. I'd give her a call just so she'd know I was there for her if she needed anything.

I crossed Cupid's Creek. Over the treetops to the left, a tower of smoke billowed skyward. I squinted, trying to pinpoint its origin. My heart plunked to my hips. My house was the only structure in the area. I stepped on the gas. My house was burning down.

I skidded onto my driveway and gunned the engine. I gripped the steering wheel, trying to stay in the seat as the vehicle bounded through potholes.

The stench of smoke blasted my nose as I neared the source. "No, no, no." Not my house. It was my childhood, my memories. It was all my tools and enough stuff to fill an SUV.

How could this be happening? I couldn't have left the iron on, since I didn't own one. I hadn't done anything different today than any other day.

I turned the last corner and slid to a stop, blinded by a cloud of gray. My eyes watered and my lungs burned.

The wind shifted. Through the hazy air, I could see that my cottage was still there. Still in one piece. It wasn't burning down.

Instead, the garden shed blazed orange and blue. Thick black smoke rose from curling shingles. As I watched, the roof collapsed and flames rose to new heights. There went my landscaping plans. There went the hangout some buyer would have deemed irresistible.

I slammed my palms on the steering wheel in frustration, then reached for my cell phone. I dialed 9-1-1.

The dispatcher answered on the second ring.

"My name is Tish Amble and I'd like to report a fire."

I gave the operator the location, then went in search of a garden hose hopefully stashed in the crawl space. I found a bucket instead. Fifteen pails of water later, help arrived. The Port Silvan volunteer firemen doused the flames in a matter of minutes.

A waist-high square of rocks was all that remained when the smoke cleared.

One of the firemen approached. His black and yellow coat hung to the top of tall boots.

"How did this get started?" he asked.

"I have no idea. I left the house around noon and when I got back about two twenty, this is what I found." I gestured toward the burnt-out shell. "I called right away."

The man nodded. "It looks like accelerants were involved."

"Accelerants?"

"Like gasoline."

I shook my head. "I don't remember seeing a can of gas in there. Maybe, but I don't think so."

"Does anybody have a reason to be angry with you?"

I looked at him in surprise.

He stared at the ashes. "The reason I ask is that the majority of crimes are committed by someone we know."

I fumbled through my data banks and came up empty handed. "I don't know anybody up here. Well, just a couple people, but they wouldn't burn down my shed."

"Weren't you tight with Melissa Belmont awhile back?"

My eyes scoped out the trees as I tried to figure out how he knew that. "I wouldn't say tight. We talked at church and bumped into each other once at the library. Why?"

His eyes were all over my face. "Drake Belmont got thrown in jail yesterday. You wouldn't have had anything to do with that, would you?"

My jaw dropped. "Absolutely not. I'd heard he dealt drugs, but I assumed that's common knowledge."

"Common knowledge or not, I think Drake's buddies are sending you a message. I imagine next time it'll be your house they burn down."

I sputtered. "If you think you know who did it, then let's go to the cops. The arsonists should be sitting behind bars next to Drake."

He shook his head. "I've seen this before. You'll never be able to prove a thing." The fireman glanced at the others winding up hoses. "I guess it pays to mind your own business, huh?"

He joined his associates. With the last of the equipment stowed, the tanker truck and engine started out the drive.

"Thank you," I called toward the last rig. One man lifted his arm in acknowledgment. The diesels roared, then were gone.

I stood alone in the yard, still shaking from the incident. The fire had scorched the grass around the ruins. I guess I was lucky the whole forest hadn't burnt to the ground. I couldn't believe someone would pick today, of all days, to do this horrible thing.

I ran inside, flopped on the bed, and dialed Candice's number.

16

"Candice, you won't believe what just happened." I blurted into the phone when she answered.

"I can't even understand you, Tish. Is everything okay?"

"They burnt my shed down. I got home and it was on fire."

"Who? Who burnt your shed?"

"Drake Belmont's buddies. The fireman said they must be mad at me for turning Drake in. But I didn't turn him in. I never said a word to anybody." I paused, remembering. "Except you and Puppa."

The other end of the line was quiet.

"Candice? Are you there?"

"I'm here, Tish."

"I can't believe they'd do this to me. I loved that shed. I had big plans for that shed."

Candice gave a big sigh. "Just be glad it wasn't your house. I'll be right over."

"Thank you, thank you."

I put on some coffee while I waited. The interior reeked of smoke. I went around and opened the windows fac-

135

ing the lake, hoping the fresh breeze would clear up the air.

Back in the kitchen, I dragged a stool to a spot near the window. I stared out at the smoldering foundation. Gray smoke wisped toward heaven, as if carrying the spirit of my precious garden shed home.

Candice arrived. Her white Impala lurched to a stop near the porch.

She raced inside. "Tish, are you alright?"

I nodded. At her show of concern, my face swelled up. Next thing I knew, tears were pouring down my cheeks. She held onto me, rocking me like a little girl, right there in the kitchen.

"Shh. It's okay. We'll get through this."

The gentle back-and-forth motion brought me back to that tragic May, years earlier.

"Do you know what today is?" I sobbed.

"I know, dear. I know."

"Why did she have to die? Why did she have to do that? Wasn't it enough just being my mom?"

Candice ran a hand along the back of my hair. "She loved you, Tish. She really did."

I pushed away from Candice and stared into her face.

"Why weren't you there, Jellybean? Why weren't you at the funeral for me? I looked and looked, but you never came."

Candice's eyes pooled. She grabbed me and held my head to her chest. "I'm sorry. I'm so sorry. I wanted to be there, I really did."

We were both crying like babies when a black pickup pulled up. Gravel flew when the driver hit the brakes.

"Oh, no." Candice wiped at her face. "I've got to make a run for it."

The passenger door opened. My grandfather stepped out. Gerard walked around from the driver's side. The two men headed for the porch.

"You're not going anywhere." I stepped in front of Candice, as if to shield her.

"What's going on around here?" My grandfather bellowed as he barged in. Gerard entered behind him.

"Hi, Puppa." I tried to act natural, though all the tears must have made my face look like I'd sunburned through a chain-link fence.

"What's she doing here?" He pointed a finger of accusation in Candice's direction.

Candice stepped out from behind me. "Hello, Bernard. I'm comforting your granddaughter in her hour of need. You know, that thing I wasn't allowed to do twenty-six years ago."

My grandfather's eyes narrowed to slits. "I'd be careful going back twenty-six years if I were you."

Candice smirked. "Interesting there should be another fire. What's this one for? To mark the anniversary?"

Puppa's fingers balled into fists. "I don't know where you got the idea I was behind the fire at your place, but it sounds like you're going to carry it to the grave."

She shimmied closer until her face was within reach of those fists. Curiosity kept me from pulling her to safety.

"Who else would have burned the place down with Paul still inside?" she asked.

I assumed Paul was Candice's husband.

She took a step closer. "And I'm sure it didn't break your heart that Sid died in the flames too."

Near the door, Gerard tensed.

My grandfather's voice softened. "They were mixed up in bad stuff, Candice. It was only a matter of time. If not a fire, then something else."

She continued on as if he hadn't even spoken. "How can you live with yourself? You wanted Paul dead so you could marry me. And Sid was responsible for ruining your career."

Puppa shook his head. "No. You could have divorced Paul. And my own stupidity cost me my job. Not Sid."

My head bobbed back and forth as I watched the two seniors match wits.

Candice's normally proud stance melted into a forlorn slouch. "You knew I couldn't get a divorce. It was against everything I believed."

Puppa leaned toward her, his hands reaching for her body but not making contact. "I'll never understand you. You were living under my roof, and you were worried about what people thought if you got a divorce?" He put a fist to his forehead as if to say *duh*. "They would have been relieved. They would have been glad for you. Nobody liked Paul. Not after what he did to you." His voice turned all raspy. "Why should you have felt guilty for starting a new life? A life with me?"

Candice dropped her head into her hands. Tufts of silver hair poked up between her fingers.

"Tish." I barely heard her say my name. "Tish. Walk me to my car."

My grandfather put out an arm. "I'll walk you to your car."

Candice glared up at him. "I don't want your help."

He put up his hands in surrender and stepped aside.

I touched one hand to her wrist and the other to her elbow and led her into the yard. "You don't have to leave, you know. This isn't Russo land. It's my land. Stay and have a cup of coffee."

Candice shook her head. "I can't be around him."

"Come on, Candice. It sounds to me like he's trying his best."

She stopped at the car door. "It's more complicated than that. There's more to it than you realize." She got in and turned the key. "I'll see you next Thursday. Treat yourself special today, Tish."

I nodded and bit my lip. She slammed the car door and drove off. I took a deep breath and went in to face my relatives.

17

I walked through the kitchen door. For a moment, the three of us just stood there looking at each other.

"Well, who's up for a cup of coffee?" I moved toward the counter.

The men nodded and I poured three mugs full. Another round of silence followed.

My grandfather spoke first. "Let's walk out to the shed and see what we can find." He bolted out the door, never looking back to see if anyone came after him.

I glanced at Gerard as we moseyed toward the ruins. "I hope you can make sense out of that whole Bernard-Candice thing," I said. "The best I can figure is they're both professional grudge holders."

"You got that right. It'd take an act of God to get one of those two to apologize to the other."

We were almost to the pile of smoldering ashes. "It seemed to me like Puppa was trying to make amends."

"It may seem that way, but there's more to it than you realize." Gerard took a sip of coffee and stared into the glowing coals.

"That's what Candice said." I stood next to him.

Through the smoke, my grandfather kicked at some charred wood.

"There's no doubt this was arson," Puppa said.

"You're sure?" I moved around to his side of the remains.

"The walls were doused in gasoline." He pointed. "See that charred trail on the ground? Gas was spilled when the container was tilted."

"How do we catch these guys?"

He shook his head. "We may not be able to. But chances are good the perpetrators would have gotten gas on their shoes and clothing, or a pair of gloves. Maybe even bragged about burning the shed. I'll ask around. And I'll have my contacts at the hospital get in touch with me if anyone comes in for burn treatment. These guys are amateurs, trying to make a statement. There's a possibility they singed more than just their eyebrows lighting this thing."

An approaching car crunched gravel on the drive behind us. I turned. A state police cruiser slowed and parked. The trooper got out and walked to the scene.

"Officer Segerstrom, nice of you to come," Puppa said with an outstretched arm.

The officer shook his hand. "Sorry to see your shed burnt down."

Puppa nodded my way. "Technically, it's her shed now. This is my granddaughter, Patricia Amble."

The officer tipped his hat in my direction. "You know my buddy Brad Walters. He's an officer in downstate Rawlings."

My eyes grew wide. "Brad? You know him?" I vaguely

remembered Brad mentioning his friend in Manistique was a state cop. This must be the guy.

"When your grandfather got a hold of me with the news about the shed, I gave Brad a call. He sounded a little worried."

"You talked to Brad?"

"He seemed surprised he hadn't heard from you. You should probably phone him sometime today."

I nodded, mute. Brad hadn't heard from me because I'd called Candice right away instead. I guess that was a big indication of where Brad and I stood with each other.

The officer looked Gerard's way and gave a terse nod. Gerard only glared back in his direction. I figured from the exchange that Gerard and his drug shenanigans had made a blip on the cop's radar. The men couldn't be anything but cool toward one another.

"Patricia," Puppa said, "Mike's got a few questions for you."

I was thoroughly confused how my grandfather, a fired ex-cop, could be on a first-name basis with the next generation of law enforcement. I guess it showed there was good breeding somewhere in the bloodlines.

I focused on answering the officer's questions: what time did you leave the house, when did you return, did you see any vehicles, did you notice anything out of the ordinary, has anyone threatened you, are you involved with local drug trafficking . . .

"Whoa." I stopped him. "I resent your implication that I'm mixed up in anything illegal. I make it a point to mind my own business. In fact, I bend over backwards to be a law-abiding citizen."

"Have you ever witnessed any drug deals?" the officer asked, undeterred.

I sputtered. "Drug deals?" My mind flashed back to the exchange on the bluff. I shot a glance toward my grandfather. "Ahh, not that I know of."

"Perhaps you can clarify that statement." Officer Segerstrom held his pen ready.

"It means, not that I know of," I repeated.

A hint of impatience settled into the officer's voice. "Whoever burnt down your shed is sending a message. It wasn't just something they did for kicks. Now, you either know or saw something they don't want you to tell. Speak up now and we may catch them, or keep it to yourself and hope you can get out before the next fire reaches your bed." He glanced at my log home. "You'd be lucky to get out alive."

"Okay, okay." I glanced at my grandfather, wishing I didn't have to hurt him by tattling on Gerard. "I did see something that looked like a drug deal. It was back in February. Some guy wearing camouflage clothes and riding a dark green four-wheeler was passing stuff off to some other guy in black on a red four-wheeler. They saw me, and the guy in camo almost ran me over."

"Did you recognize them?" Puppa asked.

I gave him a look of discouragement, hoping he wouldn't push me to answer.

"Well?" asked the cop.

"Yeah. I did." I cleared my throat. "The man wearing black was my cousin Gerard."

In my peripheral vision, I could see Gerard casually

poking at some smoking charcoal with his foot. Then he turned and walked off.

Officer Segerstrom nodded, his head bent over his notepad. He didn't even seem surprised as he jotted down my answer.

"And the other man?" he asked.

I shrugged. "I couldn't see his face. Ask Gerard."

"Did the other man get a good look at you?"

"Like I said, he practically ran me over." I thought back. "But I had a scarf over my face to block the wind. I don't think he would recognize me if he had seen me again."

"Anything else happen that would put you at risk?"

Officer Segerstrom asked the questions as if he already knew the answers. I rolled my eyes. "I did help Melissa Belmont with her kids at church one day. She said she had something to tell me and asked if I'd meet her in Manistique. I agreed. She told me her husband was dealing drugs and beating her." I tossed my head in Puppa's direction. "She thought if I told my grandfather, he could help her."

The officer glanced up from his notepad. "Does anyone else know what Melissa Belmont told you?"

My hands slashed the air. "Absolutely not. It took me awhile, but I finally got around to telling my grandfather."

"So there's nobody else who knows what she told you?"

Obviously the guy was getting at something.

I thought about it. "Uh, I guess I did tell one other person."

144

He looked at me from under his brim. "And who would that be?"

My fingers twitched. "Candice LeJeune. But I'm sure she wouldn't have said anything to anybody."

I glanced at my grandfather. His eyes narrowed into two tiny slits.

"Candice," he said under his breath.

I jumped in to explain. "Like I said, I'm sure she wouldn't have told anybody. She's a really good friend and I just wanted to get her take on the situation."

"And what was her take?" Puppa asked.

I fought against the shame that crept up. I shouldn't have to feel bad for running the scenario past Candice, but I had promised Missy that I wouldn't breathe a word to anyone but my grandfather.

I gulped. "She had a few choice words for women like Missy. She wasn't at all sympathetic."

My grandfather's face twisted with rage. "How dare she?" He paced in a mindless circle. He stopped and looked up. "If you'll excuse me, Patricia, Officer Segerstrom"—he nodded as he said our names—"I think I'll take a little ride and have a talk with Ms. LeJeune."

18

Puppa stalked toward the black truck, jumped behind the wheel, and sped off. I could only watch dumbfounded as the tires spit gravel on his way out.

I looked toward Officer Segerstrom. "That went well. I hope we don't get a report of assault and battery after he's done."

The man squeezed his brows together. "You don't know your grandfather very well, do you?"

My arms flailed with uncertainty. "Well, no. I guess not. We've only seen each other a couple times since I've been back." I gave a humph. "In fact, most of what I know about him comes from Candice."

The officer smiled. "In the future, I think you better check your source." He knelt down by the wreckage. "I'm going to play around in the dirt for a while and then drop off some stuff at the lab. I'll keep you posted if we're able to pin this on anyone."

"Thanks," I said. I headed back to the house, wondering how I was going to entertain Gerard until my grandfather returned. I looked around inside and called for him, but my cousin was nowhere to be found. I glanced out the front windows and saw him standing at the lakeshore.

"Hey, Gerard," I said, out of breath by the time I reached him.

"Hey, cuz." He stared at the rolling waves.

"Gramps up and left you. He went to give Candice a good talking-to."

Gerard shook his head and turned my way. "I hope they can finally work things out. They've been going at it for too many years."

"What's the deal with that, anyway? I got the impression that Candice left her husband for Puppa, but then she changed her mind or something?"

He sat down on a rock and motioned for me to join him. I picked a whitish, smooth-top boulder. The stone was warm from the sun.

"This family is so screwed up, I don't even know where to start," he said. "I guess you probably know that your dad's mom drowned out front of the lake house when he was only three years old."

An ant lion attacked its prey on a patch of sand in front of me. I sympathized with the unsuspecting victim. "I knew she'd died, but I had no idea so tragically," I said.

Gerard played with a stick, dragging it back and forth across the ground. "She liked to fish off the dock out front. One day she fell in. Must have hit her head or something. But nobody was around to save her. Papa B always blamed himself for not being there."

I nodded. I knew that feeling. Guilt and I were on a first-name basis.

"Anyway, Papa B had helped her get out of her marriage to a wife-abusing drunk. He put her up at the lake house. She got a divorce, then she and Papa B got married. Papa B always thought her ex was behind her drowning, but he could never prove anything. After that, he made it a point to help out women who'd gotten themselves into bad situations. He felt he owed it to his wife to always keep a fire burning for the cause."

The waves rolled in with a steady *whoosh*. The high-pitched whine of seagulls rang across the water as the birds vied for lunch just offshore.

"That's really noble of him," I said, filling the lull between us.

Gerard dropped his stick for a blade of beach grass. "Yep. He's a pretty noble guy. Anyway"—the grass went in his mouth and he chewed while he talked—"then Candice comes along. We were just kids, but I remember thinking that she was really something. Always nice, always polite, always smiling. But it turns out her husband was big into drugs, gambling, and abuse, and she was barely holding herself together. Papa B meets her, figures it out, and tries to give her an exit. I guess it took awhile, but she finally went to him for help. He let her stay up at the lake house."

I remembered the dreamlike days with Mom, Puppa, and Jellybean. The memories held a sweet aroma, like a field of wildflowers or a just-opened bar of chocolate.

Gerard shook his head. "Then, big surprise, Papa B falls in love with her. She's still married and refusing to get a divorce because it's against her religion or some-

148

thing. Next thing you know, her husband dies in that house fire. She blames it all on Papa B, of course. Motive, opportunity. You name it, he had it. And she never let him forget that."

"But Candice must have known her husband was running with a bad crowd."

Gerard flicked the grass onto the pebbly sand. "She knew. It's called denial. She's one of those people that figure if you don't look at it, it'll go away."

I slid off my rock and onto the beach. Tiny shells filled the spaces between stones. I picked at them.

No wonder Candice was so appalled with Missy's situation. Candice had once been in the exact same place and hadn't been able to save herself.

I plucked my favorite shells out of the sand and set them on my white rock. One swirled upward like a mouse-sized butter pecan ice-cream cone. "So what happened with Sid? He was your grandfather, wasn't he? How did he end up in the fire with Candice's husband?"

Gerard squinted in the sunshine. The soft crinkles around his eyes made me think of Brad.

"That's where things get complicated," Gerard said. "Here's Sid, the brother of a state trooper, and he's up to his neck in marijuana plants. The locals always figured your grandfather was covering for Sid. Anytime Papa B bought anything new or put up the white fencing or the big barn, people assumed Sid had paid him to keep his mouth shut. But far as I know, Papa B is clean." He ran a hand through short black hair. "The story goes that Paul and Sid ran up some gambling debts and pledged their harvest of Silvan Green to pay the bill." He looked at me to see if I was following. "Silvan Green is what they call marijuana grown around here."

"So I gathered," I said.

He continued. "But the bigwigs in the drug trade were counting on that harvest. Next thing you know, Paul and Sid are undergoing a joint cremation." His voice turned husky at the last words.

"I'm so sorry." The sun glinted on the water. The glaring light caused me to squint. "So my mom had something to do with turning them in?"

He gave a flip of his hand. "Olivia just needs someone to blame. If Beth did call the cops on Paul and Grandpa Sid, she was doing everyone a favor. Port Silvan is a remote community. We don't have a police force out here keeping tabs on the riffraff. It's up to us to care enough about our town to police it ourselves. The drug trade can get pretty messy."

I gave a half snort. "You should know. What were you doing that day on the bluff? Exchanging baseball cards with that guy?"

"That was no guy. Hey, I'm onto something big. But you've got to keep your mouth shut about what you saw. Let me do my job."

"Your job?"

His voice became irate. "Just forget what you saw. Sometimes things aren't what they seem."

"Fine. Whatever. I just don't like the thought of being part of some mafia family. I kind of like you guys. I don't want to have to quit hanging around you."

"We're not mafia, okay? Just drop it."

"Touchy, touchy." We watched the waves roll in. Their

rolling rhythm filled the silence. "So that's the story of Great-Uncle Sid," I said after a while. "What about your dad and mom? What's their story?"

Gerard kept his gaze on the water. "Dad died driving drunk when I was twelve. Mom took off with the milkman."

"Are you serious?" I asked, feeling sorry for him.

"No, actually it was the plumber."

I couldn't help but grin at his hopeless sense of humor. "So who raised you and Joel?"

"Papa B."

I nodded. "I guess that explains why you call him Papa B."

Gerard cracked a smile. "I guess."

I kicked back and put my hands behind my head. I lay prone and closed my eyes. With the sun beating down on me, I could almost feel the cells converting the rays to vitamin D. Gerard and I didn't talk for a while. I might have nodded off if it hadn't been for the cacophony of gulls.

"Gerard." Grandfather's voice sounded like a bare whisper in the wind.

I sat up to look. Gerard craned around next to me. My grandfather came toward us, picking his way through beach grass and rocks.

"We have to go," he said, panting. "Olivia's having another bout."

My cousin stood and stretched.

"So what happened with Candice?" I asked my grandfather.

The way his lips thinned into a long, straight line told me the meeting hadn't gone well.

"Gerard. Let's go," was all he said.

They left me. I faced the water and crossed my ankles in the sand. The breeze blew wisps of hair across my face. The gulls swooped and dove for some tasty morsels that lay just beneath the surface. The view was so peaceful. I wondered how anyone who lived in such beautiful surroundings could be driven to burn down a garden shed, or send a home up in flames. But I already knew the answer. Only hurting, desperate people did those kinds of things. I should know. I'd been there.

I watched the waves a few more minutes, then I went inside to call Brad.

19

I dialed the phone, feeling like an errant schoolgirl about to get yelled at by the principal.

"Hello?" Brad's voice came at the other end of the line.

"It's me. Tish."

"Are you okay? What's going on up there?"

"I'm fine." I sighed and rested my forehead against a kitchen cabinet. "Sorry I didn't call earlier, I've been a little distracted."

"I can imagine."

"You can?" My shoulders relaxed. "Thanks for being so understanding. Officer Segerstrom said you were pretty worried."

"I want to be there for you, but I'm stuck down here. I hate that."

I swallowed a lump in my throat and dragged my emotions away from the abyss of self-pity. I put on a smile. "Well, you're here for me now. Thanks for caring."

I looked out the kitchen window at the smoking debris as I told him the details of the afternoon, leaving

153

out the fireman's assessment that the arson was meant to be a warning.

Brad listened in silence. "Why didn't you tell me you'd witnessed a drug deal and that some dealer's wife had come to you for help?"

My heart skipped a beat. He'd been talking to Officer Segerstrom. "I didn't want you to worry."

"Well, I am worried. I thought we were closer than that. I thought you could confide in me. What else haven't you told me?"

"Nothing. That's it. That's all there is and it's nothing, really."

"A guy tries to run you over with his four-wheeler and that's nothing?"

"Don't try making me feel worse than I already do. We live a long way apart now. There's just some stuff that's not worth bringing up."

"Not worth it, huh? Why do you think that?"

"Listen to you. You're all worked up over this. That's why I don't mention it."

"I might not be so worked up if you would have told me about it back in February."

"You know, I'm doing my best." The decibels rose. "This long-distance relationship stuff—no, this relationship stuff—doesn't come naturally. I've never been very good at it. It's not as if I've had much practice, you know. Look how I botched things up last time around." My chin launched into a perpetual quiver at the memory of my ill-fated romance with David Ramsey.

"Come on, Tish." Brad's voice softened. "Don't cry.

You're doing great. Things aren't going to be like this forever. Hang in there."

"Yeah? Well, when do you think things are going to change? I look ahead and all I see is year after year of you in Rawlings and me in Port Silvan—or wherever—and the only thing between us is a phone line."

"It's just for now. It's just for today. It won't always be like this."

"How can you say that? What's ever going to change? I don't think I can take this much longer. I miss you. I need you. I feel like I'm going to die if I don't see you."

"Tish."

"Yeah?"

"Take a deep breath."

I breathed.

"Now, don't take this the wrong way. But it sounds like you're having a panic attack. It's pretty scary what those guys did to your shed. But don't give in to the fear."

I nodded. "'Kay."

"This is just a suggestion, but I think you need to get some more friends. You need to get out of the house. Get involved in a Bible study. Join an art class. Something."

I nodded, silent.

"Tish? Are you there?"

"Mm-hmm."

"Listen, I'll see you soon enough, the trials are almost over. But in the meantime, call the pastor and ask how you could get involved in the church."

I sniffled.

"Will you do that?" Brad asked.

155

My jaw jiggled back and forth defiantly. "I feel like you're avoiding the issue. I haven't seen you for two months and you want to blame my feelings on a panic attack. Can't you understand that maybe I just miss you?"

"I do understand, there's just not anything either one of us can do about it right now, short of jumping in the car."

"Well?" I said.

"Well, what?" he asked.

"Why don't you jump in the car and come see me?"

"Tish. I'm employed. I don't have that kind of flexibility. Maybe you should be the one jumping in the car."

"I did jump in the car, back in February. I'm not about to make another road trip just when I'm getting settled in."

"If you're not willing to do it, why should I be willing?"

"Well, if you're not willing and I'm not willing, then what are we even doing talking to each other on the phone? We must be the two laziest people on the planet. Too lazy to even care anymore."

"Is that how you feel?"

"Yes, that's how I feel."

"Maybe we should call it off for a while," he said.

"You can't call off something that doesn't even exist."

Brad exhaled a loud breath. "I guess I'll let you go, then."

"You can't let go of something you never had to begin with."

"Tish. I just meant I'm going to hang up now. We'll talk about it another time."

"Yeah. Maybe."

"Goodbye, Tish."

"Goodbye, Brad," I said with finality and stabbed at the disconnect, missing the button.

Panic swelled. I put the phone back to my ear. "Wait . . . Brad . . ."

Dead silence. What had I just done? Surely Brad would understand I was only talking in the heat of the moment. I hadn't really meant those words—had I?

I sucked in one of those shuddering breaths you get after you've been crying awhile and felt calm return. No. I was right and he was wrong. Our relationship was forced, not natural anymore. So, we'd had some good times together. We'd been friends. But times had changed. And that was okay. Like Brad said, that was just the way things were now. It was him down there and me up here. Nobody's fault; just the facts.

Weight lifted off my shoulders.

Everything was going to be alright. I was alone again, and alone was a good place. It felt comfortable. It felt right.

The clock read almost 6:10. The afternoon had gotten away from me and supper had come and gone. I thought of my cousin Joel and his always-delectable dinners. The thing to do was head down to the lake house and check on Olivia and the guys. I could nibble on leftovers while bidding Olivia another farewell.

But I couldn't leave the cottage. If the arsonists saw my car driving off, they'd burn down the house next. I'd already put too much effort into the renovations to let some ragtag druggies burn it down.

I looked in the cupboards and found a box of emergency mac-n-cheese. Ravished, I ate the whole pan.

Over the next couple days, I scavenged the kitchen, determined to eat every last crumb before I abandoned my watch. Sleep was a near impossibility. All night long I heard the thud of feet outside my window, the creak of someone opening the door, the splash of gasoline on the walls. I'd get up and look, but no one was there. I'd toss and turn the rest of the night. By dawn, I'd fall into slumber, sometimes staying in bed until noon.

Sunday morning, I slept in and skipped church. The pyros had known I went to Candice's every Thursday afternoon. Since I attended church regularly, a Sunday morning would be the perfect time to light up my house. I'd be down in Port Silvan sitting in the pew next to the entire volunteer fire department. There would be nothing left to save by the time church let out. I thought of Melissa Belmont and her sweet children and pictured them getting settled into their seats in the back row. With her husband in jail, Missy would be just fine. She didn't need anything from me. Besides, I'd told my grandfather her situation. That was all she'd asked me to do.

My cell phone rang a few nights that week. The caller ID said it was Brad. I finally shut the phone off, not wanting to deal with the pressure of whether or not to answer.

By Wednesday, I'd eaten the last can of food in the pantry: waxed beans. I could barely swallow the bland fare, but I forced it down, starved as I was. By three o'clock, the hunger pangs kicked in again.

I gave in to primordial necessity and started up the Explorer. I thought about heading to Port Silvan, but I figured everyone in town knew my car. One call to a cell phone somewhere, and I wouldn't have a kitchen to cook in. So I drove to Manistique instead, where I was just another face in the crowd. I shopped at full speed, stocking up with extra items this time. I raced home, searching the sky for a telltale pillar of smoke.

But everything was as I left it. I cooked myself a gourmet burger filled with onions, mushrooms, and bleu cheese. I brought it out to the deck and devoured it as the sun set. Hues of pink, purple, and orange colored the western sky. My food seemed flavorless in the presence of such beauty.

Before I went to bed, I called Candice. "Hi. I'm going to have to cancel our tea date for tomorrow."

"Is everything okay? What's going on?"

"Everything's fine. I'm just running behind after the fire and I'd like to do a little catching up. How about I see you next Thursday?"

A long sigh filtered through the earpiece. "I guess so. I can't say I'm not disappointed, though, Tish."

"I'm sorry. Next Thursday. I promise."

I hung up the phone, wishing I could have gone to tea if only to find out what had happened between Candice and my grandfather the day of the fire.

The lack of sleep finally caught up to me. I dozed through the night without my usual hauntings.

The next morning came warm and sunny. The authorities hadn't been sifting through my pile of ashes in about a week. I assumed that meant Officer Segerstrom had gotten all the evidence he'd needed from the scene. Apparently, the law was leaving it to me to clean up the mess.

I stood at the edge of the coals and stared at the remains of my adorable garden shed. The metal prongs of a rake and the blackened edge of a spade poked through the cinders. Just the items I could have used to clear out the debris. My prized ladder lay blackened under the heap.

A slight breeze toyed with the back of my hair. Birds chirped in random song around me. The sun beat down with the energy to draw thin green strands of life from the earth. I sighed. Even the old push mower I'd soon need had been destroyed by the flames.

I jerked my head up at some movement off in the woods. My breathing kicked into high gear as I scanned the forest for the perpetrator. I detected a twitch. Through a maze of branches, the face of a doe came into focus. My doe.

"Here, girl." I made the kissy sounds.

She stared at me, flicking her ears. She gave a wary toss of her tail.

"Come on," I coaxed.

Instead of running off, she turned her head and nibbled at some twigs. We were neighbors now.

I watched her awhile, then dug my gloved hands into the coals. I hauled what charred remains I could past the bushes at the far edge of the yard. I dug out the rake head and duct-taped it to a stick. I used what was left of the shovel to scoop the pile of ashes into a bucket and dump it in the woods.

I dusted the charcoal off my gloves. A few spring downpours and all evidence of the fire would be gone. Everything except the foundation, which now had to present some other use or look like an eyesore upon the sale of my cottage.

I ran a wrist across my forehead. I hated to think about selling. I loved it here in the country. My neighbors were friendly, furry, and far between. Just the way I liked it. But short of winning the lottery, staying put wasn't an option.

I turned at the sound of a car approaching. A blue state police cruiser pulled down the drive and parked next to me. Officer Segerstrom got out.

I nodded at his approach.

"Cleaning up, I see," he commented.

I looked around at the foundation. "I hope you were done here."

"I'm afraid it's going to be tough finding the folks responsible," he said. "But there's always the chance that someone will talk. Then we've got them."

"I appreciate your efforts."

He took his hat off and held it. "The reason I came by is because my buddy Brad's been trying to get in touch with you. Is something wrong with your phone?"

I pursed my lips. "Nothing is wrong with my phone."

He gave a slight nod of his head. "Well, I suggest you answer your calls, then. We don't make it a habit to check on shut-ins. We rely on their friends and neighbors to do that."

I put hands on hips. "Excuse me? Shut-ins?"

He stared at me, silent.

I waved an arm. "I've got plenty of friends and neighbors. Brad's not the only person who cares about me, you know."

He kept looking at me without saying anything.

"Besides, I can't leave," I expounded. "They'll probably burn down my house next."

"Do you keep a weapon on the premises?"

I pointed to the decapitated spade. "Right there."

"Take my advice. If they want to burn the place down, let them. Don't try to be a hero. It's not worth losing your life over." He put on his cap and adjusted it. "Whatever you decide," he said, "I think you owe Brad a call. He's tied up in court—something about a body you dug up in your basement—so he can't come up here himself to check on you."

I'd forgotten about the hearings and trials that would be taking place right around now. Thankfully, the prosecution had more than enough evidence to make the convictions without my testimony.

"Brad says call him. It's urgent." The officer climbed in his vehicle, turned it around, and drove off.

20

I waited until I was good and ready, about ten minutes later, to put in a call to Brad. It was urgent, Officer Seger-strom had said. It better be. Granted, I owed Brad the courtesy of the return phone call. But that was all. We were done. Over. Kaput. This whole past week I'd been in the process of moving on.

"Tish. Thank God you called."

His voice tore a gash in my stitched-up emotions.

"Hi." I barely formed the syllable.

"I need a really big favor," he said without formalities.

This was no time to grant favors. No. No. No. I put a hand to my temple. Just the sound of his voice made me wish I'd never left Rawlings. My earlier resolve crumbled against the power of my desires.

"Sure. What is it?" I heard myself say.

"It's Sam."

"Sam?" My voice perked up. Samantha Walters was Brad's gorgeous, spunky sister. She'd been a good friend to me back in Rawlings. "Is Sam okay?"

"No," he said without hesitation. "Her ex is scheduled to get out of prison this week and I don't want her anywhere near Rawlings when he does." He took a deep breath. "Can she come stay with you for a while?"

"Umm, ahh. . ." I launched into some foreign vowel recitation.

"It's really important. You don't know what this guy is like. They shouldn't even be letting him out."

"Well, umm, how long is a while?" I liked Sam well enough, and I hoped the best for her, but I just couldn't bear to have a daily reminder of my failed relationship with Brad lounging on my sofa. Besides, the last time I'd had a roommate was during my short stint in college. All I remembered was her penchant for soap operas during my study time and a boyfriend who should have been paying rent.

"A couple of weeks, max. Just 'til I can get a handle on him and see if he plans to cause Sam trouble."

I rubbed at my eyes. What I'd give to have Brad care for me even a smidge as much as he cared for his sister. But he'd never gone out of his way for me. I certainly didn't feel compelled to go out of my way for him, even if Sam's safety were on the line. Brad was a cop. He'd find another place to put her. "I don't know, Brad. I've got the brute squad after me as it is. I don't need to be expanding my list of miffed-off men."

There was silence on the other end.

"Maybe you don't remember," he said after a minute, "but I helped you out of a tight spot or two. The least you could do is return the favor."

My ears started clanging. GUILT TRIP, GUILT TRIP, the bells warned.

164

"Don't get me wrong. I love your sister," I said. It wasn't as if I was saying no to Samantha. It was more like I was establishing boundaries in my relationship with Brad. And in a relationship like ours, there was no obligation to return favors. My voice was firm. "It's just that I've just got too much going on in my life right now. I can't afford to get sidetracked."

"Name something."

"What do you mean?"

"I mean, name something you have going on in your life. I bet you can't think of anything."

"I can too."

"Well?"

He made it sound like I sat around and ate bonbons all day. I cleared my throat. "There's the whole upstairs that has to get finished. I just need to focus in on that."

"Sam can help you."

"What? No. I work alone. That's how I do things."

"It's time to change your policy. Sam is a good friend and she needs you. I'm still a good friend, aren't I, Tish?"

I squeezed my eyes. Guilt poured like hot coals over my head. "Of course you are."

"Then do it for me. Come on. It'll be fun."

Didn't he know I'd do anything for him—if only he wanted to be with me? I let out a sigh. "Fine. Whatever. Send her up."

"Thanks, Tish. You won't be sorry."

I gave him directions, then clicked the disconnect button. Tears coursed down my cheeks. I was already sorry.

With no clue as to when Samantha planned on showing up, I went on with life as usual. A week passed, and still no Sam. I figured she'd changed her mind about coming when she heard how unreceptive I'd been to the idea of her moving in. If Sam wanted revenge, she'd gotten it—I'd been swimming in a lake of guilt since that phone call with Brad.

Thursday morning arrived. A touch of disappointment niggled at me when I finally accepted the fact Samantha wasn't going to show. I leaned on the deck rail out front and gazed at the blue-on-blue lake and sky before me. From the direction of the driveway, I heard the sputter and cough of an engine. I jumped off a corner of the porch and raced to the source. Next to my Explorer, a 1970's-something Volkswagen van refused to die. The driver got out and ran to me.

"Tish!"

Sam slung her arms around my neck, almost taking me to the gravel. Strands of her long black hair landed between my lips.

I struggled free of the embrace. "Sam! You made it." I held her at arms' distance. "I didn't think you were coming."

The Volkswagen kept up its wheezing. I nodded toward the red and white vehicle. "What's wrong with that thing?"

Sam shrugged. "Oh, you know. Old cars."

She grabbed my arm and practically hauled me toward the cottage. Behind us, the van gave a final sputter, then was quiet.

"I've got to see this place," she bubbled. "I was ecstatic when Brad said you wanted me up for a visit."

I decided it would be rude to correct her. Brad must have spared her the details of our conversation. "I'm so glad you could make it," I settled on saying.

"The exciting part is, I can stay until the end of August." She squeezed my hand.

I ground to a halt just outside the kitchen door. My arm jerked in its socket as she kept walking.

She stopped and turned around.

"Wait a minute," I said. "Brad told me a couple of weeks. What about the diner?" Surely Sam's namesake Coney Island restaurant back in downstate Rawlings couldn't afford to shut down the whole summer.

"That's the best part." She jumped up and down, looking like a gorgeous pro football cheerleader in her cutoff denim shorts and white blouse tied over a red tank. "My awesome cousin offered to handle everything until she heads back to Michigan State in September." She squealed and flashed me a "sis boom bah" smile.

"Great." Come June, I'd probably be ready to go down and run the Coney myself. I wasn't sure I could take all this "happy, happy, smiley, smiley" 24/7 for the rest of the summer. Besides, the mention of Michigan State University always made me crabby.

Sam flung back the kitchen door and stared at the room with a look of awe on her face.

"Come on," I said. "It's not that great."

"It's perfect! Look at this countertop." She caressed the red-and-gold flecked pre-Formica. "And this floor!" She stooped to take a closer look at the rubbery tan and black tiles.

I supposed I shouldn't expect anything less from a woman who owned a '50s diner and a '70s VW bus.

"Well, where do you want me?" Sam asked, adjusting the overnight bag on her shoulder.

I swallowed. My room upstairs was my cozy haven. I wasn't about to give it up for company. That left the downstairs bedroom, the only one with a bed. But that had been my mother's snug harbor. I wasn't sure I could give it up to Sam either.

I sighed. It was only temporary.

I walked down the hall to the door. "You can sleep in here for now, I guess." I swung it open. The picture window on the far wall framed the lake view to perfection. Even with the tatty mattress showing, the room felt bright and clean.

Sam brushed past me to the window ledge. "It's gorgeous." She turned back to look at the bed. "I brought my own stuff, so you don't have to worry about sheets and towels and all that." She peeked around. "I've even got my own bathroom!"

"Uhh . . ." I followed her in while she flipped open the medicine cabinet and checked out behind the shower curtain. "This is the only bathroom that's working a hundred percent right now, so we'll have to share."

"Goody!" She slung her arms around my neck like some sugar-fed sorority sister.

All that huggy-huggy stuff had been nice once a week on Sundays back in Rawlings. But somehow now, here at the cottage, it felt more like an endurance test.

I gave her a momentary return squeeze, then pulled away. "Okay. Just so we're straight, I get the right side of the sink top and the bottom two shelves of the medicine cabinet. We each do our own laundry and we alternate cleaning up."

She stared at me, with a look of surprise on her face. "Yeah. Sure. Sounds good to me," she said.

The instructions had slipped out without much forethought. Now I wondered by her look if I had said something off-base. "You're okay with that, then?"

"I guess so. It seems kind of formal, but whatever."

I swallowed. My hands twisted. "Did you have something else in mind?" I didn't want to seem too stiff. She was Brad's sister, after all. We were practically family.

Sam shrugged. "Not really. I just figured I'd set my stuff wherever there was room. I don't want to put you out."

I nodded, glad I hadn't offended her in any way. "That's fine. I'll just leave my stuff right where it's at then."

"Okeydoke. So what's for lunch? I'm starved."

"Oh my goodness." I clamped my hand over my mouth. "I'm supposed to be at my friend's house for tea right now. Just help yourself to the fridge."

I raced out the door and headed to Candice's house, glad at least that Sam was there to guard the lodge.

"Love is patient, love is kind," I repeated over and over along the way. I pulled into Candice's drive. Heaven knew I'd need a good dose of patience and kindness to make it through the months ahead with Sam.

21

"There you are," Candice said when I arrived.

In the two weeks since I'd last visited, her porch had become an oasis of flowers. Between each white post hung pots dripping with bright pink impatiens.

"I thought you weren't planting until after Memorial Day," I said in a half-whine as we touched cheeks.

"I listen to the weather report," she said. "If there's even a chance of frost, I bring my babies indoors."

"Well, everything looks beautiful." I gave a pitiful sigh. "With my garden shed burnt to the ground, I'm ready to give up on my landscaping plans."

"Oh, pish, Tish." She waved a hand at me. "You make it sound like it's the end of the world. Plow forward. Don't give those wretched men that kind of power in your life."

We walked into the house together.

"I know you're right," I said. "But I'm feeling kind of vulnerable now. First my garden shed, then what? I can't fathom the kind of people that do that stuff."

"Welcome to Port Silvan. I warned you how things could be around here."

170

"You did. I've just been so good at minding my own business. I can't imagine this even happening to me. It wasn't my fault Drake Belmont got put in jail. But I still took the blame." My whine grew louder with Candice's sympathetic ear.

She walked toward the kitchen. "I wonder who did nark on Drake?" she asked over her shoulder.

I waited for her return before replying. The china clinked as she set it out. She poured the steaming liquid.

I sipped Candice's flavor of the day, some kind of tangy orange and cinnamon combination. "Did anyone really have to nark on Drake, or are the cops finally doing their job?" I asked.

She tilted her head, as if considering. Her long neck added grace to the movement. "The cops generally take a hands-off approach to the area. Port Silvan is too far from civilization to be much of a blip on their screen. Still, when there's a tip on a big dealer, they'll make a move." Her voice took on a cynical tone. "We wouldn't want the rest of humanity contaminated by the filth around here, now would we?"

I stared at her for a moment, amazed at her enigmatic personality. "So which is it, Candice? In one breath you condemn Port Silvan, and in the next, you defend it."

She laughed and rocked backward. "I know. I guess it's a bit of a love/hate relationship. I've had the best times of my life here on the peninsula." She paused and looked down into her tea. "And also my worst."

I nodded, empathetic.

She stirred another scoop of honey into her cup

as if to sweeten the memories. "I had so many plans when I was young. Noble plans. Good plans. But everything went wrong. I married wrong, I left my husband wrong, I never had those kids I wanted." She looked at me, misty eyed. "I even messed up royally with your grandfather. I mean"—she half smiled—"the damage was already done. I should have stayed with him and proved, if only to myself, that I could make a relationship work." She tapped the spoon on the edge of her cup and laid it back on the table. She took a sip of tea. "Instead I held a grudge against him all these years. It's as if I went out of my way to be alone and miserable my whole life."

I stared at the tray of tea and sandwiches on the table in front of me. I knew all about the psychology of self-deprivation. It was infinitely simpler to identify when it glared like a gaping wound in someone else's life. "You can't go back and do it over," I said. "But did you ever think about making another go at it with my grandfather? A fresh run?"

She waved a hand. "No, no. Too many years of hurt between us. Some things are better left the way they are. Why open a can of worms?"

I shrugged. "Maybe the label just says worms but there's really something beautiful inside."

She bit her lip and gave a nod. "Maybe. But I'm not sure at my age I have the strength to find out."

I reached across the space between us and touched her hand, lightly wrinkled but still soft and smooth. "Look at you. You have so much life. I can't believe you've gotten this far with a defeatist attitude."

She grinned. "Maybe not. But still, I'm just a crotchety old lady. I'm too old for love."

"Nobody's too old for love." I put on my choir robe and started preaching to myself. "Especially not the kind God has to offer."

I recognized the defiant set of her chin.

"Just hear me out, Candice."

She leaned back and crossed her arms.

I inhaled a breath of courage. "I still struggle with feeling worthy of love. When my mom died, my grandmother took out her anger on me and my grandfather. He was lucky. He drank himself to death. But I lived to deal with all Gram's bottled-up grief. I finally dumped my own anger onto her when she was dying. I paid a big price, but because of it, I discovered God's love. I realized He never forgets about me even when I forget about Him." I gazed into her eyes with all my strength, hoping my message might make it through the wall she'd erected. "He loves you too, Candice. I know He does."

She took a rasping breath. "God and I don't have much in common anymore."

"You're wrong." I gripped her wrist. "You walked away, not Him. He's still got big plans for you. Good plans. Maybe plans with my grandfather, if you let it happen."

She pushed my hand away. She lined up the spout of the teapot with the honey decanter. She moved a doily to the corner of the tray and set her cup on it, laying her spoon neatly on the saucer. "That's a nice sentiment, Tish," she said. "But there are things you don't know that make what you're suggesting impossible."

173

"Nothing's impossible with God." I showcased my limited knowledge of Scripture.

She glared at me. "Some things are."

Our eyes linked in a stare down. I broke contact first.

"Hey, did I mention I have a friend staying with me now?" I asked. A change of subject seemed the wisest course.

Her eyebrows arched. "A friend? And who might that be?"

"Sam Walters. From back in Rawlings."

"You never told me about Sam." Her voice had a sing-song quality to it, like she was ready to break into a round of "Tish and Sam, sitting in a tree, k-i-s-s-i-n-g . . ."

I laughed. "Sam as in Samantha. She's the sister of Brad Walters. A friend of mine."

"You never told me about Brad," she said in the same silly voice.

"Oh, he's just a friend."

"Just a friend, huh?"

I swallowed the lump that clogged my throat every time I said his name. "Yeah."

Candice became serious. "I'm sorry. I didn't realize." She looked up at the ceiling, then back at me. "Boy, don't we make a pair."

I nodded, fighting back the tears.

"Come on. Let's go for a walk." Candice stood, loaded the tea supplies on the tray, and delivered it to the kitchen. We grabbed a few finger sandwiches and walked out the back door.

The scent of fresh grass, hot from the sun, greeted us.

Winged insects hummed in the breeze as they picked their way from dandelion to dandelion across the green field. We started off down a two-track that cut next to an old barbed-wire fence.

"It's so beautiful here," I remarked as I munched.

Candice took in the view. "You should have seen it back in the good old days. We had horses and cattle and chickens."

I pictured the field bustling with livestock. "You must have loved it."

"I still love it. Maybe more now that I can get up when the whim hits instead of when the cock crows." Candice shook her head, staring at the ground in front of her as we walked. "The animals are what got me through. I could handle anything as long as my horses came running when they saw me."

"How many did you have?"

"It varied year to year. But the standbys were Brigitte—she was my favorite for saddling up—and Clint. He was a big, clumsy gelding, but gentle as anything."

"I've always wanted to ride a horse."

"You sat on them plenty when you were little."

"I barely remember."

"Your grandfather kept horses too," she said. "He still does."

We turned a corner at the end of the field and followed the trail into the woods. The sunlight dimmed beneath the infant leaves. I slapped at a mosquito buzzing in my ear.

"In fact, your mother was quite the horsewoman," Candice said.

I looked at her, thrilled. "Really? Did you ride together?"

"Now and then. Mostly I stayed behind and played with you while Bernard and Beth went riding. I couldn't bear gallivanting around with those two. My stomach couldn't take it."

I smiled. "No wonder I loved you so much, Jellybean."

She laughed with me. "We made great companions, we two." She swatted at a mosquito near her cheek.

"We still do." I smacked a bug on my arm.

"I don't know about you, but I'm getting eaten alive. Let's get out of these woods." Candice itched at a welt on her hand.

"Me first!" I whirled and ran, leaving Candice and the mosquitoes behind.

"Not so fast, young lady." Candice's voice came from only a few steps back.

I broke into the field, back in bite-free sunshine and warmth.

Candice stopped next to me seconds later. She leaned hands on knees, recovering her breath. "Not bad for an old gal, huh?" she said.

"Either you're in great shape, or I'm in lousy shape." I laughed.

"You're in lousy shape."

As we walked back to the farmhouse, I gave her the rundown on Sam.

"So the ex-husband is back on the loose." Candice shook her head.

"Brad seems pretty upset about it. But what are the chances of this guy really doing anything?"

She stopped and looked at me, her expression dead serious. "Count yourself blessed, Tish, that you've never been abused at the hands of someone you love. There's nothing harder than opening your eyes when you want only to keep them closed. There's nothing like finally admitting to yourself that you're 'one of those women'— the kind of woman you always despised for having no backbone, for not having the good sense to leave a situation that's killing you."

"I'm sorry, Candice, I didn't mean to—"

She rolled over my words as if I'd never spoken. "If Sam's ex is anything like mine was, he's going to come after her. It's as if he can't help himself. He's going to make her pay for putting him in prison, because, naturally, all his problems are her fault. And if she doesn't grovel just right and beg his forgiveness, then he's going to hurt her. He'd rather see her dead than free."

I stared in speechless horror. "Is that what happened to you?"

She nodded. "Thank God Paul died in that fire before he could hurt me one last time."

I swallowed. "Then maybe my grandfather did you a big favor and you should thank him too."

She turned and walked ahead. "Let it lie, Tish. It's a place you don't want to go."

I reached for her arm and yanked her to a halt. "I'm sick of people telling me that. I'm sick of everyone trying to protect me from the past. I just want the truth. I want to know what really happened to my mother. How can a woman who was fearless on horseback just give up on life? And I want the truth about my grandfather. Did he

177

have anything to do with my mother's death and your fire or didn't he?" My teeth ground together in exasperation. I jabbed a finger toward her. "I know you're the one who wrote 'Don't ask why' on my mother's picture and left it ripped in half on my pillow. I don't care what you say. I'm going to ask and ask and ask until I get my answers."

Her eyes were giant circles as she listened to me rant.

She pawed at me as if pleading for me to stop. "Tish, I didn't rip your mother's picture. I would never do that." She looked away. "I did write on her photo. But it was in grease pencil, easily wiped off. I wanted to warn you not to be so curious. So you wouldn't get hurt like she did."

"What do you mean, get hurt like she did? My mom killed herself."

Candice shook her head. "Perhaps. But I suspect someone helped her into that quarry."

My knees felt weak. I tried to breathe. "Why do you say that? What makes you think so?"

"There were rumors. Stories, going around at the time of her death. She'd been at the bar but had no alcohol in her system, so the crash couldn't be blamed on drunk driving. But witnesses said she drove straight through the guardrail as if she'd done it on purpose. The police took pictures and asked the usual questions. Then they tagged it a suicide and wrapped up the investigation."

"But you think there's more to it?"

"There's always more to everything."

"Oh, that's right. You think my grandfather had something to do with it."

Her eyes narrowed. "I have no doubt."

"It doesn't make sense. He loved my mother. Why would he do anything to hurt her?"

"She was meeting up with your father."

"My dad?"

"To warn him."

"Warn him about what?"

"There's so much to the story." She took a deep breath and fanned herself. "I'm feeling worn out after our sprint in the field. How about if I give you all the details another day?"

My jaw dropped. How could she even suggest putting the rest of the story on hold? But her face did look pale. Her breath did seem short. I sure didn't want her dropping dead of heart failure before I could get the whole picture.

"Yeah, of course. I'll help you in."

I settled her in the parlor with a glass of water, cleaned up the tea things in the kitchen, then left for my own cottage . . . somewhat reluctant to face my new tenant.

22

On the drive home, I mulled over Candice's denial. She admitted to writing on my mom's photo but swore she hadn't ripped it in half. I believed her, mostly. But that meant someone else had been at the lodge after she'd gussied up my bedroom. The whole idea gave me a crick in the neck.

I pulled down my driveway slow as a turtle with a bum leg, praying I wouldn't find some Woodstock revival on my front lawn. I turned the final corner and breathed a sigh of relief. The only vehicle in the yard was Sam's VW. Blankets, bags, and boxes appeared to have exploded out the back of the van. Sam's long black hair hung across her shoulders as she sifted through her months of supplies.

At my approach, she lifted her head and fluttered her hand. I parked and waded to the epicenter of my most recent disaster.

"Anything I can help with?" I asked.

She picked a box off the ground and stuffed it into my unsuspecting arms. "This can go in the closet for now," she said.

I started toward the house.

"Hurry back. There's more where that came from!"

It may have been my imagination, but it sounded like Sam's voice held a hint of evil satisfaction. I dumped the box in the bedroom closet and went outside for more.

Three hours and at least thirty boxes later, we stood at the entrance to my mother's old bedroom and surveyed our work.

"It's definitely bright," I said. An orange bedspread that looked more like a shag carpet gave the sagging mattress a much-needed boost. Neon blue and green flowers sprinkled the surface. The overall effect was of a garden experiment gone awry. At the bedside, a lava lamp bubbled, fighting with the sunshine-yellow braided rug for the room's focal point.

"Thanks." Sam leaned against the doorframe in apparent satisfaction. "I can't tell you how much I appreciate you letting me stay. You're a great friend." She reached one long arm in my direction and squeezed my shoulder.

"No problem. We're going to have fun." I repeated Brad's words, hoping if I said them enough they might come true.

"I'll look for a job tomorrow." Her voice sounded tired.

"I forgot about that. I guess you'll need one of those." We stood silent, letting our joint circumstances sink in.

I clapped my hands to break the suddenly glum atmosphere. "Let's get some food. I'm starving."

A look through the fridge revealed a stick of butter,

three eggs, and about a quarter cup of expired milk. The cupboards offered a can of corned beef hash and some baked beans.

"We could do scrambled eggs with hash and beans," I offered.

Sam scrunched her nose. "Let's go out. Is there a good restaurant in town?"

I looked at her, realizing I had no clue as to the quality of the local eateries, since I'd never tried any of them. "I have a better idea." Though I was reluctant to leave my house alone for even a short time, a lightbulb flashed across my brain. "We'll drop by my grandfather's house. My cousin Joel is the best cook in the world. You won't believe his stir-fry."

Sam seemed hesitant. "Are they expecting us?"

I gave a shrug. "No. But it's family. They won't mind. Besides, I haven't been down there in a while. I owe them a visit."

We drove down the peninsula in my Explorer. I gave Sam what limited knowledge I had of the homes we passed. She oohed and aahed over groves of lilacs bursting into bloom along the edges of farmers' fields.

"Look at that place. It's gorgeous." She spotted my grandfather's white fences, stark and straight against the vivid green grass. The white trim of the lake house stood out from the brilliant blue of Silvan Bay. I turned down the drive.

"This is it? Your family lives in the coolest houses." She perched like a cocker spaniel on the passenger seat, hands pressed against the dash.

"Thanks." I wondered what Sam would think when

she learned the sordid details of my family history. Cool houses couldn't stamp out generations of poor decisions.

I pulled onto the circle drive. Over by the detached garage, the tan car Joel drove was parked alongside my cousin Gerard's black truck.

"Looks like everyone is here. Hopefully they'll have extra food." I walked up the steps and rang the bell. Sam followed.

Joel opened the door. He looked at me, then shifted his gaze to Sam. His eyes blinked and his head jerked back as if he'd just looked upon a dazzling pile of gold.

"Hi," he said, one arm on the doorframe, blocking our way.

"Hey." I shifted my feet, waiting for him to look back in my direction. I cleared my throat. "We're wondering if it's too late to invite ourselves to supper."

Joel shrugged. I wondered if he'd even heard me.

I spoke again. "This is Sam, my friend from downstate. Sam, this is Joel."

Their hands met in a slow shake. Sam's eyes gleamed on top of her big smile.

I took a step closer to the door. "So anyway, Sam just arrived today and we were working so hard to get her moved in that we didn't have time to cook supper. Would you have enough for two more?"

Without taking his eyes off Samantha, Joel motioned for us to come in. We followed him to the dining table. Steam rose from a platter of roast beef and vegetables in the center. The scent of basil and pepper filled the air. My grandfather grinned from his place at the head of the table as we entered. Next to him, Olivia's hunched frame turned in our direction. I could sense her perusal of my new roommate.

On Puppa's other side, Gerard rose from his chair like a sergeant coming to attention. "To what do we owe the honor?"

"To Joel's great cooking," I said. "Grandma Olivia, you look well tonight." I gave her a peck on the cheek. I moved toward my grandfather and squeezed his arm. "Puppa, this is my good friend Samantha Walters. She's staying with me for the summer. Sam, this is my grandfather Bernard Russo, my great-grandmother Olivia Russo, and my second-cousins Joel and Gerard Russo."

"Nice to meet all of you," Sam said, no doubt charming them with her pleasant smile and personality, not to mention her Daisy Duke body.

"Welcome, Samantha." Puppa gestured toward two empty chairs at the table. "Have a seat, girls. There's plenty for everyone."

I thanked him and took a place next to Gerard. Sam took the slot adjacent to Joel's empty seat. In moments, my cousin the chef set plates in front of us. Scoops of beef, potatoes, and carrots spilled onto them.

I put up my hand. "That's plenty for me."

I ate the hearty fare as if it were my last meal. Sam did the same, even asking for seconds.

"So what brings you to our neck of the woods, Samantha?" my grandfather asked.

I kept my eyes on my potatoes while I listened for her answer.

She giggled and waved a hand. "Just looking for a

change this summer. I've been cooped up in Rawlings my whole life. Thanks to Tish and her awesome hospitality, I finally escaped."

I peeked at Puppa. He set his fork down. The thumb and finger of one hand rubbed together. "Exactly what is it you're escaping from?"

I dove into my carrots, enthralled by the ridges in each slice. Out of the corner of my eye, I saw Sam dab at her lips with her napkin. She took a sip of water. She crossed her arms on the table.

"I own a Coney Island restaurant in the strip mall there," she said. "Used to be my dad's, but I took it over a few years back when he died. I really love it. I guess I'll do anything to avoid burnout."

My grandfather gave a nod of his head. "Let me know if you run into any trouble. Maybe I can help."

"Thank you," Sam said. "In fact, maybe you know of a job opening around here. I wish I could afford to loaf all summer, but Tish probably wouldn't tolerate vagrancy."

I smiled but kept my eyes on the last sliver of beef on my oversized pottery plate.

"I heard the Silvan Bay Grille is looking for a waitress," Gerard piped up.

"That's right up my alley," Sam said. "I'll stop in the morning. Would you mind if I used you folks as references?"

"Dropping the Russo name won't get you very far around here," Gerard said with his half-quirk smile.

"It will if you drop my name." Olivia's voice came deep and strong from her place beside Puppa.

185

He patted her arm. "You're right, Mother. I don't know how you do it, but you've still got this town shaking in its boots."

"Somebody's got to keep the young people in line," Olivia said. She mashed a potato on her plate. She looked at Sam. "You have Nancy call me in the morning. You seem like a nice enough girl. Having a face like yours around, instead of that moose Loreen's, will do business good."

Sam blushed. Joel shifted in his seat. I checked out the etched leaf pattern on my empty plate.

"Very good, Mother," my grandfather said. "I'm sure Samantha will be a fine addition to the Grille."

We cleared our plates and moved to the living area for coffee and tiny squares of Joel's delectable English toffee bars.

Grandma Olivia settled into a straight back chair. "I heard Melissa Belmont is trying to put her house up for sale," she said with a touch of derision.

Puppa gave a nod. "Yes, she contacted Ethyl Merton about listing it. It's better if she leaves the area."

My ears perked up. "Sounds like everything is working out for her, then?" I asked, hoping to assuage my guilt.

"We'll see. It's too early to tell," Grandfather said.

"Nonsense. The girl will be fine," Olivia said. "Don't know why she wants to move at all. Those children were born here. They belong on the peninsula. Drake has plenty of family to help raise them until he gets back on his feet. And her family is just over in Escanaba."

Puppa leaned one elbow on the arm of his recliner. "Mother, Drake's been in and out of trouble most of his life. Melissa's had enough. She and those kids deserve a fresh start."

"You weren't talking that way when that Beth Amble turned up pregnant. Besides, when I was young, people got married and stayed that way. Nowadays if you don't like the way they hang the toilet paper, you get a divorce," Olivia said.

"Toilet paper isn't an issue for Melissa," my grandfather said.

"So Drake gets a little rough once in a while," Olivia said. "Your father had his moments and I never held it against him."

He humphed. "I remember his moments. You were certainly entitled to your choice to stay. And Melissa is entitled to her choice to leave."

Olivia gripped her hands together. "All I'm saying is Drake isn't that bad. I put up with a lot more than Melissa ever did. She doesn't know the meaning of hardship."

"And after what she's already been through, I'm sure she doesn't want to find out." Puppa stood and smacked his palms together. "Take a walk with me, Patricia. I want to show you the new horse."

Joel stood after him. "And I'll show Samantha the barn. We just put in more stalls."

Sam and I jumped up and followed the men out the back door. Gerard in his wisdom stayed to entertain Olivia.

23

Puppa, Joel, Samantha, and I walked past the detached garage. From behind a clump of cedars emerged a red barn with white trim and black roof. A cupola complete with a rooster weathervane topped the structure. The bronzed iron squeaked, lazy in the breeze. Next to the barn, white fencing circled the corral, then led off to green pastures. Evidence of horses greeted us on the warm spring air.

Puppa pointed me toward an enclosure past the barn. Joel and Sam wandered off in their own direction.

"There's that fine filly," he said, looking at a pretty palomino. As we approached, the horse joined us at the fence. She nuzzled my hand.

"She likes you," Puppa said, smiling.

"Her nose is so soft." I leaned my face against hers, drinking in the comforting smell of her warm coat. "How old is she?"

"Ten," Puppa said. "She's a Kentucky Mountain Horse."

"I like her size." Her back came just below my shoulders.

"She's a little over fourteen hands high," he explained.

"What's her name?"

"I call her Goldie, but her papers say Heaven Hill Gold."

"That's a pretty name."

Puppa chuckled. "It's a type of liquor. Goldie comes from a dry county down in Kentucky. The old-timers like to name these smooth-riding gaited horses after the thing they love most but can't have: whiskey."

I laughed. "Grandpa Amble would have related to that."

"She's yours, Patricia."

My smile faltered. I looked at Puppa. "What do you mean?" My hands ran through Goldie's mane, instinctively working out the knots and snarls.

"I got her for you." He patted the horse's neck. "She's the right age and height for a new rider. And her temperament is as heavenly as her name."

My eyes stung as his words sank in. "You got me a horse?"

He nodded. "I used to love riding with your mother. She was a very special lady. I hope we can enjoy the same friendship."

I wrapped my arms around his neck. "Thank you, Puppa."

His hands held me in a tight embrace. "You're welcome."

When he released me, I wiped at my eyes. "I'm so happy to have family around. I was so alone before. I feel like I finally made it home."

"You are home. And I hope you'll never leave us again."

My heart twisted with emotion as I recognized the tragedy of my profession. I had doomed myself to a perpetual fresh start. I could never settle down with family or form roots that lasted through generations. I was destined to move away time and time again from the very people who could bring stability, love, and meaning to my life. I'd left Brad, hadn't I? Was I really going to leave my grandfather, great-grandmother, and cousins too?

I choked on the ball in my throat. "I hope I never leave you again too, Puppa." I'd have to be creative, but I could figure out a way to stay in Port Silvan, and a way to stay in my family's log cabin where Mom and I spent those beautiful summers together with Puppa and Jellybean. Now if I could only get Candice back in the picture, it would be almost as good as the old days.

"Tell me about your friend," Puppa said, done with all the mushy stuff.

We started walking the fence line. I was charmed by the way Goldie stayed alongside us. "Samantha? Hmmm. She's younger than me, beautiful, gutsy, already has Joel by a nose ring . . ."

Puppa laughed. "I noticed all that. I meant tell me about her past. Sounds to me like she's on the run."

"I don't know that she's on the run so much as her brother Brad is just ultra-paranoid. He's a cop, you know."

"What's he paranoid about?"

I flipped a hand in the air. "I don't know. Something about Sam's ex-husband getting out of prison." I downplayed the man's vengeful, destructive, and insane attributes.

He stared at the ground as we walked. "What brought her to Port Silvan?"

"Oh, Brad just figured the ex would never connect the dots and Sam would be safe in the woods up here."

"How do you know these Walters siblings, anyway?"

"Ummm, Brad was my neighbor back in Rawlings. He looked in on me every now and then."

"Uh-huh." My grandfather's voice carried a note of suspicion.

I snapped a look at him. "No, he was not my boyfriend. We were friends. That's it. We walked, we talked, we skied with the church group. Then I moved up here. End of story."

"End of relationship?" Puppa asked.

"Yes."

"But now Sam's up here."

"Yeah. So?"

"I wonder if she's really got an ex to hide from or if big brother just sent her up here to keep an eye on you."

"Brad? No way. He sounded extremely shook up about the ex-husband. He really loves his sister."

"He might have been pretty shook up about your shed getting burnt down too. I'd say timing is very coincidental."

"Well, what's Sam supposed to do if the bad guys come back? Run over them with her Volkswagen bus?"

Puppa grinned. "Samantha looks like she's half Amazon. I bet she can take care of herself." He looked at me. "And watch out for you too, I imagine."

191

"Please. I have been taking care of myself practically my whole life. I do not need a babysitter."

"But having a bodyguard can't hurt any."

"That's ridiculous. I'm supposed to be keeping Sam safe. Not the other way around."

"Having a roommate at the lodge is a good thing. I feel better knowing you've got company. I'm sure your friend Brad feels the same way."

I thought of my new roomie's VW, orange shag comforter, and lava lamp. Those items didn't really affect my life in a negative way. But if she started blaring Elvis, the Beatles, or even the Beach Boys, I'd have to draw the line.

Puppa turned around. I realized we'd walked all the way to the main road. My golden horse pranced a circle on the other side of the fence, then accompanied us back toward the barn, which was barely visible through the thick row of cedars that cut the barnyard in half.

"So, what's going to happen with Melissa Belmont?" I asked him.

"Drake's sending threats from his cell to scare her into staying at the house. His dealer buddies have practically moved in to keep an eye on her and the kids."

"That's awful. I had no idea. What can we do to help her?"

"The tricky part is to get her and the kids out of town without anyone seeing them leave. Then she'll have to go somewhere Drake and Company won't think to look for her."

"Kind of a layman's witness protection program?"

"Pretty much."

"Just like Samantha has going." I cringed at the thought of Sam's ex tracking her down in Port Silvan.

"Unfortunately, yes."

"If her life is in danger, why not get Melissa into the real program?" I asked.

"Too small of potatoes, too much red tape. The feds don't really care about prosecuting a dealer like Drake. All Melissa might do is put an insignificant player behind bars for five to ten years." Grandfather bent down and uprooted a pricker plant. He flung the carcass toward the fence. "Now, if Melissa were willing to testify against bigger potatoes . . . but I can't imagine she'd do that." He kicked dirt to fill in the hole. "If Drake came forward to inform on his network, like identifying the big shot running the drug supply lines in and out of the U.P., then Drake could very well earn himself immunity and a new life."

"What? That's not fair. Melissa and her kids are the ones that deserve a new life. Doesn't anyone care if they get killed?"

"We live in a backwater county where there's only one murder a year, Patricia. Witness protection isn't a high priority. Besides, more often than not, these women go out looking like suicides."

My heart beat in my ears. "What do you mean?"

"The suicide rate is off the charts around here."

"Then my mom . . ." My voice petered into silence.

"May not have been a suicide."

I stared at him. The breeze lifted a piece of his gray hair. His blue eyes were rimmed with red.

"You didn't have anything to do with Mom's death, did you?" I couldn't forget Candice's accusations.

He shook his head. "Not directly. But I'll always wonder."

"I don't understand."

"I should have never let her go that night. It was foolish of me even to mention it." He shook his head and wiped a hand across his forehead, back in another time.

"Tell me what happened. Please. You have to." I grabbed his hands. Up in the cedars, birds chirped. My horse reached her nose over the fence and whinnied. Puppa opened his mouth to speak.

From the direction of the barn, I heard Samantha's voice. "Hey, Tish! Come and see!"

24

I tore my gaze from Puppa to watch Sam jog our way.

"Go on and visit with your friend, Patricia," he said. "We can talk later."

I gritted my teeth. Sam had terrible timing. *Go away*, I felt like telling her.

Sam reached us, bubbling over. "There's a peacock, Tish. And roosters. And a llama."

Goldie nickered again.

Sam turned. "What a gorgeous horse!"

Back away from the fence, Barbie, I seethed in my mind. Sam was driving me nuts and it hadn't even been one day. August couldn't come soon enough.

She gave Heaven Hill Gold a pat on the nose, then turned and grabbed my arm. "Come on. You're going to love it."

My feet slapped the ground in defiance at each step as she dragged me to the barn. Inside, we checked out the new stalls Joel and Puppa had put in. Even in my foul mood, I couldn't help but laugh at the roosters with their bobbleheads, and the peacock, who tried chasing us off with a shake of its plumes.

We found the llama in a high-fenced pen adjoining the back of the barn. Sam and I ran hands through the animal's thick wool.

She smiled at me. "Tish, I've never been to a farm. Thank you for bringing me along tonight."

My heart melted as I put myself in Sam's muddied shoes. She had the happiest disposition of anyone I knew, even though she'd suffered her own share of poor choices.

"I'm really glad you're here," I said. "We're going to have a great summer together."

"We really are." She rubbed the llama's ears. "I couldn't help but wonder what you were talking about tonight regarding that Melissa woman. Is there anything I can do to help her?"

"What a situation. Poor thing. My grandfather's already doing as much as he can."

"Joel caught me up on some of the details. I hate the thought of her living in that house with her husband's buddies hovering over her. Let's sneak her out of there. She can live with us at the lodge."

My hands dropped to my sides. "Absolutely not. We've got enough trouble worrying about your ex-husband. We do not need Melissa's baggage coming after us too."

"Oh. Brad told you about Gill, huh?"

"Well, yeah." I looked at her with an expression that said "duh."

"Then you see why I want to help Melissa. We have so much in common."

"I doubt it. Somehow I can't imagine you staying with Gill as long as Melissa's been with Drake. And she's still reluctant to go."

Sam stiffened, her hands tucked deep in the llama's wool. "I look like I've got it all together, don't I? But you'd be surprised. I was with Gill for almost ten years before I had the courage to break free."

I swallowed. The beautiful woman in front of me with her Grecian features and incredible black hair deserved only the finest man the world had to offer. And she'd picked Gill and stayed? "What's the story behind that?" I asked. "It just doesn't seem to fit who you are."

"It's our hardships that mold us, Tish. I wouldn't dream of trading my past for a kinder, gentler one. The choices I made led me in some weird, roundabout way to the exact place God can use me." She flipped that magnificent hair behind one shoulder. "I know this, if not for what I've gone through with Gill, my music wouldn't carry any meaning. It would be about as deep as 'Row, Row, Row Your Boat.'"

I thought back to the church in downstate Rawlings where Samantha and her band led the worship each Sunday. "You wrote those songs?"

"All except the hymns."

I recalled the many times tears had threatened as I listened to the words of gratitude and praise to the Lord. "Your lyrics are amazing."

"Thanks, but it's all God. I just made a bunch of dumb mistakes. He's the one that took what I'd messed up and turned it to something useful. Something that can help others find their way."

We left the llama with a final scratch behind the ears and latched the gate behind us. The guys had disappeared somewhere. We went back in the house, visited with Gerard and Grandma Olivia for a few minutes, then made the drive back home.

We drove past the cider mill and the turn to Candice's house. I thought about my last visit with her, wondering why I should believe her when she said she hadn't ripped my mother's picture in half.

Would the kind and gentle Joel have ripped the photo? He'd seen Candice's car leave the area that night. Maybe he went in the lodge to see what she'd been up to, saw the picture on my pillow, and in a fit of jealousy, torn it in two. He'd apologized for his behavior, hadn't he? Maybe his remorse had been more for the vicious vandalism than the callous comments.

"So what did you think about my idea to hide Melissa down at the lodge with us?" Sam said, interrupting my train of thought.

"I think I don't need one more wrench in my routine, that's what." It came out a touch snotty.

Sam's shoulders pressed back against the seat. "It seems to me like your whole life revolves around protecting your personal routine. It seems like a really dull, really unfulfilling existence."

My fingers tightened around the steering wheel. "You can just stow the guilt trip. Those don't work on me anymore."

She looked at me, eyebrows raised innocently. "No guilt trip here, honey. Just stating the facts."

"No, the fact is that I am not going to invite chaos into my life. I just climbed out of that pit and I'm not going back there."

"Come on. Haven't you ever helped someone who

needed it, Tish? Haven't you ever felt that awesome feeling that comes over you after you did something nice just because someone asked you to?"

"Yeah. I know that feeling. It bought me three years behind bars. The answer is no."

She crossed her arms and stared straight ahead. "I can't believe you'd pass up the opportunity to do a good deed."

I whipped my head in her direction. "You're my good deed, Samantha. You've only been here ten hours and I'm already sorry." I faced forward just in time to jerk the car back in my own lane and miss the set of oncoming headlights.

We made the rest of the drive in cold silence. As soon as the car stopped, Sam was out of it and running for the house.

I stayed slumped behind the wheel. Didn't Sam realize how much I'd already put on the line for her? I'd been well on my way to making Brad and Rawlings a distant memory. Instead, the life I'd turned down was now dangled before my eyes like a carrot tied to the end of Pinocchio's nose, with the distance between what I'd wanted and what I now had growing greater with each lie I told myself.

Sam had to understand. I didn't want her here. I didn't want to love her or get attached to her. I'd rather be annoyed with her. I'd rather have her go away and leave me in my misery. It wasn't as if Brad and I were ever going to get together anyway. It wasn't as if Sam would ever be my sister-in-law. I didn't need the pain she brought, let alone the agony Missy with her adorable children would pile on.

Oh, what had Brad been thinking? If ever I thought he loved me, I knew better now. He could only be out for revenge.

Friday morning, I lay in bed and listened to the plumbing as Sam got ready for her big job interview at the Silvan Bay Grille. Last night, I hadn't had the courage to apologize for the "you're my good deed" comment. A restless night's sleep hadn't made the task any more appealing this morning. When I heard the VW bus crank—and crank—then drive off, I figured the coast was clear.

Sam had made coffee and left a hairbrush on the counter—a sign that she planned to stay put despite my testy personality. The remains of the pot made a full cup. I took my steaming drink to the great room and leaned against the cool stone of the fireplace. The morning sky was a sharp blue. A few waves already lapped at the shore, promising more wind to come. Tension drained out of me with the relaxing scenery and liquid caffeine. I determined that today, I'd loosen up a little and try to enjoy Sam's company. Goodness knew I wouldn't have it for very long. After August, I'd probably never see her again.

I made the drive to Manistique for supplies. My first stop was the discount grocery. I lassoed a cart from the parking lot and started down the produce aisle. A center bin was piled with a fresh load of grapefruit. I snagged some, along with apples, bananas, and plums. Then I stocked up with veggies, salivating at the thought of stir-fry for supper. I scurried down the rows, loading up with canned goods, pasta, stuffing mix, and mac-n-cheese. Despite the long list of errands ahead of me, I paused at the meat counter and obsessed over the price difference between ground chuck and ground sirloin. I stared at the printed labels, weighing my options, and settled on the lean beef.

From the next aisle came the cries of a distraught infant. My shopping cart had a mind of its own, turning in the opposite direction, away from the ear-splitting noise. I gripped the handlebar and forced the wheels toward the sound. I had no time for detours. The cereal aisle couldn't wait.

I turned the corner. The crying got louder. Halfway up the row, a woman cradled the screaming child and waved a rattle near his face in a move to distract him from a box of sugared rings that held his full attention.

"Melissa Belmont." I left my cart askew and raced toward her.

"Tish. Hi."

She looked close to tears as she glanced around, probably looking for spies.

"Andrew, what's the matter, baby?" I reached for my church buddy and stuck him on my hip. I kissed his head. The scent of baby powder and formula niggled at a dormant female instinct. I looked at the girl clinging to the front end of the cart. "And how are you, Miss Hannah?"

She let go with one hand long enough to give a little wave.

I turned to Missy. "My grandfather says you're having a tough time. How are you holding up?"

Tears started to roll. "Not very good. Bad, in fact."

She wiped at her cheek with the back of one wrist. She put out her arms to take Andrew. "I can't talk to you. That jerk of Drake's will be back any minute. If he sees us together . . ."

I held Andrew closer. "What's going on, Missy? Why are you still there? Why don't you just get out?"

She put a hand over her mouth to hold back the squeaks. When she regained her composure, she rushed to fill in the details, whispering with her back to Hannah. "They took away my car keys. They won't let me use the phone. If they see me with anyone, they threaten to hurt that person. Anything I do, one of them goes with me. The worst thing is, Drake swears if I try to take the kids, he'll kill me." She collapsed into her hand again. "I feel like a prisoner in my own home."

I blinked, incredulous. "You don't just feel like one, you are one. Who's here with you today?" I glanced behind me, pinpointing the convex mirrors in the corners of the store.

"Bill Stigler. They call him Stick. But he just dropped us off out front and said he'd be back in an hour."

I looked at the layers of canned goods, coffee, cereal, and diapers in her cart. "How long ago was that?"

"About twenty minutes."

My brain started churning. "Let's switch carts. I'll go through the checkout, load up the groceries, then pick you guys up around back. There's an exit by the restrooms."

"Are you crazy? Drake's serious. He'll kill me." Her hands wrung together.

Puppa had said sometimes a murder could be made

to look like suicide. All Sam and I had to do was keep our eye on Missy and she'd be safe. They weren't going to do anything crazy as long as there were witnesses.

I switched Andrew to my other hip. "We'll keep you indoors for a while, just 'til they quit searching for you."

Terror crossed Missy's face. "He'll never quit looking for the kids."

"Come on. We haven't had contact since that day at the library. They won't think of looking for you at the lodge."

"That's the first place they'll go. Why do you think they burnt down your shed? The day he was arrested it was all over town that you were the one who turned him in."

Missy was right. They'd probably come nosing around my place. But we'd have several hours before they started the search—they'd scour Manistique first. And we'd hide Missy and the kids in the crawl space 'til danger passed. If all else failed, we'd turn to the pros.

"My grandfather will keep us safe." I laid the confidence on thick.

She swallowed. Then she nodded. "Okay."

"Good girl. We'll get through this just fine." I passed Andrew back to her. "Take my cart and look like you're shopping. I'll meet you out back in ten minutes."

25

I headed straight to the checkout. The lady gave me a strange look when she got to the diapers and wipes, like I had no business being a mother. I played it cool.

"Those are for my nephew," I said, stumbling over my fabrication. "He's coming for a visit."

She nodded and ran the canned goods past the laser. "How old is he?"

"Umm, almost two, I think."

She barely glanced up as she held the cereal boxes to the barcode reader. "Those diapers are for six to twelve months. Are you sure you got the right size?"

"Ahh, yeah. He was premature."

"Okay. If you messed up, you can return them as long as they're not opened."

"Thanks."

She finished the last item and gave me the total.

My face flushed red as I scrambled to count my cash. "Oh my. Diapers cost a lot more than I thought. I'll have to write you a check."

"Sure, no problem."

I scribbled the amount and signed the bottom. I passed it to her. The address box in the upper corner of the check practically blinked neon.

"You're from Port Silvan, huh?" the woman asked.

"Yeah." I didn't elaborate.

"I've got relatives in Port Silvan. Maybe you know some of them—the Belmonts?"

I guzzled some air and ended up coughing. Belmont relatives? "Yeah. I've heard the name."

"Here you go." She passed me my receipt.

"Thanks." I pushed the bagged groceries full speed toward the exit.

"Have a nice day."

I was halfway to the sliding doors as she uttered the words.

My heart pounded in my ears as I started the Explorer. *Abort mission. Abort mission*, the rushing blood screamed. But all I could think about was Missy and her kids, held prisoner by a bunch of thugs. This was America. Nobody should have to live like that.

I pulled around to the delivery door. Missy sprinted out, Andrew and diaper bag in one hand, Hannah holding the other. The Coke deliveryman almost ran them over with his handcart.

"Sorry, sir," I called through my open window. He disappeared inside the building. "Get in the back and lay on the floor." I waved my arm to hurry them along.

They loaded up. At the slam of the door, I was off, heading back to US-2 like a getaway driver.

There was silence until we crossed the Manistique River.

"Mumma? How come we're hiding on the floor?" Hannah's tiny voice asked the question.

In a sudden flashback, the windshield in front of me morphed into the broad dash of my grandmother's old Buick.

"Gram, how come we have to leave at night? Can't we wait until tomorrow?" I had the voice of an eight-year-old.

Crickets chirped all around. Gram pressed me into the middle seat. Grandpa got in on my other side. He smelled of beer and cigarettes. Car doors slammed in the cool May air. The pointer slid to the D and the car moved forward in the blackness.

"There's bad people here, Tish," Grandma said. "Lots and lots of bad people. We're leaving and we're never coming back."

"I want Mom."

Grandma made a loud breath. "She's dead. She killed herself. You're going to have to live with that, just like the rest of us."

"I want Mom." My voice quivered and my face scrunched.

"You can't undo what's been done. Try not to think about it."

I tried not to think about Mom being dead. And the harder I tried, the more the tears ran down my face and my nose leaked.

"Patricia Louise Amble, I can't drive with you making all that noise."

"Go easy on her, Eva," Grandpa said. His words came out all jiggly, like they did when he drank too much beer.

"Don't tell me what to do, you old drunk."

Grandpa turned and looked out the window.

"I want Mom," I said again. No one heard me. I looked over the seat and out the back window. The porch light disappeared behind the trees. It was the last time I saw the summerhouse.

From the back floor of the Explorer, Missy's voice soothed Hannah. "Shh. Everything's alright. We're just playing a game of hide-and-seek. It's our turn to hide. But only for a little while. Then everything will be back to normal."

I cringed at the lie. It would never be back to normal. Ever. Not for them. Not for me.

I kept my eyes open for suspicious vehicles. Heart failure nearly set in when we passed the cop hidden at the downside of a passing lane. I checked the rearview, but he stayed parked on the shoulder.

I turned at the blinking yellow light that marked the route to Port Silvan. About four miles later, I eased down my driveway, wondering how I was going to explain my change of heart to Samantha.

The VW wasn't at the house, so my roommate must have gotten the waitress slot at the Grille—and just when I needed her here to help me figure out what to do with my newly acquired guests. Surely Samantha had had some grand scheme in mind when she'd made the suggestion to hide Missy and the kids here at the lodge.

I pulled as close to the porch as I could get. Missy opened the door and scooted the kids inside. I parked and unpacked groceries. I caught up to Melissa in the living room a few minutes later.

"You guys can take one of the upstairs bedrooms. I don't have furniture in there yet, but I'll work on getting some," I said.

Missy nodded. "We'll need a crib for Andrew. Hannah can sleep in a bed with me."

I slouched in the fuzzy gold armchair and looked at Missy sitting on the green sofa, hunching Andrew against her body. Hannah sat next to them, staring at the floor. Her little arms flopped at her sides. It made a forlorn picture. Three displaced persons. I wondered if I'd done the right thing.

"Thanks, by the way," Missy said. "I don't know how much longer I could take it. And with Drake getting out of jail soon . . ." Her words ceased with a guttural moan.

"How can Drake be getting out soon? He just went in."

She nodded toward Hannah and shook her head.

"Sorry." I realized the topic would have to be put on hold until later. I stood up and clapped once. "You guys get comfortable. I'll get that room cleaned up. As soon as Sam gets back, I'll drop by Goodwill and get those items. And some clothes too."

Missy's eyes grew big. "Wait a minute. Who's Sam?" Her distrust of men was apparent in her tone.

"Sam is really Samantha. She's a good friend of mine from downstate. She's staying with me this summer." I marveled at how natural the whole arrangement sounded when I gave it an upbeat flair. Looking back, I realized what a deadbeat I was, the way I'd been treating Sam.

Melissa visibly relaxed. "Okay. I think I'll put Andrew down for a nap and maybe get a little rest myself."

"No problem. Let me know if you need anything."

I put together my cleaning supplies and headed upstairs. From the loft, I observed, fascinated, that kitchen stools made a comfy crib wall against the sofa. I kept the bumping and shuffling to a minimum while Andrew slept and Missy snoozed in the nearby armchair. Hannah had a picture book to keep her busy while the rest of the Belmonts crashed.

In the north wing, where my guests would be protected from the hot sun to come, I washed the light fixture and dusted the ceiling. Painting would have to come later. I wiped down the window and brushed off the paneling. Then I took the broom and mop and spruced up the floor.

Downstairs, I heard the kitchen door open—then slam shut with purpose.

"Hey, Tish! I'm home!" Samantha called.

Clearly she was still upset over my earlier bad manners. My delayed apology was about to cost the Belmont family a peaceful nap. I dropped my supplies and raced downstairs to warn Sam of the sleeping crew.

Too late. Andrew gave out a bellow that shook the walls. When I got to the bottom of the steps, Samantha stood at the living room arch, staring at the young family.

"Hi." Surprise colored her voice. "Are you Melissa?"

Missy nodded as she comforted the baby.

Sam glanced at me, a touch of confusion on her face. Then she turned back to Missy. "Nice to meet you. I'm Samantha Walters. Sorry I woke up the gang."

Melissa yawned and ran fingers through disheveled blonde hair. "It was time anyway."

I gave a sheepish look in Sam's direction. She returned a smile of forgiveness along with a mystified shake of her head.

Formal apology out of the way, I launched into explanation. "Sam, I heisted Missy and the kids from the grocery store in Manistique. I don't know how long before someone comes looking for them. The crawl space is hard to spot through the bushes at the end of the house, if they need to hide. Now that you're here, I'm going back to town for supplies."

I made the drive back to Manistique. Once on the highway, I called my grandfather and told him the news.

"Patricia. That was not just stupid, that was extremely stupid. Your impulse might end in disaster."

I was quiet as I processed his criticism. I'd been sure he'd support my actions. Wasn't I holding up a torch for the cause too? Trees flew past in a blur. Maybe I'd just been trying to please Samantha with my spontaneous move. Guilt can make you do crazy things. I should have gathered more information before jumping into the flames. "I'm sorry, Puppa. There they were in the supermarket and Sam had just told me her idea for sneaking them to the lodge . . . I don't know. It just seemed like the right thing at the time."

A heavy sigh. "I'll send Joel down to babysit until we figure out where to go from here."

"Thanks, Puppa." I tried to keep my voice steady. "It'll be alright, won't it?"

Prolonged silence. "It'll be alright."

I disconnected, then proceeded to give myself a mental beating for my reckless choices. About three-quarters of the way to town, I passed a vehicle that looked like Missy's minivan. A balding, round-faced man with a goatee sat behind the wheel. I exhaled in relief. He was no Stick. Besides, what were the chances? It would have taken a good dose of intelligence to talk to the checkout girl, interrogate the Coke delivery man, peek around town, and be headed to the cottage already.

I parallel parked in front of the Goodwill store. The clerk helped me speed-shop for my items. Within a half hour, I was headed back to the lodge with a portable crib, a double futon with no frame, blankets, and three bags of clothes stuffed in the back of the SUV. I felt like a Welcome Wagon gone bonkers.

Joel's car was parked in the driveway when I pulled up. I cut the engine. Joel came outside, Samantha close on his heels. Without a word, he opened the hatch and started hauling. Sam took one end of the futon as he hoisted it out.

"Hey, guys," I said. "Thanks for helping." I grabbed the paper bags and brought them in on the wake of the mattress. "I'm not so sure about this whole thing. How about you?"

Their answering silence underlined the gravity of my spur-of-the-moment decision. "Okay, so maybe I screwed up. You don't have to shun me for it."

We dumped the goodies in the upstairs bedroom. I'd expected to see Melissa and the kids, but they were nowhere in sight.

"Boy, am I nervous." I unpacked the clothes and

211

stacked them by size. "On my way to town, I thought I saw that Stick guy headed this way." I laughed and shrugged. "But what are the chances of that?"

Sam smoothed sheets over the bed on the floor. Joel stalked out for another load.

Her eyes followed him.

"He came while you were gone." Her voice was soft, with a touch of fear in it.

"Yeah, I know. I called Puppa and he said he'd have Joel come down to baby-sit."

"Not Joel. That Stick guy. He came fifteen minutes after you left."

My fingers straightened in a panic. "Where's Melissa? Is she okay?"

Sam nodded. She crumpled to the edge of the mattress. "They're in the crawl space. Joel pulled up just before Stick arrived. Joel kept him occupied while I snuck Missy and the kids into the crawl." She leaned her head on her knees. "Maybe we shouldn't have done this, Tish. I'm scared."

My instincts wanted to scream at her that the whole scheme was her idea to begin with. Instead, I reached an arm across her back. "We're strong. We'll get through this. Maybe it wasn't the smartest thing either of us has ever done, but we have good intentions. Hopefully, God will honor that."

Samantha blinked her eyes closed. "'The Lord protects the simplehearted; when I was in great need, he saved me.'" She whispered the words like a well-worn prayer. At my look, she elaborated. "It's from the book of Psalms. Got me through my divorce."

"Well, there you have it." I stood up. "Now, come on. Let's cook dinner and have a good meal. That'll make everyone feel better."

Having an audience certainly brought out the actress in me. Inside, I was scared to death.

26

Joel and Samantha took over in the kitchen while I retrieved Missy and the kids from the crawl space.

"I'm so sorry about this," I said, offering my hand.

Melissa grabbed on and climbed out with the baby. Hannah came next, her little fingers clenching mine. As I hoisted her into daylight, I noticed she couldn't have weighed more than forty pounds.

"You're a lifesaver, Tish," Missy said. "I should have left Drake a long time ago. But I didn't know how."

"It's never too late to do the right thing." I was a little weirded out by all the optimistic mumbo jumbo coming from my lips lately.

We entered the kitchen. The smell of chili sauce and hot dogs sent my taste buds soaring. "Are we seriously having Sam's Coneys tonight?" My stomach gurgled in anticipation. Samantha was held in high regard throughout the Detroit Metro area for the amazing Coney dogs served in her hole-in-the-wall restaurant.

Joel nodded. "I think I've met my match. Samantha threw supper together in all of five minutes. And boy, does it smell good."

"You aren't going to believe just how good," I said, rubbing my tummy. "I don't even eat hot dogs, but I'll eat a Sam's Coney and maybe even ask for seconds."

"Enough, already." Sam banged the spoon on the edge of the pot. "Let's eat."

Joel attacked his hot dog with vigor. On the next bite, his hot dog attacked him, earning squeals of laughter from Hannah and Andrew. Samantha got in on the fun, and I watched, enchanted, the new love kindling before my eyes.

I looked away. Where had my love gone? I'd left my one best hope in Rawlings, a love gasping for life and nearly dead from lack of proper care and feeding. I forced down my Coney, close to tears from the memory of Brad sitting next to me on a red stool at Sam's Diner. That first Coney had melted in my mouth, the delicious foretaste of a relationship comprised of down-to-earth goodness topped off with the zest of hot chili.

And I'd run from it. Too much goodness. Too much zest. I couldn't face the possibility that someone might actually love me. So here I was. Alone, comforted by the knowledge that nobody could get to my heart. No one could hurt me.

Big whoop. Where was the thrill in that? Where was the adventure, the daring, the attitude that I deserved the best life had to offer and I was going after it?

I swallowed hard and tamped down the rebel cry. There was nothing wrong with guarding my heart. It wasn't something to whip out and let others stomp all over. It was delicate, fragile, kind of feeble even. As great a guy as Brad was, it seemed like everything he said, everything he did brought acute emotional agony to my underdeveloped heart. I wasn't ready for a relationship. That was all there was to it.

"Excuse me," I mumbled and left the group to their joyous supper. Even Missy was nearly on the floor with laughter as Joel and Sam souped up their comedy routine.

I slunk to my room and set my cell phone on the bedside table. *Just dial the phone, Tish,* I chided myself. It's never too late to make a fresh start.

Picking up the cell, I passed it back and forth from hand to hand. It barely weighed anything. Yet it had the power to mend disconnected lives. I hit a button at random. The unit beeped and lit up. It would be simple to press Menu and then press Brad's name. The phone would ring, he would answer, we'd talk and laugh like two adults who admired and respected one another, then we'd hang up and go on with our lives. Five hundred miles apart.

I put the phone down. It was no use. There was no future for the two of us. He lived there. I lived here. He was a cop. I was a convict. Where could the two paths intersect for the happily-ever-after I craved?

More laughter from the kitchen. It seemed foolish to sit up here and pout over something I couldn't do anything to change. I pasted on a smile and went back downstairs.

I did my best to participate in the revelry. A little while later, Melissa went up to put the kids to bed. The rest of us cleaned the kitchen.

"What happened with Stick today, Joel?" I asked as I dried dishes.

216

"He figured Melissa came here. Maybe I convinced him she didn't, but I doubt it. Gerard's going to take the night shift. I'll take the day shift. It's hard to say what's going to happen."

"Feels like the Alamo around here," Sam said and flicked some dish bubbles at Joel.

"Hey." He laughed and sent them back in her direction. "Things will be fine. These guys aren't going to do anything too daring. They're a bunch of pussycats as long as Drake's in jail. But once he's out . . ." Joel tapered off as Melissa entered the room.

"He's going to kill me," Missy said, finishing Joel's thought.

"We're not going to let that happen." Samantha put her arms around Melissa.

"That's right." I circled them both in a hug. "All for one and one for all."

About nine p.m., the night shift arrived. We said good night to Joel and welcomed the gruffer Gerard. As Melissa and Sam shuffled off to bed, he lit a fire and pulled the armchair up to the fireplace. I leaned near the staircase, watching him as he stared into the flames, losing himself in some far-off memories.

"Well, good night," I said, hesitant to break his trail of thought.

"Good night, cuz."

"So, you're not really worried anyone's going to hurt us, are you?" I edged closer to the warmth.

"Maybe."

"Maybe, what?"

"Maybe someone will try to hurt you, but I'm not going to worry about it."

"Great. Thanks. I'll sleep better now."

"You asked me a question. Don't expect me to lie to you just so you can sleep better," he said.

"Of course not. Just so long as you don't fall asleep," I replied.

"Good night, Tish."

"Night." I padded upstairs and hopped in my snuggly twin bed. I marveled at the incongruity of having a drug dealer for a bodyguard. A good long time passed before I fell asleep.

Morning came and I felt like a flu pandemic survivor. The events of the past days had settled into my very bones.

I lay in bed listening to thumps and bumps in my normally silent home. A little voice drifted up the staircase. I flung back the covers, antsy to see Hannah's smiling face and cuddle Andrew's pudgy body. I stuck my feet into fuzzy slippers and headed downstairs. Coffee hit my nose the instant I opened my bedroom door. I heard laughter. Smelled bacon. Felt the love that only being part of a family could bring. My smile grew broader as I approached the kitchen. Maybe it wasn't so bad having a houseful of guests. I kind of liked the feel of happy chemicals floating around in my brain.

"Morning!" Samantha's hundred-watt smile lit the room.

The stove clock read 7:30. "You guys are getting an early start," I said.

Melissa fed a spoonful of something white and lumpy to Andrew. "The kids are always up by six." The bags under her eyes seemed to darken as she said it.

"And I've got my first official full day of work today." Samantha slipped on a button-up tunic with "Silvan Bay Grille" embroidered beneath a flopping perch.

"How's that working out for you?" Gerard asked from a stool, sipping on coffee and blinking hard.

"I love it. I don't have to worry if I ordered enough food, if the wait staff is feuding, or if we served enough Coneys to pay the bills. At the Grille, I just help customers feel like I've got nothing better to do than make their experience extraordinary." She gave a crooked smile. "Which is pretty much the truth. Bye, all!" With a wave and a fling of the kitchen door, she was gone.

Sam's absence left a gash in the continuum. Without her, we all drifted our separate ways, Missy and the kids to their second-floor haven, me to work on getting one more bathroom up and running. At some point, I heard a car arrive and Gerard's diesel depart during the changing of the guard.

Midafternoon, I hit a remodeling "wall" and had to quit my efforts for the day or end up dumping water or breaking a lightbulb on account of brain fatigue.

With the sun shining and temps in the upper sixties, I decided it was the perfect day for a pony ride. The thought of my new horse brought a gush of excitement.

My grandfather waved to me from the front porch as I pulled in the circle drive. He and Olivia sat in a double swing together, taking life at a leisurely pace.

219

"Hi, Grandma Olivia. Hi, Puppa." I walked up and leaned against the rail.

"Off work so early?" Olivia asked in her quavering voice.

"I finished cleaning and I thought I'd take a break." I leaned close to her and gave her cheek a kiss.

"Oh? So you're a housecleaner?" she asked.

"She doesn't have a job, Mother," Puppa explained. "She's fixing up the old lodge."

"Doesn't have a job?" Olivia sounded indignant. "Don't seem right to me."

Her criticism wiggled its way through my armor. "Well, technically, that is my job. I fix houses and sell them for a profit."

"Sell the lodge?" Olivia turned and gaped at my grandfather. "Did you know that when you let her buy the place?"

"Calm down, Mother. No one has used the lodge in years. I figured Patricia was the best one to get a hold of the place. At least she's family."

Olivia cocked her loaded finger my way. "That was my father's lodge, young lady. That stays with blood. I didn't hand Belmont property over to the Russos just to see it get sold off before I'm even dead."

"You're a Belmont?" I couldn't believe in some roundabout way I was related to that jerk Drake.

Puppa squeezed his mother's shoulders gently. "The Belmonts and Russos have always been big names on the peninsula." He met my eyes. "When Olivia Belmont married Philippe Russo, two families that had been divided by hatred were now united in marriage."

220

"Yes, I only wish someone would have told Philippe the feud had ended." Olivia's eyes teared up even as she smiled.

My grandfather held her closer.

She struggled free. "Don't change the subject. That lodge belongs to my father. You are not to sell it, young lady."

"Mother, your father built a shack that stood where the kitchen stands now. Dad built the lodge as it is today." Puppa kept his voice slow and steady.

"All the more reason for it to stay with the Russos. And if that girl"—she jabbed her finger at me—"isn't going to have children, then it should go to Joel or Gerard."

"That girl is my direct descendant and has more right to the lodge than anyone else, with or without children."

Olivia's jaw set. "The worst day of my life was the day your son brought that Beth girl around. If it hadn't been for her, Sid would still be here. And so would Jake."

"That's too dramatic, Mother." Puppa helped her to her feet and began the walk inside. I followed behind.

"Besides," he said, helping her into the living room glider, "you liked Elizabeth from the moment you met her."

"Maybe so. But I changed my mind since."

"I'm taking Patricia outside for a while. I'll check back on you in a bit." He kissed the top of her head.

We scooted out the side door.

"My goodness, you're patient," I said laughing as we veered toward the barn.

"It took years to hone my ability to stay out of her

221

drama. Poor Mother feeds on gossip and criticism. I don't get mad at her for it anymore because I realize she doesn't know any different. And I can't make her change. Only she can do that."

I hopped on the bandwagon. "My grandma Amble was the same way. It was as if she had to hate everything. Nothing was good enough for her. I'm afraid I took it personally. I think I'm still getting over the way she tore everything, including me, to shreds."

He nodded. "It's a pretty widespread phenomenon, actually. It's a family condition—or should I say a human condition. If you don't get treatment, you stay sick."

"Are you joking?" I stumbled in a rut on the lawn.

"Nope. I couldn't be more serious. I'll be in treatment for the rest of my life."

I couldn't catch what he was getting at.

"How do you get treated for a human condition? It's not like there's a cure for that or anything. I mean, we're human. Period."

"Technically you're right. But there's a loophole. Christians call it salvation. 'For God so loved the world,' and all that." His voice dropped lower, as if he was shy to speak of his faith.

Grass swished against my shoes as we cut past the garage. "Yeah," I said. "Thank God for a loophole." Goodness knew, people like me needed a Get to Heaven Free card in their wallets. I frowned as I kicked the fluff off dandelions with my feet. "Except I have a hard time believing that I only have to believe. It seems like I should have to earn my salvation."

"I used to feel the same way. Because of my upbring-

222

ing, it took a twelve-step program to get the smoke out of my eyes."

I tensed. Twelve-step program? Didn't that have something to do with drug addiction? I kept quiet, like I hadn't really heard him.

"It saved my life, Patricia. It could change yours too."

So he thought I needed "treatment." I cleared my throat as we reached the barnyard, trying not to be offended. "I'm doing really good right now. Things are under control. God and me have it all covered."

He nodded. "Let me know if you ever want to know more."

"Sure. Absolutely." I bolted through the white fence and raced toward my horse. "There's my Goldie Locks," I said, rubbing on her face. Behind me, I could feel my grandfather's stare. I brushed it off. There was nothing wrong with my way of seeing things. I didn't need twelve steps. Life was great just the way it was.

But somewhere at the back of my mind, a little voice whispered, *Liar*.

27

Through a fog of sleep, I heard Sam calling my name.

I jerked awake. "What's wrong? What happened? Who's here?"

"Come on. Time for church." Sam yanked the covers off, exposing my boxer jammies and very white legs.

I tried to sit up. I crashed back onto my pillow. "I can't go today." Every muscle in my body screamed in protest.

"Get up. You're going." Sam grabbed my ankles and swung them off the edge of the bed.

I yelled my pain. "Knock it off! I'm too sore." Yesterday, after our talk, my grandfather had saddled up Goldie. In my excitement, I'd ridden her in the round pen for hours, carefully listening to Puppa's instructions and attempting to execute them. Now, I was paying for my enthusiasm.

"It'll hurt worse tomorrow if you don't move around today."

The woman had no mercy. She sat me up and walked me down the steps, past a snoozing bodyguard, and to the bathroom where she started the shower.

"Okay, okay. I think I can take it from here."

She shut the door behind her. I moaned as I struggled out of my nightclothes. I had no idea so many muscles were involved with riding a horse. I stayed under the spray extra long, letting the hot water relax my tendons. I toweled off and went for my toothbrush. Gone. Not like I could have found it among the jars and bottles Sam had left all over the countertop. I opened the medicine cabinet. Evidence of Sam consumed every shelf. I opened the drawer. Sam. Everywhere.

"Sam!"

How could this have happened? She'd agreed not to move my stuff.

She poked her head into the misty bathroom. "Yeah?"

"My toothbrush. Where is it?"

"Oh. I put all your stuff in that basket under the sink."

"What do you mean? We talked about this and you agreed to leave my things alone."

"I said I didn't want to put you out. But by the time I got everything unpacked, there just wasn't room for your things on the countertop and I didn't want them to get mixed up with mine. So I stuck them underneath."

My face must have flashed fifty shades of red. I opened and closed my mouth so many times I must have looked like a silent Tourette's sufferer. My chest felt like a hundred-pound weight got dropped on it. Gradually, the pressure decreased. I spoke.

"Okay. Whatever, I guess."

"Great." Sam gave a fling of her hair and disappeared.

I opened the lower cupboard. The door smashed against the wall.

"You okay in there?" Sam called.

"Yep." I yanked out my basket of essentials and slammed the cupboard shut.

"You all right, Tish?"

"Hunky-dory." I brushed up and put on a dab of makeup. Finished, I stomped back to my room.

A few minutes later, I was dressed and downstairs.

"Ready?" Sam asked, looking like a knockout in her tall leather boots, short denim skirt, and white ruffled blouse. Sheesh. All I had on were tennies and jeans.

"Stand right there," Sam said and disappeared into her room.

I crossed my arms and tapped my foot. She emerged carrying a fluffy white scarf.

"Put this on. It'll look great with that T-shirt." She wrapped it once around my neck. "Perfect."

I walked to the bathroom and looked in the mirror. "Sam, this is so not me."

"Come on. You need something that screams, 'Here I am!'"

I stared at her. So. Brad was through with me. He was just using our friendship to help his sister. And in return, she was going to help me find a new boyfriend? Thanks, but no thanks. I didn't need Brad. I didn't need any man.

I pulled the scarf off. "Enough. Let's get to church."

"I'm driving," Sam said, heading out the door.

"Wait a minute. I'll drive." I had to run to keep up with her.

"No. I want to drive. I love the highway up here. There's no traffic. Besides, my vehicle gets better gas mileage."

I bit my tongue and got in the front seat of the bus. The thing lurched into drive, nearly hitting the back end of Joel's parked car. Then off we went, feeling every pothole in the road as if the tires were made of wood.

We made it to church, vertebrae intact. Once in the pew, I phased in and out of the service, too distracted by grumping ligaments to hear more than the main idea, something about loving your neighbor. If it had been about loving your roommate, I would have zoned out entirely.

Afterward, Sam flat out refused to leave without schmoozing the crowd. It seemed she had the whole coffee klatch sidling up to her, hoping for attention from those baby browns.

I stood to one side, smiling politely, wondering how I grew up to be wallflower stock, coming from a beauty like my mother.

I thought back to my conversation with my grandfather last night. We'd put Goldie back in the pasture. Above the white fences, stars popped out against the blue-black sky. The slow croak of a frog came from the direction of the lake.

"Let's take a walk, Patricia," Puppa had said.

We crossed the lawn and took the shore.

"I want to tell you about your mother." Rocks clicked under our feet. "She came into our lives like a beam of light shining through a wall of death. Jacob had lost his mom so young. I'd done my best, but it was tough going. Raising him required skills I didn't have." He rubbed at his temple. "By the time Jake was a teenager, he was out of control. He met your mom at a community-college dorm party. She was a student, he was tagging along with friends. I'm not sure what she saw in him, but there's no doubt she was in love."

I tried imagining my parents slow-dancing in a crush of college-aged kids.

Puppa continued. "She did everything for him. Even pretended she'd been driving when he crashed into a tree. She took a ticket for careless driving that night. But Jake had been drunker than a skunk." He shook his head. "They were both lucky to walk out of it alive."

My grandfather stopped and stared at the bay. The moon's reflection swam on the water. "Jake was a better person when your mother was around. But he couldn't stop the drugs. He grew marijuana right here on my land. Every summer I'd take out the gas torch and destroy any I found. I was a cop, for heaven's sake. What was he thinking?"

He turned and trekked back toward the house. I stayed beside him, careful of my footing in the near-darkness.

He finally spoke. "Then news got around that she was pregnant. I told him to marry her, but Jake had been in trouble with his ring boss. Got the headlights on his new truck smashed out. They'd even threatened Beth. She'd had enough. She was going to run on account of the baby. But I convinced her to stay. Bribed is more like it. But I didn't care. You came along and soon Candice was in my life. It was heaven on earth. But Jake couldn't keep clean. I cut a deal with his associates, my own brother one of them, to get Jake out of the loop. It cost me my job when the captain found out."

We walked silent before he started up again.

"Jake was out of the ring, but the higher-ups didn't like him running loose. If he ever decided to talk, more than one neck would hang. Next thing you know—"

"Tish. Hello? Are you going to stand there daydreaming or are you going to get in on our jam session?" Samantha's voice pierced the cloud around my brain.

"Jam session? I'm not hungry."

Sam laughed like I'd just told the funniest joke she'd ever heard. "You crack me up. Come on. We're meeting at the altar."

She dragged me down the aisle like a reluctant bride.

I looked around at the group huddled on the riser. A couple of guitars, a stand-up bass, a piano player, some fiddles . . . I looked down at my hands. And a pair of maracas.

I shook my rattles to the beat, hoping if I put on a good enough show they'd let me go home.

They were singing some song I'd never heard of. In my mind, I snuck back down to the beach with my grandfather.

We cut across the lawn toward the house. A few windows glowed with lights. What had Puppa been saying? Oh, yeah.

"Jake was out of the ring," Puppa explained, "but the higher-ups didn't like him running loose. If he ever decided to talk, more than one neck would hang. Next thing you know, my brother Sid and Candice's husband Paul

229

are stinking up the sky in that big fire. They'd been the ones covering for Jake all those years. When she heard about their deaths, Beth panicked that the goon squad would be after Jake next. He'd been keeping a low profile. But they'd been keeping an eye on Beth, figuring sooner or later, she'd lead them to Jacob. I was the one stupid enough to tell her where he was."

"Gosh, that was fun." Samantha's voice broke into the dead-of-night drama playing out in my head.

The maracas left my hands and I stumbled clueless after Sam. We got back in the VW and were at the cider mill before I even realized we'd left the church.

"Yeah. That was a good time," I said.

"Tish, are you okay? I said how fun it was back at the church, and I feel like you're just now responding."

I looked at her. Her brow was scrunched with concern.

"Wow. I'm sorry. My brain is definitely somewhere else."

"I can tell. You've been a zombie all morning. Anything you want to talk about?"

I shook my head. "Nah. I've just got a lot of thinking to do."

"The offer's always open," she said.

Back at the lodge, Joel had fixed lunch. We took turkey sandwiches and lemonade out to the lakeshore. When we finished eating, Hannah splashed around in the cool water of Valentine's Bay. Next to her, Melissa dipped Andrew's toes under the surface, earning screams of laughter.

Watching them, my smile broadened. The frolicking

children and happy adults were just what I had in mind when I bought this place.

I only wished I didn't have to sell it, even more so after Olivia's guilt trip about the property belonging to her father, my great-great-grandpa, and a Belmont, no less.

There would only be a drop of money left over after I fixed this place up, especially after the new heating system consumed its share. But if I got a job at the Grille with Samantha, I should be able to cover the taxes, mortgage, and bills. I'd have to shop at Goodwill for the rest of my life, but who cared? I'd be close to what was left of my family. And besides, Sam seemed to love her job. I was sure I would too.

As I made my plans, a nervous spasm shot across my chest. But inside my heart, I felt at peace.

28

Wednesday morning around ten, I headed down to Port Silvan. I figured I might as well get my job thing going. I could always keep working on renovations in my free time. I parked in front of the Silvan Bay Grille. Log siding disguised the building's 1960's cement block origins. A covered porch, like a Cracker Barrel wannabe, framed the entry. I walked in, nervous. I hadn't held a job since the Foodliner in Walled Lake, unless I counted three years of forced labor in prison.

It took a minute for my eyes to adjust. A bar stretched the length of one wall. Opposite me, a bank of windows overlooked Silvan Bay, glistening white in the morning sun. Tables for four scattered the center of the room with booths tucked under the windows. Several patrons occupied the dining room. From the swinging doors on my left came clanging dishes and voices. I stood at the entry, unsure of my course. The Nancy person I should talk to was probably in the kitchen. My hands sweated. I turned toward the double doors and paused, rehearsing my lines. Just as I was about to push them open,

Samantha came bustling through, a tray of food balanced gracefully on one hand.

"Tish!" she gushed. "How cool to see you! Give me a minute and I'll get you a seat by the window."

I waited, slightly annoyed, for Sam to come back my way. I shouldn't have to explain my reason for being here. It was none of Sam's business.

A moment later, a woman in a green Silvan Bay Grille apron stepped out of the kitchen, wiping her hands on a white cloth.

"Hi. Is someone helping you?" she asked.

"Well, Samantha—"

"Oh, Sam will take good care of you. She's the best waitress I've had in years." The woman pivoted and stepped behind the bar where she disappeared from sight, the tinkling of glassware the only indication of her locale.

"Uh, are you Nancy?" I stretched my body across the top of the bar to see the woman's crouched form.

"That's me." She looked up and smiled, then kept on with her task.

"I'm Patricia Amble and—"

Her head shot up in my direction. "So you're Patricia, huh? Olivia told me all about you." From the tone of her voice, she didn't sound impressed. Now standing, she plopped her cloth on the bar and rooted her hands on her hips.

I stammered for a minute, thrown off by the attitude. "I'm new to the area and I'm looking for work. Do you have anything here at the Grille?"

Her taut lips arced in a frown. "Olivia said you're not much for working."

I shook my head, dumbfounded. "That's a misunderstanding. I'm a very hard worker."

She stared at me, as if debating. "This summer I'll need an extra hand. If you want, you can train with Samantha. Then come June I might be able to put you on the schedule."

Sam approached from the dining room. "Sorry that took so long. I've got a spot all cleared for you." She smiled and squeezed my arm.

Nancy picked up her cloth. "Looks like Patricia is going to help us out here at the Grille, Sam. Why don't you show her the ropes so she'll have her head on straight when the summer crowds pull in?"

I gave Samantha a big smile, expecting to see one in return. Instead I got crossed arms and pursed lips. Nancy took off into the kitchen. Sam grabbed my arm and led me to the booth by the window. The surface was still wet from her dishcloth.

"What's going on?" Her voice was low and raspy as she slid opposite me into the booth. "I thought you were too busy with renovations to take a job?"

"Well, I've been thinking and I'd like to stay in the area. My family's here and the lodge is part of my legacy. I decided I don't want to sell it. I'm going to take a job and fix up the house as I go. Like normal people."

She tapped her fingers on the Formica tabletop. "Tish, I understand where you're coming from, but what about, you know, the rest of the people in your life?"

My lip rose in confusion. "Like who?"

She leaned close. "Like my brother. Remember him?" Her cheeks took on a heated color.

234

I looked at her like she was out of her mind. "Brad? He's not exactly in my life."

She set her jaw. "You took care of that, didn't you? I thought there was more to you, Tish. But the longer I'm here, the more I realize you're just a shallow, selfish human being who broke a guy's heart and never gave it another thought."

I sat dazed at her words. "Brad and me. We were just friends. Right?"

"He is so in love with you, and all he is to you is a passing friendship?"

The men at the center table turned in our direction. I lowered my voice to a harsh whisper. "Brad can't be in love with me. You know, not *love* love. He's got his life together and my life is such a"—I threw my hands up searching for the right term—"disaster. Guys like Brad don't settle for girls like me. They go for the ones that have things like self-esteem, confidence, a good upbringing, a real career. You know, normal."

"All I know is"—she smashed a finger on the table for emphasis—"Brad hasn't been the same since you up and left him without so much as a goodbye."

"That's not true. I said goodbye."

"Brad is not the kind of guy who gives his heart to just anybody. He's kept it on reserve for the right woman, the perfect one for him. That was you, Tish. He gave you his heart and you flattened it the day you drove off in that gas guzzler of yours."

I crossed my arms in self-defense. "Hey, he's got a gas guzzler too."

"I'm not saying he's perfect. Just that you were per-

235

fect for him. And if you're going to stay up here in that log tower of yours, how are you two ever going to get together? His life is in Rawlings. Can't you just fix up your lodge, sell it, and go back downstate?" She bobbled her head, her big eyes glued to mine.

I wasn't about to succumb to faulty logic. "In case you haven't noticed, I have a life too. And it's here in Port Silvan. If Brad wanted to be with me so bad, he'd find a job up north. Why should I be the one to compromise?"

She tapped her fingernails like she had all the answers. "Maybe because he's the one with the steady income?"

"Come June, I'll have a steady income of my own."

"Not enough to support both of you."

I humphed. "Who's supporting who? I've worked my entire life. I don't expect to kick back and sponge off a man. And I wouldn't appreciate it if a man tried sponging off me."

"I'm just saying, look down the road. If there are kids, Brad can afford to support a family. I don't think you're in the same position."

I leaned back against the vinyl cushion, overwhelmed with Sam's fortune-telling abilities. "You're skipping pretty far ahead. Last time we talked, Brad and I couldn't even figure out who should jump in the car for a visit. Besides, Brad only *thinks* I'm perfect for him. But just wait 'til he really meets Miss Right. He'll be relieved we never officially got together."

Sam crossed her arms. "I can't believe you. You're so—"

"Excuse me, miss. Can I get a warm-up on the coffee,

236

please?" one of the men at the center table asked in a booming lumberjack voice.

Sam jumped to her feet. "Absolutely. Of course. I'll be right back." She crossed to the kitchen and out of sight.

"So, you're that Amble girl, eh?" the big guy asked.

I sized him up. His orangish hair was flecked with gray. The tatty black and red flannel shirt he wore seemed overkill for the warm spring day. The dab of ketchup and flake of toast stuck in his mustache cemented the fact that whatever opinion he was about to spout could hold no water with me.

I nodded in answer to his question, then looked out the window. I could see my grandfather's house along the shore, tiny in the distance.

"Thought so," the man said. "You look like your ma. Don't she look like her ma?"

"Yep," his lunch date said.

I looked. The other man was nearly as burly as his buddy and equally unkempt.

"Sad what happened that night. I remember it plain as day," the first man said.

I snapped my head in his direction. "My mother's accident? You saw it?"

"It was no accident. She drove straight into that quarry like she wanted to die."

"You were there?" I tensed with interest.

He shifted in his chair. "Heard all about it. Later. Couple days later."

I let out my breath. I should have known he was exaggerating.

"But," he said, "I was at the bar that night and I saw her arguing with Jake before she killed herself over it."

I walked to their table and grabbed a vacant chair. "You saw my mom arguing with my dad?"

"Yep. Then she went and drove straight into that quarry."

I leaned close enough to smell the absence of deodorant. "Start from the beginning."

Sam walked up and topped off their coffees. "Here you go. Hot and fresh." She lifted the decanter and looked at me. "Ready to start your training, girl?"

I shook my head, not wanting to pass up an opportunity to investigate my mom's death. "Not today. But I'll take a cup of coffee, if you don't mind."

She gave a big sigh and twirled away.

I gazed into my informant's slightly bloodshot and red-rimmed eyes. "Okay, go."

He looked across the table at his friend. "We got to the Watering Hole around seven that night. There was a big shutdown going on at the paper mill, and we headed to the bar as soon as our shift ended. I was surprised to see Jake there. He'd pretty much quit hanging at the bars around the time he went clean. But there he was, sitting in that corner by the john. Anyway, your ma sits at the table with him. They look all lovey-dovey for a while, but pretty soon she stands up and starts yelling at him, then walks out. He tries following her, but takes one look toward the door and hightails it the other direction."

"Why? What was by the door?"

"The grim reaper, I guess." A smile flicked across his face and was gone. "I imagine he saw a couple buddies from his drug-dealing days. Probably going to set him straight for turning in that trucking guy. But before they could get a hold of him, Jake makes it out the back door and no one's seen him since. Beth made it about five minutes down the road before she called it quits on life."

A cup of coffee dropped in front of me, almost spilling. "Anything else for you, Tish?"

I looked up at Sam, somehow seeing only Mead Quarry and my mom's Ford in an endless spiral above it. "No, thanks."

The men slurped their coffee and ate their fries, silent out of respect for the dead, or because they could tell I was going to start crying any second. The scenes ran over and over in my mind. Everything my grandfather had told me combined with what these guys had said, coming together to form a movie—a poorly written and directed film that left the faces of my father and the thugs at the door blurred and unrecognizable. Even the soundtrack was damaged. Nothing could turn up the volume so I could hear the words that made my mother end her life.

I composed myself and looked at the redheaded guy. "You mentioned something about my dad turning someone in. What's that all about?" I didn't want to waste the opportunity to soak them for information.

"Majestic. Frank Majestic. He owns a trucking line other side of Escanaba. Went to prison for a few years after Jake squealed on him," Burly Man Number One said.

"Squealed on him for what?" I asked.

"Drug running. He arranged shipments of drugs along

239

with regular payloads in and out of the U.P. Don't know the details. It was in the papers."

I thought about the Witness Protection Program my grandfather and I had discussed and wondered why my father hadn't been part of it. Frank Majestic sounded like a pretty big player. I pictured life under the protection program. Me and my mom and dad could have lived together in peace and security. Somewhere tropical. Like that little island in Fiji. It would have been a different existence for me. A world of love and laughter, palm trees and coconuts. My mom would have been a photographer for *National Geographic* and my dad would have owned a sugar cane plantation and I would have been their little princess and the native children would have come over for lemonade . . .

The scrape of chairs on the tile floor snapped me out of my daydream. "Where are you going? Hey, I didn't even get your names."

"Homer Johnson," the first guy said. "And that's Cody Baker. Sorry about your mom. She was a good lady."

He flipped cash on the table to pay the bill, and they left me alone, crying in my coffee.

29

Sam found me with my head buried in my arms at the table.

"Hey, it's going to be all right," she said, rubbing slow circles on my back. "You don't have to know what happened to your mom to know that God is taking good care of her."

I shrugged her arm away. "I don't think she even knew about Jesus. She's probably rotting in hell." How many times had Grandma Amble lamented the fact that she'd never brought my mother to church as a child?

"No, no." Samantha's lulling voice tried to draw me from the dregs of self-pity. "Your mom was a special lady. God loved her very much." Sam came close and hugged me.

I brushed off her touch and stood. I didn't want comfort. I wanted a time machine with the dial set for May 6, twenty-six years ago.

I threw down some money to pay for my coffee, stormed off to my Explorer, and headed north toward home. I wished I could believe what Samantha said about God taking care of my mother. I always liked to imagine

Mom with the angels in heaven. But that was just a cop-ing mechanism, my own protective denial.

I held back the tears. Unless, like Puppa said, I had smoke in my eyes. Was there a chance my mother had somehow accepted God's love, even in an airborne Ford?

I slowed for the turn down my driveway. A rusty white Suburban was just pulling out. I stared at the driver, taking notes on the curly brown hair and handsome *GQ* face. Our eyes met as we drove past one another. I angled down the two-track, squinting to see his license plate as he headed toward Port Silvan.

HOT1. Easy enough to remember. Hopefully, the driver was a friend of Joel's just checking in. But there was the chance he was one of Drake's buddies. I stepped on the gas, afraid of what I'd find at home.

I slid to a stop, threw the car in park, and headed inside.

"Missy? Joel? Anybody here?"

Before I panicked at the silence, I looked out toward the lake. Relief flooded over me. They were building sand castles at the shore, the four of them. The guy in the Suburban could have been a tourist checking out the area. No need for alarm.

I packed a basket full of lunch goodies and joined the gang at the beach. We were still playing in the sand when Samantha showed up midafternoon. She came down to the water's edge, ignoring my wave.

She gave the group a terse hello. "Can I talk to you a minute, Tish?" The tone of her voice made me want to run the opposite direction.

"Sure."

We walked back toward the lodge in silence. Once out of sight of our friends, she lit into me.

"You are the most immature person I know. What are you thinking messing with my stuff just because we had a disagreement this morning? I don't feel safe with you tampering in my bedroom behind my back. I'm sure Missy wouldn't feel safe either after what you did. I won't tell her this time, but please don't ever do it again."

My arms flapped and my fingers pointed as I tried to defend myself without words. Finally, my mouth kicked in. "What are you talking about? I haven't gone in your room since I got the upstairs bathroom cleaned up three days ago. Believe me, your stuff is safe from me." I had no use for lava lamps and butterfly wall art.

"Then how do you explain this?" She stomped to her room and threw open the door.

I cringed at the mess in my mother's old room. Mom had always kept things so tidy. Now, there were clothes strewn in piles on the floor in front of the dresser. The bed was stripped and the blankets, sheets, and comforter scattered all over the tile.

I took a cautious step toward the bathroom. Powder covered every surface as if Sam had doused her whole body, then shook off like a dog.

"Geez, Sam. Maybe you should hire a housekeeper." I tried diffusing the situation with a little humor.

"Very funny." She crossed her arms. "You did it. You get to clean it up. And don't ever come in here again, or I'm leaving."

Her offer sounded too good to be true, but I refrained

from saying so. "Look, Sam. You know I wouldn't have done something like this. It's my house. And my mother's old room."

She looked me over. "You seriously didn't make this mess?"

I shook my head. "Why would I? It wouldn't make sense."

"Do you think Hannah might have done it?" Her voice took on an edge of unease.

Our eyes met. I could tell Hannah wasn't really on her list of suspects. My mind refused to follow her path of reasoning. "Let's talk to Missy before we jump to conclusions. Maybe Hannah got out of sight for a few minutes."

"Look at this, Tish." She pointed at a footprint made of powder just outside the bathroom door. "That looks like a man's shoe. You don't think Joel was in here?"

A creepy feeling crawled across my neck. I pictured the vehicle pulling out of my driveway. Unless the driver was one of Drake Belmont's minions, there was only one other possible explanation. Could Mr. GQ be Sam's ex-husband? "Ummm, there was a white Suburban leaving just as I was coming home. You don't think . . ."

Sam drew in a sharp breath. Her face took on a look of panic. "Heaven forbid . . ."

"What? What are you thinking?" I grabbed her arm.

"Nothing. Never mind." She gave a big, fake yawn. "I think I'll take a nap and worry about this later. Sorry to bug you."

She pushed me out the door and closed it with a bang.

I hovered. From beyond the door came the tones of a cell phone dialing. There was no napping going on in there. That probably meant my suspicions were right.

I stuck my ear to the pine. Sam's voice came low and muffled. I strained to hear the details of her call, feeling only slightly guilty for eavesdropping after she'd falsely accused me of vandalism. Her voice moved back and forth between the bathroom and the dresser. My stomach churned up an extra dose of acid. Sam was generally pleasant and perky. It had been easy to forget she'd been the victim of violence. Now, the worst had happened. Her jerk of an ex barged in and resumed his crippling power over her—just when we needed to focus our attention on keeping Missy and her kids safe.

I shuffled to the kitchen, despondent at the turn of events. The stool and countertop provided moral support while I mulled the situation.

Sometime later, Joel came in to start supper.

"Where's Samantha? I haven't seen her all afternoon."

Joel didn't know I'd already had one exile in residence before I took on the latest family of refugees. I steeled myself for a strong reaction, then told him of the day's incident and described the vehicle, right down to the boastful license plate.

His brows scrunched. "Papa B suspected as much." He hammered some numbers into his cell phone. "I'll call and get the owner's name. That should solve our mystery."

While he contacted the state police post, I finished cutting up the salad. Then, going to Sam's room, I gave a hesitant tap on her door. "Hey, supper's ready. Are you eating?"

"No." The word held the defiance of a teenager.

"Come on, Sam. You can't stay in there forever."

Bumping. Thumping. Scraping. Slamming.

"Come and eat. You'll feel better," I said.

The door opened. Sam's shirt hung out of her waistband. Her face was swollen. She looked like she'd been dragged behind a four-wheeler.

She gave a slurpy sniffle. "I can't eat right now. I'm packing."

I looked past her into the room. Boxes were strewn everywhere. The lava lamp was gone. So was the yellow rug. Even the comforter had disappeared.

Rage—and a good dose of fear—built in my chest. "What do you think you're doing? If you leave now, it would be like letting your ex control you all over again. And remember, saving Melissa was your idea. You are not ditching me."

She picked a sweatshirt off the floor, folded it, and tucked it in a box. She bent for a blouse.

I touched her shoulder, trying a gentler approach. "Come on, Sam. We're all in this together. We can keep Missy safe, and you'll be safe too. Like you said, it's kind of like the Alamo here. Together to the end."

Sam shook her head. "That's a depressing thought." She folded the garment and stowed it. "I'm sorry, Tish. I really am. I thought I'd have more time. But things just didn't work out."

I stood there, fists clenched, wanting to wring her neck. "You are not leaving me." My muscles jerked in frustration. "I'm telling Joel." I twirled and ran to the kitchen.

A door slammed behind me. The windows rattled from the vibration.

Joel followed me back to the bedroom and tapped on the door. "Sam. Open up," he said in a soft, cajoling voice.

The door opened. He went in. The door closed.

I stared at its six wood panels, fuming over the injustice of being left out. I went to the kitchen. With no Joel in sight, Melissa and I dipped into the pot of vegetable soup on the stove. Side salads and fresh bread made the meal complete. Melissa cut up a hot dog with a side of straight veggies for Hannah. Andrew got his usual runny white entrée along with a taste of mashed carrots. I told Missy as much as I could about the intruder situation, using code I hoped Hannah couldn't crack.

"Sounds like something Drake would do. Only milder," Missy said. She spooned another helping toward Andrew's waiting lips.

"How are you holding up, anyway?" I asked her.

"It's hard. I miss my life. My things. My house. You're very kind to let us stay here."

"I wish we had done it sooner. It seems foolish now that you had to suffer all those months when you could have been taking steps to get your life together."

"I know. But I guess I just wasn't ready. I'm ready now, believe me."

"Good." We sat in silence as the kids finished their meals.

With a final bite of her hot dog bun, Hannah wiggled

off the stool and put her plate in the trash. She skipped to the diaper bag by the door and reached in. A Dr. Seuss book appeared. She settled on the tile beneath the window and began to read aloud.

Missy held a cloth under warm water and cleaned up Andrew's pudgy cheeks. "Joel offered to drive me to Escanaba for my checkup this week. While we're in town, I'm going to see an attorney."

She bit her lip and gave Hannah a sidelong glance.

The girl was absorbed in her book. ". . . but the Grinch was very, very bad. He didn't like the little Who people and he wanted to make them go away . . ." She made up words for the pictures.

Missy turned back to me. "I'm going to file."

I nodded. "You're doing the right thing."

Her voice cracked. "Do you think so? God hates divorce. It says so right in the Bible."

"I can only believe that a loving God hates what Drake has done to you even worse than He hates divorce."

She sighed. "I struggle so much with that. Sometimes I feel like God's providing me the way out, like what you and your grandfather have done for me. Other times, I feel like the biggest sinner on the planet, like I'm quitting on the thing God commanded me to see through to the end. 'Til death do us part."

Behind us, Hannah turned another page. ". . . And the mean Grinch tied up his dog to the sled and went down to steal everything from the Who people . . . all their good stuff . . ."

My chin jutted out in Melissa's defense. I kept my voice to a harsh whisper. "Well, if Drake had anything to do with it, you'd be dead and he'd be the one raising those kids. I can't see God wanting that to happen. So just take this opportunity and quit trying to jump back into the pit He just pulled you from."

"I wish it was that simple," Melissa said.

I tapped my fingers on the counter. I knew where she was coming from. Self-condemnation was a tempting place to rest. It was certainly easier than coming up with a new approach to life, setting new goals, and trying to be the awesome individual God made you to be. I'd lingered in the guilt pit for years. It gave me a great excuse to check out of life and just exist. Thankfully, God made me face my sin head-on and admit the part I'd had in creating the situation. After that, I grew up a little. I quit worrying so much about what everyone else thought and started doing what was right for my life. Of course, there were casualties . . . like my relationship with Brad.

At the very thought of his name, my throat constricted and my eyes teared up. I missed his voice. And his smile. And his hand holding mine . . .

"Tish? Are you all right?" Missy touched my arm.

I wiped my eyes and nodded. "Yeah. Sorry. What a long, crazy day."

"I know what you mean."

She got up from her stool and wrapped her arms around me. Her chin rested in my hair. I clung to her for dear life, my elbows pressing against her firm belly with its little baby tucked inside. I started to cry. She cried with me.

We were still blubbering together about our own personal woes when Joel stepped into the kitchen. He looked over his shoulder toward Sam's room as if he wasn't sure which was worse: the sobbing woman he'd just left, or the two bawling females yet to face.

Melissa dropped her arms and grabbed for paper toweling. I used the hem of my T-shirt.

"How'd it go in there?" I asked.

"So-so. It's confirmed that her ex-husband was driving the vehicle you ID'd, Tish. Needless to say, she's pretty freaked out and ready to run."

I opened my mouth to interrupt, but he put up a hand and kept talking.

"Don't worry, I convinced her to stay," Joel said, a hint of triumph in his voice. "There's no reason we can't keep her safe along with Melissa. Especially since we've got extra help on the way."

"Oh? Who's that?" I asked.

"Samantha's brother is coming for a visit. He's a police officer downstate somewhere. I guess he was tied up with some big trial, but now that it's over he can take time off."

I sucked in an agonizing breath. No. Not Brad. I'd worked hard to free my mind of him. I couldn't face him. I couldn't see him. One word, one smile, one touch . . . and I'd be back at the beginning of wretched heartache.

30

"Absolutely not," I said. "There's enough people at the lodge as it is. I don't have room for tourists." There was no need for Joel to know of my past relationship with Brad.

Joel gave my face a playful squeeze with his fingers. "Not to worry. He'll be staying at the lake house with me, Papa B, and Olivia." He winked as he waltzed off.

My hands planted themselves on my hips and stayed there as I mounted the staircase. People were doing things without my consent. It might have been Sam's idea to rescue Melissa and her kids, but I was the one who'd actually done it. So, technically, everything should be my plan, my way.

I closed my door, shutting out the turn of circumstances. I went for the bedside table and picked up my mom's picture. I wiped off the remaining black letters with my bath towel. I stuck the two halves together, matching the jagged edges. Then I curled under my blankets, stared into her beautiful eyes, and cried myself to sleep.

Thursday morning, I rebelled against life by staying in

bed. Finally, about an hour before I was due at Candice's house, I bathed and dressed. I snuck out of the lodge without bumping into anyone. The drive to Candice's farmhouse lifted my spirits. The leaves were in fresh, full-blown splendor, giving testimony to hot, lazy days ahead.

I turned onto her property and parked, full of anticipation for the conversation ahead with all its distractions. I'd spent almost every Thursday over the past three months at Candice's home. It was a tradition I'd come to love, a fixture of my new life.

Candice waved me in. "Hello!"

I hurried up the walk and gave her a hug of greeting. "How are you feeling this week? Better?" I asked.

"I won't be participating in any foot races, if that's what you mean."

"Well, I just hoped you were up for talking today."

She nodded her head. "That's right. I have some explaining to do."

She served tea and sandwiches on the enclosed back porch. I settled into white wicker softened by pastel floral cushions. The view over the fields brought a sigh of contentment as I sipped the icy concoction. An occasional fly buzzed against the screen, an annoyance diminished by the barrier between us.

"I bumped into two guys at the Grille yesterday," I said. I didn't want to waste any time getting to the point just in case Candice tried to wiggle out of the conversation again. "They were there when my mom died."

She adjusted in her chair. "Oh? What guys were those?"

"Homer somebody and something Baker." What a sleuth I was turning out to be.

A nod. "Johnson and Cody. They're locals. Usually, those two are unemployed. But your mom died the year the mill hired for that big shutdown. Of course, even with a job they were doing what they do best—hanging out at the bar." Her voice of derision was back on again, and I wondered what those two men did to get on her bad side. Or did Candice even have a good side?

"So you already know about them?" I asked. I was a latecomer to the investigation, so it shouldn't surprise me that I didn't have anything new.

"Like I said, there were plenty of rumors flying around. Apparently, Johnson and Baker witnessed your mom's car driving into the quarry. They said it looked like she'd done it on purpose."

I sat forward. "No. No, they said they didn't see her drive over. They said they only heard about it later."

"It's all so long ago. I'm surprised anybody remembers anything."

"Homer Johnson said he remembered plain as day."

Candice folded her hands in her lap. "Tish. Everybody remembers things their own way. I'm sure their story has evolved over the years."

"You'd think if they'd witnessed a car driving over a cliff, they'd remember it, even twenty-six years later."

"Seems that way." She shrugged. "Maybe I'm the one with the faulty memory."

"I'm sure you remember what you were doing that night when you got the news."

She gave a slow nod. "Plain as day."

"Were you still at Puppa's?"

"No. The fire had taken place weeks earlier and I'd stormed off. I blamed Bernard for the whole thing. So I was staying in Escanaba when I got the news."

"Did Puppa call you?"

"He didn't even know where I was." She sounded like she might break into tears. "No. I heard about it later."

I swallowed. "That must have been really hard for you."

She blinked and nodded. "Yes, but that was no excuse not to attend that funeral, if only for your sake." She wiped under her eyes. "But I couldn't face your grandfather. And I couldn't face Eva and Art. And I couldn't face you." The tears started rolling. "If only Beth hadn't gone that night. I keep asking myself, why? Why?"

I scooted next to her and put my arms around her shoulders. "They said she went to meet my father at the Watering Hole. To warn him about something."

"Your mother should never have been near the place," Candice said. "Jake was in the clear. Bernard lost his career over the deal he cut to get that kid out of the loop."

I paused to get the details straight in my mind. "But the fire. Sid and Paul both died, and my grandfather supposedly cut the deal with them. With the two of them dead, my father was back in jeopardy and my mom went to warn him."

"How could she have known where he was unless your grandfather told her?" She jabbed a finger into the cushion. "That's why she's dead. It's your grandfather's fault."

254

I backed away from the enraged woman and sat in my chair. "It makes me feel better if I can blame someone too. But I don't think I'll join you in blaming my grandfather. I like him. He tries to do his best. I'm sure he thought he was doing the right thing, even back then."

Candice seethed through her teeth before calming down. "You're right. It's easy to blame. I guess we'll never know why Beth died that night, and we'll just have to accept that."

I took a sip of iced tea. I'd never accept that my mother killed herself. And I'd never stop asking why until some new, better explanation could replace that lame account of the death of a woman who lived and loved so well, yet so briefly.

"Anyway"—I set my tea on the glass-top—"I'm going to request the police report. I'll feel better after I read what the cops had to say."

Candice's tea clanked to the table. "Do you really think you're strong enough to sift through those details? I insist you let it go. For your own sake."

My stubborn streak dug in. "I think I can handle it. It'll be a lot better than making stuff up in my head. I'm ready for the truth. Hey, by the way," I changed the subject as quickly as I could, "we had an interesting adventure yesterday."

I filled her in on my visiting family and the scare we had from Sam's ex-husband.

"You have Melissa Belmont staying at your place?" Candice straightened, disapproval thick on her voice. "Does Drake know that?"

"I hope not. But I'm pretty sure he must." I told her

255

about Stick's visit and Joel's deception. "For all we know, Stick went right to Drake and told him where Missy and the kids are hiding out."

She pressed her hands together. "Tish. You don't know what you've gotten yourself into. Drake's scheduled to get out of jail in a few days. Don't think for a minute he won't go after his family." She leaned forward, elbows on knees. "And what were you thinking taking in that Sam girl? Now you've got her ex starting in. And it's only the beginning. He'll play cat and mouse awhile just for fun. Then he'll go in for the kill." She stared at me with pleading eyes. "Throw them out. Save your own life."

I shivered at the chill in her voice. But all her urging couldn't quash the defensive feeling that rose in my chest. "These are my friends. They need me. I can't let them down."

The color drained from her face. "I understand." She stood and stacked the tea things on the tray. "Now if you don't mind, I think I'll rest a bit."

I took the hint, said goodbye, and headed back to the lodge.

31

With Brad's impending arrival, my home became my enemy. I felt as if a scythe swung just above my head, ready to cut off my breath the moment I saw his face. Perhaps he'd show up for dinner. Or drop by to say hello. Or take a shift as bodyguard. Not wanting to appear interested, I'd avoided asking the details of his visit.

My waitress-training commitment provided an opportunity to escape the house, but I couldn't bear to be around Brad's sister. She'd burdened me with a guilt trip over the way I'd treated him. And my mind played right into it. I beat myself up over every perceived slight I'd given my good friend. Now, if he did show up, my only option seemed to be crawling under a rock and hiding in shame until he went away. Toss in Candice's criticism of my friends and choices, Puppa's suggestion that I needed therapy, and Joel's scorn of my very existence, and suddenly I could see how the bottom of Mead Quarry might become an attractive proposition.

But ending it all wasn't a fitting choice for me. I was a survivor. I prided myself on having lived through everything God and others threw at me. I just had to wait out this latest storm. Next time I poked my head from my hole, things would be better.

The key was getting away from my tormenters. I needed space, time to think, air to breathe—somewhere they couldn't imply how bad I was, how I should change, how I should never have been born.

Friday morning I woke early to make my escape. Snacks, water, and bug spray would be my only companions for the day. The quiet house seemed to echo with even the slightest of my movements as I snuck to the kitchen and gathered my supplies. With a final, slow zip of my backpack, I reached for the kitchen door.

"Where you going, cuz?" Gerard's voice halted me at the verge of freedom.

I froze, busted by the bodyguard on the sofa.

"Uhh, just going out for some fresh air." Even the truth had a ring of fiction to it. What was my problem? I didn't have to tell him where I was off to. I was an adult—and this was my house.

I turned the handle without waiting for a response. The porch squeaked under my boots. The door latched behind me.

Damp air, still full of the dew that covered the grass, rushed into my lungs as I put one foot in front of the other, faster . . . faster . . . until the gravel was a bouncing blur. Pavement appeared briefly, then was gone, replaced by the sharp incline of the bluff. Roots, thorns, bark, and bare earth —all passed beneath my fingers as I scrambled unthinking to the top. I paused only a moment for a glimpse of the bay. Leaves blocked the view. Before thoughts of those still sleeping could invade, I fled toward the forest, losing myself—and my mind—in the flat expanse of the Silvan Plains.

I returned in near-darkness.

"Where have you been?" Sam met me, hands on hips, at the door.

"Out for a walk." I drank down a glass of water.

"We're all worried about you. What's going on?" Sam leaned in toward me, her expression changing as her eyes shifted to my hair.

"Nothing to be worried about." I brushed past her to my room. Nice of her to show concern when she was the one to drive me from my home in the first place.

Twigs and thistles snarled my hair. I picked out the most annoying ones, then climbed under the covers and slept with my head under the pillow.

Saturday brought more of the same. I evacuated the area early, hoping to avoid brown eyes softened by those crinkles in the corners. Happy crinkles. Fun crinkles. The kind of crinkles that made you want to hang out with Brad for the rest of your life.

Sunday came. Instead of trudging to church in my negative state of mind, I trudged the plains. Every so often, my swampers sank in surprise springs, soaking my feet. I hardly noticed. At least the water washed off some of the mud caked on my jeans. And when did I tear that hole in my sweatshirt?

My slim digital camera, the one I used for before-and-after shots of my renovation projects, came along for the ride. My link to my mother . . . How would she have photographed the seed cluster clinging to that branch of the cedar tree? What angle would she have chosen to capture the circle of mushrooms in that sunny clearing? Which spring wildflower would have caught her attention and stolen her breath?

Snap. Click. I could only guess.

That night, a light supper from the kitchen. Then upstairs, exhausted. Bathe, sleep, dream. But as always, morning came. Out the door again, running . . . hiding . . . avoiding . . .

Monday found me at the Port Silvan cemetery a couple miles down the road. I meandered through headstones, reading names and dates, intent on finding one in particular. I started at the front near the highway and worked my way through family plots toward the back, like a wraith wandering over hallowed ground. Bouquets of plastic flowers, tiny American flags, and statues reminded the living that someone still cared. A few graves had elaborate displays of fencing and photos and even stuffed animals. But not the one that read ELIZABETH MARIE AMBLE. I found it along the back row, in with the Nagy family plots. Grandma Amble had insisted on burying her daughter with the rest of her family, though Mom and I had only spent summers on the peninsula and the rest of the year in Escanaba. A simple rectangular slab of granite was inscribed with my mother's name and the years of her birth and death. I crouched down. Somewhere, six feet below, lay the remains of my beautiful mother. I put my hands on the grass above her casket, imagining she could feel the pull of energy between us.

"Mom," I whispered, my lips close to the ground. The scent of rich earth greeted my nose. A black ant traversed the grassy grave top, climbing up and down through the mess of green blades. I flicked it away with my finger.

Legs tucked, I rolled onto my side and rested my cheek on the ground. "It's Tish, Mom. Your baby girl. Remember?"

I pictured her sitting on top of the grave, dressed in blue jeans and a sweatshirt, like a character from Thornton Wilder's *Our Town*.

"Of course I remember my little princess." She smoothed my hair as I rested my head in her lap. "I've missed my pumpkin. I'm glad you came to see me."

I crushed my eyes closed, but the tears came pouring out anyway. "I miss you so much, Mom. Why did you leave me? Didn't you love me?"

Her soft voice comforted me. "Tish, you have always been the most important thing to me. I made a mistake that night. Sometimes you have to let go of people so you can live. I held on to your father. But he wasn't real. Just a dream. I should have let go of him. You let go too, Tish."

"I don't want to let go. I want you back. I want to be seven again, playing in the woods. Gerard and Joel can come too. We'll all be together again. Puppa and Jellybean and the rest of us."

"Let go, Tish. It's all just a dream."

"I don't want to let go." I clawed at her lap, but got only a handful of dirt and grass. I laid there sobbing, I don't know how long, before I dusted off and headed home.

It was Tuesday. Or maybe Wednesday. Whatever the day, I left just after I heard Sam's van pull out the drive. I made it to the edge of the woods without seeing anyone. Then, there she was. My friendly doe.

"Hi, girl," I said. I kissed at her and held out a hand. She stared at me awhile. Then she casually bent her neck to eat. I smiled. She knew me. She liked me. She was comfortable around me. After a minute, she turned and walked away. I followed at a distance. Ahead, the underbrush crunched. Several times she stopped and I thought I lost her. But soon her shape emerged from the backdrop and we'd start off again.

The ground got soggy. Cupid's Creek must be just ahead. If she decided to cross it, I'd have to let her go. Water trickled. The doe stopped in a clearing and looked back at me. I waggled my fingers.

From the direction of the highway came a loud crack, like a gunshot. The doe took off running. I ducked down, arms covering my head. The reverberation died as I scanned the trees. Perhaps the report had merely been the loud snap of a branch. It sure wasn't hunting season. I stood and waited for my heartbeat to even out. I moved into the clearing ahead. A few more steps and I paused. Thumping and crunching sounded from the opposite side of the grassy area, then faded, as if something or someone were running away.

The sounds of solitude returned. I moved toward the creek. A cluster of marsh marigolds were sprinkled along the bank. A perfect photo opportunity. I stepped toward them. Halfway there, I froze in my tracks. Around me, black garbage bags filled with dirt appeared to be arranged in rows. And from the center of every bag rose the fat stumpy remains of some kind of plant. What on earth? I shrank back as if *Alien* babies would hatch from their pods at any moment.

A marijuana grove. Last year's batch of Silvan Green.

With the feeling that I was trespassing, even on my own acreage, I backed away from the clearing. The root of a towering cedar caught my swampers. I landed on my backside, fighting for calm as I crab-walked toward cover. I rested against a trunk, panting.

From the quiet of the forest came a tiny electronic beeping sound, like the alarm on a wristwatch. I looked around, confused. The tones came from a nearby clump of bushes. Beneath the tangled branches, I spotted the watch, a man's digital with chrome accents and a black band.

The wrist was still in it.

"Ahh." I grunted and scrambled away.

Adrenaline surged through me, sharpening every sound, every smell, every thought.

The hairy arm lay unmoving on the ground. A fly feasted uninterrupted on the exposed flesh. I gulped for air, wondering if the person were dead or alive. My eyes followed the logical course of a body and saw the man's work boots protruding from the other side of the bushes. He'd apparently fallen in a Nestea plunge straight backward into the brush. If not for the insistent beeping on his wrist, I would have been spared the distinction of finding him.

"Hey," I called in a half whisper, wondering now if it might have been a gunshot I'd heard after all. "Are you okay?"

I glanced over my shoulder, hoping whoever had fled the scene was a good distance away by now and not lining me up in his crosshairs.

"Hey," I said again. I crouched by the body and reached out my hand. I brushed away the fly. Then I put my fingers around the man's wrist, feeling for a pulse like they do on cop shows. The seconds passed. I had no idea whether the man was still alive, or if my own racing blood created the *dub dub* I felt.

I pulled back the branches, straining to see a face with eyes full of life. I found his eyes. They stared up at the leafy canopy, the soul they once held snuffed out by a bullet that left its mark between his brows.

I scrambled backward. Not good. Not good. The man was definitely dead. Worse, he was dead on my land. Worse still, I found him.

Experience told me that if you were the one to report a dead body, pretty much everybody figured you for the killer. Likewise, TV crime programs laid it out just as plain that if you found a dead body and didn't report it, they'll also figure you for the killer. A classic Catch-22. And even in the short time I'd been out here, I'd probably left enough DNA on the scene to seal my own conviction. They'd ignore the fact that I didn't have the murder weapon. Heaven knew I'd probably thrown it in the creek or swallowed it or something.

For a minute I wished I could be one of those famous monkeys, Hear No Evil, Speak No Evil, See No Evil. Then I could just waltz out of these woods like nothing out of the ordinary had happened today. Unfortunately, there was the guilt factor. Somewhere, the dead guy had people who loved him, perhaps a wife and kids that would wonder why Daddy didn't come home tonight.

And if it were my father lying there, I'd want someone to

264

get help right away and give him the respect he deserved for simply having lived, if not for having lived right.

I sighed and turned back toward the lodge, wishing I'd brought my cell phone along. When I left it on my bedside table this morning, I had been thinking how nice it was to be unreachable. It had never occurred to me that I might be the one in need of reaching out.

I kicked at a moss-covered log as I walked past. Dead bodies sure went out of their way to complicate my life.

The roof of the lodge poked through the trees just ahead. I neared the edge of the woods, peering through safe cover before venturing the rest of the way home. Joel's car was parked out front along with my own. And next to it was Brad's hulking silver SUV. A jolt shot through me. I took in a breath of air. Now I had to deal with Brad in addition to the dead body. I plopped to the ground. Last year's leaves crunched beneath my weight. Moisture soaked through the back end of my jeans. The wetness expanded to meet my drenched pant leg. I stared at a slug making its way across the slimy ground.

All my efforts to avoid reality only brought more reality crashing down on me. I wasn't sure how much I could take. How could I survive a rerun of my life in Rawlings, with its creepy corpse and jail jaunt? I'd come to the Silvan Peninsula for a break. But it seemed there was no escape.

A moan broke the silence. Was that me? I keeled to my side, landing almost eye to eye with my slug buddy. Who cared anyway? The forest could consume me, morsel by morsel, and that would be an improvement over my present prospects.

I must have been blubbering pretty intently because

I never heard the footsteps approaching until the size 12 Nikes were directly in front of me.

"Tish."

I sat up and wiped my tears off with muddy fingers. By now I must have looked like Rambo. A final swipe of my nose with my sleeve, then I spoke. "Hi, Brad. I heard you might be coming up for a visit."

He reached his hand toward me. "Come on. Let's go inside and get cleaned up."

I stared at him, unable to move. Unable to breathe. His blue jeans looked sexy as ever, snug across muscular thighs, then relaxed to his tennis shoes. His black T-shirt stretched over his chest, several feet above me. And his face . . . More handsome than I remembered, he gazed at me with deep brown eyes that somehow shot out rays of light. His corner crinkles were in full action with a smile that made me want to run and hide from its unmerited favor.

I fell back onto my side and curled into a ball. "Go away."

"Hey. What's wrong?" His hand touched my shoulder, giving it a gentle shake.

"You're not supposed to see me like this."

"If you want the truth, you look beautiful."

"It's not how I look, it's how I feel."

"What's going on?" His voice took on a note of apprehension.

"Today's not going so great. I just want to die."

"Hey, now. I don't like hearing you talk like that."

"Well, it's the truth. I don't think I can face life today."

"Come on. We'll face it together." He reached down.

Warm hands gently gripped my arm and back. With a nudge of encouragement, he helped me to my feet.

I made a halfhearted attempt to brush the mud from the back of my pants. He swatted at a clump of leaves stuck to my knee. I caught a whiff of his shampoo or deodorant or aftershave as he bent in front of me. I nearly swooned.

"You okay?" He grabbed my shoulders.

"I hadn't planned on seeing you today. I was going to wait in the bushes until you left. How'd you know I was here?" I barely heard him answer. His face was so close. His body so warm, so strong, so . . . manly.

"The white letters on your sweatshirt stand out pretty good against the trees," those lips were explaining.

I looked down. PROPERTY OF MSU ATHLETIC DEPARTMENT, the letters boasted. I hadn't even read the thing when I'd picked it up at Goodwill. The deep green fabric had seemed in good condition. That's all I'd cared about. But now the words reminded me that I'd failed to finish college. Another domino in the long line perched to push me over the edge.

"And we're on full alert at the lodge today," Brad was saying. "Not only has Sam's ex been spotted up and down the peninsula, but Drake Belmont was released from jail yesterday afternoon." He pulled me toward him in a partial embrace. "It's been foolish of you to be out on your own, you know." His voice was low and rumbly.

I nodded, my eyes glued to the line of his jaw, the sweep of his cheek, the arch of his brow. With the grip of his hands, the flurry in my brain calmed, replaced by clarity—or was it the return of sanity?

"I missed you, Tish." The words were nothing more

than a whisper in my ear. Then came the warm trail of his lips against my neck.

I reached up my arms and clung to him, breathing him in, soaking him in, afraid to let go. He lifted me against himself, until only my toes touched the ground. His lips nudged around until they found mine. And he kissed me. I kissed him back with long hungry gulps, lost in the moment. I shoved every thought out of my brain, determined that nothing would drag me back to reality.

But it was no use.

"Brad." I pulled my face away.

"Yes?" He gazed into my eyes, searching, ready to resume his affections at my command.

"I . . ."

"Yes?" His face took on an eager look.

"I . . . have something to tell you."

He hugged me close, his lips buried in my ear. "Tell me, Tish."

He refused to relinquish my body, so I was forced to say the news at close range. "Umm, when I was out walking this morning, I found a dead man."

He stiffened around me. Then he pushed me to arm's length. "What? Are you serious?"

I nodded.

He dropped his hands and turned his back to me, his fingers running along the back of his neck.

He pivoted in my direction and sighed. "Well, show me."

32

I looked at Brad. "Shouldn't we call 9-1-1 or something?" I asked.

Doubt clouded his eyes. "Let's see what we're dealing with, then we'll put in the call."

"You don't believe me, do you?" My shoulders sagged. Nothing had changed between us. It was just like last time. He hadn't trusted me when I told him about the body in the cistern. Then, when he actually found a body in the cistern, he hadn't believed me when I swore I hadn't put it there.

He started walking. "I believe you."

I passed in front of him in a straight line to Cupid's Creek. A little while later I spotted my marsh marigolds and the clump of bushes, still beeping.

Brad paused and perused the rows of black bags that filled the clearing. "Nice," he said with a hint of sarcasm.

He stared down through the top of the shrub at the victim's face. "Do you know the guy?"

I shook my head. "Never saw him before."

He pulled his cell phone from his pocket and dialed

a number. I crouched by the babbling creek, not caring what he said or to whom he spoke. A few minutes passed. He joined me creekside, sitting close enough for our elbows to touch.

"So how have you been, Tish?"

I nodded, satisfied with how things had been going up until my recent discovery. A small brown bird fluttered to the opposite bank, picking at something in the dirt. I figured it wouldn't be long before the turkey vultures descended on our friendly woodland corpse.

"Good. Good," he said, nodding with me. "We haven't talked in a couple weeks. I hope things are working out for you here in Port Silvan."

"Yep. It's all working out." I gave him a poke on the arm. "I even have a job lined up, if you can believe it."

"Really? Where's that?"

"The same place Sam works. She's supposed to train me. But"—I gave a sigh—"I must confess I haven't felt much like waitressing the last couple days."

"Why not?"

I shrugged. "I don't really want to hang with Sam right now. She said a few things that hit home. I'm avoiding her."

He sat quiet for a moment. "She really loves it up here. Says she's having the time of her life." He shot a glimpse of brown eyes my way. "Your cousin may have something to do with that."

I smiled. "Joel has had the hots for Sam since the first time he saw her. I wonder where that's headed?"

"Hopefully nowhere. Sam's life is in Rawlings. I'd hate to see her make any foolish choices."

I bristled. "Yeah. What a shame that would be, to leave the suburbs for a place where the air is clean and the water's clear and people aren't going around killing each other."

Brad looked over his shoulder at the body. "Yep. That'd be a shame."

I folded my arms around my knees. "Smarty pants."

We fell into silence again. I suppressed a smile, every so often sneaking a glance in Brad's direction.

He was here. I bit my lip to make sure I wasn't hallucinating. After that reunion, I couldn't believe I'd been opposed to his visit. Maybe we were a tiny bit more than just friends. Big deal. Why had I been so worked up the past few days anyway? Now, sitting there next to Brad, mountains shrank to molehills and my world of woes drifted off with the water bugs darting on the surface of Cupid's Creek.

Fifteen minutes passed before we heard the crunching of leaves and snapping of twigs. Brad stood to greet his state cop buddy from Manistique. They smiled, shook hands, and caught up on old times while the lab people collected data and snapped pictures. Then the two men approached me by the water's edge.

"Morning, Miss Amble," Officer Segerstrom said. "Brad tells me you're having a rough day."

"More like a rough millennium," I said.

He nodded. "Tell me how you found the body."

I gave him the spiel, trying not to stare as the team extracted the corpse from the shrub. My skin crawled as they laid the body in a zipper bag for removal.

Officer Segerstrom's eyes never budged during my

recitation. I knew he watched me intently, looking for clues that I might be lying or leaving out facts. Whatever. I rather hoped he did throw me in jail. Then I could avoid the topics that were sure to come up now that Brad was hanging around.

I finished my story. A few calming breaths helped ward off hyperventilation.

"Thank you," the officer said. "I'll keep in touch." He turned toward the dead man, still exposed to daylight. "Now there's a guy whose luck finally ran out."

"You know him?" Brad asked.

The state cop gave a nod of affirmation. "I was at his bail hearing just the other day. I guess Drake Belmont shouldn't have been in such a hurry to get out after all."

My heart sank to my knees. I gulped. Drake Belmont. Of all people. And on my land.

Officer Segerstrom looked my way. "His death will certainly come as a relief to some, though I'm sure those kids are going to have a tough go of it."

I gave a grunt of agreement, then glued my eyes to the patch of grass and weeds in front of me. Who could have done this thing? Sure, the guy threatened to kill Missy. But she wouldn't have beaten him to the punch, would she? Or could Joel have been the one to take out the enemy? I squinted in thought. No. This seemed more Gerard's style.

"Do you own a gun, Miss Amble?" Officer Segerstrom's voice cut through my perusal.

"No," I said, recollecting that I was the prime suspect, since I'd found the creep. The officer turned toward Brad and left me alone.

272

A little ways over, the long bag made a sound like a mournful bumblebee as the zipper closed. Two investigators lifted the body and removed it from the scene. The crew returned a few minutes later and scoured the area for more clues and, presumably, the weapon.

"Can I go now?" I interrupted Brad and Mike's intense conversation.

"Sure." Brad gave a nudge toward the lodge with his head. "I'll meet you back there." He looked toward his cop friend. "That is, if you're done with her."

"She's free to go."

I walked through the woods, running the list of suspects around and around in my mind. It could have been anybody. A good sprinkling of people would celebrate Drake's death. And perhaps some of them were willing to secure it. But to have it happen so close to the lodge, with Missy and the kids within reach . . . I shuddered to think what would have happened if he'd made it to the house this morning, instead.

I felt eyes on me as I walked across the yard.

"You look rough." Joel greeted me at the kitchen door. "Back from your walkabout so soon?"

I swept past him to the sink and ran my hands under warm water.

He followed me over. "Got a call from Papa B. He heard on the police radio that there was a possible homicide up at the creek. You know anything about that?"

"Drake Belmont got shot in the head." My voice came out monotone.

Joel stepped back. "Well. That's a twist I hadn't expected. Wait until Melissa hears."

273

I toweled off. "I'm sure the trooper will be here shortly to question everyone. I already got the third degree." Heebie-jeebies ran down my arms at the memory of the murder scene. "Is there any coffee?"

With my self-imposed exile lifted, I treated myself to the meager comfort of hot, liquid caffeine. I sat at a stool without saying much of anything. Thankfully, Joel respected my silence. At my last sip, I set the mug down with finality. "I'm going to take a bath."

The second-floor bathrooms had no showers, only old-fashioned claw-foot tubs with peeling paint around the outsides. I soaked in one, hiding my ears under-water so I couldn't hear anything but the sound of blood whooshing and an occasional thump beyond the door. I had no plans of getting out anytime soon. I wanted to wait until someone else broke the news of Drake's death to Melissa and her kids, even if it meant I suffered wrinkled-up prune-skin.

Several hot water warm-ups and at least an hour later, I finally climbed out and toweled off. I threw on fresh clothes and moseyed back downstairs.

Gerard was in the great room playing with Hannah and Andrew. Joel's voice came from the kitchen, apparently deep in conversation on his cell phone.

"Hi, kids," I said, smiling to cover any expression of pity that might show on my face. "Hello, Gerard. What are you still doing here?" His shift normally ended around six when Joel arrived.

"Melissa asked if I'd watch the kids for her this morning while she walked along the beach. When she got back a little while ago, she looked pretty wiped out. Said she

274

needed a nap. I agreed to cover for her while Joel fixed some grub."

I swallowed hard. "What time did she leave this morning?"

"Six, six thirty. Why?"

"Have you heard the latest?"

"No. Me and the kids were down at the lake until a few minutes ago."

"Uncle Gerard buried me in the sand!" Hannah jumped up and down at the thrill of it. Sand sifted off her clothing and onto the floor.

"That must have been cold this early in the day." I picked Andrew off the area rug and tickled him. "I'll take over for a while so Uncle Gerard can go talk to Uncle Joel."

Gerard left the room. A few minutes later the kitchen door opened and closed. Then all was quiet.

I could barely focus on Hannah's stories of the beach. All I could do was pray Melissa hadn't been anywhere near Cupid's Creek this morning.

33

I did whatever was necessary to entertain the two little ones the rest of the morning, short of balancing on my head. By eleven, Hannah was whining for food and Andrew was demanding it. I hauled them into the kitchen. Andrew decimated some saltines while Hannah made designs with a pile of Cheerios. I boiled hot dogs and noodles, glancing out the window a million times, wondering what the crowd on the lawn could be discussing. At some point, Brad, Officer Segerstrom, and my grandfather had shown up to chat with Joel and Gerard. Samantha rolled in with her trusty VW and joined the group.

About 11:30 the clan broke up. Sam was the first in the house.

"Tish." She grabbed my arm and pulled me out of earshot of the young Belmonts. "Can you believe Drake's dead? And that cop was asking me questions like he thought I might have done it."

I made a wry face. "Well, at least you have an alibi. I was out alone all morning."

Her eyes shifted and she looked at the floor. "Then

we're in the same boat. I thought I spotted Gill's Suburban following me on the way to work, and I took off toward Manistique. I parked the van behind some trees at a roadside park all morning. I just now got the nerve to come back." She leaned against the wall and buried her head in her palms. "I hope I still have a job."

I patted her shoulder. "Apparently, Melissa's time is unaccounted for as well. It appears we women were on a killing spree this morning. Here. Have some coffee." I crossed the room and poured her a cup. I knew from experience that it did no good to panic. The system would just have to run its course. They'd do their investigation, pick a suspect to pin it on, and the poor sap would do the time, unless evidence showed up to the contrary.

"Look at my tower, Aunt Samantha," Hannah said. The girl had layered her Cheerios one by one in a two-inch-high stack. As we oohed and aahed our approval, the whole thing toppled. "Watch me do it again," she said, undeterred. She glanced toward the doorway. "Watch this, Mom."

Melissa stood at the arch to the great room. "That's great, honey." She turned to me and Sam. "Sorry to abandon you guys. I had no energy after my walk this morning. I feel better after that nap."

Samantha and I looked at each other. Sam gave me big eyes and a nudge of her head as if to say, *Go tell her about Drake.*

I gave a swift shake of my head and a scrunch of my lips that said, *No way. You do it.*

With arms of surrender, Sam guided Melissa into the great room. Whispers. A snuffle. One good sob.

"How many Cheerios do you have, Hannah?" I said as a quick distraction from the conversation in the other room. The youngster astounded me by dividing the cereal into piles of ten and then giving me a total.

"Wow. You're so smart." I tried to devise a more complex game to occupy her attention.

Melissa and Sam came back into the room. Melissa's eyes were puffed and red. She was either sincere in her grief or a talented actress. She leaned toward her four-year-old. "Hannah, honey, Mommy has something to tell you."

The two walked out the back door. I took Andrew into the great room to play. Out the front windows, I saw mother and daughter heading toward the beach. Following slowly behind was Officer Segerstrom and Gerard. It seemed it was Melissa's turn to face the firing squad.

My heart gave a nervous plunge. What if Melissa had been the one to kill Drake? She certainly had every excuse to do the deed. But what would it ultimately benefit her if she were behind bars and strangers raised her children?

Or what about Samantha? Was she such a Good Samaritan that she would murder a man so Melissa could live safe and free?

As for me, I had neither the motive nor the gumption for the act. Besides getting the lodge to myself once more, there was no urgency to pick off Drake Belmont. I didn't even own a gun or have access to one.

But someone did.

Still, this was one case I hoped the cops left alone. Whoever murdered Drake had done a public service.

Now Melissa and her kids could get back to their lives, and there was one less drug dealer and wife beater to contaminate the community.

But somewhere deep in the back of my conscience, a thought nagged at me. Someone was playing God. And people who played God had narrow minds. There was no benevolent motive for killing Drake Belmont. Only a selfish motive. Only a dark motive.

I looked out at the beach. Gerard had taken Hannah off to build a sandcastle. Officer Segerstrom spoke with Melissa. I watched her gestures, innocent and despairing, and wondered how much fact there was in her façade and how much fiction. Perhaps Candice LeJeune had pegged Melissa correctly. Perhaps the young woman was a conniving liar. And perhaps she had us all right where she wanted us: smack dab in the middle of her murder drama, with herself as the tragic victim of abuse and Drake the deserving dead man.

I heard footsteps behind me. I turned.

"Brad. Hi." For a moment I could hardly breathe.

"How are you holding up?" he asked, bending down to pat the baby.

"Okay, I guess." I inhaled. "Did you find out anything?"

He nodded. "Yep. You, me, Melissa, Joel, and Samantha are the prime suspects. We all had motive and opportunity. But without a murder weapon or other evidence, there won't be any arrests."

"What was your supposed motive?" I asked. I had a hard time believing Brad could even be considered a suspect. He'd only just arrived in the U.P. and had no connections to the victim.

"Protecting you, apparently. Drake had threatened to burn you out for turning him in, remember? And now that you are sheltering the man's runaway wife, he had even more reason to harm you. And that's why I had no choice but to kill him before he got to you, the woman of my dreams." He gave a wink.

I smiled despite the morbid topic. "That's so romantic. But who do you think really did it?"

He threw his arms up. "Who knows? Drake lived his life like a fool. He died on your property, which makes it seem like it was one of us. But it could have had as much to do with the marijuana he was growing as anything."

I nodded. "Either way, someone did a good deed."

Brad shook his head in disagreement. "No. Murderers are capable of anything. You don't want one on the loose. Not even if it turns out to be Melissa." He stared me in the face. "Or you."

Indignation rose in my chest, even though tagging me a murderer was technically true. "Or perhaps your sister?" I shot back.

"Not even Sam."

Melissa came in. "There's my baby," she said in a chipper voice and picked up Andrew. She gave the child a kiss on the forehead. "We get to go home soon, little mister."

The two disappeared upstairs. I gave Brad a questioning look. Was it really best for everyone if the murderer was snugly behind bars?

34

Thursday came. A torrent of rain battered the roof, waking me with its drenching din. I wavered over whether to spend the day at the lodge hoping to catch a brief but wonderful moment with Brad, or to stick to my scheduled routine and visit Candice.

Downstairs, I poured a cup of coffee. I sat at the counter, watching the buzz of activity around me. Samantha had taken the day off to help Melissa with the funeral arrangements for Drake, even intervening when some of Drake's caustic family members argued on the phone about Melissa's right to handle the ceremony. Joel and Gerard both volunteered for kid duty, a job that apparently required winding the two Belmont children into a Tasmanian frenzy and then expecting them to lie down for morning naps.

By eleven o'clock, it was a no-brainer. I went to Candice's.

She seemed surprised to see me when I showed up on her doorstep.

"I thought you'd be tied up at home," she said. "Come on." Her slender figure moved to let me in.

Her makeup seemed heavier today. But as we entered the parlor, the bags beneath her eyes could not be hidden.

"How've you been this week?" I asked. "You seem a little tired."

She sighed. "A lot's happened this week. And now to top it all off with this Drake business . . . Suffice to say things are a bit stressful."

"I empathize, believe me. I can't stand the thought that I might end up back in jail for murder."

"Nonsense," Candice said with a wave of her hand. "They couldn't possibly find any proof in that respect. More likely it was something to do with drugs."

"That's what Brad said."

"Brad, huh? Did you two finally get together?"

I contemplated my relationship with the off-duty police officer before answering. "Brad's up for a visit. Which really hasn't helped matters any. He isn't sure he can believe that I didn't kill Drake."

She exhaled with indignation. "That settles it, then. He doesn't deserve you. Find someone who believes in you."

I wished it were that easy. But my record with men was a solid 0 for 2, not surprising, considering the dead bodies and unanswered questions that trailed me wherever I went.

"Thanks for the advice," I said, "but I think I'll give the guy thing a break for now. My life's a mess as it is."

Candice gestured toward a cushy chair. "Have a seat. I'll go put on the tea."

"Let me help. You're always serving me." I moved to follow her.

She hesitated, then walked to the kitchen with me close on her heels. Gray light filtered through the window over the sink, discoloring the white walls.

"I've enjoyed getting to know you these past months, Tish. I want you to know I've treasured our time together." Candice turned a dial on the stove and set the teapot on to boil.

I leaned back on the edge of the counter. "I feel the same about you. I love hearing about my mom and the great times we all had together back in the old days."

She cracked a smile. "It does seem like it all happened so long ago."

I felt the bittersweet in her voice. "Things are different now, but the two of us are still together," I said, hoping to put a pleasant twist on a depressing topic.

She looked at me with a mournful grin. "My biggest regret is that Eva and Art swept you away. I'd planned on being with you. You'd have been like the grandchild I never had."

I reached out and touched her hand. "I'm all yours now."

"But the lost years . . . Who could have known what Eva would do when your mother died? It's not so bad here, is it, Tish? We're not all evil, right?"

My grandma Amble's words floated on my memory. *"There're bad people here, Tish. Lots and lots of bad people."*

I shook my head and looked up at Candice. "No. This place is full of good people. And you're one of them."

She nodded. "Thank you." She wiped at her eyes. "I'm

just feeling a little misty today. I'm glad to know you care for me. Because I love you so very much."

On impulse, I reached out and hugged her. Just then the teapot whistled. I jumped back, heart pounding. "That scared me!"

We both laughed, the black mood broken.

She put the tea supplies on the tray. "Let's sit in the parlor. I can't stand all this gray."

She lit candles along the mantel, helping to dispel the gloom. I poured the tea, grateful to be with Candice instead of surrounded by chaos back home.

"So how is Melissa doing?" She leaned back in her chair.

I slumped against my seat. "Good. Maybe a little too good. She seems happy Drake's dead."

"Does that surprise you after what she claims to have endured?"

I stared at the swirls in the Oriental rug. "It just seems like she should be more upset. I'm worried about her."

Candice looked at me in silence. Then she spoke softly. "Do you worry that she killed Drake?"

I nodded. "Yeah. I guess I do. She was supposedly out for a walk when it happened. She could have been the one to do it."

"How would you feel if it turned out she killed him?"

I swallowed hard. "Wow. What a shock. I know she'd be justified. But murder's wrong no matter how you slice it."

Candice didn't respond.

I rushed to fill the dead air. "I mean, I thought I was

doing Grandma Amble a favor when I fed her those pills. But really I was hurting myself. And just think what will happen to Missy if she's convicted of murder. She'll lose her kids, her freedom, her future. It's just not worth it."

"What if it had been different, Tish? What if Drake had murdered Melissa? Then how would you feel?"

I didn't hesitate. "Angry. That would be so unfair. I would want Drake to be locked up for good. I'd hope those kids never had to be around him. I'd hope he was miserable for the rest of his life."

"And yet, Melissa would be dead. Nothing would change that."

"True."

"So doesn't Melissa have a right to be alive? Even if it meant Drake had to die?"

I gave a vigorous shake of my head. "It didn't have to be one or the other. They could both be alive today. Melissa should have filed for divorce like she said she was going to do. It should never have gotten to the point where murder was the only way to freedom."

"There comes a point of no return."

"I disagree. The momentum should be stopped before things ever reach that point."

"And if they are not stopped?"

"Well, then terrible things can happen."

"Like murder? Or suicide?"

Her words cut through me, opening lacerations across my heart.

"You should know better than to judge, Tish."

I knew she spoke the truth. I couldn't condemn Melissa for killing Drake. I'd also committed murder. God had forgiven me long before I'd forgiven myself. Still, I knew Melissa would have to pay for her crime as I had. I prayed the judge would be as lenient with her as mine had been with me.

"Before you think anything bad about Melissa, I want to tell you a story, Tish. A story with a very sad ending. A story of ruined lives and crushed dreams."

A yellow caution light blinked furiously in my mind. Emotional overload seemed only moments away. I stood. "I don't want to hear it, Candice. I'm sorry. I have to leave."

She reached out and grabbed my hands in a steel grip. "Sit and listen. There isn't much time."

I shrank down into the chair, submitting to the urgency in her voice.

"I was raised down the peninsula, five or so miles south of Port Silvan," Candice began. "Our house was small. Five of us in two bedrooms. Often, my brothers or my father would find their way into my bunk. But that was not to be discussed. That was not to be acknowledged. I never spoke of it after Mother explained that men were just that way and I should give it no mind."

I shuddered as she drew me into her picture.

"Indoor plumbing was a luxury my parents couldn't afford. But that was no surprise. My father was the town drunk. He'd gone to seminary as a charity case, hoping to become a priest. He claims my mother was the devil come courting, a seductress that lured him to his doom, then flaunted her pregnancy so the priests would force him to marry her. And so he punished her for her sins day after day until she was nothing but a hollow shell."

Candice spoke with a soft, singsong voice, as if she were telling a bedtime story written by the Brothers Grimm.

"So you see," she continued, "when Paul LeJeune came to the peninsula, I saw him as my savior. Yes, I knew why he was in Port Silvan. To grow marijuana. Silvan Green, they call it. The finest north of the Rio Grande. But I could close my eyes to his illegal activities if it meant a safe, clean bed and food on the table. Of course, we grew other cash crops and raised cattle as part of the farming operation. There was real dignity in being his wife."

I wanted to block my ears. I didn't want to hear anything that would make me judge Candice, not even things that had happened long ago.

She must have noticed my inner struggle. She raised her voice a fraction of a decibel. "But a few years into our marriage, times got tough. The law cracked down on marijuana growers on the peninsula. It was hard to hide the plants from helicopters. Paul got caught and did a short jail stay. He asked me to care for the plants while he served time. I barely argued with him.

"I kept things going until he got home. It was hard to put the business back in his hands. I'd done well and made good money with some new connections and growing techniques. But my personal success cut to the core of his manhood. He became abusive, beginning with mild verbal slights. It wasn't long before those slights became insults. And the insults, character assassinations.

"Then one day he hit me. But it was nothing worse than what I'd grown up with. Maybe I had it coming, like he said. So I forgave him. Another day, it happened again. I let it go. Once, he slapped me on the face so hard, I spit blood. But I turned the other cheek, like any good Christian. And he hit that one too.

"Time went on and he'd driven me back to the kitchen like a proper wife. I took up photography to give myself something to do. One day it occurred to me to start documenting Paul's activities. Maybe I'd become dissatisfied. Maybe I was bored. Maybe I was getting a conscience. Maybe I wanted revenge. Whatever it was, I secretly snapped photos of the crops, the trades, the dealers, the drop-offs, the pick-ups. I had the goods on an entire drug network. And one day, I ran. I'd heard your grandfather gave shelter to battered women. So, up the steps of his lake home and into his arms I went.

"He fell in love with me, and I with him. But my marriage to Paul would always be there, keeping us apart. Your grandfather begged me to divorce. But with the beliefs my parents had drilled into me from birth, my marriage was an irreversible mistake that God required me to live with no matter the cost to my soul.

"One day, I went back to my house. I can't remember why. I wanted to get some things I left behind on my first escape. Paul was there. He was in the garage, putting seeds into soil and setting up heat lamps. Sid was there too, helping him. Paul saw me and followed me to the bedroom.

"'Whore,' he said." Candice's voice dropped eerily low to mimic her husband. "'Did you come to steal from me to pad your love nest?' I didn't answer him. That made him angrier. He grabbed my arm."

Candice's face twisted with hate as she relived the scene. "'You filthy, low-life slut.' He'd been drinking. I could smell it on his breath. 'You don't deserve to live.'

"He wrestled me to the floor. I screamed the whole time, right up until the stockings he'd pulled from my dresser drawer were tight around my neck and I couldn't breathe. I think I passed out. When I opened my eyes, Sid was slapping my cheeks trying to get me to wake up. Paul was groaning over on the floor and holding his face. Sid had punched him to get him off me.

"'Thank you, Sid,' I said to him. 'You can go now.'

"'You sure you're going to be okay?' He was so polite and kind. I nodded yes. Then Sid left the room. I took out the pistol that I kept in my top drawer. You never know when a drug deal might go bad. I loaded it. Then I pointed it at Paul. He looked at me and started laughing. 'You crazy wench. I'm going to kill you.'

"'Kill me if you can,' I said. Then I pulled the trigger."

My hands gripped the arms of the chair. I felt as if I had been in the room with Candice. As if I'd witnessed the chilling death of her husband. Great desperate gulps of air supplied oxygen while I looked for the nearest exit. "I have to go. I have to go. Don't tell me any more." I staggered toward the front door.

She stood and came after me. "Please, Tish. Hear me out. This isn't a story about me. It's a story about Melissa."

I stopped and closed my eyes. "I don't want to hear it, Candice. I don't want the burden. I don't want the responsibility."

"Let me tell you. You'll feel better about Melissa once you know."

35

I walked on weak legs back to my seat. I clasped my hands firmly in front of me and sat down. "Whatever you're going to tell me is just hearsay," I said, hoping I could convince myself and any court of law. "It's nothing more than gossip. You made it up, for all I know."

"If that makes you feel better," Candice said.

She settled into her seat, ready to tell the rest of her morbid tale. I couldn't bear to hear the inevitable story of Melissa killing Drake in order to save her own life. And yet I adjusted to ease the crick in my neck as Candice continued.

"When he heard the gunshot, Sid came back in the bedroom. I don't know what came over me. I thought he'd try to hurt me when he saw what I'd done to Paul. So I shot Sid too. It was awful. I hadn't meant to do it. I guess some self-preservation instinct came over me. Now, of course, I had to hide what I'd done. So I dragged the bodies to the garage and set the place on fire. I went back to your grandfather's house. I showered, then cooked supper. We had a wonderful last meal together. But I knew he could never love me after what I'd done. So later, when we heard the news, I pretended to be angry with him for setting the fire. I left in a rage. In the end, the investigators called the whole thing a botched drug deal. And that was that."

I watched her thin fingers move delicately with the story. My emotions wavered somewhere between sympathy and contempt. If her goal was to make me empathize with Melissa's deed by telling me her own sordid experience, I wasn't sure she'd found success.

"I spent many long, lonely years after that, Tish," Candice said. "I was in agony over my actions. I'd broken my own heart. It is a life I would never wish on anyone." Her voice dropped to a whisper. "That's why when I heard Drake was out of jail, I arranged to meet him in the grove. I shot Drake so that Melissa could live."

I gulped and gasped and sputtered and spewed, sitting up in my chair in case the vomit rising in my esophagus should decide to erupt. Candice killed Drake? A couple minutes passed before I could see straight. Now, with indignation exhausted, I sat mute, shaking my head.

"Don't judge me too harshly, Tish." She reached her hands forward, palms up, as she pleaded her case. "It was done only out of my great love for you and the hope that your friend would have a better life than I."

"What am I supposed to do now, Candice? You tell me this stuff and . . . what? Am I supposed to keep quiet?"

"I trust you'll do what's right, whatever you decide." She stood and picked up a black box from the floor near the fireplace.

A spasm of fear came over me. I wondered if she felt the need to kill me too now that I knew her secret.

292

"I'm glad you came today," she said. She held the box out to me. It was the size and shape for storing photos. "This is for your grandfather. Would you please see that he gets it?"

"Why don't you give it to him yourself? I'm sure he'd like to hear the story from you."

Candice shook her head. "Things are already snowballing, I'm afraid. I have to leave today. I'm going to be doing some traveling. Canada, I think." She shoved the box into my arms. "There are a lot of things to put to rights before death comes calling. Please see that your grandfather gets this." She tapped a finger on the box, then reached up and clasped my face in her hands. "I love you, Tish." She kissed my forehead, then turned and left the room.

I looked at the box sitting on the passenger seat. A few errant raindrops had spattered the top like tears. I could barely fathom what Candice had done. It was a relief to know my grandfather hadn't had anything to do with that fire so long ago, but now I was in anguish trying to figure out my own course of action. In this case, perhaps it would have been better to let sleeping dogs lie. I certainly did not want the duty that came with the information now swimming in my head.

I turned down my drive. The multitude of potholes reminded me that the road was due to be graded, along with a million other things that still needed to be done. I pulled up to the house. Sam's VW was missing, along with Joel's car. I sandwiched my vehicle between Gerard's truck and Brad's SUV. I took a deep breath and got out.

Brad stepped off the back deck. I watched him come my way bringing the warm body I longed to hold, the lips I wanted to kiss, the eyes I could get lost in.

"How are you?" he asked.

I walked around to the passenger door and took out the black box. I blinked against the light rain. "My life just keeps getting better and better."

He slammed the car door for me and followed me inside. I set the box on the counter. I turned toward the noise in the great room. Hannah rode past on Gerard's shoulders, whooping and screaming in glee. I couldn't help but smile at the pair despite the gruesome knowledge tucked in my brain.

I crossed my arms and leaned against the edge of the counter. "So where's the rest of the crew?" I asked.

Brad crossed his arms and leaned next to me. "Samantha took Melissa to town. They have to pick out a casket and handle some other details."

I nodded. "How is Melissa taking all this?"

"It's like she won the lottery."

"Oh." If I hadn't known the true assailant, I would have suspected Melissa's guilt even more.

"A little strange, don't you think?" Brad said.

I shrugged. "Drake threatened to kill her. I guess she's just excited someone got to Drake before Drake got to her." I stared at the dirty dishes on the sink. If I told Brad what Candice had told me, he'd know the right thing to do. I opened my mouth.

Brad intercepted. "What do you know about your cousin Joel? Sam really seems to like him. But he has a pretty lame alibi for yesterday morning. Says he went for a drive."

294

"Joel? He's a great guy. And he can cook. What are you getting at?"

"I think him and his brother, maybe even your grandfather, are involved in off-limit activities. It's more intuition than anything. Makes me wonder if one of them had something to do with Drake's death."

I gave a vigorous shake of my head, ready to defend the only family I had. "No. Couldn't be. My grandfather does investigations on the side. Maybe Joel and Gerard help him out. I'm sure there's nothing illegal going on." A rerun of the day in the woods with Gerard trading drugs with the camo-dude plagued my mind.

"Something doesn't add up. I just can't put my finger on it." He scooted closer to me. "But enough about them. How about us, Tish?" He tipped his forehead against mine. "Are you interested in giving it a go?"

I choked on saliva. This week I found a dead body, discovered my friend was the murderer, and saw Brad for the first time in forever. And he wanted to know if I was ready to dive back into a relationship?

"Umm, yeah. Sure. Why not?" I said.

"Okay. I guess that's a yes." He slid his arm around my shoulder. "I can't believe how much I've missed you. I was pretty lonely when you left. I got up here as quick as I could."

"That's right. The trials. How did those go?"

"Guilty. Both of them. Fraud, concealing evidence, murder one, you name it."

My eyes went back to the array of plates and glasses strewn across my normally clean sink. It was hard to accept that I'd been such a poor judge of character with that hunky Brit who'd lived two doors down from me in Rawlings. But enough time had passed that I could forgive myself and allow a fresh start.

Brad's bicep rested across my back. His hand draped loosely around my upper arm. His guy scent wafted my way. The air was filled with the male pheromones that make women do and say stupid things simply so they can breathe in more male pheromones. It was like an addiction. But I didn't care. I rolled against his body and basked in the amazing feel of him. Softness and warmth as I nuzzled my face against his chest. Strength and security as he wrapped his arms around me. How could I have held a grudge against this? What form of self-hatred had made me walk away from Brad in the first place? From now on I vowed to be humble, the first to reach out, the first to offer forgiveness. Whatever it took to make it work this time.

"I love you, Tish."

The words cascaded over me like a fountain of sweet, warm life.

I gripped him more tightly and looked up into his eyes. "I love you too." It was strange to hear the words come from my lips. What did I know about loving a man, or any person? But for once I trusted myself. I believed myself. I spoke the truth, with all the accuracy of the moment.

He crushed me in his arms. His deep laughter sang in my ears and I laughed with him.

"I've been thinking about it and this is what we can do." He set me back from him, serious once more. "You come back to Rawlings with me."

I stiffened in his grip.

"Just listen. We'll keep this place as our summer home, but in the meantime, I'll apply for a position in this area. When the right offer comes along, we'll move up here. You can use the money from the sale of my house in Rawlings to renovate something nearby."

I smiled. He'd overcome every obstacle with his suggestion. "But," I squeezed his biceps, "your house belonged to your grandmother. I'm sure you don't want to part with it."

"Let me be the judge of that."

I rubbed my lips together. He would really sell the family homestead to be with me? The gesture certainly showed his willingness to commit to our relationship. And what had I done? What conciliations had I made? His plan required nothing of me, except to accompany him back to Rawlings.

It was a beautiful plan.

"So I guess there's something you want to ask me, huh?" I said, looking into his eyes.

"Yes there is." His fingers squeezed mine. "But I want to do it right. Take a drive with me to Escanaba tomorrow. Please?"

I nodded and smiled a big yes.

"Okay," he said. "I've got to get back down to your grandfather's. I promised I'd help him in the barn."

I watched him drive off. A random tune escaped my lips as I headed upstairs. I shut my bedroom door and jumped, landing on my back on the bed. What a wonderful day this had turned out to be. So what if Candice had done a terrible thing a quarter century ago? It wasn't my place to tell on her. And as for her more recent crime . . .

well, the cops could do their job and arrest Candice if they felt like it. As for me, I gave myself a giddy squeeze. I think I'd just been proposed to. And not by some con-man seeking to use me for his own gain, but by a wonderful, gentle, caring, loving—my list of modifiers could have gone on and on—man who I was going to get to spend the rest of my life with. I was about to get the very thing I longed for, and nothing could stand in the way of it. I giggled and stared into space, imagining the ceremony, the guests, the honeymoon. I dozed off somewhere between the airport and the Fiji Islands.

36

It was still daylight when I woke from my nap. Downstairs Gerard snoozed on the sofa. Andrew slept across his chest. A combination of rumbles and wheezes came from the sleeping giant and his tiny ward. Where were Samantha and Missy? And who was in charge of Hannah? I stepped into the kitchen and gasped at the sight.

Hannah had found the black box I'd left down there earlier. Photos were strewn across the countertop where she'd made rows and columns and piles.

"Hi, Aunt Tish," she said. "What is this a picture of?" She held out a 4x6 print.

I took it from her and stared at what looked like a kitchen science project. Bunsen burner–type stuff and tubing formed some kind of contraption photographed inside an old camper or trailer. I flipped the image over and read the label on the back, written in tidy handwriting. METH LAB/HIAWATHA NATIONAL FOREST. A row of numbers and letters looked like GPS coordinates.

"Just somebody's dirty kitchen," I said to answer Hannah's question, hoping she wouldn't require more detail. I picked up another photo. Two men, one holding a clear

plastic baggie containing white stuff. I didn't flip it over to see the details. I threw it on the counter with the other pictures and with a sweep of my arms gathered the photos into a messy heap and stuffed them as best I could back into the box. "Sorry, Hannah. These aren't toys. Try these playing cards instead." I found a pack in my drawer of inherited junk and tossed them on the counter.

I carted the collection of drug art up to my room.

Candice wanted my grandfather to have the assortment because he would know what to do with the information revealed. But now more than ever, I wished she'd given the box to him personally. I scratched at my forehead. Somehow having the photos in my possession made me imagine a yellow, red, and blue bull's-eye between my brows.

I flipped the lock on the bedroom door. I sat on the bed with the box and stacked the photos in neat succession so I could fit the lid on. A series near the back caught my attention. I stared at the scene—the youthful face of my mother sitting at a round table with a man who looked remarkably like my dark-haired cousin Gerard. Could it be my father? Neither looked at the camera, but rather, at each other, seemingly unaware of the photographer's presence. The setting seemed to be a bar of some sort. The walls were filled with beer advertisements disguised as décor. A sign with an arrow said RESTROOMS. My hand started to shake. It was the scene that Homer Johnson had described, of the night my mother had died. Who had taken the picture? Candice? But she'd said she hadn't been there. I flipped through the stack and found a pic-

300

ture of a twenty-some-year-younger-looking Homer and his buddy, Cody Baker. They stood in a corner of a bar by a window, near an entry door. The same round tables and tacky décor from the picture of my parents placed them at the same scene. Were Johnson and Baker the men from the past that my father had been afraid to confront that night? If so, maybe they'd lied about not being at the scene of my mother's crash.

Another shot showed a fuzzy view of the back end of a truck. Circles of light, like spotlights, illuminated the vehicle. Rescue workers wearing longish coats covered with reflective tape hovered around the wreck.

I slammed the picture facedown on the quilt. My mother's Ford. I tried to breathe. I flipped to the next shot. The profile of a crowd gazing at some sight on the ground below. In the foreground was a twisted and broken guardrail. Perhaps the spectators stood on the edge of a quarry and looked with horror or curiosity at the sight of a truck that had just crashed to the bottom. I squinted, recognizing the Johnson/Baker duo in the mix.

What did all of it mean? I stuck the last stack in the rear of the box, fit the lid, and set it on the floor beneath the window, next to the one Candice had given me earlier—the box with the photos of me and Mom and our short years together.

I opened my cell phone and dialed Candice's number. Endless ringing. Of course. She had caller ID and wasn't about to answer. Though she'd said she would be going away—Canada, wasn't it? Perhaps she'd already left.

Brad would know what to do. I craned for a peek out

301

the bedroom window, kicking the photo boxes aside to get a better view. Brad's vehicle was missing. He must still be down at Puppa's barn.

I scooped up the photo box nearest the wall and headed downstairs. The mix of voices indicated the women had returned. I stopped in the archway. Samantha and Missy worked at putting a meal together. Hannah did card tricks at the counter. Gerard was awake and leaning back against the sink with Andrew clinging to one hip. The sight seemed incongruent with my former impressions of the man. Yet over the weeks he'd become increasingly more comfortable with the Mr. Mom thing. Now he looked like a natural.

"Hey, Tish." Samantha glanced at me in between measuring flour and dumping it in a bowl.

"Hey." I gripped the box to my chest and headed toward the kitchen door. "I'm going to Puppa's for a while. See ya."

I scooted out before anyone could question my mission.

Just before I reached my vehicle, a voice called my name.

I turned. Melissa walked toward me.

She touched my free arm. "I just wanted to thank you for everything you've done. I didn't realize when I first talked to you back in February what a savior you'd be. Because of you, I'm safe. And my kids are safe. When I told Hannah that her daddy was dead, do you know what she said to me? 'Now he can't hurt us anymore, Mumma.' Even a four-year-old had more sense than me." She raised her brows and looked at me intently.

"Thank you. For everything." The last word dripped with meaning.

I looked at her pretty face, beaming with future hope, and realized from her tone that she thought I killed Drake. She assumed, like everyone else must, that once a murderer, always a murderer. I backed away from her, wordless, and got in the Explorer. In my rearview mirror I watched her practically skip back to the house. I turned the curve out of sight of the lodge and gunned the engine, flying through potholes and testing the durability of my shock absorbers.

I turned onto the highway, then a few minutes later veered left at the cider mill sign, turning down to Candice's house. I pounded on the front door. No answer.

"Candice?" I called, walking around to the back. The porch door hung open. I went in. Muddy feet had trekked through the place. I went from room to room, horrified at the chaos scattered throughout the once spotless farmhouse. The office had taken the brunt of it. Camera equipment, photos, and bills scattered the floor. Drawers had been pulled open and left askew. The pictures from the walls had been smashed against the desk, leaving a pile of glass and twisted frames on the carpet.

Someone had searched the place—no doubt looking for the black box. My heart thundered in my chest.

I raced toward the back door, but slowed at the sound of an approaching vehicle. I peered around the back corner of the house. It was Jim Hawley's rusty diesel. I made a snap decision and headed to his truck.

"Hey, Jim," I greeted him as if nothing were wrong.

"And how is Miss Amble today?" His posture and voice were laid back.

"Good. Are you looking for Candice?"

"Nope. She left earlier for a trip. I'm just here to shut the water off and check the locks."

"Someone got here before you, Jim. The place is a mess."

He swore under his breath. "Some people just can't let the past be past. Always got to be dredging up old stuff. Even when Candice is doing her best to make things right."

I wondered if he knew Candice had shot and killed somebody not long ago. Maybe in his mind that fell in the category of making things right. "Who do you think would do something like that?"

"Majestic, probably. Ever since you showed up around here again, he's been getting his undies all in a bundle. Candice kept trying to tell him you're no threat, but he quit listening to her when he figured out she was angling to fold up her end of the operation and turn him in." He blushed under his gray beard. "But you won't tell anyone I told you that, right?"

"Not a soul. Gotta go!" I waved and ran for my SUV. I put the pedal to the metal, narrowly missing an oncoming car as I blew onto the highway toward my grandfather's house.

Steam billowed out my ears. Candice hadn't so much lied to me as much as she'd sheltered me from a few important details, such as the fact that Frank Majestic—the man my father had turned in so long ago—also considered me a threat. It sure would have been nice to know that information before I took the box from Candice with a promise to deliver it to my grandfather. And what about her claim that she was a professional photographer? I hadn't realized she meant behind the lens of a spy-cam.

I glanced at the box of photos on the seat next to me. Candice had obviously catalogued a couple decades of incriminating evidence, including the night my mother met with my father at the Watering Hole. I wish Candice would have told me she'd been there. She must have known that Baker and Johnson were the men my dad saw waiting for him before he ran out the back door. And the two deadbeats had been at the edge of the quarry when there was nothing but taillights showing at the bottom. No wonder Homer Johnson had been so certain my mother had killed herself. He'd actually witnessed the crash and had the gall to lie about it.

I took the curve past Port Silvan. The pictures in the black box had been Candice's life insurance policy. What would happen now that they were out of her hands?

I stared at the road ahead. Why did I even care?

The lake house looked serene as ever against the blue backdrop of Silvan Bay. I parked in the circle drive, one front tire cockeyed on the curb. Inside, Great-Grandma Olivia sat on her high-back chair in the living room.

"Hi, Grandma." I gave her a kiss on the cheek. "Have you seen Puppa around?"

She looked at the box under my arm. "What's in there? A gun? Have you come to kill your old grandmother as well?"

I shook my head. "Don't be silly. I haven't killed anyone."

"That's not what I heard. It's all over town. Drake Belmont's dead and you killed him because of that Melissa woman."

I plunked onto the couch, the box of photos burning a hole in my lap. "Oh, Great-Gram. It's all just a bunch of gossip. Why do you even listen?"

"I make it my business to know what's going on in this town. The Belmonts and Russos were among the founding families. It's my duty to see that Port Silvan stays civilized."

I looked at the frail old woman. Her shoulders were hunched with the weight of her obligation.

"Grandma Olivia," I said softly, "did you overhear me telling Puppa about Melissa that day in your bedroom?"

She nodded and looked to the floor. "I knew a good girl like Melissa would never leave her husband. I made an anonymous call to the state police and told them what Drake was doing—and what he was doing to her." She played with the gold locket dangling from her neck. "I remember how hard it was to look in the mirror every morning when someone you loved was so cruel."

"Making that call must have been hard. But it gave Melissa the chance she needed to try to get her life together." I set the box of photos aside and kneeled next to her, patting her shoulder.

She clenched a fist in her lap. "I didn't know I'd start all this trouble. I just wanted to help Melissa. But then you tried to help and now you're in trouble too. First they burned down your little barn. Now Drake's dead. It's just like the time your mother tried to help Jacob. Look what happened to her." She wrung her hands in her lap. "I feel so terrible, Patricia. I know your mother didn't turn in Sid. I'm the one that made that phone call. I figured time in jail would convince him to stay out of the drugs. How was I to know Sid's drug boss would start that house fire? The police didn't even have a chance to arrest him or he'd still be alive today."

"No, Great-Gram, that fire had nothing to do with you. You aren't to blame for any of that. Okay?"

"I'll always feel responsible. And now I've put you in danger too. I should have learned."

I couldn't tell her about Candice's part in the fire and Drake's death without upsetting her more. "Listen." I took Olivia's hands in mine and looked her straight in the eye. "I'm a Belmont and Russo too." It felt good to claim my full heritage. "How about if I take over your job? If you hear of anything going wrong in this town, you tell me about it and I'll fix it. Okay? You deserve some time off."

Olivia's lip quivered. Her eyes teared up. "Yes. I think that will be okay. You handled Drake, didn't you? And that was the right thing to do. Melissa shouldn't have had to live like I had to all those years."

I hugged her from the side. "You've been so brave your whole life. You made it through so much. I'm so proud of you."

She was all tears by now and couldn't even open her eyes. She clung to my shoulder. "Thank you, Patricia."

After she calmed somewhat, I grabbed some tissue from

the dispenser on the end table and helped her dry her face. "I'm so lucky to know you." I dabbed at the deep crow's feet around her eyes. "I'd like to hear more about your life sometime. How about Thursdays we get together?"

Olivia nodded.

Then, despite the crushing urgency of the box of photos, I boiled water and made two cups of tea.

We were laughing over a horse named Sarge that once belonged to Olivia's father, when Puppa, Joel, and Brad walked into the room.

"What's going on?" I asked.

My grandfather answered. "I just got a call from Candice."

"Is she okay? I was just at her house, and—"

He cut me off. "She says you have a box that belongs to her."

"Yes. She asked me to give it to you. I have it right there." I pointed to the sofa.

Grandfather's eyes darted to the box and back to me. "Did you look through it?"

I swallowed. "That would be like opening somebody else's mail."

"We'll take it from here. You better get back to the lodge," Puppa said.

"Why? What's going on? Is Candice going to be alright?"

Brad gently steered me out the front door and to my vehicle. "I'll drop by later and fill you in. Everything's going to be okay." He dipped his head and kissed me. My lips tried to keep his as he pulled away. He slammed the door shut. "Hurry home, Tish."

37

In my rearview mirror, I watched Brad walk into the house. The newly awakened adult in me felt indignant at the treatment I'd gotten from the men, as if I weren't mature enough to handle the details regarding Candice's situation. Puppa hadn't spoken to her in years. And what did Joel and Brad even know about her? Maybe she'd lied to me, killed a few men in her life, and told me to get a new boyfriend, but we'd also had a lot of good times together. If she needed help, I should be the one to give it.

I drove up Puppa's drive toward the highway, slowing to see my gentle mare. Heaven Hill Gold grazed in green pastures by still waters, a place I hoped to land someday. I smiled with excitement. Tomorrow Brad and I would go to town, he'd pop the question, and then perhaps I'd begin to see glimpses of my own green pastures.

I pulled onto the main road. I hadn't spent as much time as I would have liked to with my pretty pony. Life always seemed to get in the way. I made a promise over my shoulder as I drove off that I'd be down to visit every day—starting tomorrow.

Back at the lodge, the gang was just finishing supper. I took the last of the chicken-and-dumpling soup and grilled myself a ham and cheese sandwich. I helped with the cleanup while Missy and Gerard took the kids for a stroll on the beach.

As I waited for the sink to fill with water, the little family of four walked past the kitchen window. Hannah swung between the two adults while Andrew roughed up Gerard's five-o'clock shadow from his perch on the man's hip.

"So when did Gerard start doing daylight duty, anyway?" I wasn't sure I cared to see the very pregnant and newly widowed Melissa looking so content with my rascal cousin.

"I think it's cute." Samantha soaked a dishcloth and wiped down the counters. "He's so good with those kids. And she seems happy when he's around, not afraid all the time like she used to be."

I scrubbed the soup pan. Missy was fortunate to have a protector, after what she'd been through. But was my cousin Gerard really a suitable candidate? She'd be going from one drug runner to another. Anyway, it seemed like a woman should know how to be content on her own, without a man around, before getting all cozy in a relationship.

I putzed around with the fry pan, coating it with bubbles. I scrubbed with a wire pad, wondering if my logic applied to my relationship with Brad as well. Had I ever been content on my own, or was I always looking for something more, something better, something to fill the empty ache within? Something Brad might or might not be able to provide?

I flipped the pan over and washed the back, distracted by a butterfly outside the window. It bobbed and swirled and dipped and jogged, apparently headed wherever the breeze blew. It seemed satisfied with its carefree existence. It had nothing to do, nowhere to go, no larger purpose in the universe. And yet, God cared for it and directed its path, however meaningless and circuitous the route appeared from my place at the window.

I picked up a towel and dried the pan. Was God directing my path too? I wondered if I could be happy going wherever the Spirit of God blew me. Could I accept the next situation and place God directed that I go, even if it was jail?

I looked over my shoulder at Samantha sweeping the floor, and realized that as much as I'd bellyached about her coming to stay with me, I'd had fun. And as much as I'd complained about Melissa and her kids hiding out at the lodge, they had really been a blessing to me. I took a deep breath, held it a moment, then exhaled fully. From that moment on, I determined to be content with my life, regardless of the circumstances. I decided I'd be grateful and thank God no matter what. With a smile on my face, I put away the pans and hummed a few bars of "Amazing Grace."

My new gratification washed over me, warm like dishwater. I said good night to Sam and went upstairs to get some early z's and rest up for my big day tomorrow. I fell asleep thanking God for everything and everyone in my life. And for all life's circumstances, just the way they were.

My cell phone rang, jolting me out of a deep sleep. I searched for the sound with my eyes closed, running my hand along the bedside table and knocking over the lamp. I got out of bed and tracked the ring tones to my jeans pocket.

I hit the receive button without looking at the caller ID. "Hello?" My voice croaked with exhaustion.

"Tish. It's Candice."

I sat on the edge of the bed. "Candice? Are you all right? Puppa—"

"Tish, listen," she interrupted with a stern voice. "Your grandfather brought me a black box tonight. But, Tish"— her voice was filled with something between desperation and urgency—"it's the wrong one. What did you do with the box I gave you?"

I scratched the back of my neck. "I brought it down to Puppa's today. I left it with him."

"Exactly. But it was the wrong one. I need the other box, Tish. It's life or death."

"What time is it, anyway?" I rifled around in my brain trying to understand the box conundrum.

"It's almost midnight. Concentrate. I need that box."

"I don't know where it is, Candice. Why did you give it to me if you needed it?" I set my lamp to rights on the bed stand and turned it on.

"Don't ask why. Don't ask why. Remember?" Her voice pleaded with me to understand something. But I had no idea what she was getting at.

My eyes burned in the lamplight. Over by the window, I spotted a black box. "Oh, sheesh. There it is. I'm sorry, Candice. I must have picked up the wrong one this afternoon."

"Please bring it to me."

"Tonight? It's kind of late."

"Yes, tonight. The box I have is filled with all the pictures of you and your mother. I'll trade you."

Candice must have figured I'd do anything to get my mother's photos back, even if it meant putting myself in harm's way. She was right. I pulled open the bedside drawer and toyed with the torn edges knifing across Beth Amble's young face.

My mind raced through the scenario before giving Candice an answer. Majestic's gang must have searched Candice's house for the convicting photos. When they didn't find them, they alerted backup, who managed to get a hold of Candice before she could slip away. That's when she called Puppa for the photos, hoping to buy her life. Puppa brought them to her, but it was the wrong batch of photos. And now, the person with the right box just happened to be the daughter of Majestic's nemesis, Jacob Russo.

"Tish. Please."

I was about to be delivered into the hands of the enemy.

"Why don't you tell me what's going on, Candice?" It was an order, not a question.

"Don't ask why. Don't ask why. Do it for me. Do it for Jellybean."

I leaned my head on my palm. Candice wouldn't lure me into a trap. Not deliberately. She must have some grand escape plan in mind. "Fine. Are you at home?"

"No. Meet me at the Watering Hole."

I swallowed. That was the bar my parents met at the night my mother died.

She gave me directions. "And come alone, Tish."

Don't go without Brad, my instincts warned. But Brad would never let me go at all. Then what would happen to Candice—and my box of prized snapshots? "Yeah. I'll see you there."

"Hurry."

The line went dead.

I picked up the box of narc photos and sorted through for the one of my mom and dad. It was the only one I had of them together, and the only picture of my dad I'd ever seen. I swiped it and a few others out of the pile and tucked the prints into the top drawer of the bedside table.

I put on jeans and a sweatshirt, brushed my hair, grabbed the black box, and tiptoed downstairs. A splash of water on my face at the kitchen sink gave me some energy until I could stop at a service station and pick up a cappuccino-to-go.

The kitchen door squeaked as I closed it. The boards on the deck practically shrieked as I crossed them. I'd never noticed the clatter before—but then I'd never had to sneak out on the sly in the middle of the night before. On the gravel, I looked back at the house. All seemed quiet. I walked to the Explorer, breathing in the cool night air. Stars blinked across every square inch of the sky, and I thanked God for the opportunity to be awake at midnight to see them.

I slammed the car door, flinching at the sound. The

engine churned and I drove off, hoping I hadn't disturbed my guests. Five minutes later I turned onto US-2 and set my cruise control at fifty-eight miles an hour.

Time crawled by. It seemed eternity passed before I hit Rapid River. An all-night station provided an opportunity for gas and a cappuccino—amaretto cherry. The delicious scent filled my nose as the froth filled my cup. I paid and left. Streetlamps lit a stretch of highway on the outskirts of Gladstone. A few miles later, I turned north where Candice had designated. The road ducked under a train viaduct. SOO LINE, it said in big white letters on the side.

The route curved up a hill. My headlights shone on a low cover of vegetation protected by a rail. In the distance beyond the barrier was a wall of white rock. I gasped. Mead Quarry. I shuddered at the black abyss that fell just past the edge of the road. Instinctively, I slowed and gripped the wheel. I relaxed at the top of the hill with the return of trees and a few scattered houses. Then it was fields and fences. Finally, a sign pointed the way to the Watering Hole.

The bar appeared in the middle of nowhere. A single light at the top of an electric pole illuminated the parking lot. The building itself looked like an old Western saloon that had seen better days. But the clientele didn't seem to mind its out-of-the-way location or its dilapidated state. The parking lot was packed with late-model trucks, sporty cars, and even a few minivans. I angled in next to a fancy Lincoln.

I turned off the engine and sat for a minute, looking at the box. Should I bring it in with me or leave it in the car? The photos made a valuable trade to that nasty drug runner. I'd scope out the place, and if something was amiss, I could use their safe location to buy time.

I opened the car door and stepped into the night. Country music drifted on the cool air, accompanied by crickets in the fields. Fireflies blinked in the darkness beyond the parking lot.

I took a deep breath for courage, then headed toward the entrance.

38

I entered the Watering Hole, the first saloon I'd ever been in, and God willing the last. A woman's voice twanged over top of the deafening music, creeping a tad sharp on the high notes. I winced to have been lucky enough to land at the Watering Hole on karaoke night.

I searched the myriad of faces sitting at the bar and gathered around tables scattered randomly throughout the building. A smallish dance floor, occupied by the shrill vocalist and a feisty drunk and his date, took up one corner.

Toward the back, a bright red exit sign glowed against the wall. Just in front of it, big letters spelled RESTROOMS. An arrow pointed off to the right. At the table directly beneath the sign, where my parents had sat together years earlier, were Puppa and Jellybean. A black box rested on the table between them.

My instinct was to rush over and embrace both of them and tell them how wonderful it was to see them together again. But I held back, searching the faces nearby at the door. A man locked eyes with me. Fear flashed down my spine. He could be one of the bad guys. He raised his

mug of beer and smiled, beckoning to me with lifted eyebrows to join him at his table. I shook my head and turned away, laughing inside at his come-on, despite my paranoia.

A hand grabbed my shoulder. I gave a mini-scream and turned. A huge biker-type dude wearing a black tee, tattoos, and a bandana grunted at me. "Three dollars."

"Pardon me?" Maybe he was just hoping for a hand-out. I couldn't imagine anyone actually paying to get into this place.

"Three dollars cover charge," he repeated and crossed his arms like an all-powerful genie.

I dug through my pockets and rounded up the required bills. He nodded the okay. I dodged in and out of bodies and chairs as I made my way over to the corner table. I plopped down in a vacant seat. Goose bumps crawled over my skin as if eyes watched secretly from every shadow.

I leaned toward them. "What's going on? Puppa, what are you doing here?"

Neither Puppa nor Candice made any sign of greeting. They must know which set of eyes behind me posed a threat.

"The box, Tish. Where is it?" Candice asked in a strangled whisper.

"Safe in the car. I didn't want to bring it in until I knew you were okay." I reached for the box of photos of me and my mother and pulled it toward me.

"Put it back." Candice's eyes grew large as if she'd spotted some threat over my shoulder.

I pushed it back to the middle. "So what's your big

plan? How are we all going to get out of here alive and still make sure your pictures get to the police?"

Puppa blinked in surprise.

"Yes, I peeked." I stared at them in expectation. Neither rushed to explain the strategy. "Please tell me we're going to get out of this alive."

"We are. As soon as you bring the other box inside." Candice nudged my grandfather.

Puppa nodded at me to comply.

"But if they take your box of photos, how are we going to make sure these guys end up in jail?"

"Things don't always work out like we expect." Puppa nodded toward the door. "Let's worry about getting out of here safely before we worry about what happens to Majestic. He'll get what he has coming."

Please God, please God, please God help us, I chanted with silent lips as I worked my way back through the crowd and out to my Explorer. *Bip bip.* The doors unlocked with a press of the remote. I looked at the box on the front seat, and wavered. Why would the drug runners let us live once they had the box in hand? We'd all seen the pictures. Left alive, we'd all be able to testify against the criminals. So really, in their eyes, we were better off dead.

That meant they probably planned to kill us once they had the photos anyway. So why give them the photos?

I dumped the contents of the box onto the passenger-side floorboards, mashing the prints under the seat. They pushed out the back and sides, but I kept stuffing until they stayed. Then I opened the glove box and took out my SUV owner's manual, a bunch of renovation shots

319

from the last house, and miscellaneous bills. I layered them in the box with the house photos on top, then pressed the lid over them.

I auto-locked the doors and headed back into the Watering Hole. I stepped through the entrance and began my march to the rear. A hand grabbed my shoulder and spun me around.

"What do you think you're doing?" the bouncer asked with a menacing face.

Busted. How had he known I'd switched out the photos?

"I, uh, I . . ." Only squeaks of fear came out of my mouth.

"It's three dollars."

I blinked. Slowly I let out my breath. He was just collecting the cover charge. I gave a smile of relief. "I just paid, remember?"

"Let me see your stamp." He held out his huge, gruff hand, just about the right size to wring my neck.

I cleared my throat. "I just paid to get in a few minutes ago. But then I had to go back to my car. I didn't realize I needed a stamp."

"That'll be three dollars." The genie-of-the-lamp-look appeared again.

"Okay." I dug through my pockets and coughed up just enough change and bills to get in for the second time.

"What's in the box?" he demanded.

"Just, um, pictures." At his look of doubt, I babbled on. "My aunt is sitting over there and I wanted to show them to her."

"Open it."

320

"What? I'm not going to open it." I gripped it to my chest.

"We have the right to search all items large enough to conceal a weapon."

I hesitated, looking around for bad guys. Nobody seemed to take particular interest in the box. I set it on a table and lifted the lid. "See? Just pictures."

He grabbed the top wad of photos and lifted them. Then he peeled back the bills to reveal the owner's manual.

"Fine. Go ahead." He nodded me in.

I scurried to put the lid back in place. I glanced up at my previous admirer, still sitting alone with his beer. He stared at the box and rubbed his chin. Then he looked in my eyes with a squinty glare.

I gasped and stumbled backward with the box in hand. I launched through the crowd and dove into the open seat across from Puppa and Candice.

I slammed the box on the table and switched it for the one with the photos of my mother. "Let's not hang around. I dumped the other photos out in my car, and that guy by the door figured it out."

Candice looked as if her eyes were going to pop from their sockets. "Then we're all dead."

Puppa jumped up. "Leave now, Patricia. Drive straight home."

"I can't just leave you guys. I'm sorry. I thought I was being clever. I'll go back out and get the photos."

Candice started toward the emergency exit. "Too late. Leave through the rear. Let's go!"

She and Puppa bailed toward the back door, as energetic as a pair of oldsters could be. A chair tangled my legs on the way out, bruising my shin.

Outside, darkness blinded me. I stumbled away from the building.

"Get home, Patricia," my grandfather shouted from the blackness.

I clutched my box of prized photos and sprinted around the back corner of the bar toward my vehicle. In a fog of slow motion, I threaded through parked cars under the glaring spotlight. Just ahead was the Explorer. I fumbled with my keys, hitting buttons at random on the remote. The car alarm sounded, the blaring *honk honk honk* marking me like an audio target.

I clawed for the door handle.

Disengage security. Insert key. Turn ignition. I talked myself through the process, calming my mind but not my nerves. I threw the car in reverse. The Explorer bucked as I shifted gears and shot onto the main road.

"Get me home, get me home, get me home," I uttered my desperate plea.

A truck pulled out of the parking lot behind me and hovered on my tail, its brights blinding in my mirrors. I squinted against the glare, accelerating to see if the vehicle would ease off. It stayed glued to my tail.

I pressed the gas to put some distance between us. I couldn't shake it.

"Back off!" My voice came out in a ragged scream.

I hung a right at the crossroads and picked up speed as I went downhill. The road made tight curves, then straightened out again. I swerved like a racecar driver on drugs, spilling into the opposite lane, overcompensating and hitting the dirt on the shoulder. I jerked back onto the pavement. Tears ran down my face as I hurled through the darkness, two circles of light my only guides.

What had I told myself just before going to bed earlier? That I would accept any circumstances God sent my way? This wasn't what I had in mind.

Suddenly, the truck behind me connected with my rear bumper. I jerked at the blow.

"Lunatic!"

The guardrail fenced my right side. Headlights came at me up the hill, confining me to my own lane.

Then in front of me, like a scene from a nightmare, loomed Mead Quarry. My headlamps stretched across the big nothingness to the wall of rock on the opposite side, bathing it in creepy half-light. My tormenter pulled into the lane next to me, his pickup crashing into the side of my SUV, thrusting me toward the guardrail.

A scream ripped my throat. I fought to keep the wheel straight, but the sheer force of the strike jolted me into the rail. The screech of grinding metal made my heart spasm.

"God help me!" I squeezed my eyes closed.

I felt the pressure leave my side of the vehicle. I snapped my eyes open to realize the truck had pulled behind me, apparently so he wouldn't get creamed by an oncoming car. I steered back onto the road.

The oncoming headlights passed by.

The truck made another slam into my rear.

I pitched forward against the steering wheel.

"Are you crazy?!"

I jerked the wheel and crossed the yellow line to the

opposite lane, now empty. A steep bluff fenced me in. On my right, the pickup pulled even with me. Then, from around the next bend, more headlights appeared, rushing toward us. I gripped the wheel, moving onto what little shoulder there was, and slammed on the brakes. The oncoming vehicle wavered toward the middle of the road, apparently confused by the double set of lights. With nowhere to turn, my pursuer veered away at the last moment, smashing with a sickening squeal through the guardrail. With uncontrollable jittering, I ground to a halt and watched in horror as taillights arced silently to the bottom of the quarry. Then came the stomach-turning crunch of metal on stone.

I hugged the steering wheel.

It could have been me. I could be dead in Mead Quarry right now.

My racing heart gradually slowed. After a minute, I stepped into the stillness and crossed the road toward the breach in the guardrail. The occupants of the other vehicle had beaten me to the edge of the quarry.

A man and woman leaned into each other, lit by the rays of an early summer moon. The man spoke into a cell phone, giving directions to the scene of the accident.

"I'm s-so sorry." I stumbled toward the couple, my vision blurring as tears threatened. "A-are you okay?"

"We are"—the man pointed into the quarry—"but they weren't so lucky."

I recognized that voice.

"Brad?"

The man turned. "Tish? Are you alright? What were you trying to do? You could have been killed."

324

Brad held me up as I grabbed onto him, sobbing on his shoulder.

"They tried to kill me. Just like my mother."

"Shh." He kissed the top of my head. "It's going to be okay."

Samantha scooted over and wrapped us in an embrace.

I leaned into the two of them. "What are you guys doing here? How did you know where to find me?"

I felt Brad's rumbly voice against my ear. "Your grandfather phoned me after he brought Candice the wrong box. Wanted me to get a hold of the right one and deliver it." Fingers smoothed my hair. "But I guess Candice insisted on calling you next. Said it would be quicker. He tried to stop her, but she pulled a gun on him." A kiss to my temple. "In the meantime, I'd driven up to the lodge to intercept you, but you were already gone." Brad gave a quiet chuckle. "I made Sam come along for the rescue."

Sam gave a deep sigh. "We almost killed you instead. I'm so glad you're okay."

Brad's serious demeanor returned. "Anyway, your grandfather snuck in a call to Joel from the men's room a little later. Warned him to be on the lookout for Majestic's cronies coming to do some intercepting of their own. So Joel headed up to the lodge. Called me on his way." Brad peered into the quarry at the dimming taillights. "Looks like Joel won't have anything to worry about now."

My stomach reeled as I processed all the information. "If Candice has a gun, what's going to happen to my grandfather?"

Brad aimed my body toward his vehicle and helped

me get walking. "Joel seems to think she's harmless with a gun. Says the only thing she can shoot is a camera."

I shuddered, picturing the bullet wound dead center on Drake Belmont's forehead.

"Your grandfather is a professional. He can handle her," Brad was saying. "And Majestic's crew too, if it comes to that."

All I could do was pray for Puppa as Brad and Samantha settled me onto the rear bench seat of Brad's SUV.

"The police should be here any minute," Sam said. "Then we can get you back to the house."

I reached for her arm. "Hey, I need the box from the front seat of my car. And all the pictures I put on the floor, okay?"

Samantha nodded. "We'll take care of it, hon. It's okay."

"Okay." I laid down across the seat and rested my head on the leather. Within moments I was asleep, safe from my waking nightmare.

39

My soft bed thumped and I heard road noise in my ears. Oh, yeah. I was in the back of the car. I'd climbed over the seat before we crossed the Mackinac Bridge. The Mighty Mac, Gram called it. She said it wasn't even built when she was young. Back then, they had to drive their car onto a ferryboat to get downstate.

I didn't want to wake up yet. The sun had just been coming up when we crossed the bridge awhile ago. It had looked really pretty over the lake and made the water pink and gold. Looking at it made me feel better, like things weren't going to be so bad after all. But then I had started thinking about the stuff I'd never see again. Like Puppa. And Jellybean. And the horses. And my cat Peanut Butter. And my friend Anne. Probably my dad. And for sure my mom. Every time we passed one of the big wires holding up the bridge, I'd think of something else that I could never have back. And I wondered what would happen if the big wires broke and we fell into the water so far down, like what happened with my mom when she drove into that big pit.

Then I'd started to cry. Grandma didn't yell at me for

sniffling this time. And before we made it all the way across the bridge, I had lain down on the seat and looked up at the pink sky through the back window.

I must have fallen asleep, because here I was in the backseat, just opening my eyes. Only this time there were stars shining out the window. How long had we been driving, anyway?

I sat up. There were people in the seats in front of me, but it wasn't Grandma and Grandpa Amble. I rubbed my head. The years rushed past and then there I was, in the backseat of Brad's SUV with him and Sam up front.

"Wow. Was I ever sleeping. Where are we, anyway?" I asked. The highway rolled past with nothing but pine trees as landmarks.

"About halfway home," Brad said.

"What a horrible night. I can't believe that truck tried to kill me. I don't even want to picture the shape my Explorer's in."

"It'll be fine," Brad said. "I had it towed to a body shop. The other vehicle wasn't so lucky. The driver was dead at the scene. The passenger is in critical condition and on his way to Marquette."

It seemed unfair that one of the men who tried to kill me should survive the plunge to the bottom of the quarry. My mother hadn't survived. And she'd deserved to. At least I knew for sure now. Her death was no suicide. It was murder.

Brad glanced back at me. "I talked the officers at the scene into questioning you later. I hope you're up for it when we're in town this afternoon."

I sighed and nodded. A few more hours of sleep would

help take the edge off my latest trauma before I had to cough up the play-by-play.

I leaned forward between the front seats. "Are Puppa and Candice going to be okay?"

Sam and Brad looked at each other, but neither answered.

"Hey. What's going on?"

Brad kept his hands at ten and two on the steering wheel. White knuckles shone in the glow from the dash. He cleared his throat. "We searched the vicinity of the Watering Hole for your grandfather and Candice. We couldn't find them."

"What?" I gripped the seat backs. "Where could they be?"

How had I slept through all the drama? I looked at the clock on the console. 3:36 a.m.

Brad's eyes met mine in the rearview mirror. "Hopefully it means your grandfather got away."

I chewed the inside of my cheek. "What's happening, Brad?"

He sighed. "Near as I can tell, your grandfather has been working to pinpoint a major drug connection in this area. He's set a few snares, but none have been successful. Until now. I don't know how to tell you this, but everything points to your friend Candice being a main drug pin around here."

I stared at the blur of yellow lines flashing past on the highway. Assorted conversations ran through my mind. Candice's condemnation of the entire peninsula, her avoidance of my grandfather, the confession that she'd killed Paul and Sid and Drake—all seemed to uphold

Brad's accusation. But what about her reminiscences of our time with my mother, her love of horses, her gracious hospitality, her parting kiss? How did that fit in with a lifetime of drug distribution? She had admitted that she'd taken over for Paul while he was in jail, but she'd also implied that she'd gone straight somewhere along the way, hadn't she? And yet, how did one get a box full of photos of drug manufacturing locations and dealer faces if one wasn't on the inside of the trade?

It was depressing to think the accusation was true.

"Brad." Samantha said his name low and urgent. "What is this guy doing?" Her eyes were glued to the side mirror.

Brad looked in his rearview. "Hang on."

I turned around. Headlights glared through the back window, close to our rear bumper. I held up a hand to shield my eyes. Brad sped up. The vehicle stuck with us.

"Here we go again." I sat back and tightened my safety belt.

Brad switched lanes, so did the other car. Brad slowed, the other car slowed. Brad floored it, the other driver mimicked him.

"Oh, I don't believe it," Samantha said, bracing herself against the dash.

"What?" Brad asked.

"It's Gill. I'm pretty sure it's Gill."

Sam's ex-husband drove a white, rusted-out Suburban, the one I'd seen leaving my driveway awhile back. As we passed the yard light of a rural home, the vehicle behind us shone pearly white.

"What are we going to do?" My heart raced with this latest threat.

"Like I said, hang on." Brad stepped on the gas, kicking his new-model SUV into overdrive. He floored it down the highway. The white Suburban fell behind, but stayed in sight. We flew past Hilltop Grocery and a few minutes later, Ed's Bar.

"Brad, I can't take this." I hadn't yet recovered from the high-speed chase earlier that evening. "Please slow down." I held my stomach, sure that the next jolt of the car would force me to stick my head out the window.

"It's okay, Brad," Samantha kicked in. "He's not really going to hurt us. He just likes to put on a show."

Brad lifted his foot a notch. The SUV slowed to just under break-neck speed. "I'd rather not take any chances where Gill's involved."

"Come on. You know he's all hot air." Samantha put her hand on the crook of Brad's elbow.

"Would I have sent you up here if I thought Gill was just hot air?" the older of the two siblings asked.

Sam conceded by crossing her arms and giving a big sigh.

"Fine." Brad stepped on the brakes. "You know what? Let's just see what he's full of. Let's settle this once and for all." The car slowed to fifty-five.

Behind us, Gill raced ahead, closing the gap within seconds. The Suburban pulled into the opposite lane until the passenger door was even with Brad's. Gill rolled down his window and gestured for Brad to do the same.

Brad complied. Samantha leaned forward for a full

view of her ex-husband. The two men maneuvered the vehicles to keep them from colliding.

"Samantha, baby," Gill shouted from his vehicle. "I'm sorry. Come home."

"It's over, Gill. It's been over for years. Quit following me." Her voice was sucked out the window as she yelled.

"I want you back." Gill's vehicle veered toward ours. "I'll do anything." He jerked the wheel and took it back to a safe distance. "Let's work things out."

"No. It's over. Leave me alone."

"Had enough, sis?" Brad asked Samantha.

She nodded.

Brad braked, letting Gill get ahead of us and back in the correct lane. Gill slowed and pulled his car to the shoulder. Brad parked behind him, leaving the engine running and the headlights on high beam.

"Don't get out. Lock the doors behind me." Brad stepped from the vehicle.

"Are you crazy?" Samantha asked. "What if he's got a gun?"

Brad patted under his arm. "So do I. Besides. He's all hot air, right?"

I jumped on Sam's bandwagon. "Let's just call the police and let them take care of it. Don't do anything foolish," I pleaded.

"I am the police." He slammed the car door and walked toward Gill's vehicle.

My macho cop boyfriend was about to get his Achilles' heel crushed. "Sam, do something. He's going to get hurt."

"Sit tight. He must know what he's doing." Sam didn't sound so sure herself.

"I'm calling the police." I flipped open my cell phone and dialed 9-1-1. NO SIGNAL, came the response. Why did Brad have to confront Gill smack in the middle of nowhere?

I watched with my heart in my throat as Brad approached Gill's rolled-down window. They talked for a minute, then Brad gestured with his finger for Gill to get out of the car.

Trepidation washed over me as Gill stepped out, chest puffed like a fighting cock, and rolled up his flannel sleeves. Brad pointed to the grassy shoulder. The two men walked to the shallow ditch, their huge shadows blacking out the space behind them. They took up aggressive poses, paused five seconds, then lit into each other.

40

Inside the car, Sam and I had our noses glued to the glass.

Brad made fists and did some fancy footwork. Gill danced around him making half swings. Then he lunged. Brad dodged the attack. Gill landed on his face in the grass. He stood and brushed off. They went at it again.

"This is nuts." I couldn't take the thought of Brad bleeding. The whole idea twisted my guts. So what was I doing dating a cop? I wanted to jump out of the car and separate the two ruffians.

I looked at Sam. In the backwash of headlights, a tear glinted on its way down her cheek.

"Oh, Sam." I reached over the seat and touched her shoulder. "You must feel terrible about this."

She shook her head. "No. I feel lucky."

"Why lucky?" I couldn't grasp her logic.

"Lucky to have a brother like Brad. Look at him out there, defending my freedom."

Brad was a protector. A defender. I bit my lip. It was enough to bring tears to my own eyes. I was the lucky one.

Brad ducked a punch, then lunged, taking Gill to the ground. The two grappled on the slope, nothing but black blobs rolling and tossing in the beams. Then Gill was facedown with his arms twisted behind his back. Brad bent close to Gill's ear and said something. Then he got up and brushed off. Gill stayed in the ditch while Brad walked back to the car. He got in, put the car in gear, and drove in silence.

"Well," Sam said. "What'd you say to him?"

Brad gave a smirk. "I told him your new boyfriend eats dweebs like him for breakfast and he was lucky it was me in the ditch with him."

"Do you think that's going to work? I don't even have a boyfriend." Sam sounded distraught.

He reached over and gave her a playful noogie. "Come on, sis. You think I don't know about Joel?"

Sam pouted in her seat.

"And," Brad said, his hand on her arm, "I approve. After getting to know Joel and Bernard Russo, I've decided they are the best sort of men. You're in good hands. Joel definitely comes from a good family."

Brad's sparkling eyes met mine in the rearview mirror.

I snuggled back in my seat, my stomach at rest for the moment. We drove the last ten minutes to the lodge in silence.

By the time we reached my road, the bare light of dawn cracked on the horizon. Brad parked next to Gerard's truck and Joel's car. He turned off the engine and just sat there.

"Hey. Are you okay?" I leaned forward and rubbed

his back. His neck muscles felt like clenched fists under my fingers.

"Yeah. I'm fine."

Samantha opened her door. "Are you guys coming in?"

"Give us a minute." Brad sounded as weary as I felt.

"Well, I'm hitting the sack," Sam said.

The passenger door closed and Sam walked toward the house.

"What's up?" I asked in the cushy quiet of the SUV.

He sighed. "Tish. There's more to the story than you realize."

"What story? Sam and Gill's?"

"No. Yours." He twisted in his seat until he faced me. "You can't stay here."

"What? Why?" Not stay at my own home? Maybe he thought I'd be safer down at the lake house.

He took my hand and held it to his lips. The heat lingered against my skin. "I don't know how to say it any other way. You were raised in hiding for a reason. Now that you're back, you're in more danger than ever."

"Then timing couldn't be more perfect for me to close things up here, then meet you downstate, just like we planned." I squeezed his hand in mine.

"Listen to me. Maybe your friend Candice was trying to go clean," he said. "But her timing couldn't have been worse. From what your grandfather told me on the phone, those photos contain evidence that puts a very big player in a really tight spot. The guy already has something against you because of your dad. Those pictures put you in an even touchier situation." He pulled my head toward his until our foreheads gently bumped. "I can't take any chances. Tish, I love you. I don't want to lose you."

"So, what do you think I should do?"

He patted the front seat. "Come sit up here."

I stuck my legs out over the console and squeezed between the seats until I was next to him.

He leaned toward me and looked in my eyes. "Yes. I want you to come back downstate with me. But it's not that simple. There are people that would kill you because of who and what you know. You're not even safe with me."

"This is ridiculous. I didn't ask for this."

"Shh." He put a finger over my lips. "There is a place you can be safe. It's out of the way. And as long as you don't try to contact anyone back here, they'll never think to look for you there. You could have a quiet, safe life until this whole thing washes over."

I pulled away from him and leaned against the passenger door. "I am not going into hiding again. I spent my whole life hiding from reality and didn't even know it. I'm done. Whoever wants me can come and get me. I'm going to face them head on. Just like you did with Gill. That's the only way to get my life back—the life that was stolen from me when I was eight years old."

"Trust me, Tish. If I thought we could beat these guys by taking a stand, we'd do it. But it's a huge network of dealers, suppliers, and transporters all across the state. We don't know who half of them are. A lot of lifestyles are on the line. And people are willing to kill over it. You know that better than anyone."

"Up here I'm a big nobody, Brad. So I saw a couple photos in a box. I'll just give the pictures back and forget I ever saw them. The cops could hypnotize me and I still couldn't identify any of the bad guys."

"You don't have the pictures anymore. I turned them over to the state cops at the scene. They're the ones that recommended you lay low until the investigation is wrapped up. Leave the area for a few months and then you can come back to Michigan."

"What do you mean come back to Michigan? Where were you thinking I'd go?"

"An old mentor of mine lives out in California. A little town called Del Gloria, along the coast. He's got a house that needs some fixing. He said he'd put you up in exchange for renovations."

I crossed my arms. "That's bold of you to make all these arrangements without consulting me first."

"It's about staying alive, Tish. I thought you might be interested in doing that, even if it means swallowing your pride for once."

"I just don't get it. How can I be a threat to anyone?"

"I don't understand the whole thing either. Your grandfather tried to explain as best he could, but I still don't know how everything fits together. There's some vendetta against your dad that puts you in danger. Your mom died because of it. And Candice's poor timing makes things even worse. She should never have involved you in this."

"I couldn't agree more. But I live in peace and quiet out here. They'll forget about me soon enough, when they see I'm no threat."

Brad's head dropped as he shook it. "Your thinking is so naïve." He raised his eyes and looked at me. "Luckily, that's one of the things I love best about you." He took a folded slip of paper out of his pocket. "Listen, I know you don't like anybody telling you what to do, but here's the name and phone number of that safe place to land. Don't lose it. After you go, don't contact anyone back here. I'll get a hold of you when it's safe to come home."

The whole idea seemed insane. I took the slip with reluctant fingers. I opened it and read Brad's neat, legible writing. Denton Braddock, it said, along with a phone number with an unfamiliar area code.

"Fine." I tucked the note in my jeans. "But only in case of emergency. I just got started on this place. There's still a ton of work to be done."

"Hey. That's what your family is for. They'll handle things while you're away."

"Brad, this is nuts. I'm not going anywhere, unless it's downstate with you. I don't even have the photos anymore."

"Come here, Tish." His voice was low and soothing. He pulled me to him. I buried my face in his neck and submerged myself in his comforting heat and mellow scent. I loved him. Of that I had no doubt. But that didn't mean he could take over my life and order me around. How did he know what was best for me, anyway? It was my journey. My story. If I wanted to hire a bodyguard and hole up in the woods until I got my projects done, why shouldn't I be able to? In fact—my muscles tensed at the thought—why didn't Brad just stay up here right now? If he cared so much, we could go to town tomorrow, get married, and live at my house. What made his plan the Holy Writ, anyway?

He rubbed his palm against my back. I relaxed into him. Then again, what kind of woman got mad at a man for trying to have her best interests in mind?

I sighed and pushed back until I could see his face. "I need at least eight hours of sleep before I can even think straight." I gave him a peck on the lips and reached for the door handle. "Thanks for saving my life. Call me later."

"Hang on. I'll walk you in." He scrambled to catch up with me.

I slowed and we walked up the porch steps together. He reached for the knob first and held the door open for me.

"How about a cup of coffee?" I stepped inside.

"Nah. I'm going to get back to the lake house. I'm hoping to catch up to your grandfather and figure out the missing pieces of the puzzle. Joel and Gerard are here." He nodded toward their cars parked in the driveway. "You should be safe for now."

"Okeydoke, then. I guess I'll see you this afternoon. You are still planning to take me to town later, right?" With my eyelids dragging on the floor, even the thought of choosing an engagement ring barely perked me up.

He took me by the shoulders. "You know I am. What's the date? May twenty-fifth? This is the day I'll ask the most important question of my life." He gave me a puppy-dog look that made me laugh. "You are going to say yes, aren't you?"

I wagged a finger at him. "Uh, uh, uh. That's cheating. You'll just have to wait and see."

He smiled and gave me a sleepy, lingering kiss. "Get some rest, Tish. I'll call you later."

"Night." I hugged myself and watched him walk back to his car. He turned and winked at me. I gave him an air kiss, then closed the door.

The house was quiet, though not for long with six a.m. quickly approaching. I wondered how Melissa and her kids would hold up later today, with Drake's funeral scheduled to take up the better part of it. Hoping to avoid a drug dealer convention, Melissa had arranged for the service and burial to be limited to close family members. I made no plans to attend, at Missy's suggestion.

The light over the stove lit the room with a faint glow. Someone had left a lamp on in the great room as well. Obviously they weren't the ones paying the electric bill around here.

I downed a glass of water, flicked off the stove light, then headed toward bed.

I stopped under the arch to the great room, rooted to the floor at the sight in front of me. It took me a few seconds of dumbfounded, heart-racing silence to figure out what I was looking at. Samantha and Melissa sat next to each other on the sofa against the far wall. Joel and Gerard lay prone on the floor, with their hands behind their necks. And holding pistols pointed at the women were Drake's buddy Stick and some skuzzball associate.

"'Bout time you joined us," Stick said, waving his gun my way.

41

The stout Stick gestured with his pistol toward Sam and Missy on the sofa.

"Go visit your girlfriends." His cue-ball head and goatee gave him the look of an Asian monk. All that was missing was the long robe to cover his holey jeans.

His sidekick was even scruffier.

"Welcome home, Patricia Russo," Stick's scrawny companion said in a voice that slithered down my spine. Black hair jolted from his head in random tufts. The short sleeves of his black T-shirt covered most of the tattoo on his left arm. He wore low-slung pants that showed the top of his underwear. I prayed his belt would spare us from an even more horrifying glimpse of his Hanes.

"Hey," I said with false bravado, "if you're going to break into somebody's house, you ought to get her name straight." I sat on one end of the couch and clasped Samantha's clammy hand. "The name is Patricia *Amble*."

A smile curled across Stick's chubby cheeks. "Let's give Jacob Russo some credit. He might have screwed up royally in his life, but at least he provided a daughter for collateral."

342

"What's my dad got to do with this, anyway? He hasn't been around in thirty-three years."

Stick leaned close to my face. A smell beyond morning breath gagged me. "Ever heard of a grudge? We take them seriously around here."

"What, did my dad steal your lollipop from you when you were a baby? You don't look old enough to hold a grudge for more than thirty years." The guy couldn't be a day over thirty-five himself.

"It ain't my grudge. I just get the honor of ending it. And, it will be pure justice to snuff out the woman that snuffed out Drake."

"You're going to kill five people to make up for one death?"

Upstairs, baby Andrew chose that moment to cry, flinging wails of desperation down the stairs and to his mother, at the other end of the couch.

Missy wrung her hands. "I've got to go to him. I'm sure he needs a diaper. And he'll be hungry."

Stick glanced down at Joel and Gerard cooperating peacefully on the floor. Gerard lifted his head a couple of inches from the floor and peered over his shoulder at Missy. His brow scrunched in concern. Stick gave the sign for his partner to go upstairs with Missy.

After the two disappeared along the second-floor hallway, the podgier man settled into the rickety upholstery opposite us. His weapon never pointed far from the general vicinity of our heads.

I crossed my arms, hoping to look tough. "So how long are we going to sit like this? What are you waiting for?" I asked my captor as I nudged closer to Samantha. Our shoulders touched and I felt a boost of courage.

"Couple things." Stick adjusted in his seat. The stubby '50s chair legs twisted under his weight. "First, I want to hear you apologize for killing my good friend." He rubbed a hand on his scalp and down over his eyes. "Drake was like a brother to me." He practically wept the words.

For a split second I felt sorry for him. But I got over it. Back in Rawlings, I had taken on a lunatic and won. There was no reason I couldn't outwit Stick. His intelligence quotient had to be far below that of the last villain I'd dealt with. And that person was now behind bars for life.

I scooted off the edge of the sofa and dropped to my knees on the floor.

Stick jerked his head up. "What are you doing?"

I started crawling toward him, contrite. "I'm so sorry for what I did to Drake. I wish I could undo it. I would never have told him to meet me there in the woods. I would never have taken that, um"—I quickly thought of a gun name—"that Colt forty-five and shot him. He was a good friend to you and I'm so sorry."

I'd crawled halfway to him. He simply stared at me. A few more feet and maybe I could wrestle that gun out of his hands . . .

"Wait a minute." He looked at me with squinty eyes. "You're telling me you shot him with a Colt forty-five? Drake would have never let you get close enough to him to shoot him between the eyes like that. You're lying to me. You must have used a rifle. He never even had a chance. He couldn't have seen you coming."

I paused and tried to think. "I'm a really fast draw."

He jutted out his chin, skeptical.

"Here," I held out my hand toward the gun. "I'll show you."

It may have been my imagination, but his gun hand nudged, as if he were actually going to pass me his weapon.

Instead, he stood up and reached the gun down to my temple. I jerked back, but he stayed with me. The tip of the pistol felt black and hot against my skull, as if its mere touch could shatter my bones. My body broke into a quiver. "I'm sorry. I'm sorry. I didn't mean anything by it." I dropped into a curled-up crouch.

Stick made the sound of a quiet gun report. "I ought to kill you right now."

"Don't even think about it," Joel threatened from his place on the floor.

"What are you going to do, Jimbob?" Stick asked with derision.

I watched his feet move Joel's way, passing close to Gerard. As quick as a cat on a mouse, Gerard grabbed Stick's ankle, tipping him off balance. I gasped and scuttled back to the couch. Sam and I huddled together, little screams coming out of our mouths, as Joel jumped up and tackled the gunman to the ground. Joel grabbed the arm with the gun and aimed the barrel away from us. Gerard stepped on Stick's hand, forcing him to release the weapon.

Just as Gerard's fingers touched the pistol, Skuzzball's slithery voice came from the balcony.

"Back off, lamewad, or I'll kill your girlfriend."

Gerard froze and looked up. I followed his gaze. Skuzzball had Melissa around the neck, his gun pointed at her head.

From the bedroom door came Hannah's cries. "Don't hurt my mom! Don't hurt my mom!"

My stomach curdled with the child's plea.

In the great room, Gerard put his hands in the air and stepped back. Joel gave Stick a final rough thrust, then stood, hands raised. Still cowering together on the couch, Sam and I lifted our hands on level with our ears.

Stick grunted as he stood and brushed himself off. He retrieved the gun. A few vigorous gestures of his weapon, and Joel and Gerard were back on the floor.

With order restored, Skuzzbag dropped his hold on Melissa. She ran back to the bedroom. I could hear her comforting Hannah.

"Okay, guys," my lip quivered almost uncontrollably, "if it's me you're after, then let them go."

Stick had a new look in his eye. A hard, cold look that sent fear coursing through me. "Nobody's going anywhere. And lucky for you, I don't feel like killing you yet." He looked at his wristwatch. "At least not right away."

I swallowed. "Great. What are you waiting for?"

"The only one who can save you, Mr. Jacob Russo."

"My dad?" I almost snorted. "Good luck with that."

"I guess we'll see how much he loves his own blood. Or maybe he doesn't care. And then it's *bang, bang, bang, bang.*" He swung his gun to point at each of us, as if we were ducks at an amusement park sideshow.

"Do you even know where my father is?" The last I'd heard, he was MIA.

346

"That's what you're going to tell us, darlin'," Stick said. He looked at his watch again. "Just a few more minutes and Frank will be here."

"Frank who?" I asked.

"Majestic," Joel interjected from his place on the floor. "We've already been over this before you got here."

"That's the trucking guy my dad turned in—how many years ago?" I was incredulous.

Stick looked up at the ceiling as he calculated. "Um, that would make it twenty-five, twenty-six years. Something like that."

"He's taking a pretty big risk just to get back at my dad."

"I'm sure he feels it's worth it. Things got a little out of control out here on the peninsula, what with Drake getting killed and Candice going clean and Melissa hiding out. Frank feels like a personal visit to the area might just knock some people back into shape. And if he can haul in your dad while he's at it, so much the better. He was pretty happy when he heard you turned up after all these years."

I gritted my teeth. "Is that why those guys tried killing me at Mead Quarry tonight? It'd be pretty hard to get an address out of a corpse. Anyway, Frank Majestic is wasting his time if he thinks I can tell him where my father is."

"He told me you'd say that. But no one's stupid enough to believe Jacob Russo hasn't had some contact with you over the years."

Nothing like thrusting in the knife and giving it a good twist. I lowered my head at his mocking words. "You're stupid if you believe he has."

Sam put a hand on my back. "Come on, Tish. It's alright. Your dad stayed away because he loved you so much. He never wanted you to have to bump into Bucko here."

I nodded, feeling a little better at her words.

"Hey," Stick looked up at the balcony, his voice bellowing through the house. "How long you gonna take up there?"

Skuzzbucket poked his head over the rail. "She's dressing the kids. We'll be right down."

A few minutes later, Melissa headed down the staircase with Andrew on one hip and Hannah clinging to her leg. They picked their way through Gerard and Joel and camped out at the other end of the sofa. Samantha squeezed Missy's hand as she settled in.

The room got quiet as we waited. Time crept along like a 5K race for inchworms. In Missy's lap, Andrew played with the string on his pacifier, as if he knew to sit still. Hannah sighed and leaned into her mother.

My head jerked up as I fought sleep. On my shoulder, I felt a gentle thud. Samantha's head tilted against me as if she was also catching some winks.

The sun was in full gear when the sound of a vehicle chimed in with the chirping of birds. The sleepy occupants of the great room rustled awake.

"Go see if that's Frank," Stick ordered.

Skuzzy got up and went in the kitchen. He came back a second later. "Yeah. It's Frank."

The back door opened and closed. A moment later a squat man wearing a forest-green polo over a potbelly and khaki slacks entered the great room. His thinning blondish hair was combed over the sparse area on the top of his head.

"Hey, Frank," Stick said.

"Grampa!" Hannah shouted and ran toward the man.

Grampa? If that guy was Frank Majestic, and he was Hannah's grandfather, that meant . . .

I turned my head in Melissa's direction. She looked at me, then cast her eyes to the floor. A blush crept over her face.

I'd been betrayed.

42

"Hey, little pumpkin head," Frank Majestic said, smiling. He lifted Hannah into his arms.

Safe in her grandfather's grip, the girl pointed to Stick and Skuzz. "Those are bad guys. They want to hurt my mom. And they're mean to Uncle Joel and Uncle Gerard."

The fifty-plus man set Hannah on the ground. He walked toward Skuzzo and slapped him on the back of the head. "What's wrong with you two, terrorizing my granddaughter? Put away those guns and be civilized."

The two henchmen tucked their weapons into their waistbands.

"Sure, Frank. Sorry, man," Stick said.

Melissa stood and walked with Andrew over to her father. "Dad, this is crazy."

I could only shake my head, stunned by Melissa's family connections.

"Get your stuff and get in the car," Frank Majestic said to his daughter, while giving Andrew a little squeeze on the cheek.

Betrayed. Deceived. Used. Backstabbed. If I'd had a thesaurus handy, I'd add fifteen more words to the list. How could Melissa pretend to be some damsel in distress, pleading for my help to escape her abusive, drug-dealing husband, when all along her father was Frank Majestic, the man ultimately responsible for my mother's death and my father's exile? My grandfather must have been aware of the connection. That's why he'd dragged his feet, looking at the situation from every angle before venturing to help Melissa. But then I'd gone and snatched her from the grocery store.

"I want you and these two creeps out of here. Now." Melissa's voice shook as she gave orders to her drug lord father.

"Melissa. Sweetheart. It ain't gonna happen. So just get in the car and I'll be out when I got what I came for." Frank's voice was slithery like Skuzzwad's.

Melissa latched onto Hannah and pulled her children back to the sofa. "We're not leaving. If you're going to hurt someone, you'll have to do it in front of your grandchildren."

"Honey, calm down. I'm not here to hurt anyone. I just need a little information, then we'll break this party up."

He walked toward me. I stiffened at his approach.

"Little Orphan Annie here is going to tell me where her daddy's hiding out." He put his hands on his hips and threw his shoulders back. I'm sure he meant to intimidate, but he ended up looking like the Jolly Green Giant.

"I'll never tell." I crossed my arms and clenched my

351

teeth. It was none of his business that I had no clue where the man responsible for half my genetic makeup hung out. Some days I imagined that he was dead like my mother, buried in a grave with JOHN DOE on the headstone, and that's why he couldn't come for me. Other days, I imagined that he'd been wrongly imprisoned in some foreign country for speaking out against the persecution of Christians. But, on days when reality struck, I admitted he was probably a drug addict wandering homeless in the streets of some city. That's why Frank Majestic could never track him down. How do you find a man that no longer exists?

Frank lunged toward me, sticking his steaming red face in mine. "Tell me where he is! Nobody messes with Frank Majestic and gets away with it." He wiped the back of his hand across his mouth.

In the corner of my eye, Melissa dropped Andrew into Samantha's lap, extracted Hannah from her leg, and stomped over to Frank. "Get out of here. Don't you talk to my friends like that."

"Melissa," Frank seethed, "get in the car with the kids. Now."

On the bright side, my father was not Frank Majestic, proof that things could always be worse. The thought tempered my anger.

Missy crossed her arms and got between us. "I'm staying here, you're leaving," she said to her father. "Nobody in this room did anything to you. Quit taking it out on them."

"I'll tell you what they did to me. They put ideas in my daughter's head. Made her think she could do things she shouldn't be doing. Then they broke down the line of trust between me and my associates. If I can't make a living in trucking, who do you think is going to support your lifestyle?"

"You don't make a living in trucking," Melissa said, "you make a living in trafficking. I don't want any part of it."

"How do you think you're going to survive? I can't support you from prison."

"I'll figure out a way."

"You? You never held a job in your life. You've got two kids with one on the way. Who do you think is going to hire you in that condition? And no man's going to look at you, you're all swelled up like a pig at auction. If you weren't my own daughter, I couldn't even stand the sight of you."

Missy's eyes watered at the cruel words. By the time Frank shut his mouth, she'd crumpled into a ball on the couch. Hannah ran her hands through her mother's hair. Samantha wrapped her arms around Missy's back, soothing her while she cried.

Frank watched his daughter's breakdown, smug satisfaction written all over his face.

Something inside me snapped. "You bully. You creep. You don't even deserve to have a daughter." I crossed to him in the center of the room and peered with eyes of accusation at his bulging features. It was hard to tell if I'd surprised him or if his high blood pressure was acting up.

He bared his teeth in his plumped-up head. "Neither does Jacob Russo. And I'll make sure he never sees you again, unless you feel like telling me where he is."

"Even if I knew, I'd never tell you. You killed my mother and you tried to kill me."

"I didn't kill your mother. The guys were just trying to get her to pull over so they could ask where Jacob had been hanging out. I guess she'd rather have died than told on him." Frank gave a chuckle. "How about you, toots? Are you going to die protecting a no-good son of a—" he looked at Hannah's big eyes watching him "—gun, or are you going to tell me where your daddy is so you can live to be a mommy some day?"

Behind Frank, a shadow moved near the archway. Somewhere in the kitchen, a floorboard squeaked. I put my hands on my hips. "Oh, I plan on living. But I think your luck's about to run out."

"Ooo. I'm scared." Frank looked around at his cohorts. "Aren't you scared, boys?"

The guys put on a show to impress their boss.

"Oh, yeah. I'm really shaking now," Stick said.

"Yeah. Me too," Skuzzaroni replied, knocking his knees together in fun.

I rolled my eyes at their behavior. I could swear I'd seen the episode before, while watching cop shows with Brad.

Then there was movement, a streak of color from the kitchen archway over to Frank. A slender arm wrapped Frank's neck. A gun prodded his temple. He froze, gasping. Candice's face appeared over the stubby man's shoulder. Stick and Skuzzboy floundered for their weapons.

"Put the guns on the floor." Candice gave the orders like a pro.

Stick and Skuzz hesitated, then set their weapons down.

"Hey, now, sweetheart. Let's work this out." Frank put in his plea.

"I'm done working with you, Frank. I told you if you tried to hurt my girl, it was all over." She nodded at Joel and Gerard. "Help me out."

Joel and Gerard stood, the weapons from the floor now in their hands. Joel kept his trained on Stick and Skuzz. Gerard swung his around to face Candice. She kept the gun tight to Frank's skull.

"Put it down, Candice. Nobody has to get hurt," Gerard said.

"I can't let him go again. I'm sorry, Gerard. I know you worked hard to track all the connections and players. I should have just handed you the black box. It could have put Frank away for the rest of his life. But I couldn't take the chance he'd get off on some technicality. He killed Beth and he almost killed Tish. If you think he deserves mercy, you're wrong."

"Put the gun down." The voice came from the archway.

It was Brad. With all the commotion, none of us had heard him arrive. He held a pistol in front of him, aimed at Candice.

"Are you two nuts?" I asked. "Frank's the criminal here, not Candice."

"Stay out of it, cuz," Gerard said. "There's not a whole lot of difference between these two. Justice will be served when they're both behind bars."

Could Gerard be right? I slumped over to the couch

355

and sat next to Samantha. I wanted Candice to be the friend she'd always been. I didn't want her to have some secret life, where she framed drug lords and killed dealers. She was Candice. The Tea Lady. The woman who'd dreamed of being like a grandmother to me.

"Backup's on the way," Brad was saying. "You two did a pretty lame job hiding your vehicle. Anyone could see it through the trees. And a five-year-old could spot your elephant tracks."

"You must be Brad," Candice said over her shoulder in her spider-versus-the-fly voice.

"Put the weapon down." Brad filled the archway with his imposing form.

Without a trace of fear toward the gun trained on her back, Candice ground the muzzle of her weapon into Majestic's temple.

"Ahhh!" Majestic squirmed under the pressure.

Candice threw a glance over her shoulder. "Well, Brad. You don't seem to respect the fact that I'm in charge here."

"I respect the law"—Brad's gun held steady—"which you don't seem to mind breaking."

His remark earned a smile from Candice. I held a moment of hope that the situation would be resolved.

"I'm telling you right now, Brad," she said. "You don't deserve Tish. You're just like the rest of them. No respect for women. You'll try to break her down and crush her spirit."

Brad shook his head. "You're wrong. I love Tish. And I love her spirit best of all. She'll be safe with me." He sent a split-second glance in my direction.

356

I pressed my lips between my teeth, overcome by his declaration.

Candice egged him on. "You're a man. You can't help but stomp all over us. It's in your blood. Now back away from the door. Frank and I were just leaving."

Brad stayed rooted to the floor.

"Back off or I'll kill him." She jammed the barrel against Frank's head.

Frank gave a yell. "Do what she says. She's a killer."

Brad stepped from the doorway, gun still pointed at Candice.

"Move it, Frank," Candice said. The two stumbled backward toward the kitchen archway. Candice stopped at the doorway with her hostage. Only Frank was visible from my place on the sofa.

Candice's voice drifted to me. "Tish, always remember I love you."

Then in a blink, the pistol left Frank's head and pointed in Brad's direction.

My ears exploded as she pulled the trigger.

43

When the echo cleared, the whoosh of blood in my head dampened the shrill screams coming from the vicinity of the sofa. In front of me, Joel finally reacted, jerking his gun toward the doorway, but Candice and her hostage were gone.

The next few minutes were a blur.

Across the room, Brad seemed to fall almost gracefully to the ground. One hand rested over his chest like he'd been shot. Gerard reached him first, bending to look. An oath, then he was gone, bursting through the door. I jumped as more shots rang, this time from outside.

"Joel!" Sam screamed too late as Stick and Skuzz jumped him from behind. Skuzz wrestled the gun away and cracked it across Joel's skull. My cousin collapsed to the floor, unconscious.

"Keep an eye on these guys. I'm going after Frank," Skuzz yelled and raced toward the kitchen.

Stick scooped up Brad's gun and waved Sam back to the sofa.

The rev of an engine. The spin of tires on gravel as a vehicle raced away.

Around me, screams. Shouts. A child's cry. I walked in a state of stupor through the noise until I stood over Brad. Blood rose between the fingers that gripped his chest. A sucking sound came from the wound. I hunched at his side, leaning close, feeling nothing, as if I'd been put under a trance and watched my own body move around the room.

"Tish." He said my name.

The spell was broken. My lower lip trembled. "Brad."

I rocked back and forth next to him, squeezing his hand. Breath rasped out of me, along with moans. My fingers reached toward the wound, then pulled back, helpless. The salty smell of his blood filled the air.

A scream gurgled up in my throat like vomit. "Somebody help! Somebody help him!" My lungs ached from the force of my cry. I looked around but saw nothing but the blurry wash of tears.

From behind me came Stick's threatening voice. "Back on the couch, Russo. Now."

I ignored the command.

"Do you want me to kill you?" Stick sounded dead serious.

I bent my forehead against Brad's shoulder. My answer depended on whether Brad lived or died.

"Leave her alone!" Sam yelled from the couch. "Let us get help, please."

"Stow it, bimbo."

Samantha made the growl of a mother tiger. From the corner of my eye, I saw her launch herself toward Stick. I jerked upright to see her black hair billowing behind like a witch's cape. With an oath of surprise, Stick threw his arms out. Sam landed, and the two of them plowed against the hearth. Stick's hand angled out and hit the rocks. His weapon wrenched the air with its thundering discharge.

The same moment, something hit my arm, nearly spinning me around with the force. A jolt of lightning seemed to flash through my mind as every pain receptor turned on simultaneously. I grabbed my arm. Wet heat. I held out my fingers and looked at them in horror. Sticky, hot blood. I looked at my shirt. The sleeve had a hole in it. The ragged rim seeped red. Oh, Lord. I'd been shot.

Over by the fireplace, Stick snarled and threw Samantha off of him. He jumped to his feet and hulked over her, pointing the gun at her chest.

She seethed up at him.

In the distance came the blare of sirens—Brad's backup. Help was on the way.

Stick looked at his captives as if weighing his options. Then he bolted out the deck door and ran toward the lake.

I turned to Brad, leaning over him, ignoring my own pain. My blood mingled with his like oozing lava. "Hang on. Help is coming."

His eyes were closed. His chest was still. "Brad? Oh, God, please! Brad? Hang on. Hang on."

Arms pulled me away. I reached toward him. "Brad! Brad!" My voice was hoarse, nothing more than a rattle in my throat.

Sam crouched next to me, one hand holding me back, the other sliding out of her cardigan. She wrapped my wound with the thin cotton, tying the sleeves in a tight binding around my upper arm. Then we clung to each other with grips of desperation, rocking, crying, as police entered the room, weapons sweeping from side to side.

"All clear," a trooper said into his radio. "We've got a man down. Gunshot wound to the chest. Where's the ambulance? Let's get some help in here." The trooper bent near Joel. "A second victim appears to be unconscious. Pulse is strong."

A moment later, the first response team rushed in and crowded around Brad.

"We've got another one down in here. Where's our backup?" the female rescue worker spoke into her radio.

The radio crackled a reply.

Behind us on the sofa, Missy described the ordeal to an officer, her words murky in the background of my own sobs. The trooper escorted her and the children through the arch, their forms a blur.

A woman's voice broke through the haze. "Not sure I have a pulse."

A man's bulky build obstructed my view as he barked orders. The woman raced out.

Sounds of a zipper. The whoosh of air. Then the tech's shoulders moved up and down as he started CPR.

"One, two, three . . . ," he counted under his breath.

The other EMT returned, a red case in her hand.

A zip. The tear of fabric. A ripping sound.

Then a feminine voice as emotionless as a computer. "Attach electrodes."

The AED thing was talking.

"Analyzing." A pause. "Prepare to shock." An electronic whir like a siren winding up.

The male EMT spoke. "Stand clear."

"Clear," the woman repeated.

Brad's legs jerked.

Next to me, Sam gasped and pushed away, scampering toward Joel and tucking her body next to his, as if hiding from the scene in front of her.

The man continued his pumping motions.

The woman spoke into her radio. "Medical control, we've got a gunshot wound to the chest. Confirm ALS is en route."

The radio crackled a garbled reply.

Hot pressure raced to my head. A buzzing sound filled my ears. I let out a moan.

The computer spoke again. "Analyzing." A pause. "No shock indicated. Check for pulse. If no pulse, continue CPR," the electronic voice said as callously as an answering machine.

The man pumped and counted.

I couldn't breathe.

No pulse. That meant . . .

He was dead. Brad was dead.

In silence, the workers did their obligatory repetitions.

I collapsed with my forehead against the floor. The ball of pressure in my brain had eclipsed my thinking mind. All I knew was the tiny pinpricks of light dancing behind my eyelids and the choking sound coming from my throat as time had slowed to a crawl.

I lifted my head at the sound of the kitchen door. Ordinary people in blue jeans and T-shirts came through the arch, carrying a stretcher. "Let's load."

Through my tears, vague shapes bent and hovered.

"On three," the man said. "One . . . two . . . three . . ."

Shuffling. Rustling. Then the forms rose in unison. Brad's body was gone, hidden in the circle of rescue workers.

I followed into the yard, mute. Workers clung like vultures to the stretcher as it was loaded onto a waiting ambulance. The doors slammed closed and the rig pulled away, disappearing through the trees.

I felt alone, though the lawn was a bustle of activity. Nearby, another stretcher was being loaded into a waiting ambulance. The insanity of the moment reduced me to a torrent of tears and half-laughter.

My arm throbbed. I covered the bloodstained bandage with my hand. The warmth of my palm soothed it for a moment.

A rescue worker saw me, her eyes squinched with concern. She put a finger in the air as if to say, I'll be with you in a minute. Then she turned back to the blanket-covered body on the lawn.

I wandered through the yard like a *Night of the Living Dead* costar. My heart was missing from my chest. My brain was numb.

There was nothing here for me now.

What had Brad said? Go to Del Gloria—a safe place to land. But I didn't care about safety anymore. It would have been merciful if the bullet had shot me through the heart instead of my arm.

Now all I cared about was getting away from here . . . away from the days of mourning that lay ahead. Sam could have her place next to Brad's coffin. She was his sister. His blood. And who was I? Not a wife. Not even a fiancée. Just a friend.

I didn't want to be here when my loss would become reality. Then, Cupid's Creek, my woods, my living room, all would become reminders. Reminders of this moment. This nightmare.

But if I went to Del Gloria . . . I could forget. There were no markers to jog my memory. Only strangers and strange surroundings. No Brad. No death. No grief in my wretched heart.

Fingers sticky with blood, I reached in my pocket and pulled out the note Brad had given me.

Denton Braddock, he'd written. A mentor. A quiet, obscure life for me. I half-smiled, recalling the anger I'd felt when Brad first told me about this Denton guy. But now—

The pain in my arm flared. Ahead was Brad's SUV. The door hung open and the keys were still in the ignition, as if he'd just stepped out for a moment.

I got behind the wheel, and hesitated. My driver's license. My cell phone. My checkbook. I should get them.

My foot flinched, ready to make a move.

No.

Ties to the past. Ties to my sorrow. That's all those things were. I didn't want them along. The debit card still in my back pocket from last night's fill-up was all I'd take with me.

A slam of the door. A turn of the key. The engine rumbled and I pulled ahead, past the array of emergency vehicles.

In a minute I was at the end of the driveway. Then at US-2.

I turned west. Toward Del Gloria.

With a glance at the speedometer, I set the cruise. The melodic sound of the wheels on blacktop seemed to lessen the pain in my arm. Scenery whooshed past. A soothing calm gushed through my mind. I relaxed against the leather and let all thoughts drain away.

A few more miles, and my time with Brad would be just a dream.

Acknowledgments

Thank you to Vern Annelin for his arson expertise and great stories from his years as a rescue worker.

Thanks to Ray and Kathy Young for their help with EMT details in the final scene.

Thanks to Vicki, Barb, and Kristin for their patience and inspiration during the editing process.

A SNEAK PEEK

BOOK 3

Kiss Me
If You Dare

A PATRICIA AMBLE MYSTERY

1

In the sweep of the headlights, the house on the hill looked like a gaudy mansion dating from California's gold rush era. Exhilaration surged through me. Digging my teeth into this place would make the perfect distraction. I could imagine the view of the mighty Pacific I'd have in the morning from windows overlooking the cliffs. And the thought of crumbling plaster around the panes actually got my blood pumping.

Chunks of heaving cement led to an old-fashioned carport at one side of the home. The vehicle pulled behind an older model Honda and stopped.

The driver cut the engine and touched my arm. "Miss Rigg's appearance may be disquieting, but she's here to help where she can. Please don't undermine her desire." He held my gaze for an extra beat, an Einstein look-alike with his shaggy white hair and Coke-bottle glasses. The lab-coat look with mix-n-match clothes beneath screamed "permanently out to lunch." He got out of the vehicle and disappeared inside.

Relief swept over me with his departure. We'd been cooped up in the car together on and off for the past seventy-two hours. And while Professor Denton Brad-dock obviously meant well with his endless stream of words to the wise, I felt like a four-year-old trapped in a Mr. Rogers episode.

A blast of pain shot up my arm. The moist ocean air with its tinge of salt seemed to add to the agony. I rubbed at the wrap that extended from elbow to shoulder, ready for another painkiller. I grabbed at the handle with my good arm and opened the car door.

A single bulb dangled above me in the weathered porch area. Shadows shrank and grew as the stiff breeze sent the light scuttling. I shivered, though the early summer evening was balmy.

I stared at the entry to my newest renovation project and sighed. I hadn't planned this. Fixing up houses and selling them for a profit had been my living for much of the past decade. But I'd decided to make the log cabin back in the deep woods of Michigan my final project. I'd been ready to settle down. Thanks to the redneck mafia, I now had to live with Plan B.

Ahead, warped steps led up to a screen door and into the house. I put a foot on the bottom tread. This was the first time I'd arrived at a renovation empty-handed. No cot. No sleeping bag. No coffeemaker. No tools. No Goodwill bargains. No identification.

Just the clothes on my back. I even had to go under another name while I hid out in Del Gloria. No more Patricia Louise Amble, the name on my birth certificate. I was now Alisha Marie Braddock, the professor's sup-posed niece visiting from Galveston.

"Why Galveston?" I'd asked him somewhere between Minnesota and Wyoming.

"I like how it sounds."

"I've never been to Galveston," I said.

"Then you can't give any details about your previous life, can you?"

I hated his answer. I'd once walked away from great romantic possibilities in order to dig into my past. It hadn't felt right starting a relationship when I couldn't give an intelligent account of my ancestry. According to Denton, I was now supposed to brush off any questions that would give clues to my identity.

I scuffed across the porch and through the screen door. It slammed behind me.

Beyond an entryway, I found the kitchen, tall and narrow with cupboards stretching beyond human reach along two walls. A library ladder would have been at home in the galley layout.

Far overhead, two bulbs cast a dim light on the room. The cream-colored walls seemed in perfect condition. The finish on the dark cabinetry shone to a high gloss, without a fingerprint in sight. I ran my hand along the cool stone countertop. Though clearly a replacement, the flawless surface looked original to the home. All in all, a remarkable restoration job.

I crossed my arms and leaned against the counter. When Brad set me up with this hideout, he'd assured me that Denton was offering food and shelter in exchange for my restoration skills. I could only assume the rest of the house was barely livable.

The thought of Brad delivered a new dose of pain, starting at my heart and radiating to every limb.

A door swung open at one end of the kitchen.

"Welcome, Miss Braddock," said a woman's voice.

Remembering my name change, I stood to attention at the brisk Irish accent.

"Do you need help with your bags or can you get them yourself?" The speaker shuffled into the light. She was a tiny woman wearing a black cotton dress over black socks and black sneakers. White legs poked out beneath her hem with each step. As she drew closer, I realized her small stature was due to a curved spine. The hump on her back rose almost as high as the top of her head.

Miss Rigg, I deduced. I tried not to stare. "No. I'm fine. I have no bags."

"Then what about food? You must be hungry."

I focused my mind on my stomach. It growled on cue. "Food would be great. Thanks."

The words seemed to trip a switch. The woman moved with purpose to the stove and lifted the lid on an oversize pot. "Beef stew. The professor's favorite."

Steam billowed as she stirred. The succulent scent of juicy tomatoes and spice filled the air.

"Mmmm. Smells delicious." I liked the thought of a built-in cook during my stay in Del Gloria.

She plopped the lid back and retrieved a stepping stool from a corner of the kitchen. She set it down near the sink and pulled open a cabinet. Even with the added height, she still struggled to reach the bowls. At her grunt, I intervened.

"Here. Let me help with those." I was a tall woman,

374

a feature that came in handy in the restoration business. Those hard-to-reach corners came easy for me. Long arms, long neck, long legs . . . I resembled either a supermodel or an ostrich.

The fingers of my good arm barely touched the smooth ceramic bowls before Miss Rigg swatted me away.

"Don't you be interfering in my kitchen." Her voice rose to shrill peaks. "It's bad enough the professor agreed to take you in. Barely through the door and you think you own the place." Gray hair in a bun shook loose with her anger. "Well, you don't own it yet. Relation or not, you'll not be taking my place in this house."

I recoiled at her words. "I'm sorry. I just meant to help. And please, don't worry about me. I'm not really—"

The far door swung open.

"Alisha."

Professor Braddock strode in. For a moment he seemed strong and decisive, not the awkward nerd-type I'd ridden here with.

He took me by the arm. I winced at the pressure on my bandage.

"I'm showing Alisha to her room. She can help herself to stew later." Denton led me out of the kitchen. We stopped just outside the door.

He turned me toward him, showing no mercy to my wound. "You must heed my words, Patricia. You will not survive if anyone suspects you are not who I say you are."

I shook off his grip. "Sorry." I cradled my arm. "She got so defensive. I didn't want her thinking I was here permanently."

"Perhaps you are here permanently. We won't know for some time." His lips pursed under a bushy moustache. "I warned you about Miss Rigg. I specifically asked you not to help her."

I thought back to his parting words in the car and couldn't remember him saying anything along those lines. "I had no idea she'd be so offended. I was just trying to help."

"Now you know. Don't help."

I stared at a mole on his cheek. Denton certainly offered asylum—as in loony bin, not sanctuary. What had Brad been thinking? When I found the body in my basement two projects ago, the killer had been behind bars within six months. Could I last around here for six months?

I sighed and followed Denton. It wasn't as if I had a choice.

Nicole Young resides in Garden, Michigan, with her children, cats, and tiny Yorkie. Home renovation is a way of life for the author whose first project was converting a Victorian in lower Michigan into a thriving bed & breakfast. She returned to Michigan's Upper Peninsula in 2001, where she owns and upkeeps vacation rental homes. Nicole plays fiddle and sings with two local bands and enjoys horseback riding on the beautiful Garden Peninsula.

DON'T MISS BOOK 1
in the Patricia Amble Mystery series!

A run-down house to renovate, a past to leave behind—
who has time for romance . . . *or murder*?

a division of Baker Publishing Group
www.revellbooks.com

Available wherever books are sold